HEROES' SONG

Song of Prophecy Series Book 3

P.E. PADILLA

PARTIAL MAP OF DIZHELIM

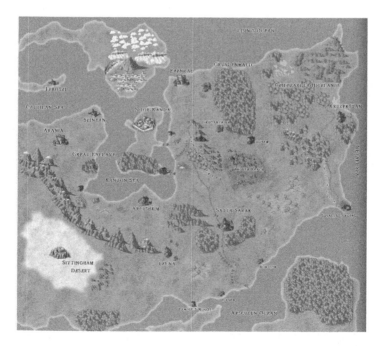

Prophecy is not a simple subject. It is the web of the greatest of arachnids, the joining of numberless strands of existence in a space the size of all the worlds. A lowly denizen may understand a small part, but to cast one's eyes upon anything but the entire spectacle is as an insect landing on a spot and believing it has explored the entire world. Beware, insects, for the spinner of the work may yet trap the unwary, beguiling them into thinking they are safe before the grand realization strikes: the doom coming is too complex for insects to perceive.

Foreword to *The Book of Prophets and Prophecy*, by Tsosin Ruus, Year 25518 AOM.

PROLOGUE

"You're not serious," Evon Desconse said, mouth hanging open.

Izhrod Benzal glanced at the young, blond-haired man and sniffed. "Of course I am. It is all so very clear to those with the mental faculties to understand it."

"And you possess such faculties?" Quentin Duzen absently flipped the pages of the book in front of him.

Izhrod gazed out the window of one of the study rooms in the grand library. In the glare of the lantern light, he caught his own reflection. He turned his head left and right, concentrating on his dark, wavy hair. With a slight nod, he shifted his attention to those sharing the room with him.

Who had let Evon into the room? He was younger than the rest of them by several years and he wasn't of the quality Izhrod typically required of those he associated with. He barely had one school mastered, for Surus's sake. And he wasn't even of noble birth.

"I do," he said. "And then some."

"Do tell." Quentin rolled his hand in the air at the wrist. He had blond hair as well, but the similarities with Evon ended there. Quentin was muscular and wore his hair very short, often accompanied by a day or two of growth on his jaw. Evon was almost pretty enough to be a woman, but Quentin would be classified as a ruggedly handsome man. At least, some of the female students described him as such.

Izhrod didn't see it.

A scoffing sound came from his left. Atwyn Iaphor had the good sense to drop her striking hazel eyes to the table and blush slightly. She wasn't of sufficient class to be in close association with him either, but she had...other assets earning the privilege of being present. The woman let her long blonde hair fall over her face. Such a shame to cover up such a magnificent work of art.

"Have you not seen the connection already?" Izhrod asked. "Surely you have studied the prophecy. It is, after all, why Sitor-Kanda exists."

Ulfaris Triban nodded his dark head. Faithful Ulfaris. If any at this gods-forsaken place could be said to be a friend, it was he. No, not friend. Ulfaris was from a noble family, but far too low to be a friend to one such as Izhrod. A close acquaintance, perhaps. Still, one of Izhrod's most solid supporters.

Quentin Duzen laughed. "Sure. For a moment, however, let us assume we are not as brilliant as you. Explain it to us, won't you? In small words."

Izhrod sighed and stood up straighter, pulling down on his tight coat. It was very fashionable with its wide lapels and tailored fit, complemented perfectly by the lace at his neck. "I will deign to educate you poor, underprivileged oafs."

Beautiful Atwyn cleared her throat. Trying to cover up another scoff? It didn't matter.

"'Hero from east and north,'" he quoted. "I, as you well know, am from Nanris, the jewel of Kruzekstan. It happens to be in the northeastern part of Promistala. That means—"

"Nothing," Quentin said. "Almost everyone can say they're from the east and north of somewhere else. The Song was written near here. There are very few places truly east and north of this location. Maybe the tip of Rhaltzheim or the border of the Grundenwald. Abyssum; it could be talking about half the beasts in that forest."

Izhrod cleared his throat, frowning at the impolite inter‐ruption. It was doubly a slight because of Izhrod's much higher station than Quentin's. "That is incorrect, but we shall assume—correctly, I might add—that you are incapable of understanding it, and move on.

"When I was seven years old, I nearly drowned in the Creslan Lake. In fact, the accounts of the servants with me that day stated that I did stop breathing briefly, but revived when one of them squeezed my chest to cause me to expel the water I had taken in."

"I remember this story," Evon said. "You had the servant beaten for assaulting you."

Izhrod glared at the young man. Who had let him into the room?

"Yes, well, you cannot allow such things. If you are lax in dealing with servants, they will soon be refusing to work at all. But you are losing sight of the topic of this conversation. I *died*, but I am living still. Just as the prophecy states. That makes two uncontestable proofs."

Atwyn looked away. Her shoulders shook slightly. Was there something wrong with her? Was she...laughing? He focused on Quentin again.

"I am the first son of two of the highest priests of Surus in Kruzekstan. My family has a long and honorable history and is very close with the royal family."

"And this is pertinent why?" Quentin asked. Ulfaris frowned at the man. Izhrod kept his face calmly blank.

"I, and my family, are very important. I am of high noble

birth. My name, in the pure language of Alaqotim, means promise. A very prophetic and fortuitous name, by the way. When I came to this place,"—he gestured at the stone around him and out toward the buildings that littered the landscape outside the window—"it could be said that I was split asunder. The noble remained at my grand home in my parents' estates near Nanris, while the more modest, scholarly half of my self came here to learn the great secrets of the world.

"In my years here, I have faced challenges, done battle with the fire of magic and physical combat, and have melded my two halves into the fine specimen you see today. As the Song of Prophecy states:

Malatirsay, split asunder
One to two, but back to one
Separated but brought whole
Welded by fire's touch

That makes the third irrefutable piece of evidence."

"Evidence," Quentin said, laughing. "That's not evidence. At best, it's merely hearsay. That's the 'irrefutable evidence' you have to prove that you are the Malatirsay, the hero prophesied three thousand years ago to fulfill the purpose of Sitor-Kanda? *You* are the one the Hero Academy was built to train, the one to save the world from destruction when the animaru come?"

"I am."

Ulfaris nodded vigorously, his mouth turned up into a proud smile. The others were...less enthusiastic.

Evon Desconse had his head cocked and his brows drawn down. He had a look of confusion about him. He was probably not able to follow the relatively simple logic Izhrod presented.

Atwyn shook her beautiful head, blonde hair swinging. Her smile was somehow sardonic, but she *was* smiling. He

4

would talk to her later. Alone. He was not above using his status as a hero from prophecy to bed her.

"Have you been to the animal pens of late, Izhrod?"

He blinked at Quentin. "What? I...no, I have not. Why?"

"Because from what I can tell, you're crammed full of sheep shit." He got up from his seat and headed out the door. "I'm going to get something to drink. After that string of *logic*, I won't be getting any studying done. Anyone want to join me?"

Atwyn leaped up from her seat and followed him. Evon formed a wry smile on his mouth and trailed after her shapely form.

That left Izhrod and Ulfaris.

"Insufferable peasants," he told his acquaintance. "Perhaps I should have used smaller words, as Quentin requested. They obviously do not understand prophecy as I do. That, or the masters have influenced them."

"Why would the masters' influence make them disbelieve you?" Ulfaris asked. He didn't speak much when they were around other people, rightfully allowing Izhrod to be the focus of conversation. It sometimes surprised Izhrod that the man even *could* speak, it was such a rare occasion.

"The masters are like any other peasant. They have a modicum of power here at Sitor-Kanda and will not give it up easily. I have approached no fewer than four of them to declare that I am the Malatirsay and have received responses ranging from outright laughter to admonitions to continue my studies. They know that, upon formal recognition that I am the purpose for which this Academy was built, they will lose much of their authority. In a word, they are jealous."

Ulfaris adopted a pensive look, eyes unfocused, head tilted slightly. "I never thought that would happen. I always assumed that when the Malatirsay was revealed, everyone would support him. Maybe it's because the other signs that we are in the end times have not come yet. Maybe it's too early to declare you to the world."

"Perhaps," Izhrod said. "Perhaps. I will not tolerate being ignored for much longer, though, Ulfaris. My destiny is nearly at hand. I will not let this place, which has grown soft and lost its purpose, to alter the way things must be.

"I will claim my rightful place as the greatest hero the world has ever known. One way or another."

eden Tannoch windmilled in the air, forcing his tired body to obey one last command. When he landed, he could rest, if briefly.

The sword in his left hand bit into the flesh of the animaru lord Suuksis, tearing a slice out of his neck and shoulder and causing the mud-colored blood within him to splash out. Before a drop hit the ground, Aeden's right sword completed a powerful forehand blow in the exact same spot, cutting all the way through flesh, tendons, cartilage, and nerves, severing the head completely.

He landed awkwardly and almost fell from his exhaustion. Suuksis's head spun off and away as his body fell near Aeden.

It was done.

Khrazhti slumped nearby, also so fatigued she could no longer stand. Nearby, Fahtin and Raki fought with the few remaining animaru. When their leader fell, the monsters ran for the stairs going down the tower.

Aeden scanned the tower's rooftop. Animaru bodies lay scattered about, most of them in piles where he'd been fighting to keep them from getting to his friends. There was blood as well, most of it dark brown, but some red, mostly on himself and the two Gypta. Not much in pools on the surface of the roof.

That was a good thing. All three humans and their animaru ally, Khrazhti, were still alive. But where was Izhrod Benzal?

"Impressive," a voice called out. "Very impressive."

Aeden jumped to his feet, swords out. He searched for the source of the voice. It sounded far away, with an echoing quality.

Izhrod Benzal was there, on the rooftop of a nearby tower, standing next to a magical doorway. It was too far to jump, especially in his exhausted condition.

The man taunted Aeden and Khrazhti, proclaimed himself the Malatirsay, and fled through the portal before the magical device beside it exploded. Aeden deflated as his eyes swept the rooftop. There was nothing left but a mangled and smoking wreck where the contraption had been. Izhrod Benzal, and those with him, had escaped.

Some time later, Aeden stepped off the uppermost stair of the large central tower. The tower where Benzal had been earlier.

It had taken the group—the others refused to allow him to go by himself—more than an hour to descend the tower where they had killed Suuksis, trudge over a few halls, and then climb up the central tower.

It felt like ten hours had passed.

Aeden dropped to the stone surface of the roof to rest for a moment before moving on. Even at rest, his eyes sought out potential dangers. It wouldn't do for them to be ambushed in their weakened state.

Surprisingly, they had found no other animaru on their trip to the other rooftop. No humans, either. Only the empty, echoing halls of Broken Reach, as abandoned as it seemed from the outside.

"Did the ones that ran from us go with Benzal?" Aeden asked no one in particular.

"No," Khrazhti answered. "We saw him step through the doorway and then watched it melt and disappear. They must have fled in a more conventional way. They will find other animaru."

Aeden grunted, too tired to comment. After several minutes, he heaved himself to his feet and crossed the roof to where they'd seen the magical doorway. The contraption that had been sitting next to it was still there, though in a much-altered state.

Before, it had looked like some kind of machine. He'd heard such things were produced—in very small quantities—at the Academy. Now...well, now it looked like it was made of wax and put on a stovetop long enough to sag and melt, but not puddle completely.

"What is it?" Raki said from right next to him. Aeden didn't jump when his young friend suddenly appeared anymore, but neither was he completely accustomed to it.

"You're getting better and better at that."

Raki smiled, but it drooped when the young man turned back to look at the melted object in front of him.

"It made the door," Fahtin said, stepping up. "Or at least maintained it. It only melted like that after the doorway flared. Benzal was expecting it. He hurried to go through when he saw how it was pulsing."

"But what *is* it?" Raki repeated.

All three turned to Khrazhti, who had knelt to inspect the object closely. She waved one of her blue hands over it, closing her eyes and setting her jaw firmly. After a few seconds, she opened her eyes and her glowing orbs found Aeden.

"Do you know?" he asked.

She shook her head. "I am afraid I do not. It is clear that it was somehow a focus for the magic that made the doorway, but I have never seen such a thing. I can feel residual power from it, but it is fading quickly. Soon, it will not be apparent it had a magical connection at all."

"Can you use it to find out where Benzal went?" Fahtin asked. "It's obvious that doorway went somewhere else far away."

"I am sorry," Khrazhti said. "I can sense no direction, only that magic passed through it. If it were whole, perhaps I could put magic back into it and make it work, though I doubt it. In this state, it is worthless. It appears to be designed to focus the magic for a limited time until it failed. This was no spontaneous means of escape. The evacuation had been planned, as a way to get the animaru and Benzal somewhere else."

"*Daeann daedos ist*," Aeden spat. "Then we are left without a means to find him. We will—" His left leg gave out beneath him and he barely stopped himself from collapsing to the stone.

"Aeden," Khrazhti said. "We are all injured and exhausted. Let us rest. Any discussion can be had later, when we are better suited to it."

"You're right.," he said. "There will be enough time to figure it out later."

They had eaten and bandaged their wounds but had been in a hurry to inspect this other roof. They were in no condition to do anything but rest and heal.

The group moved slowly down a few steps to the highest room in the tower, one they had passed through on the way up. They arranged themselves haphazardly on the floor and were soon sleeping, all but Khrazhti, who volunteered to keep watch.

Seven hours later, Aeden stirred, his multitude of cuts shocking him awake as he turned in his sleep. Khrazhti sat silently nearby, watching him with her large, glowing eyes. She looked ready to drop where she sat.

"Rest," he told her. "I'll have a bit to eat and watch for a while."

He hauled himself to his feet and shuffled to her, intending to try to heal some of the wounds she had taken. Though she'd received several sizable gashes, what he found was half-healed injuries. His eyebrows shot up as he looked into her eyes.

"I have told you that animaru regenerate, unless they are destroyed with life magic. In Aruzhelim, when we defeat a foe, it is unable to do anything until it recuperates. The time it takes to do so depends upon how extensive the damage is. Given time, I will heal."

"That's good to know, but I don't like to see you in pain. I think I've worked it out. Because you're half human, I think I can heal you without the magic doing more harm than good. Or at least let me take watch while you rest so you can recuperate more quickly."

"I...very well," she said. "For a little while."

He took the food she handed him and sat next to her, chewing. The jerk of his head was enough to remind her of his suggestion and she settled down to rest. Though she didn't need sleep, she had explained how periods of inactivity allowed their regeneration to happen more quickly. Kind of like with humans.

Aeden continued to eat, watching his friends, hoping they would regain their strength soon. They had things to do, and he had a feeling they all needed to be in their best condition to face them.

The Malatirsay, Aeden thought. *The prophesied hero of Dizhelim who will fight off the animaru and their darkness and save the world from being destroyed. Jehira told me that I am the Malatirsay, but Benzal said he was. How can he save the world from the animaru if he's the one bringing them here?* Raki's nani had told Aeden he was the Malatirsay. Who was right?

Aeden wasn't sure how he felt about the possibility. He didn't like thinking that the fate of the world was on Benzal's shoulders, but he also didn't care for the thought of it being dependent on himself. Why couldn't Raisor Tannoch or Erent Caahs have been the hero of the prophecy? Those were the type of men you could count on.

He couldn't even fulfill his promise to his clan.

Aeden gasped when another thought crossed his mind. The Epradotirum. The ancient creature had only let them go because they had insisted Aeden was the Malatirsay. It had extracted a promise from Aeden that he would fulfill his responsibility to save Dizhelim and defeat the animaru. What would the monster do when it found out Aeden was never the hero to begin with? The Croagh cared little of what happened to himself—he had already died once—but what of his friends? The thought of the powerful creature hunting them down and eating them made him grit his teeth.

On the other hand, if Benzal was wrong and Aeden truly was the Malatirsay, the responsibility he had to save the world would be overwhelming. His failure would mean the end of everyone and everything he had ever loved. He wasn't sure he could stand up to such a crushing weight.

"Are you well?" Khrazhti asked softly from a few feet away. She lay in the same position as before, but her eyes were open, glowing softly and searching his.

"Aye. I just thought of something, that's all."

"Would you tell me of it?"

"No, you don't need to bother yourself over it. I was just thinking, that's all. The silence and stillness, it's good for that. For thinking of things."

She didn't move, as still as a blue statue sculpted from a piece of exotic stone. "Very well." Her eyes closed, but not before Aeden thought he had caught pain in them.

He almost told her then, of his thoughts and his doubts, but bit down hard on his emotions and remained silent. No use in troubling his friends with his internal battles. His path would become clear soon enough. Somehow, in some way, he would be able to discern the route he should take, and whether he was important in the battle for their world.

He sighed and reached for more food. Thinking had lost its appeal, and all he wanted was to mindlessly chew and swallow. He regretted that they only had water and no wine or ale.

TERE CHIZZIT HAD BEEN LOCKED IN A CELL THREE OTHER times in his life. He hated being locked in a cell. He hated it even more this time because not only did his two companions also get pulled into the situation, but he had no idea why they had been imprisoned.

Some days, it felt like the gods had never left Dizhelim. And like they got together to make his life more difficult.

Beyond the barred window, a torch somewhere down the corridor cast its dull light. It barely reached the thick, wooden door banded with iron that kept Tere and his friends inside. Other than that imposing door, no other openings broke the stone of the walls.

The room was devoid of any of the comforts even the vilest man should be provided. Not even a bucket to use when nature called. Instead, a pile and stains indicated that one corner of the small, square room was to be used for that purpose. It had not been cleaned out in a very long time.

At least there were no rats. Well, not any longer. One had gotten in when the guards opened the door to shove them into the chamber, but Tere caught it and crushed its head. He hated rats almost as much as he hated being locked in a cell.

"Tere," Aila Ven said. She was accustomed to roughing it out on the road, but even so, she was much too pretty to be in a place like this. Tere felt doubly bad because of it. "Who is this Mayor, and what did you do to him? He seems to hate you."

"Honestly, I don't know. I am trying to remember anyone I may have slighted, but can't remember anyone. Of course, he probably wasn't called Mayor back then, and the name he called me, I've never heard before. The guards talked like it was a long time ago. As soon as he summons us, I'm sure we can come to an agreement. He's got the wrong guy."

Aila hummed to herself. Tere wasn't sure what that meant, but he wasn't in the mood for conversation, either. Luckily, Urun had gone to the opposite corner from the waste and sat down, back against the wall. He hadn't said a word since the door closed. Something was wrong with him, but it wasn't high on Tere's list to figure out what. The young man had most likely never been imprisoned before and was probably mourning his freedom.

The old archer would do his best to get them all free. If he couldn't manage that, maybe he could at least manage to get the other two released. He'd done enough to deserve being in a cell, as long as they could go free. He didn't want that option, but it was there, in the back of his mind.

He regretted most when his actions had consequences for others who should not have been involved.

Footsteps sounded outside in the hallway, echoing as if Tere was hearing them from the bottom of a well. They grew louder, and a yellow-red light bloomed in the hall as the walker carried his torch closer. Maybe they were to be released.

The bolt was drawn, then the second bolt. The man outside grunted as he slammed his shoulder into the door to open it up. It screeched its resistance, the sound of the hinges merging with the grinding of the wood on the stone floor.

One of the guards held a torch aloft. Another guard, the one who had apparently forced the door open, stepped aside.

"Out," the torch-bearer said.

Both men were of similar shape and height. Burly, heavy, with sunken knuckles. Tere was a big man himself, but each of these two probably had a dozen pounds or more on him, even if it was mostly flab and not tight muscle.

Tere got up from the floor and put his hand out to Aila to help her up, out of habit. She gave him a scathing look and scrambled to her feet without his help.

Urun stayed where he was, eyes staring unblinking at the opposite wall.

"I said out," the guard shouted. "You make me say it

again, and I'll club you and drag you unconscious. You won't enjoy either, I guarantee."

"Urun," Tere whispered as he shook the young priest's shoulder. "Come on. Get up. We'll go and clear this up."

Urun blinked and looked up as if waking. He slowly got to his feet and took a position behind Tere and Aila. The three walked out into the hallway and shuffled to where the guard pointed. Maybe they'd finally get some answers.

As the small procession marched toward their destination, Tere confirmed the layout of the town. It hadn't changed much in the decades since he'd been there. Some had been replaced or repaired, evidenced by different amounts of degradation and filth on the buildings they passed. There seemed to be some newer structures, though even those were dingy and littered with trash. It was just as Tere remembered from all those years ago.

More importantly, he plotted out everything in relation to where they were being held—a habit he had developed long ago.

They were foolish to move the prisoners around without even blindfolding them. Then again, the Mayor thought Tere was someone else, possibly someone who knew the town's layout well, so he wouldn't think to keep the prisoner from seeing what he already knew. Besides, blindfolds meant nothing to Tere's sight. Not that his captors would know that.

As he remembered, the buildings at the edge of town were set close together, making a protective wall of sorts, in addition to the literal town wall. It would keep whatever it was in the forest from entering the town in any numbers, but it would also make it difficult to leave without being seen.

Tere could see no sentries, but he wasn't counting on their absence. Maybe the Mayor was smart enough to only let the prisoners see what he wanted them to see.

They finally arrived at a large wooden structure in one of

the better parts of town. Better, relatively speaking. Mostly that meant no raw sewage in the space between buildings and no dead bodies lying in the street. The building was two stories tall and as large as the tavern Tere remembered as the biggest building when he was in the city last.

The small party climbed the stairs and entered the double doors. They passed through a small entryway and into a large room with a raised table at the end and chairs scattered throughout its length.

On the platform, behind the table, sat a massive chair. In it was a large man. The Mayor, obviously. He had the look of a street tough, similar to the guards who had led Tere and the others from their cell. His thinning brown hair, shot through with grey, sat awkwardly, as if the man had tried to hide his bare scalp by combing it on top from other areas. He was perhaps in his sixth decade, maybe the latter part of his fifth, but still vital. Dangerous.

"I think there has been a mis—" Tere started.

The Mayor raised a hand.

"Keep quiet," he said in a voice like the low growl of a bear. "I'll tell you when I want you to speak." His eyes drilled into Tere, as if he was trying to look through his prisoner. He continued this silently for several minutes. No one else in the room, which included only the two guards Tere came with, Aila, Urun, and four more guards arrayed around the Mayor, made any sound.

"Time has not been your friend, Alston," he finally said. "You look older than I am, but I know you're younger." A smile grew on his face. "It must be the guilt of your betrayal paying its toll. You do seem to have gained a little muscle, though that won't help you here."

Tere opened his mouth to speak, but the Mayor raised his hand again, the smile dropping away as if it had never been there.

"I have been looking for you for so many years. Twenty-four. Ever since you betrayed me and ran off with my treasure. You remember that, don't you Alston?"

The words died and the room became silent again. The Mayor raised his eyebrows, a cool anger boiling in his dark eyes.

Tere realized the man wanted him to speak now. He took a breath to begin. "I am not who you think I am, Mayor. I have never met you before. You have the wrong man."

The Mayor's face lost some of its tension and he looked to the guards on his left, then to the guards on his right, amusement in his eyes. "Really? Alston, there are not two men in the world who have eyes like that and who can move about without running into things. If you were a normal man, one with any color of functioning eyes, you may have gotten away. It is a testament to your clever mind that you have stayed free for so long. Clever or not, however, you surely can't expect me to believe you are anyone other than who you are."

"My name is Tere Chizzit," Tere said. "I'm just a simple woodsman who, until recently, lived at the edge of the Grundenwald. I'm afraid you have mistaken me for someone else."

"Enough!" the Mayor said, slapping the table in front of him with his palm. "I'll not waste my time any longer on this farce. You will return to me the gem you stole, or an amount in gold that is equivalent. Fifteen thousand gold marks should cover it, I would think. I will give you a few days to think about it while you enjoy your cell. If you don't give up the treasure, you will stand trial, here in this room." He swept his hand out, displaying the room as if it were a grand ballroom.

"As for your companions, I have an offer to make them, too." He turned his attention to Aila and Urun. "If you give me information about Alston here, how he evaded me all these years or where he may have hidden his treasure, I will set you free. No need for you to be involved in this unpleasantness. Think on it. If you have something to say, tell my guards and we can talk."

"For now, I have other important things to do." He flicked his hand toward the door, and the guards grabbed Tere by the shoulder and steered him toward the entryway. "Think hard on your situation, Alston. There will be no slipping out of my grasp this time. Make it easy on yourself and give me what's mine. I'm not as easygoing as I was when you took advantage of me all those years ago."

The prisoners were taken back to their cells using the same route as before. Tere hardly paid attention to his surroundings, instead focusing on his companions. Urun remained as he had been since their imprisonment a few days ago, listless and silent. He looked straight ahead and put down one foot after another as if nothing in the world mattered.

Aila darted glances at Tere, her emotions shielded. Tere could almost hear her mind grinding at what she had heard, and what it meant. There would be questions after they were locked up tight in their cell again. She had the sense not to speak in the presence of the guards. Tere appreciated that, but he didn't look forward to their conversation once the guards had retreated.

The odor of the cell hit Tere in the face like a fist. He clamped his jaw to keep from retching.

As expected, Aila waited only until the guards' footsteps disappeared down the hall and the oppressive silence and darkness had returned. The smell of the place, and of each other, took a bit longer to fade, but eventually their senses of smell became fatigued and Tere could relax his jaw without fear of losing what little food he had in his stomach.

"So?" Aila said. Her brow was drawn down, little crinkles in her forehead.

"So what?" he responded.

"So, will you tell us what's going on?"

"I would think it's fairly evident. I have never heard of this Alston Squesik and I have never heard of or met Dared Moran, with or without the title he has adopted."

Aila sighed. "Are you sure, Tere? I mean, the chance of two men with white eyes and the ability to move around and see? That's not very probable."

"Yet it's true." He wanted to get angry that she was calling him a liar, but he couldn't. He could understand her point of view—even the Mayor's—that it wasn't likely there was another man like him. Or rather, who resembled him. "I don't know about this other fellow, but I'm telling the truth, Aila. There's no need for me to lie to you about it. If I were that guy, I'd tell you."

"I don't know," she said.

He debated for a moment, but then decided to try to accommodate her curiosity. "I wasn't always like this. At the time he's talking about, my eyes were not white. They were blue."

"What?"

"Even if I could have somehow forgotten any interactions with this man, it couldn't have been me. I'm sorry, but we don't have the option of simply giving him what he wants."

"You...weren't always blind? I mean, you're not really blind now, but your eyes, they weren't always like that?"

"That's what I just said. Please, can we stop talking about this and maybe decide what we need to do?"

She shifted and edged closer to him, though she most likely couldn't see him. She was trying to examine him, searching his features like he was a new type of bug she had found.

"Tere, who are you? No, that's not the right question. Who *were* you?"

"Who were you?" he countered.

That caused her to lean away from him.

"Listen Aila," he said, "we both have secrets in our past. You don't want to share yours any more than I do mine. I promise that should it become necessary, I will talk about my past, but for now, I don't see that it is. I don't like to talk about it. Abyssum, I don't even like to think about it. I'm not sure what your secrets are, but they're *your* secrets. I'll not push you to reveal them if you respect my right for the same."

"Sometimes, I think the entire world is held together by secrets," she whispered. "Other times, I think the world is held together *despite* its secrets."

"I would have to agree."

They grew silent, accompanied by no other sounds but the skittering of some insects nearby and of Urun's breathing near the wall. Tere longed for his forest home but knew it was worse for his friends. They had to find a way out of this mess, whatever the cost.

🎇 3 🎇

Fahtin woke to the sound of Aeden and Khrazhti conversing softly in that strange animaru Alaqotim. She had learned a few phrases, but Aeden had taken to the language with a fervor he usually reserved for combat. She didn't know if he was fluent, but he could carry on a conversation. She could rarely follow one. When she spoke with Khrazhti, the blue woman kindly used Ruthrin, which she had learned even more quickly than Aeden had learned Alaqotim.

The conversation broke off as Fahtin groaned softly. Sharp pain afflicted her as she tried to move. She was sore all over, and the different cuts and bruises all over her body ached.

"How are you feeling?" Aeden asked.

"Like the cushion my mother used to keep her sewing needles in." She managed to lever herself into a sitting position and noticed the blood-soaked bandages in place on her left arm, right hand, both legs, and around her midsection. How had she slept with so many injuries and so much pain?

She hadn't noticed Aeden walking over to her, but she looked up as his shadow fell over her.

"By the gods, Aeden." His clothing was so much shredded cloth. Deep gouges and punctures marred his leather armor. Bits of red cloth—not their original color—were tied about his body. How was he even moving?

He chuckled. Chuckled! "It looks worse than it actually is. More painful than dangerous."

He handed her a waterskin and a hard cake. She took it gratefully, wetting her throat first and then biting into the food. Her stomach rumbled loudly.

"Stay still while you eat," he said. "I'll heal some of your bigger wounds."

"No. I'm f—" The icy feeling of his magic slammed into her. She sucked in air sharply, and then coughed as a bit of the cake went into her breathing tubes. Usually, when she nearly choked on food like that, she had a coughing fit and her throat grew sore. Now, though, in the midst of being healed, she coughed once to expel the food and then immediately felt no further problems.

Aeden continued for close to a full minute, his hands waving over her, mere inches from her body. She blushed furiously at the thought and turned her mind to searching the room and how good the healing felt. She could actually sense the wounds knitting together as the pain dissipated.

She was going to tell him it was enough, not to waste his energy, but then the sensation cut off and he sat down hard next to her. It was more of a controlled fall, really.

"You shouldn't use so much energy just to make me more comfortable," she said.

He smiled at her—gods how she loved that smile—gently took the water skin from her hand, gulped down a mouthful, and returned it to her. "It's fine. I slept and ate. I have trouble controlling how much magic I use, how much I heal. At times, it feels to me like I can either heal everything or nothing. I need practice. In fact, I'm hoping the more I use that spell, the stronger it'll become. I can't heal even a fraction of what Urun can.

"And no, that doesn't mean I want you to get hurt so I can heal you. I'm perfectly happy if you never have your skin damaged again. It's much too smooth and perfect for that. You are not meant for scars, Fahtin."

She rolled her eyes at him. "I'll try to keep that in mind when deciding if I want to be injured in the future." She hopped to her feet and then realized what she had done. She swung her arms in circles, stretched her back, hopped a few times to test out her legs. "You even healed my fatigue. I feel like I've slept for a week. It's amazing."

"Almost like magic, eh?" he said, eyes twinkling though they peered out at her from within a tired face.

She immediately felt bad, him trading his energy to make her feel so much better. "You need to learn to control it. I'll not have you wearing yourself out when I feel like I've never been injured in my life."

"Like I said, I'll get the hang of it eventually." He looked to the side, winked and her, and continued. "I'll practice some more on Raki when the lazy little rodent finally wakes up."

"I heard that."

"Ah, the rodent speaks. Here, have some food and water. How are you feeling?"

Fahtin sympathized with the boy as he slowly rolled to a sitting position with grunts and moans. He was a mess, too, with bandages all over, the largest wrapped around his torso. The entire back side of it was soaked in blood. It was a testament to how exhausted Aeden had been that he didn't heal it earlier. Luckily, it looked to have stopped bleeding.

"Did you see it?" he asked.

Aeden's brows drew down "See what?"

"The team of horses that stomped me into the ground.

Oh, every part of my body hurts. Did you all take turns kicking me when I was sleeping? How did I manage to sleep through this pain?"

Aeden laughed as he handed Raki another waterskin, the first real laugh she'd heard from him in some time. "When your body has gone to its limits and beyond, it can take its rest in the midst of almost anything. You've just never been tired enough."

Raki took a drink and held the skin up as if to toast Aeden. "Thank you. You know, you don't look so well off right now, either. Did you rest?"

"Aye, I did. And ate, more than I probably should have. But it takes energy to heal, and I have some yet to do."

"No," Raki said. "You don't need—"

Again, Aeden performed the gestures and mouthed the words to cast his healing spell. She had missed those when he healed her. The pain had her preoccupied.

Raki shivered as the magic went through him. Aeden kept at it for more than twice as long as he had spent on her. Fahtin figured the boy's wounds were more severe, and Aeden had to continue pumping magic into him.

Finally, Aeden slumped and Raki stopped shivering.

"I really wish you'd warn me before you do that."

"I would, but you'd argue that you don't need it and you might even try to run away from me, so it's better to simply get it over with. Let's look and see how good a job I've done."

He motioned for Raki to turn so he could find the end of the bandage about the boy's torso. He unwrapped it gently, at least as gently as he could while still tearing it from the underlying bandages and their hardened blood. Fortunately, only the top layer was dried completely, with the lower layers still damp with body fluids.

Once Aeden pulled the last bit of the bandage off, he used

it to wipe away the remaining blood so he could see Raki's skin.

Fahtin gasped. There was still evidence of the cut—a long pink gash going down the entire length of his back—but it looked to have been healing for at least several days, if not weeks.

"Damn," Aeden said. "I was hoping to be able to erase it all. A scar like that will tug when you're trying to move. It may even restrict your movement a little. I'll try to heal it some more when I've had a bit more rest."

"It's fine, Aeden. Really."

"No, it's not. I feel bad enough that you were injured, Raki. I'll not leave you with scars like that if I can help it. Urun would've erased it completely, and much more easily than I can."

Fahtin shifted her eyes to Khrazhti. She was silently watching the three interact. What was it like for the animaru woman? She had no real family; only the father who had killed her mother and tortured Khrazhti as a child. The father they had killed hours ago. The look in her eyes, it was a hunger. Longing. Did she crave interactions like the three humans were having?

"What about you, Khrazhti," Fahtin said. "Are you injured?"

"I am fine, Fahtin. Thank you." It was remarkable how easily she had learned Ruthrin. She had a discernible accent, almost like someone from Arania. That was logical, since the Aranian language was the closest thing to Alaqotim of the modern languages.

"She tells me I can't heal her," Aeden said. "I'm not sure if that's true or if she's trying the same tactic the lot of you are. I do know that life magic, which healing is, damages animaru, but she's half human, too. I intend to find out what I can do to heal her, though. Her skin is also too beautiful to carry scars."

Aeden immediately jerked, obviously realizing what he had said. "I mean, she wears revealing clothing and...that is...uh—"

"It is fine, Aeden," the animaru said. "I appreciate you wanting to aid me, but there is no need, not at this time. I am less injured than you, and you can receive no healing, so we will suffer the small pains together. You must also remember that I heal, without aid, more quickly than humans do." She smiled at him, and it struck Fahtin that her expressions lately had seemed more genuine, not scripted as they had looked before.

She liked Khrazhti, though she didn't think she would at first. The woman had been the commander of the animaru who had slaughtered Aeden's clan, killed some of Fahtin's own family. Fahtin felt justified in being suspicious of her at the start. But Khrazhti had won her over. She was not so different than many humans she knew. The good ones. Her motives seemed pure, and she had the kind of honor all the stories upheld as the ideal.

And she was a friend. Fahtin stepped over to the animaru and hugged her gently, not sure how many injuries she had.

Khrazhti's eyes widened and she looked to the ground, obviously out of sorts.

"What was that for?" Aeden asked, mouth agape.

"I'm just happy we're all safe. My friends and family." Fahtin fought off tears that were trying to fill her eyes. Why was she so emotional all of a sudden?

Aeden stared for a moment, then rushed to change the subject. "I'd like to talk about some things now that we aren't running toward our next battle."

Fahtin sat and took another drink of water. "Things? What things?"

"Well, first off, how you were struck by lightning in that last battle with the assassins and came off with nothing more than singed clothing."

"Yeah," Raki said, "and things like how Aeden did what he did against that last animaru we fought. I could swear I saw a magical shield that blocked his attack on Khrazhti."

"Yes, I would like to know about that, too," Fahtin said, mentally thanking Raki for taking the attention off her.

"Fine," Aeden said. "I'm not sure how I did it. I did make a shield, but it was more powerful than I should have been able to make. I used my spell Saving Force. I've used it before, but Suuksis's spell should have blasted through it. I don't know how I stopped magic that strong."

"I saw you," Khrazhti said. "You made gestures with your hands. Your feet were placed precisely, as if in a practiced stance. You flowed smoothly, no breaks in form, and it was impossible to determine what was one motion and what was the next because they blended into one continuous movement. It appeared to be more efficient than when I have seen you cast previously."

Aeden's mouth dropped open. "You saw all that, even though you were down and on the receiving end of magic that should have destroyed you?"

"I have been studying and using magic for thousands of years. It is second nature to notice these things. It allows me to develop my own magic."

"Amazing."

"Because of this I had determined that my father was using magic beyond his ability. S'ru must have blessed him with power he had not possessed previously.

"I have not told you of my last encounter with Suuksis, twelve hundred years ago. At that time, we were rivals for S'ru's blessing. Our god prefers it that way, that his followers squabble and contest with each other so that he can choose the most powerful to represent him. In that engagement, I struck Suuksis down. It was more than a century until he regained his full power, and he never challenged me again. It was at that time S'ru made me his high priestess.

"But this time, Suuksis used power that far outstripped what he had previously had. And what I currently have. If it were not for Aeden, I would have been destroyed, I have no doubt."

"But," Raki said, "I thought you told us that animaru aren't ever destroyed, that they only get weakened and then eventually regain their power."

"Yes. That is true, but for one exception. No, I misspoke. There are now two exceptions, one of them, of course, being Aeden or another using life magic. We knew of no such thing until recently. The other, however, we have known about. S'ru himself has the power to destroy animaru, since he is the creator of us all. I believe he endowed Suuksis with that power.

"S'ru has truly abandoned me and seeks my destruction."

The sorrow in Khrazhti's voice broke Fahtin's heart. Khrazhti had spent longer than the lifetimes of everyone Fahtin knew put together serving S'ru, only to find out her god was false to his own laws. Not only would S'ru not correct his course, but he had consciously made an enemy of Khrazhti. Fahtin couldn't imagine how it would feel if her parents not only had betrayed her, but now wanted to see to it that she was dead.

"But how *did* you make that shield? How did you know what to do? Is it one you've been practicing?" Fahtin hoped to focus Khrazhti's attention on something else.

"I don't know," Aeden answered. "I haven't been specifically working on figuring out the enhancement for that spell. It kind of just came to me. My body and my hands moved on their own, it seemed, and then it was done. I'm not sure I could repeat it even if I had to. The power going through me to make that shield, it was unlike any I've felt before. The closest thing I can remember is when the animaru first attacked the caravan and were killing our family."

Fahtin didn't want to remember that awful night. "It's the same with me. I didn't do anything to stop that lightning, and I didn't feel anything go through me, power or otherwise. It was all so fast. I was standing there, and then there was a flash, and the next thing I knew, I was getting up and you were all standing around me shocked. And I mean no pun when I say that."

"Surely you must know something," Aeden pressed.

"I'm telling you I don't."

"What do you remember doing, just before?"

"Nothing. I mean, we were in battle. I saw you fighting and I remember thinking I needed to get back behind the rock and then the flash came."

Aeden ran his fingers through his hair. "Come on, Fahtin. Think. This is important. If we can figure out how to protect ourselves, or even just you, it will make the future much easier."

"I'm telling you that I don't know anything, Aeden. Why won't you believe me? When you say you don't know how you cast that magic, we all believe you."

"It's different, Fahtin," he said through gritted teeth. "I just need you to try to—"

"You don't think I've tried? All of this scares me, Aeden. It doesn't help when you throw accusations at me as if I'm doing something wrong. I'm doing the best I can." She wiped the tears from her eyes and stood up straighter, ready to battle if that was what he wanted.

He opened his mouth to say something else, then closed it. He raised his finger and opened his mouth again, but only grunted and spun toward the doorway. "I'm going to search some of the rooms to see if there's anything we can use."

He shuffled out of the room.

Fahtin deflated and sat back down. She didn't look at the other two in the room and she hoped they wouldn't bother her. She was exhausted again, but this time the cause wasn't physical.

4

eden took his time exploring a few of the rooms on the same level of the main tower. He needed some time to think, to figure out what was going on.

He'd never had cross words with Fahtin before, not in all the years they lived together. She was his sister and he loved her. What caused him to lash out at her?

In one of the rooms he searched, he found a squat stool that was still strong enough for him to sit on. He did so, putting his elbows on his knees and his chin in his hands and thought.

Fear. Maybe it was fear that had him angry. That and bone-weary fatigue. It seemed that he hadn't had enough rest for weeks, though it was probably only days. He was strong— he knew he was—and he had been deprived of rest before, especially as part of his training with his clan. Then why? What had affected him so that he was acting this way?

He lifted his head and clenched his fists. He had not asked for this responsibility. It was fine to protect his clan and to go to battle for his family, but this was different. He either was the Malatirsay or he was not. The confusion was the worst part.

If he was honest with himself, he didn't want to be the prophesied warrior, even if it meant Benzal was the one. He had proven that he was not fit to rely upon. So many failures, starting with the largest: so disappointing his parents and his clan found him unworthy to even continue living. He had lived when he should have died; couldn't even do that right. Failing his clan was bad enough, but he had failed his adopted family, too, allowing so many of them to be killed that night with the animaru. If he had acted more quickly, he could have saved more of them. What would happen if he failed in this? The entire world would be destroyed.

And it would be his fault.

At every turn, he made the wrong decisions or faced defeat because he didn't have what he needed to be the hero everyone deserved.

Fahtin. Not only was he failing his promise to her, but he was a source of sadness to her.

Aeden sighed and lowered his head to look at the ground. He wasn't sure what he should do.

One thing he did know was that he needed to apologize to Fahtin. She had been through so much. They all had. He had no right to press her like he did.

He spent a few more minutes sitting on the stool, staring at the ground and listening to his own breaths. In and out, a rhythm, the cadence of life. It soothed him, calmed him, even gave him a bit of hope. His breaths, his heartbeat, the nearly imperceptible thrum of magic surrounding him. He closed his eyes and listened to it, shushing like the softest whisper, but in a recognizable rhythm.

That was it! The rhythm of the world's magic. He had heard it, he had moved his body to it when he had cast Saving Force. He had tapped into it, subconsciously. Maybe he could learn to do it purposely. It was worth a try; better than the trial and error method he had been using.

He jumped up from the stool, feeling a bit less exhausted, and headed out the chamber doorway. He stopped in the hall, turned around, and snatched up the stool.

When he arrived back at the room with his friends, he was greeted by all three staring off in different directions, none speaking to each other. As he came through the doorway, three sets of eyes focused on him.

"Fahtin—" he started.

"Aeden—" Fahtin said at the same time.

They both stopped, but then Aeden bulled ahead. "I'm so sorry, Fahtin. I never meant to sound angry at you. I'm out of sorts right now. I only want to understand what is happening to us." He proffered the stool, noting that she was still sitting on the stone floor.

Her smile lit up the room. "No, I overreacted. I understand why you're on edge. I'm scared. I don't know what's happening, and I got emotional. Please, let's talk. Maybe together we can figure out what we're looking for, what we need."

He set his stool down and held his hand out to her. She took it and he helped her to her feet. Then he swept her into a hug and held on tight. "I'm sorry. You are my sister and I love you. I don't like feeling that I've made you sad." He brushed her hair with his fingers, catching them on some of the tangles.

"Ouch," she said, but still hugged him back. "My hair has seen better days."

They laughed and he released her so she could sit on the stool.

"I think," she said, more serious, "that we are all changing. We should have expected something to happen. The task we have in front of us is important, saving the entire world. Did we think we would stay the same?"

Aeden's own smile dropped off his face. "No, I guess not. Still, changing is one thing, but these things..."

"It's almost like Dizhelim is giving us what we need to fight," Raki said, then flushed and looked toward the wall to avoid the others' attention.

"That's exactly it, Raki," Aeden said. "Carrying on an important task can change us as people, make us act different, but what we're seeing is magic. Why? Is it to better handle the responsibility, or is everyone in the world changing, too? Or is it something else?"

"Perhaps you always had the ability but now you are learning to use it," Khrazhti said.

Aeden wasn't sure why that suggestion chilled him. Maybe it was too close to when Jehira told him he was the object of prophecy. "I don't know. It's all so strange.

"You're the expert in magic, Khrazhti. Do you know what's happening to us? We've been dancing around it for long enough. Raki can somehow disappear, more completely than training or physical skill can account for. Fahtin took a lightning bolt full force and got up without a scratch."

"And you instinctively figure out how to cast a powerful enhanced spell when it's needed most," Fahtin added. "Don't forget that."

"That is a minor thing. I have already had use of magic. Learning to use it better is a natural progression. I fortunately figured out how to make it more efficient. That's not as mysterious as you two suddenly gaining magic."

"But that's the thing," Fahtin countered. "We're not important, Aeden. You're the one the prophecy promised, the one who can turn back the animaru. You're the Malatirsay. We're just along for the ride."

"No."

Fahtin took his hand in both of hers. "Yes. You have to face it, the three of us could die and it would not stop you from completing your mission and saving the world. You're more important than we are."

"No. You are each important. The Malatirsay, it's just a fabrication, a tool the prophecy uses as an ideal to live up to. It's not real, or if it is, it's not me."

"But," Raki said, "my nani..."

Aeden met his friend's eyes, though Raki averted his after a brief moment. "She told us what she believes, what she hopes to be true. I'm not convinced the Malatirsay is a real person. We can all be heroes. All of us can work toward saving Dizhelim. And if we do that, we are all as important as the other. I'll not hear talk about how you're less than anyone, not from any of you."

The silence was oppressive. Aeden didn't like how he sounded to himself, like a tyrannical father demanding others see things the way he did. Why were none of them speaking?

"Is your nani a prophet, Raki?" Khrazhti asked softly.

The boy turned his head toward her but kept his eyes on the ground. "I don't know if I would call her a prophet, but she has had some foretellings."

"Will you tell me about h—ugh," Khrazhti grunted. Aeden's head snapped up from his hands to the animaru woman as blinding force slammed into his mind. She had leaped to her feet and begun gyrating her body. At first Aeden thought she may be having fits, but then he noticed the space around her.

Ethereal, slightly glowing forms swirled around Khrazhti. Aeden blinked twice, his vision slowly clearing along with the ache between his eyes. At least three man-shaped spectres attacked her with ghostly swords. She tried to fight back, but her blades seemed to pass through their bodies.

Not so *their* weapons. As Aeden watched with horror, a

line of reddish brown appeared on Khrazhti's shoulder where she failed to evade a blow.

Aeden drew his swords and rushed to help her. A cut along his back pulled his attention away. More of the spirits attacked him, and his other two friends as well.

"Run," he said. "We can't fight them."

$$\maltese \quad 5 \quad \maltese$$

"How long has it been since the Mayor saw us?" Aila asked.

"Barely a day," Tere answered.

"Shouldn't they feed us soon?"

"Soon."

Aila hated waiting. That was all she seemed to be doing lately. She wasn't meant to be a prisoner. The boredom and lack of light were driving her crazy. As was the smell.

"What are we going to do, Tere?"

The old archer shifted in the darkness. She wished she could see. Imprisonment was bad enough without being blind, too.

"We'll wait and see what the Mayor does. There has to be a way for me to convince him I'm not who he thinks I am."

"No," she said. "I don't think so. He'll only accept either that treasure he goes on about, or the payment for it. Neither of which are things we could ever get our hands on."

Tere sighed. "I'm sorry this happened, that you got caught up in it."

"It's not your fault. If you're not that guy, then you didn't have anything to do with getting us captured. A person can't control how they look. Well, for the most part." She imagined how she must appear now after so many days without bathing.

"I know, but I'm sorry just the same."

"I joined your little group because I think it's probably the only chance to stop those monsters."

"No," he said. "You joined because of Aeden."

She smiled, thinking of the warrior. "Okay, yes, I originally joined because of him. I stayed because of what you...we are doing. I live in this world, too, you know. I don't want to see it destroyed by those creatures."

"All the more reason for me to regret where we are and what's happening to us."

"That's enough, Tere. Don't go down that path. If you do, you'll soon be sitting against that wall like Urun, separating yourself from reality. And then where would I be?"

He made a sound. Was that a chuckle? "Right here, same as now."

She couldn't conjure the energy to laugh, or even to smile, though he could probably see it if she did. She tried to talk to Urun, several times a day. He hardly ever responded at all. He was taking imprisonment very hard. Poor guy.

Footsteps echoed in the hall outside their door, chased by torchlight. They stopped just outside the door. She knew it was their door because as long as they'd been there, they hadn't seen any other prisoners. Was that good or bad? She didn't know; didn't really care.

The smaller door near the bottom of the main door opened, and a metal tray slid in with three metal bowls and a few crusty, hard chunks of bread. The guard pushed a shallow pan of water in after it. Oh joy, it was feeding time.

The slot the food came through would be left open so they could slide the dishes back out when they were finished.

They found out quickly that if they didn't do so, they would not be fed or given water again.

A torch waved about at the barred window, throwing light onto them. Aila blinked up at it, eyes somehow watering even though she never got enough to drink.

The guard's face peered through two of the bars, looking right at Aila.

"You're a pretty thing," he said in his rough, gravelly voice. "Need a bath, but still very pretty."

What? She had to look like a pile of rubbish, most likely smelled worse than one, and he was calling her pretty?

"How about I bring you out for a bit, let you get cleaned up? I have a bucket of clean water in the other room. I can strip you down and wash you real good. It'd be fun for both of us."

Really? How solitary and desperate was this lout that he resorted to propositioning filthy prisoners?

"Well?" he said.

"You'll let all three of us clean up?" she asked, already knowing the answer.

"No. Just you. I've no desire to see the other two with no clothes. We could even arrange getting some better food if you help me with a little problem."

I'm sure it is a little *problem*, she thought, but knew better than to say it.

"Tempting, but no thank you. I'll just sit here in the filth and dark."

The torch pulled away from the window and the face disappeared. "Have it your own way," he said as the footsteps started up again, heading back down the hall.

Aila blew out a breath. Of all the asinine things she had dealt with, this had to rate up there in the top five. Filthy pig of a man.

Tere had sat silently while the exchange occurred. Urun,

too, of course.

"You know," she said in the general direction where Tere sat, his silhouette visible through the extra light coming in through the food slot. "I could go along, have him let me out, and then kill him. We could probably escape."

"That would be a dangerous thing to try," he said. "For all you know, he'd have three or four of his buddies out there to share you."

"True, but it's worth a shot, right?"

"No, Aila. It's not worth a shot." He grabbed a bowl, took her hand in his, and then wrapped her around the dish full of slop. "At least, not until it's a last resort."

"Thanks." She wasn't sure if it was for wanting to protect her or for keeping her from spilling the food by stumbling around in the dark.

She would find a way to escape this place, though. The Mayor wasn't going to simply release him. She wasn't sure what Tere was thinking, but surely he must recognize that much.

Tere took another bowl of the food to Urun. Fortunately, the priest would still eat when given food, though he wouldn't make a move for it unless it was handed to him. The same with drinking water from the pan. It was bad enough they hardly got enough to stay alive, but it was easy to spill when trying to drink from that pan.

This was her life: scraping a bowl of slop for every drop, barely drinking enough to have to pee once or twice a day, and waiting for endless hours and days to find out what would happen to her.

The worst part was that she was getting accustomed to it. Soon, she feared, she would simply accept it and look forward to the twice daily gruel and water. She gnawed on a piece of the hard bread Tere gave her, hoping, anticipating biting into a softer, bitter spot that indicated mold.

She would be free. Somehow, eventually. She would. Even if it was only long enough for a group of the disgusting guards to use her and kill her. She would get out of this cell.

She needed to plan, come up with a scheme that gave her the best chance of escaping alive. Her *and* her friends.

Their next meal was brought by a different guard. He shoved the meal tray so forcefully into the slot in the door that some of the gruel spilled and the bread dumped onto the floor. Even worse, water sloshed from the pan, spreading across the stone floor and mixing with the muck there.

The man always glowered at her. She saw hatred in those dark, beady eyes of his. Set deep in the brow of his pock-marked face, they burned into her. The nose between was a crooked mess that had obviously been broken before. She had no doubt he would kill them were he allowed.

"I'm telling you," she heard him say to another guard after delivering their food. "If we just happen to forget to feed them, they'll die soon. The Mayor won't blame us for prisoners dying. Everyone knows some people can't survive in a cell. We can be done with them and go back to better duties, like guarding the mansion or patrolling. I'm sick of being here."

"Don't let no one hear you saying that. I'll not be blamed if something goes wrong. If they die, the Mayor will take it out of our hides. I bet he'll hang us. If that happens, if they die, I'll tell him what you just said. Maybe he'll let me live."

"Oh come on," the first guard said. "I was joking. Don't get so uptight. No need to tell the Mayor anything."

The guards went through the door at the end of the hall and it slammed shut. She couldn't hear anything else after that. Great. As if it weren't bad enough that they may die on their own before the Mayor killed them, the guards were contemplating letting the prisoners starve to death.

❧ 6 ☙

Aeden rolled out of the path of one of the translucent swords. He had tried to block the weapons with his own and received a burning cut along his hand for it. He was lucky it wasn't more serious. The blade had passed right through his weapon and then solidified just in time to inflict damage.

Coming to his feet, he scanned the room to make sure his friends had taken his direction. They had. Fahtin was leading down the stairs, pursued by two of the phantoms. Khrazhti was close on her heels, three more trying to catch her. Raki flickered in and out of Aeden's vision as he sprinted down the stairs as well.

Curiously, the ghostly warriors seemed to have difficulty tracking the young Gypta. Whatever caused Raki to fade from sight affected the apparitions as well.

Aeden's friends had grabbed their packs, even in their haste to escape. He jerked to his left and snatched his up from the ground as well. He swung it over his shoulder and thrust his arms through the straps.

The three blade wielders who had been after Aeden

rushed him as he regained his feet and raced down after the others. He noticed for the first time that they wore clothing styles from hundreds of years ago—long coats over armor made from strips of leather—though the wraiths and their clothes were fuzzy, as if seen through a fogged window.

He hoped his friends could keep ahead of the attackers, who moved at what Aeden would call a normal walking speed for a living person. He wasn't sure if there were others, down farther in the tower and heading up to cut off their escape, but he hoped not. They were taking enough injuries from the ones currently chasing them.

Aeden racked his brain, trying to come up with a way to fight off the ethereal attackers. Almost by habit, he cast Light to Conquer Darkness to imbue his weapons with life magic, assuming it would have an effect on what were plainly ghosts of the previous inhabitants of Broken Reach.

The glow settled onto his blades and he swung them toward the wraiths chasing him. They sliced through the bodies of his attackers—and their weapons—with no discernible effect.

Aeden gritted his teeth. It had been worth a try, though a long shot. Since he had learned to imbue items with a bit of life magic, all of the party's belongings were so endowed to combat the animaru. Too bad it wouldn't help in the current situation.

He took another group of steps, mind racing. What else could he do? For all he knew, the ghosts would chase them forever, until they finally overpowered and killed them. He was pretty sure ghosts wouldn't need to stop and rest like the humans would. Aeden's and his friends' deaths would mean nothing, and their opportunity to stop the animaru would have been lost.

He passed through the landing on another floor. There was no sign of other apparitions rushing up to meet them, but the racing descent down the stairs with the pursuers slicing at his friends was dangerous enough. How could he help?

Think, Aeden. Think.

An idea struck him and he began motioning with his hands, as best he could while running down the stairs. He enunciated the words of power and willed the magic toward Fahtin, who was furthest along but still within his sight, before she turned around the stairs as they spiraled down to the next landing. "*Chadu, nidar, kavach.*"

The glow he was hoping to see did not manifest.

"*Cuir aet biodh!*"

One of the wraiths got too close, slashing at Fahtin with its sword. The blade deflected at the last minute, as if it had struck something solid. Not solid like stone, because Aeden had a feeling as of something being shaved off, but still, the blade did not strike the Gypta woman.

The spell was not as powerful as when he had cast it over Khrazhti when they fought Suuksis, but it was better than nothing. He checked on Fahtin once again—she had surged forward ahead of the transparent attackers—and began casting Saving Force again, this time on Khrazhti.

He had trouble locking the magic on Raki with the boy disappearing and appearing again, but Aeden finally, with a force of will, pushed it into place on his third and final companion.

The warrior stumbled and almost fell down the stairs, but regained his balance in time to strike the wall at an angle and bounce off. He grunted, half his breath knocked from his body, righted himself, and somehow shot down the stairs again while ducking a savage slice of a ghostly blade.

Once he had caught his breath, mostly, he cast the spell one more time, this time on himself. He put the shield in place barely in time to deflect the sword of another wraith.

They reached the ground floor. Aeden's legs almost buckled on the transition from stairs to the regular surface of the entry corridor. He ran across the tower hall and shot out the doorway into the mid-afternoon air.

Though injured and exhausted, Aeden closed the gap on his friends, coming up behind them quickly on the level ground. There were no longer any ghostly attackers between himself and those slightly ahead of him. He chanced a glance over his shoulder and saw none following him, either.

When he turned his eyes forward again, he nearly slammed into Khrazhti's back. Only a lightning-fast evasion that almost caused him to lose his balance completely kept him from doing it.

He stopped, panting.

"Where did they go?" he asked, hands on his knees while he tried to pull air into his lungs.

"They vanished when we crossed through the door out of the fortress," Khrazhti said. She wasn't even breathing hard. In fact, Aeden tried to remember ever seeing her breath *at all* and couldn't.

Fahtin leaned against the broken remains of a short wall and Raki was sitting on the ground a few feet away. Both of them looked exhausted, and both had new sources of blood leaking out.

"They are bound to the fortress then," Aeden said. "Lucky for us."

He went to Fahtin first to check her new wounds and to bandage them with the remains of the clothes they had shredded for that use. Raki had far fewer wounds because of his ability to evade the phantoms.

Finally, Aeden went to Khrazhti and looked her over. It was easier to see any cuts on her because she wore so little clothing. He had tried to convince her to wear armor—or at least more rugged clothing—but she said it inhibited her movements and could interfere with her magic. Aeden hadn't found that to be the case with himself, but he grew up and trained his whole life with armor.

The blue woman had a few new cuts, but none of them were deep. Until he could rest again, he wouldn't be healing any of them. He still wanted to try his magic on Khrazhti. He believed he could heal her despite her animaru side.

Fahtin looked around nervously. "We should probably leave. Those things can't leave the fortress, but what if there are others that are not tied to a building?"

"That's a good point," Aeden admitted. He hadn't seen anything else, not even animals, but that didn't mean there weren't any. "It's past time we left anyway. Khrazhti, did you see any of those spectres when you used the fortress as your headquarters?"

"No. I have never seen them before. Perhaps they do not like living beings. Since animaru are unalive, they may not offend the warriors as live people do."

"Hmm," Aeden said. "That sounds reasonable." He took a drink from his water skin and returned it to his pack. Noting the position of the sun and the ancient ruin of the road they were on, he searched out any sign for what they should do next.

"Which way?" Raki asked.

"What are our plans?" Fahtin asked in turn. "I mean, before we decide which way to go, we probably need to figure out what we intend to do next."

"Well," Aeden said. "We still need to meet up with Tere. Then again, if there's a chance to find Benzal and finish our job, that would be good. I think those are the only two options, if we discount running somewhere and hiding until this whole mess is finished."

Khrazhti gasped. "You would abandon our mission to save your world from S'ru's influence?"

"What? Oh, no. It was a joke, Khrazhti. I meant it to break the tension. To be funny. I wasn't serious."

"I see."

"So, huh," Aeden said. "Two options: go toward the Academy, or see if we can find Benzal before he can prepare and open another portal. If we go west to meet with Tere, we may not get back to Benzal for a month or so."

"We promised Tere we'd meet him when we could," Fahtin said.

"You still need to get to the Academy," Raki added.

"I can help you find Izhrod Benzal," Khrazhti said.

Aeden's attention was snatched from his internal thoughts to the animaru. "You can?"

"Yes. Now that my father's influence is gone, I can sense Izhrod Benzal again." She pointed toward the east. "He is that way."

"Do you know how far?"

"I am sorry. I do not. I only know that he is in that direction."

Aeden considered their options. On the one hand, he did want to get back together with Tere, Aila, and Urun. But if Khrazhti could lead them to Benzal, especially since he was in the opposite direction, they might be much closer to him than to where they would meet up with Tere.

There was also the matter of the Academy. The village where he would meet Tere was close to the Academy. They would finally get to Sitor-Kanda and he would get his answers, one way or another.

Was he ready for that?

"Benzal could be just a few miles away," he said.

It wasn't quite a question, but Khrazhti recognized he wanted some kind of answer. "Yes. He could be close or he could be very far away."

"So if we turned around to go and meet Tere, we'd only

have to come all the way back here, wasting time when we might be close enough to get to him in a day or two."

"What you say is possible," Khrazhti confirmed.

"Do you know the next time he will be able to open a portal?"

"No, I am sorry. From what I have seen, the opportunities are several weeks to several months apart."

Aeden ran his fingers through his hair. He knew what he wanted to do, but was that because it was the wise choice or because of how he felt about the two options?

"I think we should go after Benzal," he said.

Fahtin frowned, but said, "I think you're right, though I don't like it."

"It sounds like the smart thing to do," Raki said.

"I will go where you go," Khrazhti said.

"We might as well start immediately," Aeden said with a nod. "No telling if there are more phantoms about. We'll find a suitable place and make camp at least a few hours from here."

They started off again, heading in the direction Khrazhti sensed Benzal. Travel was relatively easy in the barren landscape of the Broken Reach. They skirted a few small hills and jagged rocks that thrust up through the surface of the dirt, but there were no obstructions to keep them from heading in a straight line toward their goal.

No other phantoms appeared and they saw no other creature, neither human nor beast nor animaru, though there were towers in that direction as well as the one they had come from. Four hours from the fortress, they stopped to make camp in the shelter of two large boulders in an otherwise flat area. If there were towers that far out, they weren't anywhere the party could see them.

They stayed there for the remainder of the day and the entire night. Each took a turn at watch, but even so, they were able to sleep more than at any one time during the previous weeks. It was glorious. Wounds, torn clothing, and unbathed bodies notwithstanding, it was glorious.

Aeden cast Life to Unlife a few more times to heal the new wounds his friends had received. When he was done, he felt a bit more tired, but it was nothing compared to the exhaustion he had been battling for the last few days.

"I want to try," Aeden told Khrazhti. "Just a small test."

"No, Aeden. You must reserve your strength. Also, I believe you would damage me more than help me. I am animaru."

"You're *half* animaru."

"I have lived for almost three thousand years. Humans cannot do that. My mother may have been human, but my body has become fully animaru. It will not work."

Aeden sighed. He had to try another approach. "Do you trust me?"

"Of course."

"Then, please, let me try. Just a little test. You let me know if it feels that you are being hurt and I'll stop."

Khrazhti bit her lower lip. Aeden had never seen the woman do that before. She was picking up habits from them. This one was Fahtin, through and through. "You cannot control how much you heal, how much magic you use. You have complained about this."

"I've had some practice and I think I can let loose just a trickle, if I concentrate hard enough. Look at it as helping me to develop my magic. You know I would never hurt you on purpose. Just a little test."

Khrazhti looked at the others. Fahtin smiled at her, a hopeful expression on her face. Raki shrugged. Aeden waited expectantly.

"Very well. A small test. Do not use too much of your

magical energy, however. You still must rest. You have been exerting yourself too strongly lately."

She didn't have to remind him. The Croagh in him accepted the hardship, though. The best way to become stronger was to test your limits, and then push past them. The entire way of life of the clans was based on this philosophy.

"I think I can focus my power on just one wound. I'll try... on *that* one." He gently brushed a two-inch cut on her cheek. It wasn't the most serious of her injuries, but it broke the smooth skin of her face, and he'd come to enjoy looking at that face.

Khrazhti cleared her throat and Aeden realized he was still stroking her cheek, around the cut. He pulled his hand away, feeling his neck and cheeks go warm.

Not only the cut on her cheek, but others she had received were already healing on their own, much more quickly than human wounds did. He knew that was how animaru healed and it made him apprehensive about what he was about to do. He convinced himself it was a harmless test, though. They needed to know if he could heal her if she got more seriously injured. When she had critical wounds was not be the time to find out that it harmed her further.

Aeden moved his arms outward and then brought them back toward the center of his chest a few inches in front of him, allowing his wrists to flex as his movement flowed. It was like he was moving his arms through water. As he repeated the motions, he could feel the magic warming his hands, especially when close together where they formed a shape like he was holding a ball. He intoned the words, "*Jiva, karana, jivana,*" then moved his hands up.

He brought his right hand to Khrazhti's face, letting it hover so close to her skin, he could feel her warmth. As he felt the power trickle out of him, he wondered why she was warm. Were all animaru that way, or was it because she was half human? If they were unalive, why would they be warm?

Khrazhti's eyes widened, and her fists clenched and unclenched in the corner of his vision.

"Am I hurting you?"

"No. I am simply...anxious."

He continued, maneuvering his hand to aim the power more directly at the cut he was trying to heal. Their eyes met, his bright azure and hers a pale, glowing blue. He smiled at her and she, despite the nervous energy in her eyes, smiled back.

Then she gasped and he lost his focus, control of the magic fleeing from him.

"Did I—"

"No," she said. "It was a good thing, a surge of energy I felt. It merely surprised me."

Aeden blew out a nervous breath. Then he noticed her face.

Her unblemished, perfect face.

His mouth dropped open. She noticed and her hand flew to her cheek.

"It does not sting any longer," she said with wonder in her voice.

Fahtin nudged Aeden aside and put her face close to Khrazhti's. "It's gone. The cut is gone. You did it, Aeden. You healed her."

"Woo!" Raki said.

"Aye."

"But," Khrazhti said, "it is impossible. Animaru cannot be healed, not even by S'ru's hand. Only time and our natural rejuvenation can undo injuries we receive."

"I told you," Aeden said. "I can feel the human part of you when I am holding the magic. I focused on that and used the spell differently than I do for the others. More concentrated, more precise, more careful. Now that I've done it, I think I know how to heal you as well as the others. Let me—" He reached for her.

"No," she said. "I believe you. You have done what I thought was impossible and I admit I was mistaken. However, my wounds are not severe and your energy is not limitless. Leave these others. Their small stings and aches will teach me to do better next time."

Fahtin rolled her eyes. "That's what he always says. Injury and pain are great teachers and they allow us to become better."

"Then I agree with him."

Aeden reluctantly gave over, knowing he would not convince her. He was elated, though, that he could heal her in the future, should she be injured on the long road ahead of them.

Soon after, they finished their meager meal and started off again. Khrazhti aimed them toward Benzal and they continued on their way, the land unobstructed and wide open.

Over the next two days, the terrain changed gradually from the barren, broken, dry ground they had been traversing. It transformed to plains with first scrub, then occasional bushes, to the edge of grasslands that seemed to stretch out for miles before breaking into a series of smooth hills. The horizon itself was obscured by clouds and mist.

Evening was coming upon them and Aeden scanned the land ahead of them for a place to camp. The terrain had changed drastically this close to the hills—foothills to the mountains now visible. They were traveling through the outskirts of loose stands of trees, if not a proper forest.

As they came around a grouping of three short trees with close-packed leaves, motion from ahead and to the left caught Aeden's eye. He turned in time to lock gazes with a short, squat, humanoid creature rising up from the ground.

It looked at him with wide, black eyes, then squealed and took off at a sprint, disappearing into the brush.

Khrazhti had her swords out. She studied the surrounding foliage as if she expected an army to jump out at them.

"It's fine," Aeden said.

"That creature," she responded, still looking for danger. "What is it? I have not seen one such as that."

"Pouran," he said. "A youngling. We frightened him. There must be a village nearby."

"A village? It was not a beast?"

Aeden chuckled. "No. They're smart, smart as humans. They're sort of human, as far as their thoughts and their communities are concerned."

"But it did not have smooth skin. It was covered with stiff dark hair, and it had long teeth protruding from its mouth."

"Tusks," Raki corrected. "They look different, but they're not so bad. I've seen a few as the caravan traveled, but they mostly stay away from human settlements. People normally don't treat them well. We Gypta know the feeling."

Khrazhti lowered her swords but didn't sheath them. "It will not bring back more of them to attack us?"

"Even if he does bring back adults," Aeden said, "they won't attack us without finding out who we are and what we're doing here. The best thing we can do is to wait here so we don't run into any guards they may have around their village. They'll come to us soon enough."

Khrazhti didn't look convinced. Fahtin stepped over to the blue woman and put a hand on her shoulder. "It'll be okay. Relax. Let's stop right here and have something to eat. We don't want to appear hostile. We may scare them."

The animaru finally put her swords into their scabbards.

"I learned that many things in this world are dangerous. These creatures, they look formidable, with their...tusks, and their compact form."

Aeden sat down on a rock. "They can be, just like humans can be. Do you not have different types of animaru?"

"Yes, there are different forms animaru can take. There are sixteen main types."

"And do you have other creatures, ones who are not of the main types? More animal than animaru?"

"Animal?"

"You know, beasts. Or rather, creatures that are like animaru but that keep themselves apart, living their own lives and not associating with the rest of the animaru."

Khrazhti cocked her head at him. "No. In Aruzhelim, there are animaru. Some lesser forms are little more than beasts, but they serve the more powerful. All are engaged in the wars that constantly rage between factions. None are held aside."

"That sounds very sad," Fahtin said. "Is that all there is to Aruzhelim? It's just war and fighting between yourselves all the time?"

"Such is as it has been for thousands of years. Until now."

"Oh," Fahtin said. "Right."

Raki sat down on the ground next to Aeden's rock. "Well, here there are more varieties. There are different types of humans, there are beasts and insects, there are things some would call monsters—though most of those are gone from the world—and there are other people that are not human. The pouran are one of these, just like the encali, astridae, and arba."

"People?" Khrazhti said. "You call them people, but they are not human? I do not believe we have a word for these in my language."

Aeden waved toward a tree that had fallen and continued to grow, making a bench of living tree trunk. "Sit. We'll wait to see if the pouran come to us."

She hesitated, darting looks in the direction the small pouran had gone, then finally sat down.

"While we wait, maybe Raki can tell us how the pouran were created."

Raki started and twisted around to face Aeden. "Me?"

"Of course," Aeden said. "I know you like them, and I've heard you talk about how they came to be more than once in the last several years. You'll tell the story better than I."

Raki leveled a skeptical gaze at him, then shrugged. "Okay. I do like them. Or maybe it's that I sympathize with them. Either way, I'll tell the story." He turned to face Khrazhti.

"Thousands of years ago, during the War of Magic, lived a great wizard named Sarketh of Golonir. The kingdom to which he belonged was relatively small when compared to others in the Souveni Empire, but he had made a name for himself with his magical prowess.

"Unfortunately, he had also become famous for his temper and the way he manifested his anger.

"He was allowed a short time to return home to visit his family during a lull in the endless string of battles. After several hard days of travel, he arrived and wanted nothing more than to soak in a bath and rest.

"When he came through his door, however, a servant he had never seen met him at the door and demanded to know what he wanted. Before the situation got out of hand, another servant, one who had worked for the household for many years, interrupted and greeted his lord.

"Sarketh was so weary, he didn't continue further with berating the new servant, instead commanding his attendants to bring hot water for his bath in his upstairs bathing chamber.

"When he arrived, however, he found his rooms in less than ideal condition. He found dust on the mantel and even on the table he used to read his correspondence each morning.

"Sarketh's anger from earlier was still smoldering, and when he found that the new servant, the one who failed to recognize him, was the one responsible for keeping these rooms clean, he called the man to an accounting.

"The head servant went to fetch the man as others brought up the buckets of heated water. One of the women, another servant he didn't recognize, brought soap and oils for Sarketh's bath. On the way inside the room, she tripped and fell, scattering the items she had brought. Two of the bottles of fragrant oils broke and sprayed across the floor rugs.

"Sarketh had just about had enough. He was preparing to give the clumsy woman a tongue-lashing when the servant he had called for entered the room. Sarketh looked down to see that the man's hands were dirty. He was attending his lord with dirty hands!

"The servant spotted the woman, still sprawled on the ground from her tumble, and he reached down to help her up. She smiled at him and scurried to clean up the items she had dropped.

"The master observed all this, his anger building. 'What is this familiarity with which these two servants interact with each other?'

"'I'm sorry, master,' the older servant said. 'They are married. The lady of the house hired them as a team.'

"'Two troublesome servants at once? They do not recognize their own master, they cannot perform simple tasks such as bringing soap and oils to my bath, and he dares to come into my presence with dirty hands? This is unacceptable.'

"The two bowed to their master, pleading with him to be merciful, that they would show him he could rely on them. But he'd had enough.

"'You snuffle around my home and you are clumsy and filthy. I will give you a form more befitting your natures.'

"Sarketh cast a spell on them and they began to change. Their bodies became squatter and shorter. They grew coarse hair. And their noses, ears, and heads transformed. Within seconds, the two stood before him, both resembling boars of the forest. They still thought and spoke like humans, and stood on two legs, but they were now something other than human.

"'I name your kind pouran,' Sarketh said. 'Perhaps now you will serve me better. Leave my sight before I decide your punishment is not yet complete.'

"The newly made pouran fled down the stairs. They continued in his employ—who would hire those who looked like monsters?—hoping against hope that the master would feel sorry for what he did and change them back if they became ideal servants.

"Unfortunately, soon after Sarketh returned to the fighting, he was killed by enemy wizards. The two transformed servants remained in their boar-like forms for the rest of their lives.

"Unknown at first, possibly even to Sarketh, the pouran could not procreate with humans, only other pouran. The original pair produced seven children, who had to marry their own brothers or sisters in order to create children of their own. This continued down until our day, with every family of pouran being descendants of that original pair.

"Of course, like anyone a little different, the pouran faced abuse and mistrust. A few remained servants for this lord or that, but most of them fled human communities and made their own, far away from the towns and villages of men."

Raki looked embarrassed for having spoken so much. He studied the ground in front of him. "And that's how the pouran were created."

Khrazhti, who had been motionless, her attention rapt, blinked like she was coming out from under a spell. "Thank you, Raki. I did not know about any of that."

"Sure."

It wasn't more than a few minutes after that when a rustling in the bushes revealed a group of the pouran coming to visit them. The small one they had seen, his fur a lighter brown than the dark grey of the adults, stayed at the rear of the group. When one of the adults in the front of the pack turned to the smaller one, the youngster nodded. He took a look at the humans and slid behind one of the other adults. Aeden would bet it was the child's mother.

"Tisig told us of your presence," the large pouran at the front said. He was a bit larger than most of the others, and his face and arms showed old scars. "I am Cherun. What is your intention?"

"We are just passing through," Aeden said, "on the way to somewhere else. We didn't mean to frighten him. We'll cause you no trouble."

While Aeden was speaking, Cherun noticed Khrazhti and tightened his grip on the spear in his hand.

"Who is that one?" Cherun pointed his spear at her.

"She is my friend and traveling companion. She is of no concern to you."

"She resembles creatures we have seen recently. A very few of them destroyed nearly half my tribe. If she is one of them, she is a concern."

"You have seen animaru?" Khrazhti asked.

The entire group of pouran backed up a step when she spoke.

"You speak Ruthrin?" Cherun said.

"I do. My friends have taught me."

Cherun turned to face Aeden again. "I have never seen a creature like this, except for those that attacked my tribe."

"Aye. It's a long story, but we have been fighting those creatures you speak of. They're called animaru. Khrazhti here has been helping us. We're hunting the man who brought them to our world."

"To our world?" Cherun asked.

"Yes. I told you, it's a long story."

Cherun whispered softly with the others with him for a moment, then turned back to the humans. "Are you Raisor Tannoch, the great hero?" At the name, Tisig, the smaller one, bounced excitedly.

Aeden laughed. "No, I'm afraid not. My name is Aeden Tannoch. Raisor was my kinsman. How do you know of him?"

Cherun drew his lips back in the semblance of a smile, though with his tusks and sharp teeth, it looked more feral than friendly. "We are not savages, no matter what we look like. We have few books, but one has stories of heroes in it, including Raisor Tannoch and Erent Caahs."

Aeden was surprised, though he didn't know why he should be. He grew up listening to stories of great heroes, as did Raki and Fahtin. He supposed it was just a normal part of life. It made him feel more comfortable with the pouran.

"Your red hair," Cherun continued, "and your armor and weapons. It's how Raisor Tannoch was described. I meant no offense."

"No offense taken. I grew up with stories of Raisor's adventures and always wanted to be just like him. It's a compliment and I thank you."

Cherun whispered with his companions again. "Would you have a meal with us? We were about to prepare dinner. We brought down a large deer today and have plenty of food."

Aeden looked toward the others. Raki and Fahtin had expectant looks on their faces and Khrazhti simply stared at the pouran with no emotion displayed on her face. "We would be honored. It's been quite some time since we have eaten a full meal."

"Very well," Cherun said. "Please follow us. It's not far."

The humans followed Cherun while the other pouran spread out. They were not exactly surrounding the humans, but Aeden knew they were trying to do that without looking like they were. He smiled. The pouran were people like any others he had met. Better than some, and more practical.

During their short journey, the smaller pouran, Tisig, drifted toward Raki. They were of similar size, though Aeden thought Raki was probably older. Tisig was wider, of course, but they were more alike than any of the others in their party.

"I love stories of Erent Caahs," Raki told the pouran.

"Me too, but I like Raisor Tannoch better."

"Why?"

They drifted to the edge of the group and started whispering animatedly. Aeden shot a look to Fahtin and jerked his head toward the two young ones. She smiled at them like a proud mother.

A tap on her shoulder from the pouran who Tisig had hidden behind drew her attention and she began to converse with the one who Aeden figured was the boy's mother, making her Cherun's wife? He was sure he'd find out soon.

Khrazhti walked alone with several of the pouran in what looked like a formation surrounding her. Aeden slowed down to match pace with the blue woman. They spoke softly as the group made their way to the pouran camp.

❧ 8 ❧

"I t's about damn time," the big man with the huge axe grumped as the Falxen came across the bridge into Praesturi.

Keenseeker. His name was Keenseeker. But he was awful big. Shadeglide always referred to him in her mind that way: "the awful big one."

She didn't have much respect for him. Indeed, he didn't command much. He was fierce, she'd give him that, and he knew how to use that weapon he carried, but at best he was a raging warrior. At worst, he was simply a dumb brute with anger issues.

Shadeglide shook her head. She was being too judgmental. The man was on her team, so she should be positive about it. It was so hard, though, with how much he complained.

Darkcaller lifted her chin, as she normally did when addressing Keenseeker. "I'll not explain it again. We needed to make sure we didn't tip off our targets. Praesturi is a small town, and our arrival would no doubt be the subject of conversation immediately. We needed Shadeglide to scout it out first to make sure we didn't blunder."

The Falxen leader turned toward Shadeglide and nodded. "Shadeglide completed her task admirably. *She* follows instructions and does her job. *She* found that the three we chase were imprisoned and not likely to hear of our arrival. And thus we are here."

Keenseeker scowled. It was his default expression. "Like I said, it's about damn time. I haven't had anything to drink but water for weeks. I'll be at the tavern." He walked away from the group, scowling even harder at the townsmen staring at the women in his group.

They were staring at Darkcaller, who wore little underneath her thrown-back cloak, and Phoenixarrow, who displayed so much skin it was hard to believe she engaged in combat as her primary profession.

Keenseeker's scowls made some of the watchers avert their eyes to other things, but men would be men, and Shadeglide did have to admit both women were beautiful. And very shapely. Fireshard was, too, and Shadeglide herself took pride in her taut, athletic body, but she and Fireshard covered their forms more completely.

Keenseeker turned a corner and headed down an intersecting street, unhesitating in his direction. Maybe he'd been in this town before.

Edge's silent, looming presence quelled the flurry of attention even more than Keenseeker's glares. He was a compact man, but the way he moved, the confidence he displayed, made people think twice about challenging the man. Though she found him very polite, he did have an air of danger about him. Others could sense it, even if they were generally not perceptive.

Shadeglide stepped over to Phoenixarrow.

"Have you been here before?"

The statuesque redhead flipped a lock of hair from her face, glaring at the retreating form of Keenseeker. Her mouth twisted up on one side. "Someday, I'm going to put an arrow in that arrogant ass."

"In his arrogant ass?" Shadeglide asked with a straight face.

Phoenixarrow blinked and shifted her gaze to the smaller, black-haired woman. A slow smile appeared on her face and she chuckled. "Yeah, maybe that, too." She shook her head while scanning the crowd ahead of her for danger. "No. I've never had the pleasure of coming here. Too close to the Academy for my taste."

Shadeglide wondered how the taller woman could be so perceptive to dangers but completely miss the hungry looks men threw her way. She probably didn't miss them, but ignored them.

"It's exciting, though, right?" Shadeglide was almost bouncing with excitement. "Sitor-Kanda, the Hero Academy, the biggest concentration of magic left on Dizhelim."

"The *Hero* Academy," Phoenixarrow said. "We're assassins for hire. We're the type of people heroes hunt down and kill."

Shadeglide smiled. "Nah. That hero stuff is just in reference to the prophesied hero for whom the Academy was built. They're no more heroic than anyone else, just more effective in doing stuff. I'd love to fight one of their graduates to see if their combat skills are really as good as they say."

"You are a special kind of crazy, you know. And why are you always so happy?"

"I'm talking to you—my friend—and exploring a new place I've never been to before. What is not to be happy about?"

The taller woman shook her head. "A special kind of crazy."

Darkcaller came up to them, Edge following on her heels. Fireshard drifted over as well.

"There are two inns in the town," Shadeglide said. "One is just over there. The other is a few streets over."

"Thank you, Shadeglide." Darkcaller was perfectly polite, not to mention frighteningly efficient, when she didn't have to deal with dissenters like Keenseeker. "I have been here once before. The farther inn will do nicely. When did you say the trial was?"

"A few days from now."

"Fine. Then we have that amount of time to prepare. Let's go and see if we can get rooms at the inn."

"They have four left, as of two hours ago."

Darkcaller smiled, a woefully rare event. "You are a good one to have around, aren't you?"

"I try to be."

The five headed toward the inn. There would be work to do in the next few days, but that was fine. Shadeglide got along well with all of them—except Keenseeker, of course, who tolerated her—so the time would go quickly. And not only would she be able to ply her craft, but she could explore more of the town, maybe even the surrounding area. It would be exciting and fun. Maybe Phoenixarrow would join her. That would be wonderful.

⚜ 9 ⚜

Khrazhti followed the others, Aeden at her side, as they made their way to the pouran camp. She pretended to ignore the creatures surrounding her, their hands clasped tightly around their weapons—spears and clubs.

She found it interesting that the three humans would cooperate so easily with the hairy creatures, treating them as if they were also human. If what Raki said was true, there was no human blood left in the pouran, but one couldn't tell by the way they interacted with each other. It would not work this way with animaru. As a commander, she knew the value of her troops and treated each one according to their station, but she would never treat them as equals unless they were a type that *were* her equals, such as the semhominus.

Without her friends, she would feel isolated in this world. They had taught her much already, and she learned more each day. She glanced next to her without moving her head. Aeden had positioned himself to walk beside her. He answered her questions and engaged her in conversation when he noticed she was being shunned by the pouran. How could he do such things for her, his former enemy? She still didn't understand.

But she wanted to.

Up ahead, the group split, widening out so she could see what was in front of them. It was a camp not too unlike one of her war camps when she had been on campaign. Much smaller, to be sure, but it had the same feeling.

All told, there were probably only thirty pouran. Tents and lean-tos dotted the little clearing, with a few small fires spread around the area distributed in a loose ring around a larger, central fire.

The scent was musky, much like the lesna animaru. It was neither good nor bad, but it was noticeable. Tinier hairy figures darted around the area, some of them laughing. Small ones at play. Seeing such things still surprised her. She had seen few small humans—a glimpse or two when they were in the city—but the entire thing fascinated her. Who would have thought small versions of creatures existed and grew to be the large versions she was used to seeing?

Another scent permeated a portion of the camp as she passed. A bad smell, this one. She wondered what it was.

Aeden stopped walking and looked around. He crinkled his nose, apparently detecting the odor as well. The pouran in front of him stopped, noticing he had done so.

Aeden sniffed and headed for a large tent set off from the others. It had a small fire in front of it, a structure of rods of iron holding a large pot. The smell was not coming from that pot, she noted as she followed him and came close enough to see it was merely water. No, the tent itself, or what was in it, was the source.

Cherun stepped quickly to Aeden. "It's this way," he said, trying to grab hold of Aeden's shoulder. Khrazhti knew as well as anyone that laying hands upon the young warrior was not as easy as some would like. He slithered out of the way, leaving Cherun to grasp at empty air, then pulled open the tent flap to enter.

Cherun hissed and the other pouran went on alert. Khrazhti made no moves toward her weapons, but she mentally plotted out which she would kill first if they tried to attack Aeden or the other humans.

The leader of the pouran sighed and followed Aeden into the tent. "Please, Aeden. The food is at the central fire. Do not bother them."

Khrazhti waited long enough to register that the other pouran, looking at each other in confusion, relaxed their grips slightly on their weapons and took up positions as if to guard the tent, then she entered behind them.

The pungent aroma she had detected washed over her as soon as she entered the dark confines of the tent. Lit candles didn't brighten the space more than dimly.

Greater than a dozen forms lay around the floor, blankets underneath and over them. Pouran faces poked from some of the blankets, some of them moaning.

Khrazhti understood now. This was a tent of injured pouran. Bundles of cloth, some of them dyed red and others still light-colored, were off to the side. One pouran—Khrazhti thought it was female—ministered to a young one in the corner of the tent. She had grey shot through her black bristly fur, and though Khrazhti couldn't see it as well as on a human, it was obvious the pouran was exhausted. Her black eyes were sad and tired.

"What is this?" Aeden asked Cherun.

"These are the injured from the attack by those dark creatures. The others have died. Most of these will, too."

"How did you fight them off?"

"We didn't. The few that attacked tore through us, ravaged even the corpses, and then suddenly left, as if someone had called them. If they hadn't left, we would all be dead. Nothing we could do hurt them."

Aeden nodded. "I know. It was like that with my clan. Slaughtered to a man. There is a...trick to killing them."

Cherun's eyes widened. The first time Khrazhti had seen the emotion on any of the pouran. "You can kill them?"

"Yes."

"Will you teach us? I have no doubt they will come back. We have seen others. We have been able to evade them so far, but we will not be lucky forever."

"I'm sorry, Cherun, but it's nothing I can teach." Noticing the fallen expression on the pouran's face, he continued. "I might be able to do something, though. After I help with these."

"Help?" Cherun asked. "Are you a healer?"

"Not really. I'm a warrior, but I can do a little, I think."

Cherun didn't answer, simply looked at the young pouran in front of them.

Aeden quietly moved up to the older pouran and looked down at her patient. "May I?"

The healer looked to Cherun and the leader nodded, so she stepped over to the wall of the tent, sad eyes locking onto Aeden. Khrazhti thought that if the pouran woman saw Aeden do anything harmful, she would throw herself at him. This instinct some humans—and apparently some pouran—had to sacrifice themselves needlessly for certain people confused her. It was something she planned on asking Aeden about.

Aeden paused, right above the young patient. Then he gently pulled back the blanket.

The sour scent intensified. The injured pouran had gashes down its torso, covering the full length of its body. She recognized injuries such as this. Claws. Seren claws. But was the skin and the fluid coming from it supposed to be that color? Dark red and black, it didn't look natural.

Fahtin gasped from beside Khrazhti. The former high priestess hadn't even realized the girl had come into the tent, she was so engrossed in what was happening.

"Aeden," Fahtin said.

He turned to her. "Sh. It's all right."

He quickly adopted the proper stance and performed the gestures that were by now familiar to Khrazhti. The expected words of power sounded loud in the small tent. Then Aeden knelt beside the injured youngster. In the dim light in the tent, his hands glowed softly as he moved them over the worst of the injuries. Movement behind Khrazhti tickled her danger sense, but not enough for her to take her eyes from what was happening.

Aeden kept at it for several minutes, moving slowly from one area to the next. As he did, the color of the pouran's skin changed. Inch by inch, it went to a light grey, apparently the natural color of their skin underneath the hair. The light on the warrior's hands finally winked out and he slumped, catching himself with one hand so he didn't fall on top of his patient.

The young pouran took a sharp breath and opened its black eyes to look at the human so close to it.

"Hello," it said in a voice Khrazhti thought was female.

"Hello," Aeden said, tired but gently. "How are you feeling?"

"Good. Hungry."

Aeden laughed. "Me too."

A sound from beside her made Khrazhti look, only to find Fahtin weeping.

"Are you well," Khrazhti whispered. "Did someone hurt you?"

"No," Fahtin said with a sniff. "They're happy tears."

Happy tears. Khrazhti didn't know what those were, but she was satisfied that Fahtin had not been attacked.

"You," Cherun said. "You healed her? We thought she was already gone."

Aeden sat back on his heels. "Not yet." He looked around the tent, searching for...something. "Who is the next worse off?"

The old healer was inspecting the young pouran, tears in her own eyes. At Aeden's question, she moved more quickly than Khrazhti would have expected of one who looked so frail, going to another blanketed form. Aeden looked toward Khrazhti and Fahtin and smiled, shuffling after the healer.

"I might be a little while," he said. "Fahtin, Khrazhti, Raki, you should go eat."

"No," Fahtin said, wiping her cheeks. "I want to help."

Aeden used his healing spell on three other pouran, bringing them back from their serious condition to a more stable one. By the time he was finished with the fourth, he could barely stand.

"That's enough, Aeden," Fahtin said. "You'll do no one any good if you collapse from exhaustion trying to help everyone."

"She's right," Cherun said. He stood at the opening to the tent, helping to keep others from coming in to see what was happening. "We appreciate your help. You have saved lives here tonight. The others are not injured as seriously."

Aeden nodded tiredly. "I wish I could help more. If my friend Urun was here..."

"Come," Cherun said, putting his hand out to Aeden. "Lean on me and we will go sit by the fire where you can eat and rest."

All the pouran gathered around stepped back and watched him as he shuffled toward the fire, leaning heavily on Cherun on the one side and Fahtin on the other. Khrazhti made to step toward him twice, but then backed up into the crowd both times. He was being taken care of. He had no need of her. She followed the procession to the fire.

When Aeden finally sat down, he swung his head, looking around. He caught sight of Khrazhti, his eyes meeting hers, and he motioned for her to come join him. Fahtin was on his left, retrieving a plate of meat for him, and Raki stood behind him, still talking with his new pouran friend. There was an empty spot on the log bench next to Aeden, on his right.

As she approached, Cherun sat down in the spot next to Aeden and Khrazhti stopped. She didn't know what to do, so she stood there, considering. Aeden leaned over to say something to Cherun, who turned toward Khrazhti. He spoke to Aeden and got up from his seat, looking at Khrazhti and motioning for her to sit down.

A warm feeling flooded her body, confusing her. She wasn't so close to the fire that she should have felt such a drastic temperature difference. Aeden motioned again for her to join him and she did so.

"Don't get lost in the crowd," he said to her.

Fahtin handed Khrazhti a plate of food and a cup of water, which Khrazhti accepted thankfully.

"You helped them," she said softly so that others wouldn't hear. There was little chance of that. Everyone seemed to be chattering with each other excitedly. "Why?"

"Because they were suffering and because I was able to. Do you think I shouldn't have?"

"I...no. I mean, no, that is not what I was saying. I just find it difficult to understand you at times."

He cocked his head. "Really? I think I'm pretty simple."

"But you are trained as a warrior, to kill."

"Aye."

"Yet you put yourself at risk to help these ones you have never met before."

"I do."

"Why? What makes you do what you do? You seem to decide immediately, but I cannot understand the reasoning."

"My honor," he said. "I kill, yes, when I have to. Mostly it's to help, though. To protect my clan, my family, my friends."

"Which are these?" She was missing something but could not figure out what.

"None of them. They are simply people who have been hurt. People I could help."

She still did not understand but didn't want to seem stupid.

He smiled at her. "I can see you're still confused. Did you...feel anything when we helped them?"

"I could discern a change in the mood," she said. "Especially the older pouran, the woman who was in the tent. She became happy."

"And how did that make you feel?"

She had to think about it for a moment. "Perhaps it made me less tired. It made me think of what S'ru wants to do to this world."

"And..."

"And I became angry that he would do so, but grateful he did not destroy the little one you healed."

He took a drink from his cup. "I see. When you felt grateful, did it make you feel better or make your opinion of the day or our mission or anything else change?"

"I...yes." She thought for a moment, drinking from her own cup. "Fahtin cried but said they were happy tears. She was happy, too, that the little one was repaired?"

"Yes. So, what we did made the girl happy, the healer happy, and Fahtin happy. I'd say it was time and effort well spent to make so many people feel better. Wouldn't you agree?"

She nodded as she took another drink, then smiled at him. "I would. Thank you."

"It wasn't too much trouble to explain it to you."

"No," she said. "I did not mean our conversation. Thank you for expending your energy and making me happy."

"You're very welcome."

Another pouran female tapped Aeden on the arm and spoke to him. He conversed with her, looking back to Khrazhti occasionally to make sure she was still there.

Soon, other pouran spoke to her. The young ones seemed to be fascinated with her blue skin. They asked her questions, which she answered the best she could with Fahtin's help. The Gypta girl had squeezed onto the bench on the other side of Khrazhti and shared in her conversations. By the time the evening was done and they were offered two tents to sleep in, Khrazhti was smiling and chatting with a small group of pouran surrounding her.

She could not remember ever feeling such things, except maybe during the evenings as she and her new friends were traveling from the fortress to Satta Sarak. These humans— and the pouran, who were essentially hairy humans—were a complex and wonderful race. She was proud to be half human, but felt a pang of regret that she wasn't pure of blood.

In the morning, Aeden was the first awake, as was his custom. Khrazhti heard him in the open space at the edge of the clearing, performing the exercises he rarely missed. She went out to join him, swinging her own swords about in an imaginary battle.

He nodded at her and continued his exercise. She sneaked looks at him when her position allowed it and decided he was still not fully recovered from the energy he had expended the night before. He was still fluid and almost jarringly fast, but he lagged through some of the movements, compared to how he typically performed them.

The camp began to wake up and Aeden cut his workout short, nodding to the pouran sentries who turned to look at him when they heard a change in the sounds he made. Khrazhti stopped, too, and followed him to the central fire, where a few of the pouran were starting to cook breakfast.

Cherun soon appeared, and Aeden asked the leader permission to go help in the healing tent again. The pouran looked uncomfortable.

"Please don't take offense at this, but we would prefer that you didn't help."

Aeden's eyes widened and his mouth drooped down into a slight frown. "Why?"

Cherun looked nervously toward Khrazhti and then to a few of the pouran gathering around the fire. "Well, you see, we appreciate what you did last night. We also saw how much it tired you out. You helped with those worst-off last night. The rest are not in danger of dying. They just need time to heal. We...well, that is...we don't want you to sap your strength too much. You're passing through dangerous lands, even more so with those dark creatures roaming around. I'd hate it if something happened to you because you're too tired to fight."

The worried look cleared off of Aeden's face and his eyes became sympathetic. "I see. It's really no trouble. I want to help."

"I know you do," the leader said. "And we respect you all the more, but I must insist. Tiring yourself out will only speed up the healing of those left. We'll not have you waste precious strength on that. Those in the healing tent can rest for the time necessary for them to heal completely."

Aeden lifted his hands toward the pouran. "But I—"

"If you would like to do something else for us," Cherun said, "you could teach us how to kill those monsters."

Aeden's arms dropped. "Yes, actually. I forgot about that. I can't teach you, but I think I can help. Gather up your weapons and bring them to me. I can cast a spell that will allow your weapons to harm the animaru." He shot Khrazhti a look and shrugged.

A pile of spears, a few knives, and some clubs and staffs were soon in a pile in front of Aeden. He cast his spell Light to Conquer Darkness to imbue them with life energy. They glowed softly for a moment and then returned to normal.

"You can't see the glow anymore, but the magic is still

there," he told them. "I'm not sure how long it will last, but it should last for a fair amount of time, maybe a few weeks."

"Again," Cherun said, "we are in your debt. This will save lives if we're attacked again. Please, let us fill your water skins and give you food to carry with you so you won't have to hunt for at least a few days."

"We will accept it gladly. Thank you."

"There is one more thing I would like to give you." Cherun took something from a pouch at his waist. It was something spherical tied on a leather strand. "This is a *fylacta*. It's made from woven pouran hair. My hair, in fact. It is a small token of our thanks to you. It also shows anyone seeing it that you are favored by my tribe. Any pouran family who sees it will treat you as one of their own. You have saved the lives of some of my people and given us the tools to save more. You are one of our family." He turned to Khrazhti, Fahtin, and Raki. "You all are."

Aeden accepted the gift with thanks and slipped it around his neck. They accepted the food and water, said some quick goodbyes, and soon headed east from the camp.

Raki took one last look, waving to Tisig, and the party was swallowed up by the thickening foliage.

They sheltered that evening under a large shield tree, a massive thing with a trunk easily four feet across and a canopy that stretched out twenty feet all around the base. The humans seemed to be in a good mood. The day's travel had been easy and relatively slow, weaving between trees that were still spaced wide enough apart to keep them from slowing the party too much. With the addition of the food given to them by the pouran, the day was almost leisurely.

They set a watch, with Aeden taking the first, Khrazhti the second, Raki the third, and Fahtin the fourth. They woke well rested and set out again.

Just after midday, the sky seemed to swirl and press in on

Khrazhti. She found herself falling to the ground. Off to the side, Aeden began a curse, but it cut off abruptly.

As she fell, she wondered how enemies had snuck up on them. She toppled to the ground, luckily padded by grass and soft bushes, and waited for her vision to clear of the maelstrom around her. Hoping it would do so before whatever had attacked them killed them all.

"Khrazhti," a voice said. "Khrazhti!" It was Fahtin. Khrazhti opened her eyes and saw the woman, her face just inches away. "Are you okay?"

"I...I think so," Khrazhti said. "Where are the attackers?"

"Attackers? There are no attackers."

"Then what knocked me down?"

A pause. "I don't know," Fahtin said.

"Khrazhti." This time it was Aeden's voice. "Did you feel it, too? Did the world spin?"

"Yes."

"Ach. It's still moving a little. Just a moment."

She heard movement and turned her head slowly toward it. Aeden was stumbling to her. He sat down next to her in the grass.

"I haven't felt anything like that before," he said. "But it seems to be passing." He shook his head and blinked several times. "Yes. It's getting better."

It was for her, too.

"I thought someone attacked us with magic," she said. "I felt...something."

"Aye, that makes sense. I guess it felt kind of like when someone does magic around me. A sort of tingling, along with some pain. What was it?"

"I don't know, but...no. No."

"What? Are you well?"

"I can't sense Benzal any longer," she said. "I can't sense *any* magic."

❧ 11 ❧

"I'm attached to my weapons, too," Aila said, "but I'm more attached to my head. If getting free means leaving my weapons, then I'll do it. If I have to."

"No," Tere argued. "The only way we can escape and stay free is if we head north toward Sitor-Kanda. Through the forest. We'd have to be half-mad to do it, but we'd be completely mad to try it without our weapons."

"I just don't see how we can get them. It'll be hard enough to get ourselves out."

"I think they're still there, at the guard station. Do you remember the chest they put them into? I saw the chest, still right where it was, when they took us out the other day."

Aila shook her head, though it was dark. "That doesn't mean they're still in there. They could have taken them out and stored them somewhere else. Or taken them home for themselves."

"If that's the case, then we'll have to take their weapons. We cannot go into that forest without some type of protection. I'd feel more comfortable if it was my bow and my knives, along with your...whatever you call them."

80

"Vinci," she said.

"Vinci?" Tere asked.

"Yeah. One is a vincus, but two are vinci. Anyway, I think you're exaggerating the danger the forest presents. You lived in the Grundenwald, for Vanda's sake. And not the edges like you told the Mayor. You lived inside it, where all the monsters and magic were."

"It wasn't like that. Not much anyway. Once you learn and get used to it, it's just like anywhere else. But here, in Verlisaru Forest, it's a different thing altogether."

Aila huffed. "Different how? In my travels, I've found that most reputations are highly exaggerated. I'm thinking it's the same thing here. We'll be fine."

"We will not. Even with our own weapons, even if Urun comes out of his stupor, it will be dangerous. We don't know anything about the specific dangers of the forest because no one ever comes out. No one."

"Sure, sure. I've heard that about the Grundenwald, too."

"It's different."

"How?"

"Do you know anything about Verlisaru? Anything at all?"

"Just what you've said," she said. "It separates the Academy from Praesturi and no one who ever goes in comes out. Pretty vague."

"There's a lot more to it."

"Really? Like what?"

Tere shifted, looking directly at Aila, though it wouldn't have an effect on her in the darkness. "It was put there for a reason. It has magic. Real magic, not just the kind that people make up to explain things they don't understand.

"Here, I'll tell you about it. Maybe you'll understand how dangerous it is when you know more about it.

"You know how the Academy came to be on Munsahtiz Island, right?"

"Yeah," she said. "Everyone knows that. The Prophet, Tsosin Ruus, wanted to build an academy to train the one he made the prophecy about. The Malatirsay. He gathered all his resources and purchased the island from several different landholders who owned parts of it each."

"Yes and no," he said. "What you said is basically correct, but you're missing a key point. He could never get all the landholders to agree on prices. Since the island was not the ancestral home of any of them—it was only land they owned and sometimes hunted—he wasn't asking for the seat of their power or anything. They were simply greedy because they knew he wanted it badly.

"He was instrumental in the War of Magic and brokered several deals between factions that prevented even more death and damage. He appealed to the king of Salamus, telling him of the prophecy and the Prophet's plans. The king responded by seizing the island for himself, trading lands or giving the previous landholders good prices for their portion. Then he sold it to Tsosin Ruus.

"But he didn't sell the entire island to him. The king was shrewd and he knew that things often change with time. To prevent the possibility of a new nation rising on the island in the future and carrying out surprise attacks, he held one small part back from the sale. He put a fort there to monitor the construction of the Sitor-Kanda.

"The magical resonance of the island was abnormally strong, which was one reason the Prophet wanted it to begin with. The fort was to keep a rival to the Salamusian Empire from growing, especially if the Prophet were to die.

"So, the king—he required all to use that title, and not emperor—had the fort built, and he called it Praesturi. The construction of Sitor-Kanda soon started and the king turned his attention to other things, such as the war that appeared to be winding down.

"The first commander of Fort Praesturi was a tyrant of a man. In fact, he was stationed there as punishment for some past misdeeds, adding to his anger at the position. He demanded respect from the mages and artisans building the main building at Sitor-Kanda and would visit unannounced, obviously trying to find incriminating evidence. Evidence of what, no one was sure, but the commander seemed to think some type of conspiracy was afoot. Or maybe he was just power hungry and enjoyed feeling important.

"In any case, the mages complained to Tsosin Ruus. He was still busy with the war effort and with gathering materials to build the Academy, but he would visit the island occasionally to be sure progress was being made. On one such visit, he tired of the complaints and rode out to the area south of where the Academy was being built.

"Just north of Praesturi, he sensed a magically powerful area in terrain that was ill-suited for building. It had twisted hills with deep gullies, too difficult to level for placing structures. He got an idea. Taking a few species of local trees, he used his magic to make them grow more quickly.

"He pointed them toward Praesturi. More accurately, he set magic within them that caused them to want to grow from the western edge of the island to the eastern edge, all while moving toward the south.

"His goal, of course, was to grow a forest that would block off Praesturi from Sitor-Kanda. Satisfied with his solution, and telling the mages building the Academy to be patient, he went back to his work of providing for the Academy's construction."

Tere stopped at the sound of a door closing farther down the hallway. He waited, listening for footsteps that would announce one of the guards coming. No further sound reached his ears. He turned to look at Aila again and found her staring at the small barred window and the paltry amount of light leaking from the hallway.

"Where was I?" he said. "Oh, right. It was several years before the Prophet was able to make his way back to Sitor-Kanda. When he arrived, he was shocked at what had happened.

"The head mage on the building project told him that at first the trees did as Tsosin Ruus commanded them. They grew more quickly than trees unaffected by magic would, but not alarmingly so. Remembering that the Prophet had told the builders to be patient, they continued their work but monitored the spell's effects.

"The handful of twisted, stunted trees Tsosin Ruus had started with gradually stretched toward the eastern shore, as directed. At the same time, the stands of trees thickened from north to south, widening at a marked rate.

"The commander of Fort Praesturi may have noticed the abnormal growth of the trees but wasn't alarmed. After all, it was the Age of Magic, and the rapid growth of vegetation was most likely not the most surprising thing he had seen. He set up lumber crews to clear a wide swath of the trees he could use as a corridor for his travels to inspect the building project. Much to the chagrin of the builders, he didn't let up on interfering with their project.

"Then something strange happened. Or, should I say, something stranger. The trees, almost as if in response to their fellows being cut down, began to grow faster. Soon, the fort commander had more than half his men on lumber duty and still they were falling behind. It can be assumed that he dedicated all his troops to the task in a last attempt to keep the way clear, but we can't be sure. His contact with Sitor-Kanda was cut off completely, so the builders only knew he never bothered them again.

"Rumor had it that the commander tried to burn the

entire forest down when axes wouldn't do the trick. Whatever happened, the forest remained and the commander gave
up his commission, retired, and was not heard from again.
The new commander was a more practical man and settled
into the boring task of guarding the fort itself, never actually
setting foot on the northern part of the island but once. He
took the long way around, going to the mainland and over the
northern bridge to introduce himself and offer his services
should the builders ever need it.

"They did not.

"Once the parts of the island were separated by the forest,
there was no further conflict between the two. The builders
controlled the majority of Munsahtiz completely, and few
people who were not part of the construction crew were
allowed to set foot there. The fort, though, eventually was
manned by fewer and fewer soldiers, while accepting civilians
—tradesmen, merchants, others who happened upon the fort
and decided to stay—until finally, the last soldier was assigned
duties elsewhere and Praesturi became a civilian outpost.

"Praesturi was still out of the way, and being so separated
from the rest of the empire, living day to day was rough. It
never enjoyed a high population, and eventually people of
questionable relationships with law were attracted to the
borderland town.

"Our story isn't there, but north of the town. The forest
changed over the years. It became thicker, more congested,
and darker. An almost perpetual mist hung over it, and tales
spread of strange happenings. People entering to hunt or seek
lumber disappeared. The reports were few at first and
increased with time.

"It's not clear who actually named the forest, whether it
was when the Prophet created his spell or much later, but it
came to be known as Verlisaru, the South Dark. By this time,
the War of Magic, as well as the Age of Magic, was over.

Tsosin Ruus himself had died and the main part of Sitor-Kanda had been built.

"Never again did the Academy have to worry about intruders from the south. The forest itself, now dark, twisted, and full of some kind of power that has never been accurately identified, cleanly and effectively separated the southern tip of the island from the rest.

"Though magic waned all over Dizhelim, more remained at Sitor-Kanda than at any other single place in all the world. As such, several expeditions were mounted to investigate the forest. They ranged from expert explorers to groups of mages taken from the Academy graduates and masters themselves. None returned.

"One thing is sure: Verlisaru has magic of some type. Whether it is the forest itself, a great wizard within, or something else is not clear. No one really knows what hazards it contains. At least, no one who knows has ever returned to tell anyone else.

"So when I say we need weapons to enter that place, I'm not speaking idly. Even with our favorite weapons, we may never leave."

Aila sat still, her eyes closed. Tere wondered what she was thinking.

After a moment, she opened her eyes. "Yeah, it might as well be something like that. It figures. If it's so dangerous, why would we go that way?"

"It's simple. We'd likely not be able to get through the town and away without being killed. Even if we did, those assassins are still tracking us. I can feel it. Too, if we somehow get through both of those obstacles, we would have to travel through all the animaru to go north to meet Aeden. It's not just our lives at stake here. If we don't meet up with Aeden and help him, the world itself may fall."

"But what if Aeden has already won? What if they caught

up to Benzal and killed him, stopping the one who was bringing the animaru over? We'll be risking that monster forest for no reason."

"Yes. It's true. We could be doing it for nothing. I guess that's the decision we have to make. Do we chance the forest or chance the other three dangers? Myself, I am leaning toward north. Urun could help us with the forest, I think, but the other options are too risky."

Tere patted Aila on the shoulder. "Think about it. We have a little time. One thing is for sure: we're going to need to get out of here. I'd give myself over to the Mayor if I thought it would help, but that's not the way he operates. He would execute the two of you as well unless you deliver his treasure to him. I'm sorry again that this is happening."

"Yeah, well, it makes life interesting," she said. "You know?"

❦ 12 ❦

Shadeglide slipped into the room where the rest of the Falxen waited. It was the smaller of the two rooms they had rented, the one the men were staying in. She bowed her head to Darkcaller, an apology for being a few minutes late.

"I found out more about the trial," she said.

"There's gossip all over the place about the trial," Keenseeker said from the bed he was sitting on. "There hasn't been talk of anything else. What's so special about the information you have?"

"I know when it will be held."

Darkcaller glared at Keenseeker but directed her words to Shadeglide. "You know for sure, or it's the proposed time?"

"It is certain. I heard the Mayor command his men about it just minutes ago. It's why I'm late."

Darkcaller's look turned triumphant and she raised her chin as she met Keenseeker's eyes. Those two could barely tolerate each other's company. Shadeglide understood, but professionals should be able to get past any disagreements they had.

"When is it?" their leader asked.

"Two days from now. At noon."

"Excellent."

"It's a formality. The sentence is death, and from the way the Mayor is talking about it, the verdict is already determined."

"That's strange," Phoenixarrow said. "Why even have it, then?"

"Because," Darkcaller answered, "the Mayor wants to make a show of his power to put people to death. It'll do wonders in keeping people in line. He will also tell the prisoners they have two days, so whatever it is he wants, now it becomes more urgent for the ones imprisoned. He's likely working them against each other, making offers to let one go if they betray the others."

"Yes, that is correct," Shadeglide said. "It apparently involves something one of them took from him. The older one, I think."

"Very good," Darkcaller told her. "We may be able to sit back and allow the Mayor to do our job for us."

"Not wise," Fireshard said.

"What?"

"Leaving it in their hands, it's not wise. They may fail, the prisoners may do what the Mayor wants, it's even possible they might escape. We've seen how resourceful those prisoners can be. We should plan to kill them ourselves, leave nothing to chance. I want to be done and out of here."

"I'm with her," Keenseeker said. "The sooner we finish, the sooner we can get back to see if that scrawny runt of a leader has held up his half of the deal. I want to get back to working solo. Too many people involved in this one."

Phoenixarrow muttered something Shadeglide was too far to hear clearly. Keenseeker scowled at the red-haired woman.

"What you say has some merit, Fireshard," Darkcaller

said. "We will plan on killing them. No doubt, the execution won't be carried out right away. We'll be able to listen to their judgment and then decide on our course. If there's nothing else—"

"Pardon, but there is a problem," Shadeglide said. "The trial will be held in a room in the Mayor's building. It will be closed to all but a few of the Mayor's people."

"And?"

"I have already investigated the building and...some of us do not have the skill to infiltrate and spy on the proceedings."

"Some of us?"

"Yes. Er, I don't believe anyone in this group but me could do it successfully without being discovered."

Keenseeker scoffed and looked around at the others, obviously looking for someone to agree with him. "Oh, that's convenient. Only you can get in to watch the trial. What's your angle, girl?"

Shadeglide locked eyes with the man, communicating to him in no uncertain terms that he did not frighten her. "I have no angle, *man*. I am simply stating that you are too clumsy to move stealthily, and not smart enough to carry out subterfuge acceptably."

She held his eyes with her intensity for a moment, then dropped her emotionless mien to flash a big smile. "No insult intended."

He blinked at her. She knew the thought process. He was wondering if he saw what he thought he did. It was enough to keep him confused, and wary. He hadn't seen even a fraction of her talents. If he were to initiate combat, she could do anything from rendering him unconscious to taking his life before he could swing that tree trunk of a weapon he carried around, especially in this small room.

"That's fine, Shadeglide," Darkcaller said. "We'll formulate a plan, and when the trial happens, you will observe it and report back to us."

"As you say," she said, maintaining her smile. "Anyone hungry? I smelled food coming through the common room. I'm going to go get some."

She turned and left the room.

"Shadeglide," someone said. It was Edge, the only other man in their brace. "May I join you?"

"Of course. Come on."

He followed her silently, the other women leaving the room more slowly. She heard the bed creak as Keenseeker got up, but he didn't seem in a hurry to associate with them. He would probably go drinking at the tavern again.

"You have Shinyin blood in you," Edge said. He didn't talk much, and when he did, he was always straight to the point. Shadeglide couldn't remember ever seeing him smile.

"Yes. My father was Shinyin."

"And your mother?"

"Aranian."

They reached the bottom landing of the stairs and found a table in the corner of the common room. There were people scattered about, but it wasn't too full yet.

"Were you trained by the Sike?"

The Sike, the assassin clans of Shinyan.

"Nope. My grandfather taught me all I know. He was an assassin in Arania for decades. When my parents died, he took me in, trained me to take care of myself."

"I see," he said. They told the woman who came by they wanted food and drinks—Edge specified water for him—and they continued talking. "Have you had any dealings with the Shaku?"

"The assassins of Teroshi? No. Teroshi don't typically appreciate my Shinyin heritage."

Edge grunted. "Do you find the Teroshi unacceptable companions? Many Shinyin do."

"I was raised in Arania, on the border. My grandfather didn't believe in treating people differently because of where they came from, and I don't either. Do you dislike Shinyin like many Teroshi do?"

"No. I appreciate skill, no matter where it comes from. And honor. Shinyin know more of it than many other peoples. Honor is most important."

She smiled at him. "I was taught that as well. I try to be honorable."

"Many people," he said, "many around us, have no such honor. Keenseeker is one without honor. He has skill and strength, but no honor. You must think carefully before making an enemy of him."

Shadeglide laughed. "I'm not worried about him. He would not survive attacking me. But, yes, I agree, honor is woefully lacking in many people. Still, I find it occasionally in the strangest places." She jerked her head toward Phoenixarrow, who was crossing the common room floor toward them. "Women,"—she nodded to Edge—"men. It doesn't matter. I respect honorable people and consider them my friends."

"Yes. It is good."

"May I ask you, Edge, why are you here? Why did you join the Falxen? The Blades are not known for their honor."

"No, they are not. As you may have deduced, I was born into one of the great Shaku clans in Teroshi. I will not tell you which one, for I do not want to tarnish my family name with my past mistakes.

"I had the privilege of serving a great warlord there. While I was on a mission he gave to me, a rival clan assassinated him. I discovered this when I returned.

"Though I had no part in his protection, and therefore was not required to give up my life, I was masterless, without an honorable profession. Masterless Shaku are not respected members of society. Without it, I was a blemish on the name of my family. I chose to leave Teroshi after I had taken care of some important business.

"When I arrived on the mainland, coming through lands belonging to Shinyan to do so, I realized I was disrespected in this land as well, though it confused me as to why. Had they heard of my failure, of my shame?

"I witnessed an assassination by a man. I chased him down as he fled, intending to ask him if he belonged to a guild. I had heard guilds of assassins were much like families on the mainland.

"He thought I had sought him out to kill him, and he attacked. He was fairly skilled, but his movements lacked refinement. I did not draw my swords on him, for it would have brought shame to me to do so. Instead, I defended myself, disarmed him, and knocked him to the ground. Once he realized he could not be victorious, I explained that I merely had questions as I offered to return his weapons.

"From him, I learned of the Falxen, and though he told me he could not lead me to their headquarters, I simply followed him without him being aware of it. After infiltrating the headquarters at Vatheca, I convinced them to accept me into their number. That was seven years ago."

Shadeglide wasn't surprised. The Shaku were legendary assassins, but they were more. Many of the Shaku clans were of high birth, like the noble families on the main continent of Promistala. He would have been trained to read and write early in his life, and to enjoy art, music, poetry, and other activities only participated in by nobles.

"What was the work you had to complete before you left? Was it so important?"

"Yes. I hunted down the clan that had killed my master and made sure that for every one of my brothers they had killed, I eliminated five of theirs. Ten for my warlord. It will be a long time, if ever, before they will assassinate another lord. There are very few remaining."

Shadeglide whistled softly. "And have you found honor among the Falxen?"

He turned his dark eyes to her. "I have not, but I will continue to search. At times, honor may be found in the most curious of places." He raised his cup to hers, then drank as Phoenixarrow and Fireshard joined them.

Two days later, Shadeglide was nestled comfortably in the ceiling of the court room. She hadn't even needed to disguise herself to enter the building; she merely snuck in. The prisoners shuffled in, wearing chains and covered with cloaks to hide their identity for some reason. They were forced to kneel on the floor to the side of the main stage where the Mayor and a few other people sat.

"Let's get this over with," the large man who called himself the Mayor said. "I have things to do. Alston Squesik, you are charged with stealing my possession, the ruby called the Eye of Codaghan that I had obtained. You fled with it, and I never saw it or you again, until you wandered into my town. Do you deny it?"

The taller of the three spoke. "I've told you that I'm not the person you think I am. My name is Tere Chizzit, and I have never wronged you or even met you."

The Mayor nodded and one of the burly guards swung a fist at the man, throwing him to the floor. Shadeglide smiled. He was good, but she could tell he had rolled with the strike, barely taking any force while raising his shoulder enough to fool the guard into thinking he had struck the man's face.

"I didn't ask for commentary. Guilty or innocent? We have to follow the procedures."

"Innocent," the man said. He even made it sound as if he

said it through a hurt jaw. Shadeglide found herself respecting the man's skills. Why had she been hired to kill him?

Then she remembered that she hadn't. They had been given the mission to kill the blue woman. They had followed these three because they weren't sure which group had contained their target. Technically, they weren't even required to kill them, though it was Darkcaller's decision to make as their leader.

"And you other two," the Mayor continued. "You got anything to say to my offer? Give me information about Alston here and where he hid the treasure, or any other treasure, and I'll let you go free."

The other two might have been statues under those robes for all the sound they made.

"Fine. I find the prisoners guilty of stealing, lying, and whatever else sounds good when we announce it to the town. You'll all be executed in three days, maybe two. It depends on how long it takes to build the new gibbet. It's been a while since we executed anyone, and the old gibbet fell apart in the last storm. Damn bad construction. That's all. We're done. Put them back in their cell."

The prisoners were taken out and the few people in the chairs set up in the main part of the room filed out, leaving only the Mayor and three of his minions.

"It was worth a try," the Mayor said. "I figured old Alston would be too much of a coward to resist and accept a death sentence. Maybe he'll still have a change of heart before we kill him."

"If you execute him," one of the others said, another large man, this one with thinning dark hair on his massive head, "you'll never get the gem back."

"He would have sold it long ago anyway, and he's not the type of man who saves up wealth so he could pay me back. He probably had it spent within weeks of when he stole it.

Whores for miles probably had new purses to carry all the gold he gave them. We'll use them as an example and put the whole thing behind us."

"As you say, Mayor."

The Mayor and his companions finally left the room as well. Shadeglide stayed where she was for a time, thinking over what she had heard and seen. It was probably better she hadn't seen more of the prisoners than their hoods. She'd found if she learned too much about some of the people she killed, she would begin to imagine that they didn't deserve their deaths. Better to do the job and not think too much about it.

With a final look at the farce of a courtroom, she snuck out of the building and headed back to the inn to fill in the other Falxen.

13

Aeden watched as Fahtin helped Khrazhti up. He had felt whatever had hit them, too, but it didn't seem as if it affected Fahtin and Raki.

"What do you mean you can't sense magic anymore?" Fahtin asked Khrazhti.

Oh no, Aeden thought. Did magic somehow fail completely after being a weak shadow of itself for so many hundreds of years?

He quickly made the gestures for Pieces of Evil, pronouncing the words to call the magic of the Raibrech into being. A swirling maelstrom of colored lights appeared over them. As it moved, the glowing collection of magic formed a wedge pointing toward the north. It remained for several seconds, then faded slowly until the last few sparkles died in the air.

No, there was still magic that could be called upon.

"What was that for?" Raki asked, eyeing Aeden as if maybe he had lost his mind.

"I wanted to check to make sure magic still worked."

Khrazhti sat up. "Then it is not magic itself but my ability to sense it. And more importantly, to sense Izhrod Benzal. What is happening, Aeden? Did you feel it, too?"

"I did, though not as strongly as you did, I think. Raki, Fahtin, you didn't feel anything just now?"

They both shook their heads.

"It's clear that something happened to the magic of the world. We are sensitive to it, you more so. Can you focus, try to point out where Benzal is?"

"I can try," Khrazhti said, "but it does not work like that. Before, I sensed him the way you can hear something or see it. You don't have to try, it just happens. I will try, though."

She closed her glowing eyes for a moment. Her face was expressionless, appearing calm and in control. When she opened her eyes again, though, Aeden saw the disappointment in them.

"No. I cannot sense him. Everything seems so quiet. I am accustomed to the soft buzz of magic surrounding me. Now it is gone."

"*Cachtionn daedos d'estaigh*," Aeden spat. "Do you feel okay? The effects have already passed for me, but I'm not as sensitive to magic as you are."

"I am well, other than not being able to sense magic. It did not harm me. It merely surprised me."

He paused. "Do you think that maybe Benzal attacked us somehow? Maybe he's the cause of it."

Khrazhti got up and brushed the stray blades of grass from her legs and side. "I do not think so. He would have to be more powerful than I believe he is to do such a thing from a distance. I may be wrong, however. I am not familiar with magic in this world, though I have never heard of a power that could do such a thing. What will we do? I cannot lead us to Benzal if I cannot sense him."

"We should continue on the way we were going," Aeden said. "Maybe it's just this area where the magic is strange. If we pass through it, we'll already be that much farther on the path. The most we'll have to do is make some corrections to our destination."

The three agreed with him and they continued toward the mountains. Another day of picking their way through the foliage and the increasingly difficult terrain and Aeden stopped them.

He looked through the trees as the land tilted upward into the sky. "I know we're still going the same way because we have the mountains ahead of us to aim for. But I'm not so sure we should tackle them if you won't be able to sense Benzal again."

"What are you suggesting, Aeden?" Fahtin asked.

"We could backtrack past where Khrazhti's senses failed. If we pass that point and she can sense Benzal again, maybe we can choose a different path to bypass this pocket of strange magic."

"That would mean wasting time by going back over land we've already traveled, maybe twice more," Raki pointed out.

"Aye, I know. It might be worth it to find out what's happening to us. To figure out if it's simply a matter of location."

"And what if she never regains the ability to sense him?" Fahtin asked.

"Then we're going to need to find another way to locate Benzal anyway. The sooner we know that, the better, I'm thinking."

All three of the humans looked to Khrazhti.

"It is a good plan," she said. "I am sorry."

"Nonsense," Aeden said. "It's not your fault. We'll figure it out and we'll work around it. It's not your fault."

They hiked back the way they had come, or at least as close as they could tell. Aeden picked out signs of their trail and tried to keep them on the path, but they veered off due to the terrain and then intersected their path, then deviated again. After a few hours, they were all ready to rest.

Late the next day, they passed the location where they all agreed Khrazhti and he had felt the magical spike of power. As they went farther west, Aeden's nervous energy zipped around inside him like a swarm of angry wasps. Any minute, he thought, they might be struck with that magical jolt again. The anticipation made him jittery.

It never came. Neither did Khrazhti's sense of where Benzal was. Another full day of travel and she still couldn't sense their enemy or any magic.

"I think we have to admit that it wasn't a localized thing," Aeden said. "We'll have to do whatever we're going to do without being able to sense Benzal. Any ideas?"

They were sitting around a clearing with boulders scattered throughout. It almost appeared as if a very large rock dropped from the sky, shattering into smaller—but still large —pieces of rock, killing the foliage around it.

"What if we just headed the way we were going and tried to find where he's hiding when we get over the mountains," Raki suggested.

"There are hundreds of square miles between the mountains and the ocean," Aeden said. "We'd be wandering blind, hoping to chance upon a clue to his whereabouts."

Fahtin perked up. "Your magic! Aeden, can't you use your magic to find where he is?"

He frowned. "I don't think so. My spell, Pieces of Evil, will point toward the closest source of enemies, but there could be any number of them between us and Benzal. I could keep casting it and we'd have to fight through every group of enemies until we finally get close enough to him for it to point the way. It would be like we're hunting down all the animaru in Dizhelim to finally get to him. Plus all the bandits and anyone else that could be hostile to us. With just the four of us, that would take weeks or months, if we even survived it."

Khrazhti didn't have any suggestions. She huddled off to the side, arms wrapped about herself as if she was cold.

"It's not your fault, Khrazhti," he said. "I'm more concerned that the jolt of magic did something to you than if you can sense Benzal. Are you sure you are well?"

"I am well, though disappointed that I have failed my friends."

Fahtin went over to her and put an arm around her. "You haven't failed anyone. It wasn't your fault. Besides, we'll get around this. It's just one more thing to deal with. Not even a big thing."

"Thank you."

"I wish Tere was here," Aeden said. "He'd be able to track Benzal."

"That's it," Raki said. "We go and get Tere. We were supposed to meet him at Dartford anyway."

"We talked about that before," Aeden said. "We didn't want to waste the time going all the way west only to turn around and head east again."

"Yeah, but things have changed. Now, our choices are to wander around aimlessly or go back and get Tere and probably go straight to Benzal. I bet we save time doing that, and I bet it's a whole lot safer than poking around without knowing where we're going."

"Hmmm," Aeden said.

"It would be nice to see Tere again," Fahtin said. "And Aila. I wonder how she's doing."

"It sounds logical to me," Khrazhti said. "Perhaps the best of two undesirable choices. I can think of nothing that would be more appropriate."

Aeden ran his fingers through his hair. "Aye, you're probably right about that. I'm not fond of having to hike all that way, but it may be our only choice."

"We still need to go to the Academy, too," Fahtin said. "After we meet Tere, it will be a short trip to get there."

A lump formed in Aeden's chest at the thought. He didn't trust himself to comment on that point.

"So, is that what we're going to do?" Raki asked, eyes alight with excitement.

"It sounds like our best choice. What say you, Fahtin, and you, Khrazhti?"

"Yes," Fahtin said.

"I agree," Khrazhti said.

"Fine. We'll rest up and start off in the morning. If I remember correctly, the North Road should be fairly close. That will make traveling easier."

He couldn't argue with the logic of their destination, and the others were obviously excited about it, but something still bothered him. Mentally shrugging, he unwrapped some of the food they had left from the pouran and ate mechanically, his mind trying to go through all the angles. He hoped Tere could find Benzal for them or they would be wasting precious time.

14

Urun Chinowa had only ever wanted to be a bigger part of the natural world. Even as a child, he was more comfortable with plants and animals than with other people. With nature, there were no lies. With people, it was *all* lies.

Sure, nature had its deceptions. Camouflage, disguise, even outright imitation to avoid being eaten, or to eat others. But it was a simple deception, pure and with easily defined motives. When dealing with people, nothing was simple.

He was moving now, walking. His head was covered with something. A cloak with a hood? When had he put that on? Why? He was barely aware of what happened to him anymore. Were they going somewhere, or returning? He vaguely recalled people around him, something important happening, but...no, he couldn't recall how he had come to be outside the cell.

Light leaked around the buildings surrounding him. Some of it even made it past the hood covering most of his face. It wasn't the sunlight of a forest filtered through the trees or the bright, almost glaring sunlight of an open field during summer. It was the sterile, heartless light that bounced off so many horrible man-made structures that it felt dirty.

But at least it was light. He turned his face upward, hoping to feel the warmth on his skin. All he felt was the sticky, stagnant air that settled in between the buildings. Even outside, he got no relief.

How long had it been since he'd been outside? He had lost track of the days, locked away in the dark cell, removed not only from Osulin's sweet light but also from nature itself. Surrounded by stone and dead wood, he felt his life force draining from him. Was that possible?

He had lived in the forest so long, he wasn't sure. It was really the only life he knew. All of his adult years had been spent in Osulin's service. The time before that, before he had settled into his little house in the Grundenwald, was hazy to him, mostly unimportant.

It had been a long time since Osulin had spoken to him. He prayed to her, entreated her, begged her for her help and guidance.

Nothing. She hadn't responded for what must have been years. No, that wasn't right. Weeks? Surely it had been that long. Since before he had been thrown in that dark place with Tere and Aila.

Had he been eating? He must have, or he would have died. His magic could sustain him for a time, but without food and water, he would eventually die like anyone else. It was rumored that the priests of old, in the height of the Age of Magic, could survive indefinitely without physical sustenance, living only on the power from their gods. Of course, their deities would have to grant them that power, not ignore them.

He wondered if he had done something wrong, something

to drive Osulin away from him. The magic still tingled within him. He thought he could still use it, if necessary, though he had no stomach for trying. Better to sit in the dark and hum to himself of better days. Maybe his goddess would oblige him and simply put an end to his life. He was too much of a coward to do it himself.

What had he been thinking about? Oh, yes. Eating. He remembered little snippets of his time in the dark room. Tere and Aila encouraged him to eat, spoke to him, asked if they could do anything to help. It was a gargantuan task to summon the energy to speak, so he didn't. Maybe they would stop feeding him and he could be free of his mortal prison as well as the one of stone he had been locked in.

He vaguely registered having his robe pulled off him, causing him to stumble and almost fall. Tere caught his arm, steadied him. The guards said something, hateful words in an angry tone. One of them swung open a heavy wooden door with a barred window at its center and kicked him hard in the back, making him stumble into the room and fall onto his face. Pain blossomed across his cheek as he struck the stone floor at an angle and slid a little. He remained there, not comfortable but at least not needing to walk anymore.

The door closed, snuffing out most of the light from the hallway. Tere and Aila turned him over and sat him up in his normal place, against the wall. One of them wiped his face with some cloth, cleaning the muck that seemed to be over most of the stones of the cell. He let them. He didn't care one way or another.

Urun plunged into deeper despair as the light dimmed to nearly pitch black. His eyes would adjust and he'd be able to see silhouettes eventually, but it didn't matter. He would die in this place, sooner or later. He might as well already be dead.

Osulin, he whispered in his mind. *Why? Why have you left me?*

Tere and Aila began to discuss something, but he didn't listen. He began humming to himself, shutting himself off from the rest of the merciless world.

❧ 15 ❧

Aeden scanned the roadway ahead, swiveling his head from left and right for any sign of danger. Nothing of concern was present. He stepped from the foliage along the hard-packed dirt and sighed. How long had it been since he'd been on a proper road?

The others joined him. Fahtin squinted toward the left—westward—with a resigned expression around her squinting eyes. The mid-afternoon sun was getting lower in the sky. They would be walking toward it.

"Where are we?" Raki asked.

"My best guess," Aeden said, "is that the highlands are off that way"—he pointed toward the northeast—"and not too far away. My birthplace, the home of my clan. Former home of my clan."

"Then this is the North Road?" Fahtin asked.

"Aye, I believe so."

"It's a long way to Dartford," Raki said, "especially on foot."

"Yes," Aeden agreed, "so we best get started."

They headed toward the sun. No one seemed to feel much

like talking. The original excitement about going to meet Tere had been ground down by their daily traveling through rough terrain. It would take some time to recover on their easier route. Aeden had things he needed to think over anyway.

"Oh," Raki said suddenly, causing Aeden's hands to fly to his swords. He was relieved to see that he wasn't the only one. Khrazhti had one of her swords half out of the scabbard and Fahtin had wrapped her hands around two of the knives strapped to her.

There were no dangers on the empty road in front of the Croagh. "What?"

Raki looked back at him abashedly. "Sorry. I just thought of something."

Khrazhti's sword clicked as she seated it in the scabbard again.

"Raki, if you do that again, I'll swat your bottom like I used to a few years ago. Fahtin glared at the young man.

He stared at the ground as they began walking again.

After a moment, Aeden spoke. "Out with it. What was so important that you made us think we were under attack?"

A smile replaced Raki's sulking face. "Going on this road, we're going to go through Hosen."

The statement was greeted with silence until Khrazhti, switching her attention from face to face, asked, "What is a Hosen?"

Raki beamed triumphantly. "It's the hometown of Erent Caahs."

"Erent Caahs was from Arcusheim," Aeden said.

"No. His family moved to Arcusheim when he was seven years old. He was born in Hosen and lived there with his mother, father, and sister before they were forced to flee to Arcusheim."

"Huh," Aeden said. He knew better than to argue with

Raki about Erent Caahs. The boy idolized the hero and knew the most obscure tales about him.

"Do you think they have a monument? We never stopped there with the caravan, something about it being too small to bother."

Aeden caught Fahtin rolling her eyes. "Raki, we're not on a sightseeing trip. We have to get to Tere. There's no time for stopping."

"I know." His gaze shifted to the ground once more. "I just thought we could see it as we pass through. That's all."

"We'll see," Aeden said. "We may have to get supplies there. We're running low on—what is that?"

A shape up ahead resolved itself into a man. He was sitting on the side of the road, a horse grazing nearby. He looked familiar, but Aeden couldn't quite place him. The Croagh inspected the surrounding bushes closely, hands on the hilts of his swords poking up above his shoulders. He had heard of bandits using ruses such as this to ambush travelers.

The man hadn't noticed them yet. He seemed to be speaking to his horse.

"Is that...?" Fahtin sped up to reach the man first. Aeden reached out to her as she passed, but she was already too far in front of him.

"Dannel Powfrey?" she said as she got to within ten feet of the man and stopped.

"Yes?" The man looked up. His pale face was shaded by a large-brimmed hat, but even shadowed, Aeden recognized him, the Academy graduate they met when their adventure had first started. Hadn't they met him close to where they were now? Why would he still be there?

"Oh," Dannel said. "It's..." he snapped his fingers repeatedly, his lower lip in his teeth. "Ah. Fahtin, Raki, and Aeden. That's it."

Aeden relaxed. The man was harmless and besides, he was

friendly to them. He had given them good advice the last time they met.

"But who is your beautiful blue friend?" Dannel asked, as if it was the most normal thing in the world for someone to have an azure hue.

Khrazhti looked back and forth from Aeden to Dannel, then finally stepped closer to the scholar. "I am Khrazhti."

"Ah, Khrazhti," he said, then spoke to her in her own dialect of Alaqotim so quickly and fluently that Aeden could hardly follow. "And what is one of the animaru doing traveling with fessani?"

Khrazhti's mouth dropped open, the most expressive gesture Aeden had ever seen on the woman. "I..." She looked toward Aeden as if asking permission. After his nod, she continued, "...have realized the path I was on was not honorable. I have sworn to help Aeden."

"And she's our friend," Aeden added in his broken animaru Alaqotim.

Dannel Powfrey clapped as he stood up. "Oh, bravo," he said in Ruthrin. "You are learning the pure Alaqotim. Very good, Aeden. And Khrazhti, are you learning the crude language common to humans?" He took her hand in his and kissed it.

Khrazhti, looking confused about the entire thing, stared at her hand, then at Dannel, and finally gave Aeden a look of pure stupefaction. "Yes. My friends have been teaching me this and other things."

"Quite remarkable. What did the masters say, Aeden? Did they provide enlightenment?"

Aeden blinked. It was hard to follow Dannel sometimes, with the way he jumped around in conversation. "I haven't made it to the Academy yet. We ran into some complications."

"Yes. Complications. I myself haven't been back since we

last met. Other things have pulled me this way and that. Such is the life of a historian and scholar. Ah, but I'm being rude. Here you have visited my humble abode and I haven't offered you anything to eat or drink. Will you join me for both? Blennus here will be glad to shed a few of my supplies to make her load lighter."

Khrazhti's eyes widened when Dannel said the name of his horse.

The scholar winked at the animaru. "You should hear what he calls me. It's all in fun, of course."

"That would be great," Raki said. "Do you know anything about Hosen?"

Dannel smiled at the boy. "I know it's the home village of Erent Caahs. Is that what you're referring to?" He winked.

"Yes," Raki said with a smile.

Dannel led the group to a small clearing a stone's throw away from where he had been sitting by the roadside. It had a fallen tree, several rocks that had been rolled into position to provide perfect sitting places, and a ring of stones which had obviously been used as a fire pit. He soon had a fire burning brightly, a kettle hanging over it from a tripod, and a spit with cuts of meat roasting. Aeden scratched his head, wondering how Dannel had kept all of that in his saddlebags without spoiling. And where had the water come from to fill the kettle?

"It looks as if you've seen some adventures," Dannel said. "Just the quantity of dust on your clothing would tell me you have traveled far. How goes the mission?"

"Mission?" Aeden said.

"Of course. The Malatirsay was not to appear solely for others to look upon him. That one has things to do, missions to complete."

"I...uh..."

"Have you heard the story of the false Malatirsay?" Dannel asked, as if he hadn't asked the other question.

Aeden shook his head. It was difficult to keep up with conversation with this man. "False Malatirsay?"

"Yes," Dannel said, testing a chunk of meat with his knife to see if it was cooked thoroughly. "It was two centuries ago. One hundred ninety-seven years, to be exact."

"No. I've never heard of such a thing. Then again, I never heard of the Malatirsay until a few months ago."

"Ah, yes. True enough. Don't feel bad, however. Few seem to remember what happened. In fact, I can say with some authority that some purposely try to keep the tale hidden. Would you like to hear of it?"

Aeden accepted a plate of food from Dannel. Fahtin and Raki had already gotten theirs. He handed his to Khrazhti and waited for Dannel to make up another "Aye, if it would not be too much trouble."

"No trouble at all. I'm a historian after all. Part of my life is relating the histories I have uncovered so people may learn from the past."

Raki fidgeted on the log he was using as a seat, apparently trying to get comfortable. He loved stories of all kinds, especially ones about heroes. Aeden hoped this was one of those.

"Have any of you heard of Campastra?"

They shook their heads, all but Khrazhti. She merely focused on Dannel's mouth and the words he was speaking. Though she was capable with Ruthrin, she was not fluent. For some people, she had to pay close attention as they spoke so she could understand.

"It's not unexpected," Dannel said. "Even those as widely traveled as the Gypta don't usually travel that way. The name Campastra signifies an area on the very southwestern edge of Promistala. It means, roughly, *dark plains*, or *black plains*. It's south even of the Sittingham Desert, which you no doubt *have* heard of.

"The area is configured as you would expect with a name like that. It's mostly plains of grass and low vegetation, but it also includes twisting ravines and some small hills. It is the home of the Arunai people.

"But I get ahead of myself. Allow me to step back and start again. During that time, a man rose to prominence farther to the north and east. He was a charismatic man, a great orator who could sway crowds with his words. More, he claimed he had been prophesied.

"He was the Malatirsay, he said.

"By the time he had gained some notoriety, he already had a sizable force following him, solely on the merits of his speaking ability. He, with his followers, traveled from the east to Sitor-Kanda to present himself to the masters. He claimed to be the one who was prophesied by the Song of Prophecy and he entreated them to validate his claim and provide for him the aid the Academy was built for.

"Well, this was a shock to the masters, who had become complacent in watching for the signs of the Age of Darkness. When he came to them, he spoke for hours, laying out his claim that he was the one they were waiting for.

"Some of the masters believed immediately, while others had to be convinced and, in fact, became so as he presented his case to them. Some third of the masters still did not believe him, if only because they felt they should meditate upon the evidence for a suitable time before making their decision.

"The man was dissatisfied that they did not all accept him immediately. He spoke enthusiastically about the enemy arriving and the danger they posed to Dizhelim. He told them he was disappointed that they did not fulfill their purpose but swore he would carry on and complete his task even without their help, for that was the purpose of *his* existence.

"Some of the students at Sitor-Kanda abandoned their tutelage and joined him, and though none of the masters did, divisions sprang up and threw all of the Academy into disarray.

"As quickly as he had arrived, he departed, taking his forces and the newly added with him. He took them south, and then east, and threaded his way between the Shadowed Pinnacles and Ianthra's Breasts, skirting the Sittingham Desert. He finally came to what was known as Campastra.

"You see, the residents of Campastra were dark of color. Indeed, the term Arunai means *the darkness* in Alaqotim, and it was originally meant as a derogatory term. This man, this so-called Malatirsay, claimed that the Arunai were the dark forces of the prophecy, that errors in spelling had crept into the words of the prophecy. Arunai or animaru, he was sure the enemy was upon them, and it was his job to root them out and destroy them.

"The Arunai, for their part, were a solitary people, their nation made up of many different tribes, all self-sufficient and led by their own chieftains. Their dark skin and their isolationist tendencies had kept them distinctive through the ages, though they did take part in the Great War on the side of Salamus. Now, though, they faced the forces of this Malatirsay, who attacked them relentlessly and showed no mercy.

"And that would have been the end, but for a brave man among the Arunai. His name was Jintu Devexo. Jintu the Render, he was called. He was able to bring the tribes together to act as one. Alone, none of the tribes could have resisted the large number of the false Malatirsay's soldiers, but together, they were formidable. All the chieftains swore allegiance to him as high-chieftain and they pushed the invaders back, footstep by footstep.

"In the end, the attacking armies were routed and, in one glorious final battle, Jintu slew the so-called Malatirsay in single combat on the battlefield while their followers slaughtered each other around them.

"Only after the blood had soaked into the ground and the dust clouds dissipated did people consider what the one who called himself Malatirsay had attempted. What remained of his forces scattered to the winds and never rose up again.

"The Arunai settled back into their regular lives, though their population had been reduced considerably. Since then, they have been wary, protective of their borders. Violently so. They learned, as have so many other groups in this world, that to be different often means you are a target for hatred." He nodded toward Fahtin and Raki, who both raised their chins as if they had planned to do it in unison.

"But," Aeden said, "how could that have happened? The man—what was his name?—fooled even the masters? It was obvious he wasn't the Malatirsay because that was two hundred years ago and the world wasn't consumed by darkness."

"His name?" Dannel said. "No one is sure. It was either never recorded or it was struck from the histories. Believe me, I've looked, but there seems to be no record of what he called himself, other than Malatirsay. We do know the name Jintu Devexo, however. His gathering of the tribes, along with his battle prowess, are legendary, as are his tactics. For one who some considered primitive, he won battle after battle against greater numbers by sheer excellence in strategy.

"There are lessons there, as there are in all history. We have but to think upon them and derive them."

Aeden considered the story. He had never thought about someone claiming they were the Malatirsay when they weren't. It *was* something to think about. "What is the lesson?"

Dannel cocked his head and squinted at Aeden. "That's for each person to decide, Aeden. What is the lesson for *you*? That's the question."

His words hung on the air and no one else spoke, each contemplating what he'd said. The historian stood, stretching. "But I have once again taken too much of your time. I should get back on the road. Lots of ground to cover."

Fahtin washed the plates and handed them to Dannel while Aeden disassembled the tripod and wrapped the pieces in a leather strip for the purpose.

"Are you sure you won't stay with us for the night?" Aeden asked. "The sun will go down soon, so we'll make camp right here and start out early tomorrow."

"I thank you, but I must be going. My task is rather urgent and I've whiled away too much of my time already. Not with you, I might add, but before that. I seem to get lazier and lazier as time passes."

"Thank you for the food and the story," Fahtin told him. "We hope to see you again. Maybe at the Academy."

"It is possible, my lady. It is very possible." He clapped Aeden on the shoulder. Gods' speed on your journey, Aeden. Think on the story. Who knows, it may have a lesson for you."

He kissed Khrazhti's hand again—the blue woman didn't look as uncomfortable as she had the first time—and he gathered up the reins of his horse and headed back toward the road, then went east.

"Always going the opposite way as us, that one," Aeden said. He said it with a smile, though, watching the historian disappear from view.

"Aeden," Khrazhti said. "Why did that man put his mouth on my hand?"

❧ 16 ❧

"The waiting is the worst part," Phoenixarrow told Shadeglide, falling onto her bed in the room they shared with the other two women. Darkcaller and Fireshard were in the common room, taking their turns listening for any gossip that might be helpful.

"Really?" Shadeglide responded.

"Yeah. The combat, the travel, all that other stuff, it's fine. The waiting, though, I hate it."

"I don't mind it so much."

"You don't mind most things. You are the single most upbeat person I have ever met. You do realize you're an assassin, right?"

"Yep."

Phoenixarrow shook her head. "Listen to me. I sound like all those people who ask me if I know *I'm* an assassin."

Shadeglide sat up in her bed, bouncing slightly. Her eyes sparkled with curiosity Phoenixarrow almost laughed at the sight.

"Why would people ask you that?" the smaller woman asked.

She really ought to watch her tongue. For a professional killer, Phoenixarrow seemed to say too much. "Oh, it's just my preoccupation with Erent Caahs."

"Preoccupation?"

"Okay, maybe they use the word obsession more often. I can't help it. He's everything I want to be."

"Including a hero?"

Yeah, she really had to work on thinking before she spoke, especially with people as smart as Shadeglide. "That's why they ask me that question."

Shadeglide bounced out of her bed and sat down next to Phoenixarrow on hers. "Don't worry so much about what people say. Do what you want to do and be what you want to be."

The red-haired woman arched her back, stretching. "Someday, maybe. For now, this job pays the bills."

The smaller woman studied Phoenixarrow's face for a long moment.

"What?" the archer asked.

"Why do you idolize him so much?"

Her immediate reaction was to retreat, change the subject, even be rude to push the woman away. Then she looked into Shadeglide's dark eyes and found genuine interest there. She was the most sincere person Phoenixarrow had ever met. Either that, or she was the best at faking sincerity.

"It's just...well, he could do anything. Tracking, fighting, outthinking his enemies. He had drive. When he was committed to something, he didn't let anything get in his way. Even if things didn't turn out the way he wanted, he didn't consider it a failure, but used the experience to try again and win. He was..." She trailed off, feeling her face go warm.

"A hero," Shadeglide finished. Her eyes twinkled and she asked, "You know you're an assassin, right?"

Phoenixarrow mock-scowled at her. "Oh, go back to your own side of the room, you little terror."

Shadeglide did as she asked, chuckling as she did so. When she was settled onto her own bed, her face grew more serious. "Tell me another story about this hero. I've heard some, but not as many as you know."

"Hmmm," Phoenixarrow said. "Do you want to hear about his special move, something only he could do?"

"Ooh, yes. I don't think I've heard about that."

"Okay. I'll tell you one of the stories a lot of people don't know, and how he used his special technique to win.

"Erent Caahs was in between tasks. In addition to helping people wherever he happened to be, he would often take bounties on particularly dangerous criminals. It wasn't because he wanted the money, but because few of the others hunting bounties could handle them. He saw his fellow hunters as a type of hero in their own right, though many of them were not nice human beings.

"Anyway, he had just finished a job and was traveling the River Road, going north from Arcusheim, taking his time and enjoying the fresh air. He rarely rode horses, instead relying on his own two feet. That was when the messenger found him.

"'Are you master Erent Caahs?' the messenger asked from his horse.

"'I am.'

"'I have a message for you from Amir Keya.' The young man proffered the envelope and Erent took it from him, flipping a coin to him in payment. The young man nodded to Erent and rode back the way he had come.

"The message was from a friend, one who apparently knew he had just finished a bounty in the area. It begged him to come to him in the small town of Leafburrow. A fierce group of bandits had taken the town for its entertainment.

They had misused several women in the town and were getting more violent. Already there were five dead.

"Amir was older, though still a formidable fighter, but Erent understood. One man alone against a group of bandits was not odds any sane man would take. *Good thing I'm not sane*, he thought to himself, and changed direction to head toward the town.

"He didn't make it as far as Leafburrow, though. A few miles from his destination, he passed through an area where the narrow road was pressed in on by heavy foliage on one side and a rock face on the other. He would have normally trod carefully in such an area, but his worry for his friend and the short distance he had left to go occupied his mind.

"As he passed, several men crowded behind him. Erent sensed them, but too late. More men jumped into the roadway ahead of him. There were ten in all, and all of them began running at him with weapons waving, as if it was a contest for who would be the first to strike.

"It was Erent's habit to carry his bow strung for such occasions. Without a thought, he drew three arrows from his quiver, the fletching laced between his fingers. In a blur of movement, he nocked them, drew, and released. As he did, he twisted his bow around, rotating his left arm so that each arrow went to a slightly different location.

"The arrows had barely left the string before Erent withdrew two more arrows, nocked them, drew, spun, and released them in the same manner, his bow rotating again to send each arrow off in a separate direction. He pulled another shaft, nocked, drew, and released a single arrow. In the space of less than two seconds, six men dropped lifelessly to the dirt.

"The remaining men were all in front of him. They weren't within range to use their weapons yet, but were getting close. Three lightning-fast movements and three single arrows punctured two eyes and one throat.

"There was one bandit left, but he hadn't charged. Instead, while the others did so, he reached behind a tree near him and pulled out a young boy. The bandit put a knife to the boy's throat and positioned himself so he was mostly covered by the tree and the boy was held in front of him like a shield.

"'Drop your weapons or I slice his throat,' the bandit said.

"Erent weighed his options. The bandit seemed cautious enough that he would leave no vital target exposed. The archer could shoot him, but he was afraid the boy would still be harmed in the bandit's death throes. The way the man's hand twitched, Erent figured he might kill the boy, even if he knew he'd die an instant later. The archer had a good sense of what people would do, and he had no doubt the bandit would carry out his threat.

"Erent raised his bow, then dropped it in front of him.

"'The knives, too.' So the bandit knew about his knives. Erent realized this wasn't a random robbery. He drew his knives and dropped them near the bow.

"'Now step back three steps,' the bandit told him. When Erent didn't do so quickly enough, the bandit flexed the arm around the boy, causing him to grunt as air was expelled from his lungs. The knife moved closer to the boy's throat.

"Erent stepped back and waited as the bandit came to him. When the man was close enough, he pushed the boy at Erent, drew another knife, and lunged at Erent.

"But Erent Caahs was more than an archer or a knife wielder. He was fast as a striking snake, and rumor had it that he knew exactly where an opponent would strike at him. He sidestepped one knife, ducked under another, and then straightened while he pulled an arrow from his quiver.

"The bandit spun and slashed at Erent again, managing to

catch a piece of Erent's tunic with his knife, but that's all. Erent slammed the arrow slightly upward at an angle, piercing the man's eye and driving the point into his brain. The bandit's body went slack and he toppled to the ground, the last casualty of the battle.

"Erent searched the bandits and found some gold, which he gave to the boy. Behind the tree were several other prisoners, a woman who had been beaten so severely she couldn't walk without help, and three more children—one boy and two girls.

"He escorted them the few miles to the village only to find his friend there, both legs broken and cuts and bruises all over his body. The bandits had concocted the entire plan to kill Erent and collect the bounty set on him by several bandit lords. The gold went a long way to helping the town recover, but it didn't bring back those who had been killed. Erent left after a time, heavy at heart that he couldn't do more, but satisfied that at least he had eliminated the bandit problem for the time being."

Shadeglide had her hand on her chin, deep in thought. She looked up to Phoenixarrow. "Is it real? Do you really think he could do that with arrows? That fast? That accurate?"

"Yes. Since I heard that story when I was a child, I have practiced my entire life to duplicate it. I failed. I can shoot several arrows at a time, and I can even aim some of them fairly accurately, but I can't do all of that quickly, and hit all the targets. It is possible, though. Maybe one day I'll be able to do it. If I can come close, I know he could achieve it."

"Ten men in seconds," Shadeglide said. "Very efficient." She smiled at the archer. "I can see why you idolize him so. Anyone that proficient deserves adoration."

Darkcaller stepped through the open doorway into the room. "Are you telling tales about Erent Caahs again?"

Phoenixarrow looked down at her hands.

"Just girl talk," Shadeglide said. "Trying to keep from being bored. You know, the waiting is the worst part."

"Hmm," Darkcaller said, sitting on her own bed. "There won't be too much more of that. Soon, we'll carry out our plan, eliminate the targets, and be on our way to meet the others. All this will be far behind us."

"That will be wonderful," Shadeglide said. "On to new and exciting missions."

Phoenixarrow watched the smaller woman from the corner of her eye. Just when she was sure about that one, she began to doubt herself again. The archer wished she knew what part of Shadeglide's personality was real and which was an act.

17

"**A**re you sure about this, Aila?" Tere asked. "If anything goes wrong, there will be no one else to help out."

"I'm sure. We need to get out of here. Unless you think we can break down the door or dig through solid stone, it's the only option I can see. It's dangerous, yes, but staying here until they come to execute us is more dangerous. At least there's a chance with our plan."

"I don't know," he said. "I don't like it. I should be the one risking himself, not you."

Aila shook her head violently. "Don't even start with that. You think you should play the hero because I'm a woman and can't be the one who saves us?"

"What? No, it's nothing of the kind. I'm old. I can die and it won't matter much. You're young. You have a lot of life left to live. I don't like my friends to put themselves in danger."

She patted the man's shoulder. "Aww, that's sweet, Tere, but you know as well as I there are no other options. We've talked about it, thought over it, tried to come up with anything else. We couldn't. It's this plan or nothing, and nothing means we get executed. And not just executed, but hanged. I've seen people hanged that didn't die right away. They suffered as they slowly suffocated, even with the gibbets that drop the condemned. Sometimes their necks don't break. Nope. Give me a clean, quick death."

"That's what I'm afraid of, but I'm afraid it won't even be clean. If you fail, it's going to be...bad. Worse than hanging."

Aila's hand traveled down Tere's arm until she reached his hand, then took it in her own. "We're doing this. Wish me luck and stop trying to make me nervous. If we're lucky, we'll be out of here and on our way in a little while. If we're not lucky, I'll either have the worst day of my life or I'll be dead, to be remembered by you as a hero. At least until they come for you to kill you, too. See, it's really very simple."

He squeezed her hand. "I don't like it, but thank you. You're a hero to me already. Try to not be killed or...used."

"I intend to give my best effort to avoid those things. So, are you ready?"

"I don't really have anything to be ready for, but yes. If you insist on doing this, do it quickly. Be careful."

She laughed and stepped up to the window in the cell's door.

It was nearly time.

A few minutes later, footsteps echoed in the hall, accompanied by the growing light of a torch. Aila looked behind her, trying to make out Tere's face, but she couldn't see a thing, not after her dark vision had been ruined by looking out the window.

The guard came about an hour after their feeding time to retrieve the dishes. Each time this particular guard was on duty, he always took the opportunity to ask her if she was ready to bathe.

A cold chill skittered up her spine at the thought of what

she was doing. She said a quick prayer to Vanda and took a deep breath.

The guard—he had never said his name and she had never asked—plodded up to the door. When the torch got close enough to illuminate the window, he started as he saw her face.

"I'm ready for that bath now," she said, trying hard not to allow her voice to shudder.

He smiled, crooked yellow teeth glinting in the torch light. "Good. We'll have a good time, you'll see."

Aila swallowed to keep the bile from rising in her throat. "Just you and me," she said. "I'm shy."

His grin turned wicked. "Just you and me." He reached to his key ring, his movements jerky and quick, nearly fumbling the metal ring. His excitement was plain, and it terrified Aila. She stepped back from the door as he looked in to check the positions of the others.

"Be strong, be careful," Tere whispered soft enough that it was covered by the sound of the key grinding in the lock and then the door scraping open just enough to let her out.

The guard was not a complete idiot. He had stepped back to give himself room, and he had his sword in his hand, the torch placed in a sconce near the doorway. She stepped out timidly, face down. She blinked at the bright light, the brightest she'd seen since the trial.

He nudged her aside and closed the door with a thunk. The key ground in the lock mechanism again, and the guard withdrew the key and replaced the ring on his belt. Aila looked up to find him leering at her and licking his lips.

He was a particularly ugly man, as were most of the rest of the men who worked for the Mayor. They all looked to have gained their positions by engaging in tavern brawls. She hadn't paid enough attention to be able to describe any of them, but they all seemed to have noses that had been broken repeatedly and scars criss-crossing their faces. This one had a single eyebrow that described an unbroken line above his beady eyes. Aila suppressed another shudder.

"Come on," he said. "I've got a bucket all ready, and some cloth to wash you. I can't wait to...um, help you get clean."

She wasn't able to keep from trembling this time. He saw it but misunderstood.

"Don't worry. There's a fire in the guard room. You won't be cold for long. I'll..." He licked his lips again, moving his tongue over the stubble he didn't care enough to shave. "Make sure you're warmed up."

He took his torch from the wall and pushed Aila's shoulder so she was facing the corridor to the guard room.

She couldn't do this. It was too much. She calculated her chances of killing the man in the hallway and opening the cell with his key. Could she act quickly enough that she could kill him—or at least incapacitate him—and open the cell before the other guards got to her?

He still had his sword out, wary of any betrayal by her. She had hoped that her feigned interest would have put him at ease, but he was a thug, a criminal. He was untrustworthy and so probably didn't trust others. His paranoia made what she needed to do all that much more difficult.

"Go on," he said, pushing her shoulder again, this time with the side of his sword. "You'll soon be clean, warm, and happy. I'll even let you have some of our food leftover from our morning meal."

"Thank you," she said, hating herself for doing it. Her gorge rose up and threatened to make her vomit.

"You can thank me when we get to the room."

They moved slowly down the hallway. Aila tried to use the opportunity to stretch out her legs to prepare for what she needed to do. What was she doing? Did she really believe she'd be able to do this?

She took a deep breath to calm herself. He was only one man. She only needed to knock him out, not kill him. They would be insulated in their own room and she would render him unconscious, take his keys, and let her friends out. She had done many more difficult things.

They passed other cell doors, none of which held prisoners as far as she knew, and finally arrived at the door at the end of the hallway. The guard reached around her to push it open and then nudged her to go inside.

"It's about time," one of the other guards said. He shared a wicked grin with the guard who had brought her. The third man in the room stood from the chair he had been sitting in and ran his eyes over Aila.

The guard who brought Aila was bigger than the other two, which was probably a good thing, because the way the other two stared at Aila, she was pretty sure they would have attacked her if the larger man wasn't there.

"You...you said it would just be the two of us," she said to her escort.

"Yeah, well, it's kinda true. I get to go first, and it'll be just us two. They'll wait patiently until I'm done and then they'll have their turn. It'll be real civilized."

Inside Aila's mind, she screamed.

❧ 18 ❧

F ahtin's breath misted in front of her face as she cleared the final rise in the Cleft of Surus. The hike was as hard as she remembered it, though at least this time she wasn't being chased by dark monsters. As far as she knew.

Aeden and Khrazhti had stopped ahead of her on the hard-packed dirt road that was, thankfully, devoid of snow this time of year. Raki plodded along at her side.

She stepped up next to Aeden and looked out over the lands to the west of Heaven's Teeth. It was beautiful, the sinuous blue line of the Alvaspirtu, the green of the vegetation split by the thin brown line. The River Road was a welcome sight. Farther to the west, the dark blue of the Kanton Sea glimmered, Munsahtiz Island breaking up the azure expanse, an emerald bobbing in a bowl of water.

"We didn't have time to enjoy the view last time," she said.

"Aye, but we don't really have time to enjoy it now, either. Come on, we best get going. I'd not like to have to make camp in the mountains tonight. It'll get cold."

"*Get* cold?" She blew out a breath, a white cloud growing from her.

"This isn't cold, Fahtin. The nights in the highlands are much colder than this, even in the spring."

"You haven't spent a night in the open in the highlands since you were a young boy," she said. "I don't think you're remembering it correctly."

He laughed. "Maybe you're right. Still, it will get colder when the sun goes down, and I want to be lower when that happens."

"Yeah," she said, her shoulders slumping.

They made it down to a lower elevation with plenty of time to spare and started down Tarsun's Trail, the road they had to abandon the last time they came this way. Fahtin shivered at the thought of plunging into the river again.

But they wouldn't need to. There had been an army of animaru chasing them then, and nothing pursued them now. At least, nothing obvious. She knew because she constantly looked back to make sure.

They weren't able to get quite so far as the river before the sun went down, but the flat clearing they found a short distance off the road was warmer than the land above and looked inviting. It was obviously used by travelers often because there was a large ring of stones with ash in the middle and small remains of wood and what looked like rabbit bones.

A little stream was nearby, another tiny tributary to the grand Alvaspirtu. She scooped up a pot full of water and brought it back to camp while Aeden and Raki searched for deadwood for a fire. It was a nice luxury to have a fire. She missed sitting around the flames in the evening, talking and telling stories. For a Gypta, those things were necessities in life, things that had been sorely missed as she ran from one danger to another since they had left the caravan.

"Are you thinking of the family?" Raki asked her.

"Yes."

"Me, too. How do you think they're doing? Are they safe?"

"I hope so, Raki. There was no reason for the animaru to hunt them after we left, but the world is a dangerous place right now. Hopefully they went as far west as they could. We'll see them again."

"I know," he said.

Aeden lit the fire and the three humans watched it grow into a nice warm blaze.

Khrazhti sat off a little from the others, as was her habit. Fahtin went over to her and sat down next to her on the ground.

"How are you doing?" Fahtin asked.

"I am well."

"Do your people sit by fires and tell stories?"

Khrazhti shook her head. "No. We have no things such as this. In Aruzhelim, on campaign, we retreat into our own shelters and regain our power and our health. We talk only to convey important information, never for no reason."

Fahtin hunched down, sorry she had mentioned it.

Khrazhti observed her for a moment. "I am sorry. Am I being impolite? I did not mean offense."

Fahtin tried to smile and was half successful. "It's fine. I understand. It makes me sad to hear about the place you came from. No light, no stories, no conversation. It just seems so..."

"Unalive?" Khrazhti offered.

Fahtin's eyebrows shot up. "Oh. I'm sorry. Now I'm the one being insensitive."

"I take no offense. It is true, Aruzhelim has no light, no life. I never realized what we did not have. I never missed it. I think I would if I had to go back. Or if S'ru is successful into making this world like my own. I would be...sad to see the world lose these things."

Fahtin smiled at her. "Me too. Come on, let's move closer to the fire. Maybe we can tell stories."

Khrazhti scooted alongside Fahtin until they were near enough the fire to feel its warmth, but not so close it was uncomfortable.

"Ah," Fahtin said. "That's better."

There were a few short stories that night as the fire grew smaller, but everyone was tired from their travel and soon they drifted off to sleep. All except Aeden, who took the first watch.

Fahtin, wrapped in her cloak for warmth, with her back toward the fire, plunged into the comfortable darkness of sleep.

Her eyes suddenly snapped open. Something was wrong. No, not so much wrong as different. She could feel something had changed but it wasn't immediately apparent. She turned her head to see where Aeden was, but the young Croagh was not there, nor was the fire.

What was there was a large glowing disc, floating in the air.

She started in surprise but she wasn't afraid for some reason, peering into the depths of the swirling light within the circle in front of her, curious. As she did so, shapes formed and a rush washed over her, as if she was being pulled forward quickly. Into the shapes.

Animaru moved in groups, transitioning from the foliage to the road, looking, searching.

The scene shattered and she was surrounded by darkness. Faint light came from a hole in a door. A window. It had bars on it. In the faint light Tere and Aila huddled in the cold, talking quietly while dressed in little but rags. Urun was slumped against a wall nearby, his mouth moving but no sound coming out. Outside the walls, the crash of waves against rock echoed.

Blood. There was blood on the walls of another room, men lying dead, one with a dagger in his eye.

A forest of twisted trees and dark things sprung up around her. A voice called, inviting her to go to it. She resisted, barely, but Tere, Aila, and Urun walked toward it, shapes made of teeth and fur prowling around them.

Fire. A flash of flame in a large clearing showed the faces of several people that should have been familiar, Fahtin thought, but that she couldn't remember. Tere, face gaunt and body unsteady, raised his bow and fired an arrow. The entire world flashed in firelight and burned, including Fahtin.

The young Gypta woman screamed and sat up.

Aeden was there in an instant, holding her and scanning the area for enemies.

"Shhh," he said. "A dream, Fahtin. Just a dream. Shhh. It's all right. I'm here."

Fahtin's head swung wildly from side to side, eyes darting to find the dangers she knew had been there. Khrazhti was on her feet, swords in hand, looking anxious. Raki was off to the edge of the firelight, his own daggers out.

There were no enemies. No flame other than their low campfire.

She breathed out. "It seemed so real."

"What was it?" Aeden asked.

"Just a dream."

"No," Khrazhti said. "Not just a dream. I felt magic before you cried out, the first magic I have felt since losing my ability to sense Izhrod Benzal. A small surge, but unmistakable. What did you see?"

Fahtin explained the images she saw to them, trying to be detailed.

"I'm sorry, but that's all I remember," she said.

"You did great," Aeden told her. "It's probably just your fear running away with you, making those images in your mind. I'm sure Tere and the others are just fine."

Fahtin shivered. "It doesn't feel like it. I've had dreams before, but never like these. They seemed more real, as if I was really there. More vivid than any dreams I've ever had."

"I'm sure everything's fine," Aeden said, squeezing her with one arm. "You'll see. We'll get to Dartford in another day or two and they'll be waiting there for us, asking what took us so long."

She sank into his hug. "You're probably right. I hope so, anyway."

"Try to get back to sleep. There's plenty of time for you to get some rest still tonight."

She nodded, lay back down on her cloak, and pulled it up around her. As she settled in, she wondered what had caused the dream. Aeden was probably right. It was nothing but her body telling her it was too tired.

Khrazhti's concerned eyes seemed to argue otherwise, but the animaru woman didn't say anything else. Fahtin appreciated that.

❧ 19 ❧

The guard placed his torch in a bracket and pushed Aila toward the corner of the room, where a bucket and a few rags waited. He sheathed his sword, then unbuckled his sword belt and set it, with the scabbarded sword and sheathed knife, on the table against the wall.

His eyes were alight...and hungry. They roamed across her hair and face and then seemed to stick to her as they reached her tunic. Then they made a slow circuit down her body as his twisted smile grew. Aila could swear she felt the tracks of that gaze, fiery lines burning her skin as they scanned her, leaving filthy tracks of muddy ash.

"Take off the tunic so I can wash you," he said. "My mama taught me to always make sure a woman's clean before...before."

Goosebumps prickled Aila's back, though the room was warm. She swallowed, mind whirling to figure out what she could do.

It was plain that there was no turning back now. She had the choice between cooperating with their vile acts or risking their ire and possibly being maimed or killed. They would definitely hurt her if she resisted.

She stepped over to the bucket and put her finger in the water. It was cold, though not as cold as the stone in the cell she had been in. She sipped the air in a long breath and tried to gather up her courage. She had hard choices to make, but she would do what she needed to.

Long ago, Aila swore to herself she wouldn't allow someone to tell her what to do. She was her own person and she would die before losing her freedom. But she had to be smart. Best to get on with it.

Aila turned to look the guard in the eyes. She gave him a smoky gaze and licked the water off her finger, letting it linger between her lips.

The guard looked ready to mount her that instant.

"You're right," she said, changing her voice to a lower, sultry tone. "I do need to be clean, what with all the dirty thoughts in this room."

She faced the bucket again, back to the men, and clenched her muscles so they wouldn't see her tremble. Then she unlaced the tunic they had given her to wear and slowly peeled it off her, exposing her back to them.

"Turn around," the guard told her breathlessly. "We'll start with cleaning your front."

Aila did as he asked, turning slowly so they could see her bare chest. Again, it seemed that the men might jump on top of her at any moment, but between the heavy breaths of the guard who brought her and his glares at the other two, they restrained themselves.

If she thought his stares were uncomfortable before, she had been mistaken. He focused on her breasts, eyes fixing and staying on her left nipple. Another shudder racked her, causing it to visibly harden. The man's eyes nearly popped out of his head.

He took a breath, keeping control of himself, and went to her, reaching toward her chest to stroke her. His breath skipped and he readjusted his hand to take up a rag and soak it in the bucket, then brought it back up to her.

Aila closed her eyes briefly, but they flew open again when he began to wash her chest with slow, gentle strokes. He did it almost reverently, which almost made it worse. The man had closed his eyes, too, head tilted up. In the corner of her vision, she saw the other two guards, wide-eyed and anxious. One of them took a step toward her.

Now, she told herself. There would never be a better time.

Aila's hands darted out, grabbing the sword on the table in her right hand and the knife in her left. She spun, slashing the guard's throat with the knife. He didn't even have a chance to scream, eyes wide and dripping rag still clutched in his hand.

Aila lunged at the guard who had been stepping toward her. Before he could draw the sword at his side, she rammed her own through his belly. It stuck there and she had to kick at him to pull it free, allowing the other guard to draw his own sword.

Aila danced backward, avoiding the slash that would have taken her head off. The man she faced was very large, and she had no doubt he was strong as well. She hoped he wasn't fast, too, or she was in trouble.

She blocked another swing of his sword with her own blade. The blow almost ripped it from her hand, causing her to be thrown to the side, off balance. He chased her around the room and she barely kept ahead of his weapon, parrying when she could and evading as best she knew how. Another block would definitely end the fight. Her arm was numb from the first one.

The room wasn't large, and they used every inch of it. Aila stayed on the defensive, never quite regaining her balance as he cut at her time and time again. She was weak after the long imprisonment and tiring fast. She needed to end it soon.

The guard lunged at her and she wasn't quick enough to get out of the way completely. His sword tore into her side and a blaze of pain exploded in her, making her vision go red at the edges.

Aila spun with the direction of the sword and brought her own down, point at the floor and blade outward. Her spin was enough to force the sharp edge toward the guard's arm. The one holding the sword.

Her weapon cut through his wrist, severing tendon and bone, and removing the hand from his arm. He screamed as blood pulsed from the wound, reaching for her with his other hand to finish her off.

Aila changed direction, tearing out the sword that had gone through her flesh and allowing it to drop to the floor. She almost blacked out. Before she did, though, she swung the knife in her left hand wide, over her shoulder and downward.

Into the guard's right eye.

There was a sickening crunch and a wet slapping sound as the blade's point punctured her enemy's eye socket and brain. He dropped to the floor, dead before his body reached it.

Aila's eyes blurred and she stumbled, barely regaining her balance. The room was a mess, with items strewn about and three bodies on the floor. No, make that two. The guard she stabbed in the belly was still alive, breathing in quick, whistling rasps.

He looked up at her and took one of his hands from his ruined midsection. It was covered with his blood.

"Please," he panted. "Please, help me."

She should probably put the bastard out of his misery, give him a quick, clean death like his companions.

No. Not only didn't he deserve it, she couldn't spare the

strength. Already, her knees were about to give out beneath her. All of it would have been for nothing if she didn't get back to let Tere and Urun out of the cell.

She shuffled toward the first guard she'd killed. Thankfully, he fell in such a way that the keys were visible and she didn't need to move the body. She put her hand on the table to steady herself, then bent over to take them off his belt.

"Please," the barely living guard begged again.

Aila straightened, pain shooting through her like lightning as all her muscles went weak. She only barely caught herself on the table. She turned without even looking in the other guard's direction and stumbled out the door to the long hallway, bumping into the doorframe as she passed through. She cried out in pain, then clenched her teeth to silence herself. No one else would be coming, but she would be damned if she was going to cry and whimper.

Her entire world became her mission: to reach the door and let her friends out. She blinked, realizing the hall was growing darker ahead of her. At first, she thought she might be dying, but realized it was simply that there were no torches lit at the end of the corridor.

She dropped the sword. No need for it now. Taking a torch from a wall sconce almost caused her to cry out again, but she ground her teeth together, her breaths hissing through them, and slid along the wall. Closer, closer.

By the time she reached the door, her jaw was quivering from clenching it for so long and she could barely push herself along, grinding her injury along the stone blocks. She stopped in front of the cell by pure friction.

Torch in her left hand, hanging down so it came dangerously close to burning her as she held it, she fingered the keys with her right hand. The first key didn't work, nor did the second. She was having trouble concentrating. The keys in front of her were blurring in her vision and she was tired. So tired.

Almost, she was almost finished. Then she could die, her task complete. An unfamiliar sound reverberated near her head. What was that?

"Aila." It was Tere's voice. "Aila, by the gods." An arm came through the window, but it couldn't fit more than part of the forearm through. "I can't help you, can't reach. Unlock it and we can help you."

The fourth key she tried finally worked. It fit into the hole and seemed to want to turn, but wouldn't. She didn't have the strength to twist the small piece of metal. She was so close. So close.

She felt herself falling, but barely felt the impact with the stone floor. She had been so close. *I'm sorry, Tere*, she thought, not having the energy even to speak. *I did the best I could.*

20

Tere had been a nervous wreck. Aila went off alone with that guard, taking the risk to try to get them all free. Even as she had stepped out of the cell, he had wanted to call her back, tell her to abort the plan.

But he didn't.

The minutes seemed hours as he waited. He thought he heard the buzz of voices, bodies moving around energetically, far up the corridor. He hoped it didn't mean what he was afraid it did. The guard was a hulking brute. Tere never should have let Aila go alone. They should have found another way.

In the silence of his torture, a door up the hallway opened, but the familiar sound of footsteps didn't follow, nor did the brighter glow of a torch approaching. He sat in the dark, barely breathing, waiting for something to make sense.

What was that scraping noise, like leather being dragged across stone? The light finally approached, but erratically. The scraping grew louder, the light brighter, until it stopped in front of the cell door. He looked out and only saw a piece of dark hair below the window. Aila!

"Aila? Is that you? What happened? Are you all right? Aila?"

She didn't answer. Something was wrong. Tere put his face right up against the bars in the window and tilted his head to look down. Was that blood on the floor?

It was Aila, but she was slumped against the door, her entire focus on the keys in her hand. She fingered them one by one, slowly putting them into the hole on the door. Even that small action seemed more than she was capable of.

"Aila," he said. "Aila, by the gods." He tried to reach out, to steady her or to manipulate the keys to get the door open, but the bars were spaced so he could only get part of his forearm out, not enough to reach her or the lock. "I can't help you, can't reach. Unlock it and we can help you."

She didn't seem to hear him. She chose the next key, the previous one not fitting the lock. It took her three tries to actually insert it into the hole. She grunted and tried to twist it, but seemed to lack the strength to actually move the mechanism.

"Come on, Aila. That's the one. Just turn it and you'll be done."

She fell, and as she did, Tere's hopes went with her. He cried out at the thought of her dying so close to him, just on the other side of the door.

Aila seemed to get hung up on something, bouncing once before she finally hit the floor. A grating click echoed in the hall and Tere felt it through the bars pressed against his face. Praying to every god he'd ever heard of, he pushed on the door.

It swung open an inch and then stopped, butting up against Aila's crumpled form.

"Urun!" Tere yelled. "Urun, we need you. Snap out of it, man. Aila is dying. You need to heal her."

He didn't bother to turn to see if the priest reacted.

Instead, he firmly, but as gently as possible, pushed the door farther open, sliding Aila a little along the floor.

"I'm sorry, girl," he said, "but we have to get out to you to help you."

Tere squeezed out the door and took Aila into his arms. She was a mess of cuts and blood. She wasn't moving. He picked her up easily and set her down gently in the doorway.

"Urun, you gods-forsaken son of a bitch. If you don't get over here and heal this girl right now, we're going to have two corpses here."

He finally turned to the priest and found him with his knees to his chest and his arms wrapped around them, rocking back and forth, slamming his back into the wall with each backward motion. He was muttering.

"Can't. No power. Why have you left me? Why? Can't..."

Tere went to him and grabbed his shoulders. He shook the young priest violently. Urun was limp, like a bundle of rags, and only flopped this way and that with Tere's shaking.

"Urun," he begged. "Please. Help her. Urun. Aila will die if you don't help her. Please!"

The young man's grey eyes flashed as he looked up, the dim torchlight in the hall reflecting off them. "Aila?" he said.

"Yes, Aila." Tere grabbed Urun's chin and forced his head in the direction of the woman's unmoving form.

"Aila." Urun's eyes became more lucid. He scrambled toward her, his face a mask of horror. Tere left him to it, watching intently.

Urun skimmed his hand over Aila's body. When it came to her torn side, he gasped and his fingers trembled. He began to mouth words, barely making any sound at all. Prayers to his goddess, Osulin.

Nothing happened. Tere was about to shake the young man again when Aila sucked in breath suddenly, a rushing, hissing sound that sounded like the first breath she had ever taken. Then she coughed repeatedly and cried out in pain.

None of it fazed Urun. He continued his whispered prayers and his hand continued to hover over her side. After what seemed to Tere to be hours, the priest finally slumped and leaned against the doorway.

"Urun?" Aila said. "Tere? Did I make it?"

"You did," Tere said, falling against the wall. "By the gods, you did."

21

Tere Chizzit had been in pickles before, no doubt, but his current situation had his hackles rising. Maybe he was growing too old for such foolishness, or it could be that others were involved. Others who he worried over, and with good reason.

Aila had very nearly died. Urun broke out of his stupor to heal her—though he seemed to have immediately lapsed back into it—but the entire situation was too close to a disaster. If that key ring hadn't caught and twisted as she fell...

But that was done, and he had a job to do. He slipped down the corridor to the door leading to the guards' room. He went on silent feet, second nature to one who tracked and stalked in the forest. Moving on stone without so much as a scrape was child's play.

Tere swung the door open slowly, crouching low to peer through the gap where the door met the frame. His mouth dropped open. Nothing moved, so he stepped around the door and got a good look at the room.

There was blood everywhere. The trail of Aila's blood that stretched along the wall all the way down the hallway was not evident here, but red painted much of the floor and many of the objects in the room as well. Table, chairs, the hearth rug near the fire, all had at least a bit of the crimson. Pools of it had settled in the uneven flagstones.

Three.

There were three corpses in the room, all bigger men even than Tere. It was no wonder Aila was injured so severely. The wonder was how she survived at all.

A hiss caused Tere to spin, bringing up the sword he had found in the hallway.

"Please," one of the guards said in barely a whisper. He had a nasty belly wound that had almost done its job. The man wasn't moving anywhere, so Tere ignored him for the time being. He held his sword at the ready and kicked the first body, the one by the table. It didn't move, nor would it ever. The savage slash that split his throat made sure of that.

The other body had no life in it, either. The severed wrist barely dribbled blood, and the dagger rammed into its eye made that no surprise to Tere.

He finally turned his attention back to the barely alive guard. "Where is our gear?"

"Please," he whispered again, then jerked from the pain it caused.

This was the guard who hated them most, the one who constantly threatened to stop feeding them or to kill them outright because they were such a nuisance. He was not worth even getting the sword bloody over. Tere had no feelings for the man's pain, unless it was a sense of justice. But he didn't need to be vindictive.

"Tell me where our gear is and I'll end you quickly. You have to know not even the best healer in the world could save you now."

The man's eyes were glazed in pain, tears leaking from them. "Trunk," he wheezed. "Next room." He turned his head slightly, trying unsuccessfully to focus on the door to what looked like a side room.

Tere hefted his sword and walked over to the door. It didn't have a lock, only a simple latch. He lifted it and slowly cracked the door. It creaked and Tere cursed under his breath.

There was no need for worry, though. The room was darkened, but opening the door a bit wider showed it to be a large closet with a few barrels, some crates, and a chest. His bow stave leaned against the wall in a corner. He swung the chest's lid up and breathed out a sigh of relief. Their weapons, armor, even their purses were within. He picked through it to find his knives and drew one, leaving the other for the time being.

The man was still in the same position, his head still turned toward the closet, when Tere returned. "A deal is a deal. I'd like to let you suffer more, but I'm a man of my word. Burn in the deepest layer of Percipius's realm."

He stabbed the sword into the guard's chest, at the perfect angle to puncture the heart. The guard's eyelids fluttered and then his eyes lost their light.

Tere left the sword in the man's chest, and then headed back to get Aila and Urun, carrying the knife he had grabbed. It was past time for them to be out of this place.

The group was in sorry shape after having not eaten anything but the slop they were fed only twice a day and being dehydrated from their time in the cell. Still, with Aila healed of her serious injuries by Urun, they were as ready as they'd ever be to escape to the forest.

Possibly to a gruesome death.

"I found our things," Tere told them as he led them back to the guards' room. "At least we have that. There's some food left over from the guards' last meal, so we can have something to eat, and the crates in the storage room look like they contain rations. We'll be thinner than we were, but we should be able to make it to Dartford. If we can get through the forest alive."

Urun had returned to his unresponsive state and Aila plainly was too tired for conversation. Healing took its toll, and she was weakened by the long captivity. Tere showed them the trunk and they changed out of the rags their captors had given them into their own clothes and armor.

Tere's bow strings were in the pouch still attached to his belt. He strung his bow with a practiced hand and had to admit that it felt good to hold it again. For a time, he thought he never would.

Aila and Urun ate what food they could find that hadn't been splashed with blood while Tere opened two of the crates, finding the rations he expected. Several water skins, two of them full of wine, were in the room, too, and he put those in his pack. When he finished that, he went to the table to eat the food Aila had left aside for him as she went into the storage room to change behind the closed door.

"My purse is empty," she said when she came out fully dressed. "The bastards took all the gold I had."

"From me, too," Tere said. He and Aila both looked toward Urun, but he didn't so much as register their existence, let alone give them the status of his purse.

"On the other hand," Aila said, "they didn't find the secret purse I had hidden in my armor." She tossed a small leather pouch up in her hand. "Not as much as we had, but enough to get by on, I think."

Tere eyed her, wondering if she'd leave it at that.

She didn't. "Of course, there's also this." She drew one of her weapons and sliced the strings off the purse on the closest corpse, the one with only one hand. She opened the pouch and displayed a wicked grin. "Yep, here's some of it." She gathered the purses the other men had carried, handed one to

Tere, and poured the contents of the last one into Urun's pouch, which was tied to his own belt.

"That's almost as much as we had when they took us," Tere said. "Minus what they probably spent on drinking and whoring."

Aila spit on the corpse near the table for some reason, but Tere didn't ask about it. That one was the one who had offered to bathe her.

"Are you ready?" she said. "I want to get out of here."

"Let's go." Tere turned Urun's shoulder toward the entrance of the building.

He was surprised to find daylight streaming in the windows when they reached the entryway. Being in the cell for so long had made him lose track of the time of day completely, but he thought it was night for some reason. It would be harder to move around unseen in the crowded town during the daylight. There was nothing he could do about it, though. They couldn't very well wait for darkness to fall when the missing guards could be detected at any time.

"Are you sure we can't go around the edge of the town and over the bridge instead of trying the forest," Aila asked. "We could swim instead of going over the bridge."

"We'd be seen going through the town to the entrance, and I don't think we're in any kind of shape to swim to the mainland. The Kanton grey sharks are thick here, so even if we could swim it easily, we'd never make it alive. The forest is our only chance, the slim chance that it is."

"I was afraid you'd say something like that. Fine. Let's get this over with. I won't survive another minute in that cell." She turned to Urun. "Urun, we're going to need to escape, probably run. We need you to keep up with us. We can't drag you along or we'll all be captured. Do you understand?"

Urun nodded silently. It was probably the only response

they'd get from him, so Tere accepted it and opened the front door of the building.

It seemed that this structure was built over an older one. Tere wasn't sure what happened to it, but the stone basement and cells were of a more ancient design, and better built. They were close to the north edge of the town, which was fortuitous, but there were still plenty of opportunities to be spotted and caught.

"How are we going to get out?" Aila asked. "I have some rope in my pack, but it'll take too long for one of us to climb up with it, set it, and for the others to follow. We'll be spotted for sure."

"There was a breach in the wall when I came here before. It was already old then, made decades ago by a violent storm that uprooted a tree and slammed it through a section. The tree was long gone, but they hadn't repaired the wall when I was here last. Hopefully they still haven't. It was this way."

He sprinted toward the wall, visible through an alley nearby, scanning the other darkened alleys as he went. Between the shadow of the wall and that of the buildings around them, it was darker than the rest of the town, though still with plenty of daylight to see by.

Once he reached the wall, he skirted along it, at one point having to turn sideways to squeeze between the back of some building and the wall itself. He kept checking to make sure Aila and Urun kept up with him.

"If we get separated for any reason," he whispered to her, "meet me at the edge of the forest. Don't go in, if you can help it. We need to do that together."

Aila nodded and he continued to where he remembered the hole in the wall.

He let out a breath he had been holding once it came into view. It was as he remembered, a notch cut in the wall where the tree had fallen and been rammed into the stone by the storm. The opening of the V was five feet from the ground, but it was less than half the height of the wall itself, so it was their best bet. Tere checked to see if any guards or watchmen were around who could see them. He didn't see a soul.

"We're in luck," he told her. "Go ahead. You two go first. I'll follow right behind you."

Aila crouch-ran up to the opening, jumped without slowing down, and grabbed hold of a jagged tear in one of the stones making up the wall. Without seeming to strain at all, she pulled herself up, lodged her foot into a gap, and bounded over the notch and disappeared, only to lie on her belly and push her arm down toward Urun, who had followed her up to the wall but was making no attempt to climb.

"Take my hand, Urun," Aila hissed. "Come on. We have to get out of this town. If we don't, they'll put us back in the cell."

Urun's eyebrows shot up at that and he reached up to take Aila's hands in both of his. With some grunting and scrabbling, the young priest finally climbed up over Aila and dropped to the other side.

Tere had just turned to scan the area again when an arrow rebounded off the stone near him, shattering in the process. A loud curse from behind him and to his right exploded in the air.

He spun, nocking an arrow, drawing, and releasing as he completed his spin. The sound of the bowstring slapping his bracer was followed closely by a wet sucking sound as the arrow's tip found the other man's eye. Before the soft thump of the body hitting the ground reached Tere, he was already in motion, jumping for the stone Aila had used to pull herself up. Thankfully, she had already dropped to the other side with Urun, so he didn't collide with her.

"They saw us," he said. "I don't know if they alerted

others, but I'm not going to stick around to find out. Let's go, into the forest."

He plunged into the trees ten feet away. As soon as he stepped out of the open space, he was surrounded by darkness. He was barely able to stop Aila from running past him as he snatched her arm and wrapped one of his own around Urun's chest as he followed two steps later.

They paused, listening. It was eerie how little sound traveled to where they were. The trees were thick, their twisting trunks seeming to reach to their fellows, but not dense enough to explain why there was no sound from outside the forest.

Tere didn't like the feeling, like someone was dragging a sponge soaked with cold honey over his body, the gel-like liquid clinging to him and making him feel not only chilled, but dirty and sticky.

"Tere?" Aila said.

"I know. It's magic; it has to be. We need to get out of this forest as quickly as we can. Straight north. It should only be ten miles or so across going south to north on this side. We can go ten miles. We're going to have to."

22

"What are we doing?" Urun said. Tere's head snapped around to look at the nature priest.

"We're trying to escape the town," Tere told him.

"I don't like this place."

"None of us do, but we have to go through it to get away."

"I don't want to be here."

"We don't want to be here, either, but we have no choice. Let's start moving. The sooner we get to the other side, the better."

"It's"—Urun gave a visible shiver—"not right. Not natural. I can hear nature screaming here."

Tere found himself stepping toward Urun, his fingers twitching like they would curl into a fist and strike the younger man of their own volition.

"Come on, Urun." Aila took his hand. "We'll be out of it soon."

"I don't think so." Urun began mumbling to himself in a quiet voice.

Tere headed toward where he thought north was, perpendicular to the trees lining the city wall. "Stay close. I have a feeling if we lose each other in here, we'll never find one another again."

Travel was slow. With the thick trees and vegetation to crowd them and trip them, and the eerie lack of light, they stumbled along at a snail's pace. Tere could see well, but it almost seemed that the vegetation went out of its way to snatch at their feet, though he never actually saw it move.

Less than a quarter mile in, a thick fog enveloped them as well, making it difficult to see each other even at arm's length. Even Tere's vision was affected by the fog, which should have been impossible.

Tere was about to suggest they tie themselves to each other with rope when scratching sounds reached his ears from several different directions.

"Something is out there." He nocked an arrow. Scuffs emanated from the fog around them, but he could see nothing other than his two friends floating in a sea of grey, roiling cloud.

Something flashed to his left, a shadowy shape as big as a man but on all fours. When it repeated the movement straight ahead of him, he released an arrow and was rewarded by the thump of the projectile hitting something soft and the grunt of whatever the four-legged creature was. The scuffling sounds came again, but this time retreating.

They waited for several minutes, Tere's nocked arrow waiting for release. When they heard or saw nothing more, they started out again, going toward where Tere guessed was north. With no sun to guide them and no landmarks, it was little more than speculation.

Urun was having trouble keeping his feet. He tripped on vines and bushes, got snagged on thorns, and wasn't efficient in skirting other hazards in the foliage. Tere had never seen the priest suffer this way in vegetation. It always moved out of the way for him, leaving a clear path for him to walk. This forest, it seemed, resisted that skill. It meant nothing good for the party that it did so.

They plodded along for hours in the bubble of greyness. Finally, the light failed completely and they were soon walking in total darkness. Tere stopped them and found a few branches of deadwood that lay nearby. He broke them and stripped them with his knives, then lit them with the help of some dried moss and his flint and steel to make crude torches.

"I'd normally suggest we set up camp and not try to travel in the darkness, but I really don't want to spend a minute longer in here than we have to and I don't think it would be a good idea to stay in one place, fire or no."

"I agree," Aila said, taking the torch he handed her.

Urun took the proffered torch as well, but said nothing. In the torchlight, his eyes were wide and darting around them, very different than the glazed look they had in the cell.

Soon after, the sounds of scraping and shuffling returned. This time, however, there was definitely more than one of whatever it was they encountered earlier. They didn't surround the humans, but approached from the right. Inadvertently, Tere swayed toward the left as they continued, meaning to circle around a dense clump of trees and then center the party again.

When they had skirted the obstacle, though, more of the sounds and movement came from the right, pressing them to the left again. A few more adjustments as whatever creatures were hunting them chased them in other directions, and Tere realized he had no idea any longer where north was. For all he knew, they were traveling south.

"Maybe it's time to take a stand," he suggested.

The others had nothing to say, both of them wide-eyed

and scanning the mist around them, Aila with her weapons out and Urun with his staff in front of him.

Come, a voice said directly into Tere's mind. *Come, and I will protect you. Food I have, and water. You may rest safely.*

"Did you hear that?" Tere asked.

"The voice, in my mind?" Aila asked in return.

"Yes."

"I heard it."

"Urun," Tere prompted.

"I heard it, but I don't believe it."

Come! The voice was more insistent. *Do not make me send my minions to retrieve you. I would not like to see you damaged.*

"We don't know where to go," Tere said out loud.

I will show you the way.

A faint light appeared in the fog, streaming off in front of them.

"Tere?" Aila said.

"I don't know, Aila. I can't tell which direction is which. Those things in the mist seem to be able to see us. Urun? Do you know where we should go? Do you know what's happening?"

"No."

Tere waited for more, but the priest had his hands to his head and his eyes closed as if trying to force the voice out.

Come.

"Damn it," Tere said. "I think we have to go. I can't think of anything else to do."

Aila huffed. "Me either. Let's see where the light goes, shall we?"

They followed the light through the forest, surrounded in the impenetrable bubble that didn't allow them to see anything but each other and the glowing signal ahead of them. It was as if the fog itself was somehow illuminated, the light traveling in front of them and dimming just as they reached it, only to light up farther toward their destination.

Tere didn't hear any more of the scuffs and didn't detect any movement. They were going the way the voice had told them and it seemed that was enough for whatever had spoken.

Urun whimpered, muttering frantic, unintelligible things. Occasionally, something would jump out in his babble, things like *unnatural*, *wrong*, and *help*. It didn't make Tere feel any better about their situation. He tried to think of something they could do, but he kept coming back to one thing: they were within the realm of something more powerful than they. Even if they bolted, they didn't even know which way they were traveling.

After a time—Tere couldn't even guess how long it was—the light seemed to stop progressing and created a pool ahead of them.

Come, the voice said.

The light expanded and it seemed the fog thinned enough to see to the other side of a clearing. It was about twenty feet across and consisted only of grass and vines, the former waving in a nonexistent breeze and the latter quivering and occasionally jerking in the midst of the grass.

"No, no, no," Urun chattered. He dropped to his knees and covered his head with his arms.

Figures rose from the ground all around them, standing on two legs and swaying slightly. They each had the form of a person, but were made of bits of plants and covered with clothes that were falling apart even as they stood there.

Welcome, the voice said. *Welcome home.*

23

"Damn it all to Abyssum," Darkcaller said when Shadeglide gave her the news. The strike team— Shadeglide, Edge, and Fireshard—had gone to where the prisoners were being held. Shadeglide had found the location earlier that day and Darkcaller had decided to eliminate them as soon as it was dark. They needed to do it before the Mayor carried out his execution.

When the team got to the jail, they found the guards slaughtered and the only cell that had evidence of recent occupants empty.

They had escaped, hours before the Falxen went to kill them.

"Did you scout the area and find out where they went?" Darkcaller asked, rising from a bed in the women's room at the inn.

"We did," Shadeglide answered. It was strange to Darkcaller that the other two allowed her to take the lead like this. They probably recognized that when it came to sneaking around, the small woman was several levels above the normal assassin. Edge may have had more experience, but he was fine with following. So Shadeglide answered for the group. "They couldn't be tracked over stone, of course, but when we widened our search, we found another body."

"You found a body where?"

"In the north wall. Near an old breach. They made no attempt to hide it. If it weren't for how secluded the area is, others would have found it already and reported it. That may have happened in the time it took us to come back here, though."

Darkcaller glared at the floor. "Are you saying they went outside the town wall, *on the north side?*"

"Yes."

"Into the forest?"

"We are assuming that, yes. I saw some scuff marks that would indicate such."

Darkcaller growled.

"Are we going to track them and chase them down?" Phoenixarrow asked.

Darkcaller's frown grew more pronounced. "There's no tracking in the Verlisaru Forest. There's only dying there."

"It can't be that bad," the red-haired archer said.

"It can. While I was at the Academy, a group of high-level students and a master tried to study the forest. Others, including most of the other masters, tried to discourage them, but the core group were scholars. Though they were all competent combatants—either physically or magically— several were avid knowledge-seekers. They paid no attention to the warnings.

"They outfitted twelve of our number. Honestly, it seemed like they were preparing for an expedition from one side of Promistala to the other, through every hostile territory in between. They had plenty of gear; weapons, magical elixirs, amulets, spells, and an abundance of paper and supplies for drawing and writing. They thought they had considered all things.

"I remember them setting out. They caused quite a stir as they left. The mood was light, within their party in any case, but I wasn't so sure. I'd heard the stories, read others, and didn't think I would have the courage to brave the forest as they did.

"As it turns out, I was wiser than they. None were ever seen again. Not one trace of their party was ever discovered. Not that anyone went into the forest to look, mind you. If there was one thing their example taught us, it was that no amount of combat prowess or magical power would equip someone sufficiently to plunge into those trees. They were never seen or heard from again."

The others stared at Darkcaller as if waiting for her to continue. She had nothing else to say about it. A chill filled her with ice as she remembered the sheer amount of power the group wielded. And how it didn't help them in the end.

"So, we're going to give up on the mission?" Shadeglide asked. "Go back to the others?"

"A bunch of cowards," Keenseeker said before Darkcaller could answer. "Some spooky stories about ghosts or such nonsense. I thought I was in a group of professional assassins, not girls who had not developed breasts yet." He conspicuously eyed Darkcaller's chest as he said it.

The Falxen leader clenched her jaw and counted to three in her mind. It kept her from blasting the bastard to ash right where he stood, but it did nothing to temper her voice. "Perhaps you would like to try following their trail."

"Yeah, I would. Problem is, I'm shit when it comes to tracking. All those little details and having to remember all that information about what's important, it's not my strong point."

"Do tell," Darkcaller said.

"I *am* telling you. If one of these fine ladies who is good at that stuff wants to come with me, well, that'll be okay. How about the redhead? At least I'll have something to look at while she's looking for footprints."

Phoenixarrow's hand twitched and Darkcaller was afraid an arrow was going to be loosed any moment.

"No," the leader said loudly—probably too loudly—and the archer looked to her, the fire for Keenseeker plain in her eyes. "We're not going to split up, especially if we're to try to follow the targets."

"I thought you just said we're not going into the forest," Fireshard said, motioning with her hand and conjuring a knife made out of flame, which she used to scratch at her fingernails.

"No, that is not what I said. We can't blindly go into the forest hoping that we'll be able to follow their trail. But then, we don't need to. There is only one thing they can do if they're using the forest to escape. They're trying to get to the northern part of the island where they can get back to the mainland using the northern bridge. They may even be trying to get to the Academy. What they won't do is come back out and try to get to the Praesturi Bridge. They'd have to go through the town, which they would have already done if that was their goal."

Phoenixarrow nodded, but Keenseeker wasn't done.

"You can't know that they won't try that."

Darkcaller sighed. Gods, she hated dealing with this man. "You're right. It seems our choices are to try to catch them when they come out of the northern edge of the forest—if they survive that long—or we can wait around here to see if we can catch them as they try to get through town and back to the bridge."

"They won't do that," Phoenixarrow said. "The older guy is too smart for that. I thought he'd be too smart to go into the forest, but deciding between the two options, I'd choose the forest, too."

Darkcaller considered the rationale. "Time is wasting. We'll make this simple. Give me your opinion on which way you think is best. I'll consider them and make a decision as to what we'll do."

"North," Fireshard said. "I ain't afraid of a bunch of trees."

Keenseeker glared at the woman, probably because he wanted to say the same thing. "The forest."

"I will go where you tell me," Edge said.

"North," Phoenixarrow said.

"I'd prefer staying in the city and waiting," Shadeglide said, "but I think Phoenixarrow is correct that they won't try going through town, so I choose the forest as well. I think we can compromise on exactly how we do that, though."

Darkcaller's lips formed into a wry smile. She was really beginning to think Shadeglide had a lot of potential as a brace leader. "I'm glad we're all in agreement, but Shadeglide is correct. Plowing through the center of the forest is foolhardy. Whether the targets make it out alive or not, I intend to.

"So, we will be going north, but taking a route along the eastern edge of the island, hugging the shore as much as possible. If I remember correctly, the trees go right up to the cliffs dropping into the water, but they are at least a little less condensed there so travel should be easier. And staying on the edge may limit the interaction we have with whatever lives in the forest."

"Or it may trap us between the cliffs and whatever wants to attack us from the trees," Phoenixarrow said. "I agree, though. Your plan sounds like the best choice."

"Good. Anything else anyone needs to say? No? Then let's gather supplies and prepare to leave. One hour and we will start off. We'll need to find a way to get over or through the walls on the northeast section of the town..."

"I'll find it," Shadeglide said, as Darkcaller knew she would. "I already have all my gear and rations in my pack, so I can go now. I'm assuming there will be guards near the breach in the wall now because of the body there. I'll be back in less than an hour." She nodded to Darkcaller and headed out the door.

"This is a strange mission," Darkcaller said, almost as if she was talking to herself. "First dealing with the one bringing those dark monsters over from that other world and now chasing targets through the Verlisaru. Our employer better give us a bonus for this one."

"Wait," Phoenixarrow said. "Dark monsters? You mean the ones in the rumors, the creatures that tear people apart? We're on the same side as those things?"

"Does it matter?" Fireshard said. "As long as there's killing to be done and we have money in our purses, who cares?"

"Enough," Darkcaller said. "Forget I said anything. It's none of our concern right now. Those people fleeing into the forest are. After we've killed them, we'll deal with any other issues that come up. We have our orders."

Phoenixarrow's look of disgust wasn't a welcome sight. Would her hero worship cause her to question her loyalties? Darkcaller would have to watch the archer. The brace leader couldn't afford for any of her blades to have an attack of conscience.

Almost exactly an hour later, the assassins left the inn, following Shadeglide. It was a simple enough thing. The small woman had simply bribed one of the few sentries that patrolled the walls to let them out of a locked gate. It was positioned in a narrow alley on the far east section of the north wall.

The guard shook the coins in his fist as the six assassins filed through. "I can't let you back in, you know. Going out is one thing, but coming in, well, I can't do it. The Mayor'd have my head for sure."

Shadeglide nodded as Phoenixarrow—the last of them aside from Shadeglide and Darkcaller herself—passed through the doorway. "We understand. Thank you."

The two remaining women stepped across to the north side of the wall and the man didn't waste any time in closing and locking it behind them.

Darkcaller looked over at Shadeglide. The woman smiled at her and pranced up to the front of the group, where Phoenixarrow was already taking her place to lead them. The dark witch shook her head at the small assassin and joined the rest of the Falxen in entering the forest.

24

A ila gasped and Tere trained his eyes on the figure closest to them. No, they weren't made only of bits of plants. He picked out pieces of rotting flesh in the amalgamation that made up their bodies. At a few points —an elbow, a head, an ankle—Tere noticed what looked to be white branches peeking out.

No, not branches. Bones. These creatures were human. Were.

That was when Tere noticed the vines crawling up Urun's legs and others coming toward him and Aila.

"Urun!" he said, drawing his knives and slashing at the vines quickly moving toward him. "Urun. Get up. Don't let the vines get you. They'll take your body. Urun! You're going to die."

Aila had her own weapons out, cutting at the vines. The once-humans were moving in a slow, rhythmic gait, closing in around them. Tere cursed, slashing alternately at the vines and the creatures. His blades cut bits off the humanoids, but the vines were tough, and they were moving more and more quickly, some dodging his blows.

"Urun!" Tere yelled again.

The priest finally came out of his stupor, shaking his head to clear it. He looked around, eyes going wide and mouth dropping open. He leaped up, swinging his staff at the closest vines with a flare of light. The vines shriveled at the light's touch.

"Tere? Aila?"

"Urun, can you do something?" Aila asked, dodging a vine and cutting at one of the lumbering creatures. "We can't hold them off with our weapons. A spell. Can you do something to help?"

"Osulin," Urun said. "She has forsaken me. I can't...feel her power."

"You have it." Aila jumped back from two vines crossing in front of her, barely evading them. "You just shriveled those vines. You have the power. Use it."

Urun looked at her blankly as one of the vines reached for his leg. Out of reflex, he slammed his staff into it, charring it to ash.

"You have the power of nature," Tere said. "These things are unnatural. They're vulnerable to your spell. Please, Urun, do something or we'll become like those shambling things."

Urun swiveled and trained his gaze on one of the humanoids. He had apparently not seen them before. "You." He grabbed his staff in two hands. "Are." Light flared on the tip of the long shaft of wood. "An abomination!" A bright lance of pure white light shot out of the staff and struck the former human in the chest. It glowed for a second, then exploded into ash.

No! the voice shouted in their heads. *You will not undo my work.*

The fog rolled over them again, smothering the light that had been there. Tere felt the vines grow more energetic, move faster. One tried to slither up his leg and he cut it down, depositing a shallow slash on his own limb as he did it.

"Urun!" he shouted.

Muttering sounded to Tere's right. It grew in volume and Tere realized it wasn't muttering at all, but another language, one he didn't understand. Urun was soon shouting, the sounds reverberating in the air. At the source of the sound, a glowing ball winked into existence and grew rapidly. It doubled, then doubled again, and continued to do so until it exploded outward.

The creatures around them came apart at the flash of power, and then the entire area was drowned in darkness again. A hand grabbed his shoulder, and he almost slashed out with his knife but realized just in time it was Urun's.

In the soft glow of the light coming from Urun himself, he was able to pick out Aila on the other side of the priest.

"Come on," Urun said. "We have to go now. I'll confuse it, but we have to escape. I can't hold it off long."

Tere nodded and the three of them moved out at a run. A few times in their mad flight, he caught glimpses of the creatures that had surrounded them before. They looked like a cross between a giant wolf and a hunting cat. They pawed at the ground, seeming not to see them, chasing after things that Tere couldn't see himself.

After what seemed like hours, the three stumbled out of the trees and onto a grassy meadow. A glance backward showed the trees of the Verlisaru Forest, clear as could be in the moonlight, without a trace of fog. A growl echoed across the meadow from the forest, and Tere shivered, but nothing followed them.

"That was too close," he said.

A flare off to his right caught the archer's attention. It was a reddish light, like someone had built a fire, but the flame was moving. Around the fire, he saw movement of several other figures.

Tere jumped to the side to confuse anyone targeting him, drew and launched an arrow as he moved.

❧ 25 ❧

It was nearly dark by the time the assassins crossed the line of trees into the Verlisaru Forest. It was as if the only light in the world was a candle and it was immediately snuffed out, leaving them in deep blackness. A fiery sword appeared in the midst of them, Fireshard holding its hilt.

"Get the torches out," Darkcaller commanded. Her voice was steady, but she shivered inside. She hadn't even detected the magic of the forest and it had sprung up instantly, blocking out light and even the sound of the waves crashing against the foot of the cliffs below them.

Once they lit the torches off Fireshard's blade, they started the arduous trek northward. They could see barely enough to keep to the edge of the cliff without walking off, but they had to pay constant attention. The fog wasn't natural, didn't swirl or have substance or a damp feeling, and Darkcaller hated it all the more because of it. Still, if a little mist was the worst they'd face, she would accept it gratefully.

They kept at it for hours. Whether it was many hours or a few, Darkcaller had trouble determining, but they were definitely making progress. Even paying close attention, there were times she found herself walking due south, based on the direction of the cliff's edge. She would correct herself, turn around, and begin moving the way she should have, but it happened entirely too often for her comfort.

A movement to her left drew her eyes. She peered through the mist, trying to find what had caused the disturbance.

"There are...things around us," Phoenixarrow said, nocking an arrow and narrowing her eyes. "I'm not sure what, but be prepared."

Small sounds found their ears, where there hadn't been any noise before. Twice more Darkcaller saw movement, but whatever was out there hadn't revealed its intentions yet. At one point, she was sure they were going to be attacked, but then there was a sense of the things around her rushing off, heading somewhere more important to them. She released a held breath and loosened the grip on her staff.

When it seemed to her that it should be growing daylight soon, the things in the mist returned and finally showed themselves. They were huge, almost as large as the great bears that roamed the forests in Artuyeska, shoulders at the height of Keenseeker's head and solid bodies, bristling with fur, that seemed to move contrary to the laws of nature. Sharing a form with both wolves and predator cats, they slinked along gracefully, rarely looking at the humans. There were at least five of them.

Without any outward sign, the creatures leaped to the attack.

One of the monsters flew through the air at Darkcaller, moving faster than she had seen anything move before, except maybe Featherblade. With a thought, she pulled darkness from her surroundings and forced her will upon it. It coalesced into a thick bubble of dark magic, surrounding her and protecting her.

The beast slammed into her shield and bowled her over with the sheer force of its leap. It's claws and teeth, visible through the smoky shield, weren't able to penetrate, but Darkcaller was surprised at the effect the creature had on her protective bubble; it should have resisted the force of its leap, not knocked her down. It bounced off the shield and bounded to the side, turning to charge again.

While Darkcaller was scrambling back to her feet, she saw that one of the attackers had lunged toward Shadeglide and Edge, who were standing next to each other. As the monster approached, Shadeglide flickered, reappeared to the side of the creature, and slashed out with her knives. Edge dodged the main brunt of the attack and sliced down with his sword, which appeared suddenly in his hand like magic. The blades seemed to pass through the creature's body without doing any damage.

Fireshard was having a bit better luck, two fiery longswords in her hands, spinning in a pattern that left little room for the monster confronting her to swipe at her. A gout of fire lashed out from between the two blades, forming into a throwing knife made of flame, already in motion. It sank into the creature's shoulder. The beast opened its mouth as if to cry out, but no sound issued forth. It changed its direction and rolled on the ground to put out the singed fur where the knife had injured it.

Keenseeker swung his axe around, trying to cut two of the creatures in half, but to no avail. The blow passed harmlessly through the monsters' bodies, though it did disrupt their movements.

Phoenixarrow, obviously seeing the success Fireshard had, dipped a pitch-tipped arrow into the flame of a torch, lit a small pot of the same pitch she had dropped in front of her, and loosed the arrow. The red tip streaked across the distance between her and one of the creatures attacking Keenseeker and plunged into it, upsetting its balance and keeping it from sinking its teeth into the axe-wielder's neck. She drew another arrow, dipped it into the little pot, and shot another fiery brand at the same creature.

They did not have the upper hand in this battle. Darkcaller launched a blast of dark magic toward the beast that was coming in to attack her again and it bounced from the thing's fur, barely upsetting its run toward her. While she watched it, her breath caught. Three more of the monsters had appeared behind Shadeglide. That made at least eight, and Darkcaller doubted they could even kill half of those if they all cooperated.

"Run," she said. "Go north. Maybe they're territorial and they'll give up the chase."

Shadeglide, performing an impressive flip with a twist to avoid another leaping creature, landed lightly and sprinted along the cliff, keeping her eyes down at her feet. Edge followed closely on her heels, his sword licking out to lop off branches to trip the beasts chasing them. Surprisingly, one of the monsters stumbled.

Keenseeker, of course, ignored Darkcaller's command. That was fine with her. She swung her staff, sprayed a curtain of dark power toward the creatures targeting her, and rushed after the others. As she passed, Phoenixarrow put two more arrows into the same creature. Several spots on its body were on fire, but it didn't seem slowed. The red-haired archer nocked another arrow, lit it, and raced along next to Darkcaller.

Darkcaller's entire world narrowed down to the space right in front of her feet. Luckily, they were in a patch of the forest that was less tangled than many they had passed through during the night, so she could keep the edge of the cliff in sight and still move fairly quickly. She couldn't chance the break in focus to see where everyone else was, nor could she try to detect anything about to pounce on her. She maintained her shield and ran as fast as she could, hoping she—and at least some of the others—would survive.

When she burst out of the undergrowth and onto a grassy field, she nearly tripped and fell. She continued running for several more seconds before she realized the fog was gone and she could see Shadeglide and Edge in the moonlight as she passed them.

Finally stopping, she turned, staff up and words of power on her lips.

Phoenixarrow almost ran into her, dodging at the last moment reflexively and sliding to a halt nearby. She raised her bow and moved it back and forth, looking for a target to train her arrow on.

The creatures were nowhere to be seen, nor was the fog. Even looking back into the trees, she could detect no trace of the mist. Suddenly, a bright orange light shot out of the forest. Fireshard and her two swords made of fire. They shrank as Darkcaller watched, from long swords to the size of shortswords.

Darkcaller ticked off a list in her head. She could see Shadeglide, Edge, Phoenixarrow, and Fireshard on this side of the trees. Where was Keenseeker? Did the stupid bastard stubbornly stay to fight the creatures?

As she thought it, the mountain of a man stumbled from the trees, tripped on his own feet, and slid to a stop. She had to give him credit for half-rolling—without cutting himself on his weapon—to get back to his feet and twisting to face the forest again, axe held ready.

A soft evening breeze ruffled the grass around Darkcaller as she stood, waiting to see how many of the monsters chased them down. Her staff crackled with dark energy as if anxious to try again to injure its foes.

Seconds ticked by, all six of the Falxen waiting, on guard.

Darkcaller put her staff on the ground and slumped, holding onto it. "They can't leave the forest, apparently," she said. "I, for one, plan on making an offering to whatever god I can think of. That was too close."

Shadeglide smiled in the moonlight, of course, and the others showed their relief in various ways, some sitting down and others putting their hands on their knees and panting. Fireshard stood still, her fiery weapons still held up. But she wasn't looking where they had come from. She was looking at the edge of the forest more to the west.

What was...?

Three figures burst out of the trees, one of them glowing with magic in her power-sensitive sight.

26

Khrazhti watched Fahtin carefully during the day and a half it took them to arrive at their destination. The others seemed to take the young woman's dreams as something normal, non-magical. The animaru wasn't so sure.

She felt as if her sensitivity to magic had flip-flopped and she wasn't sure if she could count on it anymore. She had experimented with her spells and they seemed to work the same as they always had. She had disappointed her friends, failed them. She seemed to still be able to sense some magic, but not Benzal.

Thinking on the changing magic made her even more concerned over what was happening with Fahtin. Visions were not to be ignored. Of course, her thousands of years of experience were with animaru, who do not sleep, so she was not sure if it was the same for humans, who *did* sleep. And dream, apparently.

She would watch Fahtin. The girl was her friend, and if she was being affected by magic, Khrazhti would try to help.

It could be an attack, but that was probably simply Khrazhti's animaru upbringing and wariness showing through.

Things were much simpler in Aruzhelim. You assumed that every other animaru was preparing to assassinate you or otherwise betray you, and the vast majority of the time, you were correct. Things were different here on Dizhelim. The concept of friendship was enough to confuse her for at least a hundred years. She thought she understood it one moment and then all her assumptions were challenged the next. She wanted badly to comprehend it.

Khrazhti stared blankly at Fahtin as they walked. The younger woman smiled at her, but it slipped when Khrazhti didn't respond. She shook her head and smiled back, solidifying Fahtin's.

"How are you feeling?" Khrazhti asked.

"I'm fine, maybe a little tired. We'll be in Dartford soon. I'll be able to sleep in a real bed and sit at a table to eat a meal. That will be wonderful."

Khrazhti nodded. She still wasn't sure why such things made so much difference to humans, but if they made her friends happy, that was enough for her.

"Ooh," Fahtin said. "There it is."

Khrazhti looked up from the hard-packed dirt road to see a grouping of structures in the distance, streams of smoke rising up from several. She checked to make sure she was completely covered by her cloak and hood.

Dartford was nowhere near the size of Satta Sarak, one of the only other real cities she'd seen. They passed through or near a few others after they had taken to the road, but nothing like the first one she had seen.

The buildings appeared to be made of wood instead of the stone she had observed previously. What was the difference between using one material over another? Was one easier to work with, lasted longer, had other benefits, or was it simply convenience that dictated building materials?

She estimated that they were no more than a half hour from the place. They would meet the others she had not seen in weeks and then they would plan their assault on Izhrod Benzal. It would be good to finally be working toward something rather than reacting to disappointments. Like her losing her ability to find Benzal for them.

"I'm going to take a bath tonight," Fahtin said, a bounce in her step that Khrazhti had not seen for some time. "Yes, hot water, a clean body, and a bed with blankets. Oh, and a nice warm fire I don't have to build." She giggled and Khrazhti found herself feeling better because of it.

They crossed into the buildings at least two hours before sunset and headed for an inn called the Wolfen's Rest. It seemed like the other inns she had observed or stayed in since she had joined her friends. There was a common room with a roaring fire and chairs arranged around tables scattered throughout the room. Food smells wafted around and mixed with the slightly peppery scent of the smoke. The pungent odor she had come to recognize as ale and wine permeated throughout, the bar maids flitting about as if swimming in all of it.

"We need two rooms," Aeden told the inn keeper. They talked about the prices and other things as Khrazhti searched the common room for Tere, Urun, or Aila. She couldn't find them.

"I don't see them either," Raki said from next to her. "Maybe they're in their rooms."

Fahtin frowned but continued looking around the room anyway.

Aeden stepped up to them. "Okay, we have our rooms. He handed a key to Fahtin, along with two wooden tokens. These are for the bathhouse next door. You give them to the attendant and they'll take care of whatever you need."

"Oooh." Fahtin held up her token like it was the most valuable of treasures. She handed the other one to Khrazhti. "I can't wait to get clean. Finally."

"What are we going to do?" Raki said. "Eat, bathe, or find Tere?"

"It's up to you," Aeden said. "I think I could stand to get cleaned up before I eat. As for Tere, I asked the inn keeper and he hasn't seen anyone with the descriptions I gave him. Tere's eyes are pretty distinctive, and no man in his right mind would overlook Aila, so I'll take that to mean we beat them here. Somehow."

Fahtin's face went pale, then her brows drew down and her eyes narrowed. Khrazhti had thought she had figured that expression out, and it meant someone was angry. Perhaps she was mistaken.

"No, no," Aeden said. "Don't jump to conclusions. We ran into things on the road, too. They may have been delayed for some reason other than dangerous ones."

"Like ours?" Fahtin said pointedly. "Or maybe Aila convinced them to go west to Sarania to get a new outfit or something. Men!"

Aeden scratched his head. "Uh...just don't get too paranoid. They can take care of themselves. Go get your bath. I'm going to go up and put my pack in my room. Meet back here in an hour?"

"Yes." Fahtin didn't sound as joyous as she had a few minutes before.

"It will be fine, Fahtin," Khrazhti told her. "We should go and get the baths. If we hurry, we will have longer to stay in the hot water." She didn't quite understand why that made Fahtin happy, but she had observed enough to know that it did. Sure enough, the young woman smiled again, took

Khrazhti's hand, and dragged her off to the appointment with a large quantity of this water they were so obsessed with.

After their baths, the travelers met in the common room and took a table in one corner. Aeden had a habit of choosing places near a wall or corner. Khrazhti wondered if it was because the location provided superior placement in case of attack or because of the necessity to hide her from view. Most likely both. He was a practical man.

She disliked wearing the cloak they had gotten for her in Satta Sarak, but she donned it whenever they were in a settlement of humans. Despite the variety in form she had observed, apparently none of them included blue skin or ears shaped similar to hers. They explained early on that they were not embarrassed by her, but that they could avoid trouble if she would wear the cloak when in public. She acquiesced, being practical herself.

Khrazhti partook of some of the food, but drank water and not the foul concoction they called ale. She had developed the habit of eating and drinking, though she merely nibbled the food as the others attacked it with the ferocity of an animaru in battle. She smiled. For some reason, that amused her.

"We need to decide what we're going to do," Aeden said between mouthfuls. "I've asked around a bit, and I don't think Tere and the others arrived. Not one person saw them, so it isn't just that they came and then left again."

"Maybe we should wait for them," Fahtin said. "I'm sure they—"

"I'm telling you," a man at a nearby table said loudly, "it's monsters."

"That's not what I heard," his companion said, a thin man with a mop of dark hair covering half his face. "They say up in Gyuralsk, it were soldiers."

"Are you stupid?" the first man said. "Why would soldiers go and attack a town and kill all the people?"

"Maybe because there's a war starting."

"A war with who? Kruzekstan is all one big place. The king and the nobles up there have it all worked out. There's no one around to have a war with."

The thin man flipped his hair from his face, revealing reddening cheeks. "I don't know. I heard it were soldiers."

"Maybe it was the Crows," a third man got out through a mouth full of food. "That's right close to Crow territory."

The first man slammed a meaty fist on the table. His dark eyes set in a blockish head glittered. "I'm surrounded by idiots. We heard last month that the Crows were killing each other off and being attacked by wild beasts. They never cared about the Kruzek border towns, so why would they attack now when they got their own troubles?"

"What about Dmirgan?" the thin man asked. "I heard they had trouble, too. They're south of Gyuralsk."

A woman at another table piped up. "I heard that one was beasts and monsters. Dark and twisted things that came from Abyssum itself to feed on the bodies of people. Men, women, and children alike. It's a sign the world is ending. It's the Age of Darkness, just like the priests used to tell us about."

The three arguing men muttered amongst themselves, not addressing the woman directly. That was strange to Khrazhti. She still hadn't figured out why the genders treated each other differently than they did those of the same sex.

"They're talking about the areas bordering the highlands," Aeden said.

"We know about the trouble your clansmen faced," Raki said. "They have it wrong, and it's been longer than a month."

"Aye, but they got some of it right. It takes time for news to travel. This other, though, about the towns in Kruzekstan, I think it's more recent."

Fahtin pursed her lips. "They probably came from the same person or people in a caravan. That's the way news passes. You have to separate out the core of it from the embellishments each teller adds. It's one of the first things I learned traveling with the family."

Aeden put his fork down and rubbed his chin, which had several days growth of reddish-brown hair on it. "Yes, but the bit about the beasts...I'd hazard a guess that the tales all have a little truth in them. It sounds to me like Benzal has not only been sending out animaru but also some of that army we passed. They're taking over towns one at a time. Once they gain footholds, they'll probably start attacking cities."

"Do you really think so?" Fahtin asked.

"I agree with Aeden," Khrazhti said. "It is a good strategy. I am afraid that if I were in command, it is what I would have done. After eliminating the Gneisprumay, of course." She showed her teeth to the others, trying to indicate that it was a joke.

Aeden laughed, Fahtin looked horrified, and Raki simply stared at his food.

"I wonder where the family is," Raki said. "I hope they're all right."

"They won't be in a town in Kruzekstan," Fahtin said. "Those towns barely tolerate our presence. They won't let the caravan camp within the cities."

"That's true. I hope they went west."

Aeden huffed. "So, Benzal has started his attacks in Kruzekstan. He's probably there, somewhere. We need to find Tere and have him lead us to where Benzal is hiding. We're running out of time. Every day gets closer to when he can bring more animaru over. He already has an army. We can't afford to let him make it larger.

"We'll give it another full day. If we can't find any good leads on where Tere might be, we'll go looking for him. The most logical path would be coming straight north on the River Road. It'll give us time to rest and resupply. One way or another, we'll be moving again after tomorrow. Agreed?"

"Agreed," Raki said.

"Yes," Fahtin replied.

"I agree," Khrazhti said.

One more day and then they would be traveling again. She hoped they'd find Tere. She was worthless now when it came to finding Benzal, and she had a feeling that, as Aeden said, they were running out of time.

27

I t took a moment for Phoenixarrow to understand what was happening. She and the rest of the brace had just finished a harrowing run through the forest, at the edge of a cliff, being chased by creatures that took several of the assassins working together to stop even one of them. And the monsters outnumbered them.

They had made it, though, sprinting out of the trees—which the creatures couldn't or wouldn't leave—and into a meadow. But now, now something was coming out of the trees, a little distance west of them.

The moon was bright, and after being in the fog for most of the night, her eyes picked up the movement easily, and some of the detail as well.

Three people fled the forest. One, a dark-haired man, carried a staff. A woman in black clothes, hardly visible, ran alongside him, something she carried glinting in the moon-light. Then there was the taller man, the white-bearded archer she had seen before.

She recognized the three from the short battle they had in Satta Sarak, but she had not been completely sure which of their targets were here and which were being chased by the other half of the larger brace until Shadeglide reported on the prisoners in Praesturi.

The archer's head jerked to the side.

"Put out those flames, you idiot," Phoenixarrow told Fireshard, but it was too late. An arrow zipped from the enemy archer toward the Falxen. Phoenixarrow's eyes widened. That shot had to be three hundred yards. In the dark.

The arrow clanged off one of Fireshard's short swords. It was incredible. How could anyone aim that precisely under such conditions? It had to be luck.

"We've been seen," Darkcaller called out. "Attack."

It wasn't normal operations to enter battle instead of killing from cover or in darkness, but occasionally situations fell apart and it was necessary. Now was apparently one of those situations.

Phoenixarrow began running, fitting an arrow to her bowstring and firing on the move. She thought at first to incapacitate the archer, but then shifted her bow to target the staff wielder at the last moment. She wasn't sure why.

A brief flare of light showed the arrow flashing to ash as it bounced off something.

Of course, the man with the staff had cast a shield.

"Caster. The guy with the staff." She felt foolish after saying it, since it should have been evident, but a little embarrassment at this point wouldn't kill her. The other archer, though, now *that* could end her.

They closed the distance quickly, though the targets remained where they were. No use helping out the ones that would kill them. Phoenixarrow drew back another arrow and was about to release it when another shaft came out of the darkness and embedded itself in her bow stave. The shock of it caused her to fumble her own arrow, releasing it into the darkness around them where it wouldn't cause harm to her or her enemies. What was that old man? She was still too far for him to be accurate to more than a few inches, but a finger's width to the side and that shaft would have parted her skull.

He was much more dangerous than the others.

She took a moment to pull the arrow free from her bow, since it off-balanced the weapon. She lost several steps doing so, allowing her companions to pass her.

Darkcaller was within range for her spells, so she began throwing dark missiles—nearly invisible in the night air—toward the enemy caster. As the projectiles impacted the man's shield, they puffed out of existence, but each one reached a little farther before it did so. That shield would come down quickly under such an onslaught.

Edge and Fireshard headed for the woman, closing the distance so they could cut her down. One of Fireshard's swords shrank into a throwing knife and she launched it ahead of her.

The woman batted the flying blade out of the air and flicked her other hand. Surprisingly, Fireshard cried out and stumbled, sliding on the grass before righting herself and scrambling back onto her feet. Was that blood on her arm?

Edge noted his companion's fall with a shift of his eyes and charged ahead, longer sword in his right hand and shorter sword in his left.

Where was Keenseeker?

Oh, she thought, as she spotted the man. He was huffing breath like he was going to pass out, but he had built up momentum and was actually moving at a fair speed, heading toward the archer.

It was a foregone conclusion that the six would be victorious over the three. They had to be powerful to have made it through the forest, especially going through the middle as they had instead of the edges like the Falxen, but still, the odds were overwhelming. Phoenixarrow felt a pang of sadness at that. She would have liked to have matched skills with that archer, maybe dueled him on her own.

Such was the way things worked out, though. Her bow unencumbered, she nocked another arrow and picked up speed again. There was still a chance for her to be the one who killed the man.

Edge was almost to the woman. It was surprising someone his age could run so quickly. Both of the woman's hands flicked out and Edge reacted immediately, shifting his swords strangely. Dual clangs sounded as something struck his blades.

The woman moved her hands again, as if she was catching something. Then she twisted and slashed at the air. Another sound of metal on metal rang out. Phoenixarrow blinked and squinted, finally seeing another swirling shadow as she got closer. Shadeglide had somehow outrun them all and was fighting the woman face-to-face.

"Livia?" Shadeglide's voice called out and then something Phoenixarrow had never seen before happened. Shadeglide rolled backwards and disappeared into the darkness, breaking off the battle.

"What the—" Phoenixarrow said, but she didn't finish. She opened her mouth wide when she saw what the old archer was doing. It surprised her so much, she forgot to draw the arrow she had nocked.

The man reached over his shoulder and drew out three arrows at a time. It was as if she blinked and they were suddenly there on the bowstring. He torqued his hips as he drew them back, then he dropped his shoulder as he released, spinning the bow stave clockwise.

Before she could see where they had landed, he had two more arrows nocked, drawn, and released, this time with his bow spinning in a counterclockwise direction. Finally, his hand blurred as he pulled, nocked, drew, and released a single arrow, and then another.

The last arrow had left his string when Phoenixarrow realized what he had done. One of the first arrows slammed into her shoulder, causing her to release the second wild arrow of the battle.

Sounds from nearby called attention to two arrows sprouting from Keenseeker's shoulders, one in each. A fraction of a second later, arrows appeared in the big man's throat and Edge's chest. Darkness coalesced in front of Darkcaller as one of the other arrows was stopped by her shield.

The last arrow made it through the shield in exactly the same spot as the previous arrow and punched through Darkcaller's forehead.

Phoenixarrow dropped her bow to her side, her right arm no longer able to pull the string. She watched in horror as the female target flicked her arms out again and Fireshard grunted. She seemed to be stunned somehow, not generating her fire weapons as she normally did. She dropped to her knees and then flopped onto her face, but not before Phoenixarrow saw the dark line across her throat.

The red-haired archer threw her bow down. She drew her knife with her left hand, but she had no chance with that archer in front of her. She stood, as tall and proudly as she could, waiting for the arrow that would end her life.

<hr />

"LIVIA?" SHADEGLIDE'S VOICE CALLED OUT, SOFT AS A whisper but seeming loud in the sudden silence after the battle. "Is that you?"

"Rina?" a familiar voice asked.

"Yes."

"Urun, some light please," a man's voice said. The archer.

The soft glow of a misty sphere of light appeared near Shadeglide.

"Step into the light and drop your weapons," the archer said.

She could see him, a few dozen feet away. His white eyes glinted in the light in front of her, but he looked through it as if it didn't affect his sight.

She did as instructed, raising her hands above her shoulders.

"Rina, you're an assassin?" Livia asked.

"Yes, pretty much always have been. Even when I knew you, I was. And you were a thief."

Livia tried to hide a smile. "I pretty much always was." Her face grew serious, though. "You tried to kill us."

"I didn't know it was you. It was a job. The last one I was going to do."

"Convenient," the archer said. He was eyeing Phoenixarrow. She didn't like the look on his face. "You just happen to be on your last job. No doubt you are changing professions to take care of orphans and help old widows."

"No," Shadeglide said. "We've heard some things that we don't agree with. We don't like some of the allies or employers the Falxen are connecting with. It's time to leave."

"We?" Livia asked.

"Me and Phoenixarrow over there."

"Phoenixarrow," the archer said. "Very pretty."

"My Falxen name is Shadeglide."

"A bunch of power-hungry killers trying to make a social club. Normal people don't need fake names."

"Is that true?" Shadeglide asked. She turned—slowly—to Livia. "Is Livia your real name?"

"No, not any more than Rina was yours. Or Shadeglide, for that matter."

"Fair enough. May I ask what you call yourself now?"

Livia—or the woman who she knew as Livia—darted a glance at the archer. He didn't respond, simply kept looking at Phoenixarrow. "I'm Aila. Aila Ven."

Shadeglide smiled. "That's...actually very pretty. I like it better than Livia. I think it suits you."

"Yeah, yeah," the archer said. "Enough of the chatter." He scanned the area. The rest of the Falxen were unmoving. "I'm figuring I'll need to put arrows in both of you so we can be on our way. No offense, *Shadeglide*."

"Tere?" Livia—Aila—said.

"What would you have me do? They tried to kill us."

"I...trust Rina. She has honor, one of the few people I've ever met that did. Until I met you and Aeden. Please. Can't we do something else?"

"Tell you what," the archer said. "You two keep an eye on her. I'm going to make sure these others don't pop up and attack us. Does your conscience say anything about that?"

"No. We'll be here."

"Urun. Urun!" The archer snapped his fingers in front of the dark-haired young man and he blinked, then focused on the man in front of him. "Keep an eye on these. Any quick movements and I want you to strike them dead with your magic."

The young man's eyes narrowed, but he nodded.

The archer made the circuit, checking on the bodies surrounding them. He had killed most of those himself. How had he done that? She barely saw his hands move, but it sounded a lot like Phoenixarrow had described in her story. She guessed maybe moves like that were possible. How had he moved so fast? And the accuracy!

"This one is still alive," he called out. He was standing over Edge. Poor, honorable Edge. "What?" the archer cocked his head and considered the prostrate man. He ran his hand through his hair, then reached down to retrieve the dagger from Edge's belt sheath. He handed it to the man and stepped back.

Edge said something, dipped his head, as if in thanks, and slipped the knife into his own heart. He spasmed once and then lay still.

"Crazy bastard," the archer said. "Those Teroshi and their honor and glorious deaths and such nonsense."

Shadeglide bowed to him—slowly—as he passed her on his way to Phoenixarrow. He stopped. "What is that for?"

"Thank you."

"For what?"

"For allowing him to end his life honorably instead of dying slowly in this field."

He stared at her, or stared through her, with those white eyes, then shook his head and stepped up to Phoenixarrow.

"What about this one, Aila? Do you know her, too? You all belonged to some sewing guild or animal fighting club or something?"

"No. I only know Rina here."

"What am I going to do with you?" the archer asked Phoenixarrow.

"You're him."

"What?"

"You're him. No one can perform that move. No one. I've practiced it my entire life and even I can't do it."

"What are you going on about?" the archer snapped. "Give me one reason why I shouldn't slice your throat right now."

"I have none, other than that heroes don't act that way. I am unarmed, no longer a threat. You won't kill me."

"I won't, eh?" He drew one of his long knives and stepped toward her.

"Please," Shadeglide said. "Don't kill us. What I said was true. We found out very recently that the Falxen have been working with someone who has dark monsters, beasts that are ready to take over our whole world. We were going to quit, after this last job. I'm telling the truth. We just found out in Praesturi."

The archer stopped, inspecting Phoenixarrow's face in the moonlight. "Is that true?"

"Yes," the redhead said immediately. "Killing for money is one thing. Selling out the human race, that's another. We were going to strike out on our own, maybe try to help in some way. There'll be a need for mercenaries, right? It's not glamorous, but it feels more right than...this." She gestured with her left hand toward the bodies lying in the grass.

"The assassins you were with were really working for the animaru?" Aila asked.

"I don't know that name, but our leader, the woman in black over there, said the one who hired us has a bunch of dark beasts he brought from somewhere else and they're going to take over, so there will be lots of work for us."

"Damn," the archer said, slamming his knife into its scabbard. "As if we didn't have enough to deal with. Give us your weapons and start walking that way," he pointed toward the northwest, "and we'll let you live. You'll get to the Academy in a day or so." He looked Phoenixarrow over one more time. "You're not going to die from that arrow. They can fix you up so you will be able to shoot again. But if you ever shoot at me, that's the day your life ends. Do you understand?"

"Yes," Phoenixarrow said. She seemed somehow subdued to Shadeglide. Maybe it was the shock from the arrow.

"Agreed, *Shadeglide*?" he asked.

"Agreed. Thank you, Tere. Aila."

"Go. You can pull the arrow first and dress it. Do you know field medicine?"

"Rina—I mean Shadeglide—does," Aila said. "We discussed it when we worked together."

The archer gave Aila a strange look. "You'll have to tell me about it later."

Aila didn't look happy about that.

Shadeglide dressed Phoenixarrow's shoulder and gathered some of the food from the others' packs. The archer and Aila gathered the weapons from the Falxen and took them, then set off to the northeast.

Shadeglide's eyes met Phoenixarrow's. The taller woman gave her a small smile and Shadeglide returned it. "Follow them in a few hours?" she asked.

"Definitely."

28

After escaping from the jail, the dangers of the forest, and the attack by the assassins, Tere was exhausted. He knew the others felt the same.

"We'll go for another couple hours and then we'll stop and sleep," he told them.

Urun had lapsed back into his own silent world, and Aila shuffled along as if will power was the only thing holding her up. Her head would dip as she walked, and Tere was sure she'd fall down, but after a few stumbling steps, she'd right herself and lift her chin, only to repeat the entire thing again.

He kept an eye out for a place they could defend easily and also for anything coming up behind them. He argued with himself at letting the two assassins live. He was definitely getting soft in his old age. The smaller woman was Aila's friend and the other one, well there was something about her. Maybe he was missing a woman's company and that was it. She was quite a beauty, and her *armor* didn't really leave anything to the imagination. A tiny bit of mail covering the important bits had never been so distracting. It could be as simple as a pretty face swaying his judgment.

If so, he needed to retire right now. Again. That way held only disappointment and betrayal.

They'd have a tough time overpowering him and his companions, though. They had no weapons and the archer was injured. No, he didn't think they'd sneak up and kill them, but he'd keep watch, just in case.

He found a place they could use to get a few hours of sleep. It was in a stand of trees with a large boulder to one side and thornbushes on another, just big enough for them to squeeze in. The place wouldn't be the best they'd camped at, but it wouldn't be the worst, either.

"I'll take first watch," he told them. "Aila, unfortunately, I think we'll be the only ones taking turn. I'm not sure Urun will remain lucid for an entire watch."

"Yeah," she mumbled. "I figured. Wake me in a few hours, or earlier if you're going to fall asleep."

"Will do." He sat on a stump near a trunk that looked to have been struck by lightning and then pushed over by the wind. Bow on his lap, he tried to picture a map of the area in his mind. He had pored over the map books his teacher had when he was a boy. Most times, he could still recall them well enough that he didn't have to use a physical map.

Those maps were old when he saw them, so they were of limited use. In this case, though, they'd do fine. Sitor-Kanda and the immediate area hadn't changed in decades, if not hundreds of years. The maps he had seen would be accurate enough.

Tere had a pretty good idea where they were. By the time a few hours had passed and he woke Aila for her turn at watch, he had determined that it would be two days or so to Dartford. He wondered how long Aeden and the others had been waiting for them. Had they gone, tired of the waiting? Maybe they went to the Academy. If so, he might actually see them before Dartford. He would have to go near the

Academy and then swing toward the east to take the bridge across to the mainland.

He settled in to sleep as Aila—looking much less exhausted than before—took up the watch. He woke three hours later, the sun already up over the horizon.

"Anything?" he asked.

"Nope. Pretty quiet."

"I like quiet."

"Yeah."

Tere shook Urun awake and they ate a hurried breakfast. They didn't bother with a fire; they wouldn't be at the place for long.

As they traveled, Tere saw that he had been correct about where they were. The world seemed a better place with some sleep and some food in him. He couldn't wait for an inn and to be able to sleep in a real bed. There shouldn't be any real dangers between them and Dartford. Who in their right mind would cause trouble so close to the Academy?

Urun carried the gear from the assassins in his pack. They had found that, though he didn't respond often, he also didn't seem to mind carrying his share—or a bit more—of the load.

The girl's bow, though, Tere carried. It was too large for a pack and tall enough to use as a walking stick—unstrung—while still keeping his bow strung. He inspected the other bow as they went. It was fine work, almost as good as his own. There was the issue of an arrow hole midway down its length, but it was still serviceable. That had been his arrow, last night.

He spat to the side, disgusted. He'd have never missed a shot like that, even in total darkness, if he had his magical sight. He could see, so he should probably be satisfied with that, but he wasn't. Not after a lifetime of being able to see where people and things would be.

What was it that girl had said, something about it being

impossible to make those shots? She didn't know anything. Until recently, he wouldn't have needed any more than six arrows to kill the lot of them.

Still, the bow was fine work, and she seemed to know her way around it. Her focus was lacking, though. If it wasn't, he might be the one dead. An arrow striking her bow shattered her concentration and gave him the edge. Piss poor concentration, that was. But she was young. If she really did give up her pay-for-blood profession, she might grow into a formidable archer.

While they stopped for a few minutes so Aila could fish something out of her pack, Tere got a sense of something watching him. He dropped his ruminations and scanned the terrain. That had been something behind them, moving carefully. A deer? He didn't think so.

They continued and Tere scanned the area behind him every few minutes. He had to do it without looking like he was looking back, but that wasn't really a problem with the way his sight worked.

"Let's stop for a moment up here," he told the others. "I need to check on something."

Tere left his pack and the woman's bow and headed out into the grasses, angling toward the west. The blades reached his knees, not nearly high enough for most people to disappear in.

Tere Chizzit was not most people.

After a time, he circled back around to the southeast and then swept into a more northerly direction. As he thought, there were tracks in the grasses. Two sets, to be exact. One from Aila and Urun and the other...well, he knew what he'd find when he caught up to the track makers.

He spotted a blaze of red hair and a head of darker hair sitting in a depression they had made in the plants. He watched them for a moment and was about to confront them when the archer woman's head snapped up and looked around. Tere dropped to his belly. Did she see him?

He was impressed that she had detected him at all, if in fact she had. It could have been a stray sound or movement from an animal in the grasses, but he didn't think so.

Enough games, he thought, and headed toward the women. He didn't exactly walk normally, but he wasn't being as stealthy as he was capable of either.

They sat silently, looking abashed, as he stepped up to them, bow held up and arrow nocked.

"I told you to go to the northwest, toward the Academy," he said.

"We want to join you," the archer said bluntly.

Tere blinked. "You want to what, now?"

"Join you," the darker-haired woman—Shadeglide, that was her name—said. "We're not sure what you're doing, but if the one who's working with those dark monsters wants you dead, we think you're on our side."

"On *your* side?" Tere spat, bow still at the ready. "You've been chasing us for weeks now and last night you tried to kill us."

Shadeglide looked to her feet, her cheeks coloring. "Yeah. We're awfully sorry about that. Like I told you before, we didn't know everything until recently. Before, it was just another job. I'm sure you've done things that you regretted later."

"He has," Phoenixarrow said. "He regretted that time he killed a man in Dmirgan who wasn't guilty of the murder the townsfolk thought he was, and then there was Dartran Finis's son, who he spared but had to kill later on after he grew to be a worse monster than his father."

Tere's heart jumped. How did she...?

"Doing something you regret is one thing," he said. "Being a professional assassin is another. I have only your word that you've changed your mind. I'm beginning to regret letting you live last night. Maybe I'll remedy that now, out of sight of your friend who will speak for you."

The redhead stood up straight, impressive chest out and back straight. "Then be done with it. I know who you are and I know you won't kill an unarmed woman who is trying to do the right thing. You're not a cold-hearted killer."

"You don't know me," he said. "To me, both of you are cold-hearted killers, and the world would be a better place without you and all of your type."

"Please," Shadeglide said. "Give us a chance. Put us in ropes or chains if you like. Make us carry your gear. Make us carry *you*, for all we care. We may not be the best of people, but we are human, and we will not stand by while other humans give our world away to monsters. Let us show you we can be of help. We have skills..."

"How many times did you talk Raisor Tannoch out of killing someone when it wasn't necessary? Have you really changed that much?"

Tere's knees went weak and he had to lock his legs to keep from stumbling. Gods, it was true. The woman did know. He let out a sigh. "You are going to leave me no choice, are you? I'll have to kill the both of you, or cripple you, to keep you from following."

The archer nodded at him.

"Damn you," he said. "And damn me and my stupid senti-mentality. Aila's been through the flames lately and I'd not like to do something that will upset her." He motioned with his bow. "Go on, get moving. You know where the others are."

Shadeglide smiled at him. An honest, simple smile that made her look like the type of young woman who lived next door to you, one who had a kind word or a "good morning" always ready on her lips. Yeah, right before she punched a dagger through your eye.

The archer woman nodded to him, then winced as she turned to follow her friend. Ah, right, the shoulder wound. He'd have to take a look at that. If he wasn't going to kill her, he should probably make sure she wouldn't die from infection either.

He kept his distance from them, ten feet or so, as the trio headed toward Aila and Urun. Distance enough to put an arrow in each of them if they tried anything tricky. They wouldn't, though. He'd distilled his ability to judge people decades ago, even without his magic. Though it seemed unlikely, he thought they were sincere; otherwise he would have finished them the night before.

Tere stomped on the grass as they went. More complications, that's all this was.

When Aila caught sight of the two women, with Tere trailing, she barked out a laugh and waited for them near Urun.

"What have you found, Tere?"

"Your friend and her cohort were following us, against my orders."

Aila turned to the dark-haired assassin. Tere hadn't really paid attention before, but was her hair blue?

"What are your intentions, Ri—Shadeglide?"

"Please," the woman said, "my real name is Jia. Jia Toun. I would rather not use my Falxen name any longer."

The redhead's head snapped toward her fellow assassin. Tere suppressed a smile. She hadn't known the girl's real name.

"It's as we described last night, Aila," Jia continued. "We will not work for an organization that supports those who are trying to destroy humans. We only wish we had left the brace before last night's ill-fated attack. We want to help in whatever way we can."

Aila eyed Tere, but he schooled his expression so it was completely neutral.

Aila turned to the female archer. "Phoenixarrow, huh? Is that because of your red hair?"

The woman opened her mouth to speak, but Tere beat her to it. "It's because she likes to shoot fire arrows."

The woman's eyebrows shot up to meet her hair. "How did you know that?"

"You think I don't recognize a fire arrow or an oil pot? We have your weapons, remember?"

"Oh, right." She sighed. "I suppose I shouldn't use my Falxen name any longer, either, though I really liked the sound of it. My real name is boring. I'm Lily Fisher."

Tere actually stumbled at that. Lily.

That woman's eyes grew sad for a moment before she clenched her jaw and shook her head slightly. "I'm sorry," she said to him. "My actual name is just Lily, though. Not Lilianor."

The pressure in Tere's head grew and he felt as if it was going to explode. Damn his broken eyes and his inability to cry. A picture of a beautiful girl seared his mind. His sister. She was so young when...

"So, where are we at, Tere?" Aila asked, eyeing Tere in confusion.

He grasped at the conversation as if it was a lifeline and he was drowning in a stormy sea. "I don't know. They won't stop following us. We can try to make them go somewhere else—though that won't work—or we can let them travel with us so we can keep an eye on them. Or we can kill them and be done with it."

Neither of the assassins said anything. At least they had some sense.

"I can vouch for Jia. We actually were friends, unless that was all an act." She looked at the assassin.

"You will make your own decision, Aila. Remember, though, there was no benefit in me tricking you or becoming your friend. Why would I waste the time and effort for no gain?"

"You do have a point there," Aila conceded.

"And this one?" Tere pointed at Lily.

"You won't kill me," she said. "I don't know why you are going by a different name, but you are the same man, the same hero. You will not kill an unarmed woman for no reason." She raised her chin and stood proudly. He had to give her credit; she was an imposing figure.

"You said something like that last night, too," Aila said. "What are you talking about? Why do you say he's not who he says he is?"

Red hair swung as the woman looked back and forth from Tere to Aila. "What? Do you mean you don't know?"

"Know what?"

"This man is Erent Caahs."

❧ 29 ❧

"We've waited long enough," Aeden said.

Half of the morning sun peeked above the horizon, the other half yet to make its appearance. They had eaten and were preparing to go out looking for Tere and the others.

"Are you sure about this, Aeden?" Fahtin said. "Maybe one of us should stay here and wait for him in case he arrives. We could miss him and travel all the way back to Satta Sarak and never know he was close the whole time."

"I've thought of that," Aeden said. "I left a note with the inn keeper to give to Tere. It tells where we've gone and that we'll come back after we've looked around for a few days."

"Oh. That was good thinking," she said.

"Thank you. I don't like it, either, Fahtin, but we need to find him as quickly as we can. If you'd like to stay here and wait, you can do so. In fact, any or all of you can. I can look for him myself. I've no problem with that."

"But you'd be alone. It's dangerous out there."

"Aye," he said. "It is. I am a fair hand at taking care of myself, though."

She gazed out toward the south, then to the west, shifting her eyes to rest on the ground in front of her. "I'll go with you."

"Fine. We should get started, then. We'll head south on the River Road. That's the way they should have come. I'm not sure where whatever is keeping them happened, but we'll start with that."

"But my dream showed them on Munsahtiz," she said.

"I know. We can't make decisions based on dreams, though. You know that, Fahtin."

He tried to say it a gently as possible, but her eyes still shone as if she was going to cry. He went to try to console her, but Raki interrupted him.

"Aeden?"

"A moment." He was more concerned about Fahtin's feelings at this point. She had been emotional the last few days and he seemed to have said the wrong thing.

"Aeden."

"Yes, Raki. Just a moment. Fahtin—"

Raki's voice became more insistent. "Aeden, look."

Aeden swung his head. A small group of people walked toward them from the west, the direction the bridge to the Academy was. One was bald with a white goatee and one, almost as tall as the first, had red hair. The others had dark hair and one carried a staff.

Aeden blinked. Was that...?

"Tere!" Fahtin yelled and ran toward the group. It did look like Tere, but who were the others?

Fahtin threw herself at Tere, who accepted the hug stoically as they continued toward Aeden. The Gypta whirled and latched onto Aila, who was a bit more expressive and returned the embrace. Urun strode along as if none of it was happening.

The other two women looked on questioningly, the one

with the red hair moving stiffly, no doubt because of her bandaged right shoulder, red seeping through the cloth.

Tere stepped up to Aeden and put his hand out. Aeden clasped wrists with the archer, smiling. "It's good to see you," he said. "We were worried when we arrived and you weren't here. We were just about to go looking for you."

"How long have you been waiting?" Tere asked.

"Not quite two days."

"Really? You must have been held up, too. Let's go to the inn to talk about it. I'm thirsty and hungry and want to get off my feet." He nodded toward Khrazhti and gave a little wave at Raki.

"Aye." Aeden looked at the unknown women like staring at them would solve the mystery of their presence. "We've a lot to talk about. We need your help."

Fahtin whispered with Aila as they walked, darting looks at the women and Urun in turn. Tere chatted softly with Raki. It sounded like he was quizzing the boy on how his practice was going. Aeden smiled at Khrazhti. It felt good to be back with his friends.

"That's her?" Aeden heard the red-haired woman say. "That means the others failed."

Aeden's swords were out in a flash. He spun and stopped his blades just in time to keep from cutting into the taller woman. The smaller one had ducked and rolled backward, coming into a ready stance, then looked embarrassed that she did so.

"That's where I've seen you before," Aeden said to the redhead. "You're one of the assassins." He turned to his friend. "Tere?"

"It's a bit complex," the old archer said. "Let's sit down and we'll talk about it. I took their weapons. They won't cause trouble or they'll be sprouting arrows." He glared at the assassin who had rolled and she assumed a normal standing pose.

Aeden looked them both over again, then slammed his swords into their scabbards. "We'll talk, and it better be good."

They soon settled into a private dining room, one the inn keeper was more than willing to provide since they'd rented five rooms. Food was brought, as well as ale, wine, and water for them to drink.

"Now," Aeden said, "what about these two?"

"Fine, fine," Tere said. "We'll talk about them first so you can ease your mind. Yes, they were with the group of assassins who tried to kill us. They claim they got some information a couple of days ago that made them change their mind about being with the Falxen."

"People don't just quit the Falxen," Aeden said. "Even the Croagh know that."

"Yes, well, this news...affected them. Apparently, the one who paid the contract was Izhrod Benzal."

Jia's head snapped up. "How did you know that? We didn't say his name."

"You didn't have to, girl. You explained him well enough."

"I only told you that the one who paid us was working with those dark creatures," she said.

"I know. Let us get through this without too many interruptions, all right?"

She nodded, turning her attention back to her food.

"Anyway," Tere said, "they said they were going to quit after this job—"

"Convenient," Aeden said.

Tere laughed. "That's what I said. There was still doubt, but Aila vouched for the talkative one."

"What?" Aeden met the beautiful thief's eyes.

Aila raised her chin and fluttered her eyelashes at him. "I knew her. Before."

"You knew a Falxen assassin. Before. You're going to need to give me more than that, Aila. It's our lives we're risking here."

"I was with her for several months," she said. "In a thieves guild."

"Which thieves guild?" Tere asked.

"The Hooded Shadows."

"When?"

"About three years ago. And before you go and doubt me, yes, that was around the time the Sutanian government attacked and destroyed the guild. We escaped since they didn't know about us. In any case, we got to know each other and became friends."

"Supposedly," Aeden put in.

"As I explained yesterday," the assassin said, "there was no benefit for me to befriend Aila. I was sent to infiltrate the guild to assassinate one of its leaders. There was no reason to become friends with her other than we seemed to connect right away. We were like sisters."

Aila's faint smile irritated Aeden, but he let it go.

"And this one?" He pointed toward the redhead. "Is she your sister, too?" Why was the woman wearing little more than a small mail piece covering her chest and another sheet of mail fashioned into what looked like a very short undergarment?

"She and I discussed our employer's loyalties," the smaller assassin said, "and we agreed we would leave the Falxen after the current job. One does not quit in the middle of a job or the rest of the brace will turn on you and execute you."

"Lovely," Aeden said. He turned back to Tere. "How can we trust them?"

"I don't know. For what it's worth, I have a good sense of them and I think they're telling the truth."

"What happened to your shoulder?" Fahtin asked the taller woman.

"Uh, that would be my fault," Tere said. "When they were still fighting us, I put an arrow in her."

"Why is she still alive, then?" Aeden asked.

"Aeden!" Fahtin huffed and moved over to the woman, inspecting the bandages. Fool woman didn't have any sense of danger.

"I..." Tere said, "ran into some trouble a week or so back. I lost my magical sight."

"You can't see?" Raki asked, sitting up straighter in his chair so he could see better.

"No, Raki. I can see. I can't see the magical signatures anymore."

"Wait," Aeden said. "You can't track people by seeing their movements in the magical field anymore? But we need you to find Benzal for us. It's why we came back."

"I knew it," the redhead said, gently pushing Fahtin's hand away. "You are—"

"Enough," Tere said loudly, building to a shout. "Be quiet or—"

Fahtin had jumped when he raised his voice. Now she was staring at his white eyes. "Tere, what's wrong with you? Why are you acting like that?"

He refused to say anything. Fahtin pivoted to the woman, who was fixed on Tere.

"Oh, damn it," he said. "Fine, go ahead and tell them. For all the good it'll do." He pushed his chair back from the table and headed out the door. "I need to use the privy anyway."

All eyes went to the door as it closed behind Tere. The room was silent, not even the sound of chewing to be heard.

"What is this secret Tere is so upset about?" Aeden asked.

The assassin blew out a breath. "Is it really true? None of you know who he is?"

"He's Tere Chizzit," Fahtin said. "He's our friend."

"Maybe I'm asking the wrong question," the woman said. "Do none of you know who he *was*?"

Aeden ran his fingers through his hair and moved his head from side to side, his neck emitting a slight popping sound. "Let's skip the theatrics. Tell us plainly what you want to say."

"He's Erent Caahs," she said.

"But Erent Caahs is dead," Raki said.

"Is he?"

"And you know this how?" Aeden asked.

"She's obsessed with Erent Caahs," the other assassin said. "She knows everything about him. She has tried her whole life to be like him."

The red-haired woman's face flushed so furiously, it would match her hair soon. "I...he was the greatest hero ever to live. I try to emulate him."

"You know you're an assassin, right?" Aila asked, getting a glare that seemed altogether too harsh for what she'd said.

Aeden tried to rein in the conversation. "So, you're an admirer and you want to be like him. That doesn't give you insight into someone you just met."

"Over the course of our tracking him," she said, "I observed his competency. I have been all over Dizhelim and believe me, he is very, very good."

"So am I," Aeden answered.

"Then a few nights ago," she continued as if he hadn't spoken, "he did something that removed all my doubts. He used his famous three-two-one attack."

"He used what?"

Raki spoke up. "The three-two-one attack. He's famous for it. He fires three arrows at a time, then two, then one, but he spins his bow when he does it and actually kills six different people, all in less than two seconds."

"That's nonsense," Aeden said. "Exaggerated tales."

"I saw him do it," the woman said.

"I did, too," the smaller assassin said.

"You saw him kill six people with six arrows, all in under two seconds?"

She crinkled her forehead. "Uh, no. Not exactly that."

"Then what?" Aeden pressed.

"Well, it was dark and—"

"Erent Caahs is said to have been able to see in the dark like it was daylight," Aeden interrupted.

"—and one of the men was a good three times the size of an ordinary man—"

"So he didn't do what you claimed he could do." Aeden finished, slapping his hand on the table.

"No one could have made those shots like that. No one. I have practiced my entire life to master that technique and I couldn't have done half as well or as quickly in broad daylight."

"Then maybe you're not as good as you think you are."

She glared at Aeden, but didn't say anything else.

"He also knew about a very rarely heard tale," the smaller assassin said. "Phoenixarrow—I mean, Lily—here used it to prove a point and he knew. Have you observed him knowing obscure facts about Erent Caahs?"

"He does know a lot about him," Raki said.

"Raki?" Aeden asked.

Tere stepped back into the room and everyone went silent again. He took his seat, took a drink from his mug, and began eating again as if he was the only one in the dining room.

"Tere?" Raki said, pulling the archer's eyes to him. "Is it true? Are you Erent Caahs?"

"Erent Caahs is dead," he said. "I'm Tere Chizzit. You know that, Raki."

"*Were* you Erent Caahs?" Fahtin asked. Her large, glistening eyes seemed to grab hold of the older man and wrench him.

He shuddered once, took a long drink from his mug, then set it down. He glanced over at the red-haired assassin, frowned at her, and shifted his white eyes to Fahtin's, one of the few people who actually looked him in the eyes. "Yes."

✣ 30 ✣

If the silence before was deafening, Aeden could only equate the current lack of sound to death.

"How?" Raki asked.

"Why?" Aila said at the same time.

"You've gotten enough out of me for now," he said. "I spoke true. That man is dead. I've put up with as much as I'm going to. No more questions. You've wrung me out." He looked up from his cup, and though Aeden knew his eyes could no longer tear up, he thought he could see pain there. "Please."

"Let me tell you what has happened with us over the last few weeks, and then you can catch us up on your adventures," Aeden said. Relief washed over Tere's face and he nodded to the younger man. "We're still in a bit of trouble and could use all the help we can get."

Aeden explained what had happened to him, Fahtin, Raki, and Khrazhti since they had split from Tere and his group at Satta Sarak. The others added details as he wended his way through the tale. Fleeing the animaru, assassins on their heels, the human army, Suuksis, how Benzal escaped, and trying to track the magic user down, he covered it all.

When he reached the part about the battle with the assassins, he noticed Fahtin watching the two former Falxen intently. When he paused to gather his thoughts on how to tell the next part, she spoke to them.

"You don't seem to be too upset that your friends were killed."

Phoenixarrow—Lily—calmly looked up and said, "They were not our friends. They were simply part of our brace. That's what we call a team of Falxen. Death is part of the job. I've seen a few of my fellow assassins die over the years. It's constantly there, waiting for us to make a mistake. My time could have been a couple of days ago. None of the ones in my team would have mourned my passing."

"I would have," Jia said quietly.

Aeden continued. When he reached the point in his story where Khrazhti lost her ability to sense Benzal, he finished quickly. "So, once we were sure it wasn't simply a localized thing, we knew our only choice was to come back and get Tere so he could hunt down Benzal for us. The most important thing we can do is to find and kill that man before he can open another portal and bring more animaru over."

"I'm sorry, Aeden," Tere said. "I wish I could help, but without my ability to see disruptions in the magical field, I am only as good as my mundane tracking skills are. Granted, I'm good, but I don't know that I can sniff out Benzal from hundreds of miles away."

Aeden's mood grew even more sour. "That's about it for what happened to us. What did you go through, Tere? You should have reached Dartford long before us."

"Yes, we should have," Tere said. "There were complications."

Tere launched into an explanation of what had

happened to them. Aeden could tell they felt a similar tension as he with the assassins dogging their steps. The part about the animaru searching for something near the area they were in at the moment made him wonder if they would have run into them if they'd gone out to search for Tere.

Through the entire tale, Aeden watched Urun. There seemed to be something wrong with the young priest. He'd never been the most social of people, but now he was more withdrawn, sitting at the end of the table and eating mechanically. He hadn't said a word since the two halves of their group had gotten back together.

Soon enough, Tere addressed the issue, telling the others how Urun didn't react well to being imprisoned, away from nature. The others darted looks Urun's way, and Fahtin took his hand and squeezed it, but Urun didn't say a word, though he did meet Aeden's and Fahtin's eyes.

"Then we got stuck with these two," Tere said. "They've been traveling with us since yesterday."

Aeden put his hands on the table, considering what he'd heard. "It's a miracle we're all here together in one piece, thank Codaghan for that. It seems to me we have two things we need to decide.

"We have to figure out what we'll do next and we have to decide what to do with these two." He gestured toward Lily and Jia.

"Please," Jia said, "let us go with you, wherever you decide to go."

"Why should we let you and why would you want to do so to begin with?" Aeden asked.

"I don't have any family left," she said, "but I'm still human. If I understand correctly—and your experiences have given me more information on the subject—those dark monsters have come from another place to destroy our world, to kill everything alive." Khrazhti nodded at that. "We may not be the most upstanding of people—"

"You're assassins!" Raki said, then immediately put his head down to try to hide his face.

"Yes," Jia continued. "We're assassins. But we're human. We don't want our world to end, for everyone we've ever known"—she nodded toward Aila—"to be killed. We want to help prevent that. We'll do so in whatever way we can, even if you don't let us join you, but we can add our strength and skills to yours, making us all stronger."

"You'd not be able to harm them permanently if you went off on your own," Aeden said. "It takes a special magic to destroy them."

"All the more reason to let us go with you," Lily said. She had been trying to surreptitiously peek under Khrazhti's hood the entire time they had been talking. Khrazhti was in the corner of the room, still fully covered. "That one, there, she's one of those creatures."

"Her name is Khrazhti," Aeden growled, "not *that one there*."

"I meant no offense," she said. "Khrazhti is one of them, one of the enemy, but she travels with you and you treat her as one of your own."

"She's our friend," Fahtin said. "She has sworn an oath and has proven herself to be a good and honorable friend."

"We'll swear any oath you require," Lily said. "If you can accept one of those—what did you call them, animaru?—then why can't you at least give two humans a chance?"

"It's not about human or animaru," Aeden said. "It's about personality and character. You two hunted us simply because someone was going to pay you."

"Erent Caahs did the same thing," Lily said. "No offense meant, but he hunted down and killed people for pay. Is that not correct?" She said the last while looking toward Tere.

Tere looked away, though the woman was trying to meet his eyes. "He did, yes, though not as blatantly as you make it sound." He looked to Aeden. "They're right, I think. They should be given the privilege of fighting for their world. Whether that means casting your spell on their weapons and sending them on their way or taking them into our group, they should have that chance."

"Let's all think about it overnight," Aeden said. "We don't have to make the decision right now. While we're thinking, we should consider what the rest of us will do. Where do we go now?"

"Wasn't your plan all along to go to the Academy?" Aila asked.

"Aye," Aeden said. He was going to say more, but stopped himself.

Fahtin took up the discussion. "Then maybe that's what we should do. We're very close and they will have answers. Maybe they'll even know how we can find Benzal."

"At the very least," Aila said, "we can report the animaru to them."

"About that," Aeden said. "We heard yesterday about a few towns being attacked and destroyed in Kruzekstan. I'm sure they have heard the rumors at the Academy as well. Merchants go there, too. I don't think there's a need to tell them something is happening."

"Yeah, but we know a lot more about what's going on than some rumors."

"Let's think about it," Aeden said. "You make good points. We can decide tomorrow. Why don't we rest and think it over?"

The others filed out of the room, some to their own rooms and others to the bath. Aeden stayed where he was. What *would* they do? He had been sure that once they reached the others, his problems would be solved. At least as far as being able to track down Benzal. He'd been certain that Tere would save the day as he seemed so capable of doing.

But Tere couldn't. Erent Caahs. Codaghan's balls, was his friend really the hero he had grown up hearing tales about, the only man who could overshadow Raisor Tannoch, even in the minds of young Croaghs? What was Aeden doing rubbing shoulders with such a man? And he had the audacity to tell Tere what to do on occasion, never mind that the archer complied.

But that was neither here nor there. They would make a decision in the morning, something that would dictate the near future. Maybe the far future, too. He didn't really care one way or another about the former assassins. They seemed...human. Somehow, he'd thought a professional assassin would be different. If he had to answer truthfully, he liked the women, or at least liked them better than many other people he'd met.

Of course, maybe that was their skill as assassins, fooling him into complacency.

Still, that decision paled in comparison to the one about where they would go and what they would do. What would happen if they finally went to the Academy? Would they tell him he wasn't the Malatirsay? Even worse, would they tell him he was? That thought frightened him more than two assassins traveling with them and being at his back.

He slammed his palm on the table, making the plate and mug near him jump. Standing, he swept out of the room, suddenly needing fresh air. The last thing he wanted at the moment was to be enclosed, with a building around him blocking the breeze and the sunlight.

Aeden slipped out the inn's door and headed for an area overlooking a nearby stream. It was raised, with logs fashioned into benches—a perfect place for thinking. He had crested the small rise, heading for one of the benches, when he realized someone was already sitting on one. The last thing he wanted was for some stranger to ask him questions. He turned to go, but was drawn back when the other person spoke.

"Aeden?" It was Urun's voice. "You don't have to leave. I'll...I'll go. You can stay if you want."

"Urun? Are you okay?"

"It's a good place to think, right? You can look out over the stream and see some of the surrounding terrain. A deer was drinking a moment ago. She darted off into those bushes when she heard you."

Aeden walked over to the priest and sat on the bench next to him. They sat silently together for a time before Urun got up to leave.

"No," Aeden said. "You don't have to leave. You were here first. I'll find another place."

Urun sat down again, looking out at the stream.

"Urun, what's going on? Tere told us about the prison. Is that what's bothering you? Does being out here in nature not help?"

Urun sighed and slumped, putting his hands between his knees. "She left me, Aeden."

"Who?"

"Osulin. She doesn't answer my prayers, won't contact me or respond in any way. She has rejected me."

"I don't think that's true."

"I can't feel her presence. I have always felt her presence, since she first took me as her priest. I..." He choked on his breath, then regained his composure. "...don't know what I've done to become disapproved. Why won't she answer, tell me how I've failed?"

"You haven't failed, Urun."

The young priest didn't speak, simply sat there, slumped, breathing in and out.

Aeden tried another approach. "In Tere's story, he told me you healed Aila. She was close to death, but you healed her."

"Aila is my friend. She was injured."

"Yes," Aeden said. "And then, when the assassins attacked, you put up your shield and defended against that dark woman's magic."

Urun grunted.

"Don't you see, Urun? If Osulin had rejected you, if she left you, you wouldn't be able to do magic. You're no mage; you're a priest. Your magic comes from your goddess. Tell me how you think you could heal Aila or shield against magic and other attacks if you didn't have the blessing of your goddess."

Urun cocked his head. "You...you're right. I couldn't use

her power if she didn't let me. But why, then, won't she talk to me?"

"I know nothing of how gods act," Aeden said. "I'm sure there's a reason, though I probably couldn't guess it."

"I don't know." Urun put his head in his hands. "I *feel* unworthy. It wasn't just being locked up, away from nature. I felt like I was losing my connection, like it was slipping away because I didn't deserve it."

"That's nonsense. You are the most loyal person to any god or goddess I know. Don't doubt yourself so. Tere lost his magic, but do you think it's because he's not worthy of it?"

"Of course not, but it's not the same thing."

"I think it is. Things happen to us in life. Not all of them are because of something we did—or didn't—do. Don't be afraid you're not worthy. Instead, do your best and try to see if there is a way to rectify what you think the problem is."

Urun sat up and looked into Aeden's eyes. There seemed to be something going on behind those grey orbs, his mind biting off chunks of what Aeden said and chewing them. Tasting them.

After a time, he finally said, "Maybe you're right. Maybe it has something to do with all these other crazy things that are going on with magic right now."

"The question you have to ask," Aeden said, "is not if others think you're worthy. It's whether *you* think you're worthy and if *you* are committed to doing what needs to be done. If you focus on that, I think things will be a lot easier."

The priest's mouth turned up into a smile, barely more than a flat, neutral expression. But it *was* more. "I'll think about it. Thank you, Aeden. That helped. Excuse me. I have to go into those trees over there and pray. It works better when I'm surrounded by natural things."

He got up and walked toward where he had said the deer went. Soon, he was swallowed up by the trees.

Aeden smiled. He felt good, useful. What he said seemed to have helped. All Urun needed was to stop feeling inadequate and get rid of his fear of failing his goddess and...

"*Cuir aet biodh!*"

Hadn't he been doing the same thing? All this time, dreading going to the Academy because he was afraid of what they'd tell him, afraid it would change things. It was exactly the same thing Urun had been doing. Aeden hadn't withdrawn from everyone else, but he was just as surely avoiding going where he should have gone first and doing what he should have been doing.

It was time he took his own advice. No longer could he hypocritically worry about whether or not the Academy would slap a title on him. The best chance of finding Benzal and for beating the animaru invasion lay in getting the help from the Academy.

He jumped up from the bench and strode back into the inn. He had made his decision. In the morning, he would tell them he wanted to go to the Hero Academy, no matter how it turned out.

He thanked Urun mentally as he headed up to his room. In trying to help the priest, the young man had actually helped him. Life was funny that way sometimes.

The morning came and the travelers all met in the private dining room again. The innkeeper had food brought in and the fire was already stoked and burning brightly when Aeden stepped into the room, the first except for Tere. The man looked exhausted.

"Good morning, Tere," Aeden said, finding a pitcher with milk and pouring a cup of it for himself.

"Morning, yes. Good? We'll have to wait and see about that."

"Are you...okay, Tere?"

The archer shook his head and blinked several times.

When he turned to face Aeden, he didn't look so despondent as he had a moment before. "I'm fine. Thoughts are shooting through my head faster than any arrow I could shoot. I'm just too old for this life anymore."

"No. You just don't let yourself be human. You have decades left before you slow down."

"Oh, gods help me, I hope not. The way things are going, I expect I'll be killed before too long. Getting involved in trying to save the world. What is wrong with me?"

Aeden chuckled. "The same thing that's wrong with the rest of us, I expect."

"We're all crazy," Tere said as Fahtin walked in, Raki and Khrazhti just behind her.

"Crazy?" she said. "Did your mother never teach you how to be polite, Tere Chizzit?"

The old archer finally cracked a smile. "She tried, but it didn't stick." His lips turned down in an instant and a pained look washed over his face, but he recovered and schooled his expression to a more neutral one.

Raki stared at Tere with wide eyes.

"Did *your* mother never teach you it's not polite to stare?" Tere asked the boy.

Fahtin headed off the conversation before it got into more painful territory for the boy. "His *nani* did teach him that, yes."

"Raki," Tere said in all seriousness, "I'm the same person I was before. The one who taught you to move more silently, the one you sat around the fire with, telling stories."

"Yeah," Raki said. "Telling stories about *you*. You're the most famous hero ever."

"Not hardly. I could name a dozen others that are more famous, and I figure some in this room will be even more famous yet. It means nothing. People are people. King, peasants, warriors, *assassins*," he said that last as the other three women walked in the room, "they're all just people. Don't forget that. Don't let anyone ever tell you otherwise."

Raki dropped his head to look at his shoes.

Urun stepped into the room, looked around and noticed everyone else was already there, and closed the door.

"It seems that everyone had their baths and cleaned up yesterday," Aeden said. "Nothing like soaking in hot water after so many days on the trail."

The silence greeting his statement made him think maybe he had said something wrong.

"Lily," Urun said. The beautiful red-haired archer turned toward the priest. "May I?" He pointed toward the bandages on her shoulder. They didn't have blood leaking through, which Aeden thought was a good sign, but her injury was obviously still causing her pain, if the way she moved carefully was any indication.

She stood up straighter and nodded, letting him fiddle with the bandages. She raised her eyebrows when he slipped a wad of cloth saturated with a dull green liquid from his pouch. He peeled back the bandage and gently placed his compress on the wound. It was still an angry red.

Urun chanted something under his breath and clasped his staff tightly with one hand while hovering the other over the wound. After half a minute, he stopped and relaxed his grip on the wood. When he took the compress off, it had turned a reddish brown. Aeden could smell the rot from across the table. The priest casually tossed it into the fire, where it smoldered for a moment and then burst into flames.

Lily took the rest of the bandages off her shoulder, revealing her pale, unblemished skin. There remained only a slight pink spot, the color of a mild sunburn, but Aeden didn't think it would leave any kind of permanent mark. The only way one could tell anything had happened at all was the lack of freckles on the spot, whereas they dusted the rest of the shoulder. The assassin gasped, then promptly swept Urun into a hug, only to jump back a second later, her fair skin flushing.

"Uh, sorry," she said. "Thank you, though. I hardly slept a wink last night because it was irritating me. That's amazing."

Urun couldn't seem to meet her eyes. "It's nothing. I mean, it's what I do. I'm a priest of Osulin. She has given me power to help others."

Aeden smiled, but not nearly as widely as Fahtin. She told the priest how nice he was and how thoughtful. It wasn't the act that made Aeden happy so much as the confidence Urun had shown. It appeared that his prayers—and his talk with Aeden—the night before had helped.

"No use in dragging this on," Tere said. "It's clear Urun approves of letting the Falxen—"

"Former Falxen, if you please," Jia said.

"Former Falxen join us. What about the rest of you?"

Fahtin was in favor, but that had been a given. She never had a suspicious hair on her head. Raki nodded bashfully, as he normally did around women of any type, especially beautiful ones. Aila smiled her affirmation as well. Khrazhti gave a small nod, almost as if she didn't know if her vote would count. She did, Aeden noticed, allow her cloak and hood to reveal much of her face and skin this morning, at least after they had closed the door to the dining room.

Aeden wasn't sure how he felt about letting the women travel with them. They seemed to be sincere, and they had to have skills to have been accepted by the Falxen. When it came down to it, the feeling he got from them was a good one. His senses and his friends' judgment were good enough for him.

"I suppose we have two more to help us take down Benzal. Welcome to our little circle of friends."

Jia whooped and gave a little hop. Lily tried to catch

Tere's eye, but the archer had put his head down and was eating his breakfast. Aeden realized the man had not stated what he thought. He immediately felt bad about acting the leader again. He'd have to talk to Tere about it later, apologize.

"Now that that's out of the way," Aeden said, "we need to talk about what we're going to do. Tere? What's your opinion?"

The archer finished chewing his food, then slowly took a drink from his cup. Only then did he look up to Aeden. "The way I see it, I'm shit for finding Benzal. We could go and search the east for the next year and still not find him. I know how that works, believe me. I've spent most of my life hunting people, and that was with magic to help me.

"The only chance I see is to go to the Academy and ask their help. Besides, they still need to know about the animaru —from people who have actually fought them—and they need to know about you. I say we go there next."

There was no sense in asking each person what they thought. Every one of them was nodding their head or verbally affirming Tere's comments.

"It looks like we're going to Sitor-Kanda," Aeden said. "We can leave as soon as we finish eating."

32

The trip to the Academy took a day and a half on foot. The group made good time to the town of Bridgeguard, where they took rooms at an inn. Most of them had never seen the little community before and Aeden noted right away that it wasn't like any place he'd ever visited.

First, there were seven inns in a town with barely four times that many buildings total. Seven! Tere had explained to them that the residents made their living catering to the visitors to the Academy, though there were fewer of those than at one time. It was also unique in that the town straddled the road that emptied onto the bridge to Munsahtiz itself.

The townsfolk whose professions were not involved with visitors engaged in trade. The Academy, in addition to training warriors and mages, had the most advanced manufactories in the world and were on the cutting edge of modern technology. Many of their crafts went through Bridgeguard or the Academy's own port on the west of the island to sell to the wider world. A handful of the town's residents had made a nice living for themselves in such trade.

As the party strolled down the main roadway—a paved street large enough for four wagons to pass at once—Aeden spied the variety of stalls and shops. He could find anything he could ever want to buy here. But that wasn't what was on his mind.

As they approached the inn Tere had recommended, Aeden caught his first glance at the Academy itself, off across the narrows strip of the Kanton Sea. He stopped in the street and gaped.

He was not alone. Most of his friends were frozen in place as well.

The main building at the Academy was a massive stone structure, larger than any castle or fortress Aeden had ever seen. It looked to be constructed of huge blocks of stone, but from that distance, he couldn't see even a hint of the individual pieces that made it up. It rose into the sky, a behemoth of white stone, glistening though the sun was slowly making its way behind it, heading toward the horizon.

Around the main building were many other large structures that, if he had seen them alone, would have awed him with their size. Surrounding the main building, though, they looked like ducklings swarming around their mother duck, interesting but not particularly impressive. Smoke rose from several of the structures, but one belched out enough that at first Aeden thought it might be on fire.

Tere noticed which way Aeden was looking. "Those buildings over there are the manufactories. They have forges aplenty and looms and tanning racks and whatever else you may have ever seen or thought of to make crafted items."

"You'll see it much closer tomorrow." Tere slapped a hand on Aeden's shoulder. "We can leave early in the morning and enjoy the leisurely walk. Then maybe we'll get some of the answers we've been wanting, eh?"

Aeden nodded woodenly at him, then turned and followed the others to the inn.

The next day, they were already on the bridge, crossing to the island, when the sun had been up for a little over an hour. Aeden stayed near the back of the group, in the midst of them, but still apart. He was surprised to see other people on the road with them, heading toward the Academy.

Fahtin chatted with Aila, Jia jumping into the conversation when there was an opportunity. The three of them seemed to think it was a grand adventure to go to the Academy. Lily, her bow and quiver returned to her, walked alongside them but didn't take part in the conversation. Raki peppered Tere with questions, Urun at their side.

Khrazhti seemed to be left out of all of it. No doubt she felt self-conscious in her cloak and hood, especially with how little clothing Lily wore. She hovered between the others and Aeden, eyes forward when she wasn't scanning for danger.

In the silence between his companions quietly chatting about what they saw and the sound of the surf crashing at the bottom of the cliffs, Aeden thought he heard something else. Something he recognized. Try as he might, the young Croagh couldn't place where the sound was coming from.

Tere's mouth turned up into a smile as he drifted back to Aeden. "Yes, your ears are not playing you false. That's the clash of steel you hear in between the hammer blows in the smithies." He pointed to an area free of structures to the north of one of the larger manufactory buildings, though the wall blocked most of the view. "The largest of the practice yards is over there. They sometimes perform mock battles there as training."

Just how big was this place? He let out a breath. The Hero Academy. He'd heard about it as a child, but he never thought he'd see it. Though his Croagh pride told him he never *needed* to see it, the wonder of the place struck him hard. He swallowed, not knowing what to say. What was *he* doing here?

He was thinking about what he'd do when they arrived at the Academy. He couldn't very well go up to the first person he saw and say, "Hello, I'm the Malatirsay. Take me to whoever is in charge here." As much as he's like to—he preferred the direct approach in most cases—that wouldn't do much but alienate all around him. But what *would* he do?

He mechanically put one foot after the other and stayed silent. Within his mind, thoughts slammed together like soldiers on the front line of a heated battle. It was making him dizzy. Looking over at Khrazhti, he noticed her shoulders were slumped slightly when she usually had perfect posture. He was getting too wrapped up in himself.

"How are you doing, Khrazhti?" he said. Her head snapped up in surprise.

"I...am well. How are you? Nervous to talk to these *masters?*"

"Not really nervous about them, but I'm concerned about how I'll present what I want to say to them."

Her forehead scrunched up. He could barely see it under the shadow of her hood. "I do not understand. The Academy was built for this purpose, was it not? To aid you in your work? Why do you not simply walk up and tell them what they must do?"

He let out a short laugh, which felt very good. "I wish it were that easy. They don't know me, and I'll need to be able to get to the masters to really talk to them about what's going on. They have assistants, no doubt, to keep people from wasting their time. I need to figure out a way to get past them and to the masters."

"Will you sneak through? Your stealth skills are not as impressive as Raki's, but you move well and quietly, when you desire to."

He shook his head. "No. If I do that and get caught, they may think I'm an assassin or something. I might see the masters after that, but I'll be in chains. No, I need to come up with a convincing argument as to why I need to talk to the masters."

"I see. I cannot think of a way to help you. I am sorry."

He took her hand and clapped his other on top of it. "Don't be sorry. I don't expect you—or anyone else for that matter—to solve it for me. I'll think of something. In the meantime, please let me tell you that *I'm* sorry that you have to wear that cloak and hood all the time. It's just that—"

"I understand. I am too...different. Some will not understand and may be afraid. They may try to hurt me and I would have to defend myself. It is little trouble. When we travel again, away from the towns and villages, I will put the cloak in my bag and feel the air on my skin again."

He squeezed her hand and let it go. "Yes. Thank you for understanding. I appreciate that."

She nodded and stepped aside so they were a little farther apart. She became silent again, allowing him time to think. But when they approached the wall surrounding the main building, he still hadn't decided what he would say.

As soon as they passed through the gate, it was plain they were not the only ones who had come to see the Academy. More than a dozen people already waited near the double doors into the structure Tere had called the administration building.

A young man wearing charcoal grey robes approached them. He carried a board with sheets of paper clamped between two pieces of wood. On the corner of the board was an inkpot secured into a hole. The young man had a quill in his hand. He seemed too young to Aeden. Maybe he was a student.

"What is the purpose of your visit to Sitor-Kanda?"

"I need to speak with the masters," Aeden said.

"About...?"

"About the Song of Prophecy." He was about to explain further, but the young man jotted down something on his paper and began to turn toward the next person in line.

"The Master of Prophecy will see you when he is able. Stay in this area and one of the aides will call for you. Your name?"

"Aeden Tannoch."

"Very well. I cannot estimate when the master will be available, but we shall call for you three times. If you do not respond, we will assume you have changed your mind and will strike your name from the roster. Good day to you."

The young man moved over to another group just arriving. "What is the purpose of your visit to Sitor-Kanda?"

"Well," Aeden said. "I guess we wait."

Lily stood like the statue of some ancient hero, her green eyes blazing in the sunlight streaming in the windows. "I can make them see you now."

Aeden didn't doubt she could. Besides her obvious presence and strength, she received quite a lot of attention for her choice in clothing.

"No, Lily," he said. "Thank you, but we can wait."

"Fine," she said. "Let me know if you change your mind."

Aeden figured they would be waiting for at least a little while, so rather than to worry over what to say, he would ask the question that had been on his mind.

"Lily, you said you studied Erent Caahs, tried to pattern yourself after him?"

"Yes." She narrowed her eyes.

"I am confused. What does"—he waved his hand to take in her whole appearance—"your wardrobe have to do with him? He didn't wear, well, that."

It surprised Aeden when she smiled. "Of all the things I

thought you might say, that wasn't one of them. What I wear doesn't have anything to do with Erent Caahs, neither who he was—" She jerked her head toward Tere, off to the side talking with Raki. "Or who he is now. I wear what I like."

"You have to know that what you wear leaves you vulnerable in battle. I mean, I understand that what little you do wear is covered with mail, but you have so much skin unprotected...um, isn't that a bit dangerous?"

"How many scars do you see, Aeden?"

"I don't...I mean I haven't...uh, you don't seem to have a lot of scars visible."

She got a wicked smile on her face. "Have you looked closely? Do you want me to point some out?"

"No! I mean, no, that's okay."

She laughed. "I do have a few, but my point is that I don't have many. I'm an archer. I try to stay out of face-to-face combat as much as I can. I can use the long knives, mainly because Erent could, and I trained to be very good with them, but I'd prefer to put arrows in my enemies. To me, it's more important that I can move freely and 'what little I wear' suits me just fine."

"I can understand that. Thank you. I didn't mean to embarrass you."

She tossed her full head of red hair and laughed again. "You, embarrass me? Not likely. Have you seen what I wear?" She winked at him, then looked over his shoulder to smile at someone else.

Aeden turned to see Aila standing there, a wide smile on her face.

"You're blushing, Aeden," she said. "Such a pretty color."

"*Daeann daedos ist*," he muttered, and sat on an empty space on one of the benches arranged in rows in the reception hall.

Fifteen minutes later, one of the aides, a young woman

dressed in the same charcoal robes the young man from earlier wore, called out, "Aeden Tannoch to see the Master of Prophecy."

Aeden stood up from sitting on one of the benches and shouldered his pack. He raised his hand and headed toward the aide, smiling at the pretty young woman. When he stopped in front of her, she raised one eyebrow at him. He looked down at himself, wondering what the problem was, but she was focusing behind him. He turned to see all his friends a step behind, waiting to accompany him.

"Is it okay for them to come in, too?"

The girl sighed. "Audiences are typically for one alone, but there are no others to see the Master of Prophecy, and he is in one of the lecture halls, so I'll allow it."

"Thank you," he said, still smiling. She smiled back coquettishly and motioned for him to follow her. Something softly swatted the back of his head, or at least tried to. His reflexes took over and he ducked, spun and prepared to counterattack. His right-hand sword was halfway out of the scabbard before Aeden realized it was only his friends around him.

Aila's hand was still in the air.

"You're mine," she said as if he hadn't caught her trying to strike him. "Keep your eyes—and that fantastic smile of yours —pointed toward me, not every young girl who bats her eyelashes at you."

Aeden worked his mouth, wanting to say something but not knowing what. Fahtin giggled into her hand, as did the two former assassins. Khrazhti looked confused and the men's expressions ranged from brows drawn toward Aila to Urun's rolling eyes.

Instead of addressing the issue, Aeden followed the aide through the large double doors through an entryway, into a hallway, and to a side room that turned out to be the promised lecture hall.

It was a largish room with tables lined up in rows, three chairs behind each. It was empty but for a man behind a podium on a little dais at the front. He was older, probably nearing or into his fifties. His pointed beard was a mix of black and grey while his mustache was almost entirely black, like the remaining hair on his head. His forehead seemed to have grown backward and now split the hair into two parts, lining the side of his head. His dark eyes looked at his visitors over sagging skin with dark circles on either side of his nose.

"These visitors requested to see the Master of Prophecy, Master Tiscomb," the aide said. She turned to Aeden, gave him another smile, and said, "Master Marn Tiscomb, the Master of Prophecy, this is Aeden Tannoch." She bowed to the master and then left the room.

"If you wish to have your fortune read, you are mistaken. I do not do foretelling." The man's voice made Aeden think of taking a nap. It wasn't quite monotone, but neither did it evoke interest in what the man was saying.

"No, I'm not here for that. I'd like to talk about the Bhav-isyaganant, the Song of Prophecy."

"That name is Dantogyptain. Do you know that, boy? Scholars sometimes refer to the Prophet's work in that manner. You are no scholar."

"I am not. I am something quite different."

"And what would that be?"

"I have been told I am the Malatirsay."

The master scoffed. "You've been *told* you are the Malatirsay."

"Yes."

"Is this some kind of joke? Have the students put you up to this? I've no time for your foolishness. Please leave."

Aeden immediately regretted the way the conversation

had gotten away from him. "No. Please, Master Tiscomb, hear me out. The animaru are here. We have fought them. We have valuable information about them."

"You do, do you?" the master asked. "And what makes you think we don't already have all the information you could tell us?"

Aeden tried to think quickly. He had to bring this conversation back to where he wanted it to go. What could he say?

"He knows because I was their leader," Khrazhti said, dropping her cloak to the ground and stepping up next to Aeden in all her blue-skinned glory. "I was the high priestess of S'ru and commanded three thousand animaru."

The master stared at Khrazhti for a moment. Then he chuckled. "You're very good. I hope they paid you well. You have earned every copper. You've had your fun, now begone before I call the guards."

"Please," Aeden said. "A Gypta seer told me the prophecy points to me. I was born into one of the highland Croagh clans and then was adopted by the Gypta. I can tell you how each of the points of the prophecy apply to me. I just want help in battling the animaru. All Dizhelim is at stake."

"Listen, boy. I am the Master of Prophecy. There is nothing you can tell me about the Song I do not know. You are *not* the Malatirsay, and all your wishing will not make it so. I already know who the prophesied one is, and it is not you. Stop pretending and go home. Leave dealing with these so-called animaru to those who can do it best: us. Leave now, and don't let me see you on this campus again. Is that clear?"

Aeden nodded sadly, turned, and walked out of the room.

✥ 33 ✥

Aeden stumbled out of the front doors to the Academy. He bumped several people on the way out, but the fact didn't register in his mind until he was already out on the grounds. He was vaguely aware of his friends following in his wake.

That was it. The Master of Prophecy of the Hero Academy had told him he was not the Malatirsay. If there was one person on all of Dizhelim who would know, it would be that man.

It all came crashing down on Aeden. His stomach roiled and he became light-headed, like he'd had too much strong ale. All the things he had believed, all the things he had thought he came to know as the truth about him and about his destiny, they were all false. One thought shone brightly amid all others.

His clan was right. He was not worthy.

Aeden felt physical pain in his chest when the words rang in his head. Pain greater than that which almost killed him when he was a boy and his clan beat him nearly to death. How could he have been so stupid to believe he could be some hero from a prophecy thousands of years old? Ludicrous, ridiculous. He must have seemed mad to the master.

Well, at least it was done. His quest was over, his responsibility ended. He didn't have to hunt down Benzal or stop the animaru. Not him. Not Aeden Tannoch. He was just a boy who knew how to fight, but not even well enough for his clan to accept him.

He was a failure, through and through.

Aeden sat, huddled into a ball with his arms hugging his knees, for a long time. An hour, two, more? He blinked and looked up to see his friends' concerned faces looking back at him. Where was he?

That's right, he had made his way out of the gates to the other side of the wall. There, he sat and had been there since. Had his friends tried to talk to him? He couldn't remember.

"Aeden?" Fahtin's soft voice said. "Aeden. Are you well?"

"I'm sorry, Fahtin," he said.

"Sorry?"

"I failed you, just like I failed my clan, my..." His voice broke. "Parents."

"Oh, no, no, no." She sat in the dirt next to him and wrapped her arms around him. "No, Aeden, you haven't failed anyone."

"I'm no hero," he said. "I'm not who I convinced myself I was. I'm just an orphan, a nobody."

"Shh. No. You *are* a hero. Look around you. All your friends are here because of you. You saved each of us a number of times, as well as many more people. Our entire family would have been slaughtered without you. The people of Drugancairn. Hundreds, thousands that we don't even know about because you were a hero, and because of your heroism, you brought Khrazhti to our side. Once our enemy, now our friend. All because of you."

Aeden couldn't listen. He shut his ears to her argument.

He was too confused for discussion. "I will still do what I can. I won't fail in the promise I made you. I will give what I can until I am dead or the threat is gone. I promised, though I had no right to."

Fahtin held him and he sank into her embrace. After a time, he gently extricated himself from her and stood.

"We should head back," he said. "We can decide what to do after we get some rest. I don't really want to talk about it right now."

They respected his wishes and followed him back across the bridge to the inn. Conversation between his friends was muted, but it didn't matter. Even if it was loud, he wouldn't have listened to any of it. The only thing he kept hearing was the master's voice: *You are* not *the Malatirsay and all your wishing will not make it so. I already know who the prophesied one is, and it is not you. Stop pretending and go home.*

He ate a quick dinner in the common room of the inn, not speaking or responding to the others in any way. When he finished, he trudged up to his room and got into bed. He lay there for a long time before sleep took him.

By the time the light of the morning sun filtered through the windows of the inn, Aeden had been up for more than an hour. He was shirtless, behind and to the side of the building, performing his training exercises. He had long ago removed his tunic and undershirt and was sweating freely in the cool morning air.

Turn, cut, parry, block, spin, kick. He moved through his techniques precisely and at great speed. The whistle of his blades cutting the air soothed him, and he got lost in the feeling of pure movement and explosive energy. He didn't think of imaginary opponents, though he often did when performing his exercises. Instead, he let the power of his body moving in efficient combinations of lethal moves calm his nerves and relax his thoughts. There was nothing but him and his weapons.

He opted for an alternate sequence, one more acrobatic in nature than the standard routine. With a flip to gain power in his cut, he split a target in half that was not there then spun and cut it into quarters, striking out with kicks to scatter the pieces and attack the next target. Again, he pictured nothing but a cool, calm field of green, a symbol of his home.

With a furious flurry of slashes and attacks with feet, pommel, and elbows, he stopped, standing in exactly the same place he had started dozens of minutes ago. He brought his swords up to salute the empty air and dropped them, relaxing.

"You *are* good," a voice said.

He spun, swords at the ready, only to find Jia sitting on the ground, legs crossed in front of her, a stalk of grass in between her teeth.

"Are all the Crows as good as you?" she asked.

He walked over to his scabbards and slid his swords into them. "I was found unworthy by my clan," he gave her as his answer. "They beat me nearly to death and left me to die, expelling me from my family and my home. If Fahtin hadn't found me and her family taken me in, I would be dead."

Jia nodded slowly, chewing on her piece of grass. "That's unfortunate and I'm sorry, but you didn't answer my question."

Aeden cocked his head at the woman, then one side of his mouth twitched up and threatened to smile before he forced it back down. "I was unable to master all the skills. That's why they expelled me."

Jia opened her mouth to speak again, but Fahtin's voice cut her off.

"He's being difficult," she said. "He's never said so, but I think he was exceptional even in his clan. All except the little failure with the magic. But he's remedied that." She turned and threw him a towel. "Haven't you?"

Aeden growled under his breath, but snatched the towel out of the air. "Can't a man get a little practice in without being pestered?"

"No." Fahtin stepped up to him and kissed his cheek. "Not when we're concerned about you."

"I'm fine," he said. "We'll figure out what to do during breakfast. We'll put all this behind us."

"If you say so. Come on, Jia. Let's get some food. Aeden's going to be grumpy until he's had his breakfast." She put her hand up to her mouth like it would keep him from hearing her and whispered, "He's always like that."

Jia chuckled and flipped up onto her feet. She spat the grass out onto the ground. "I hope it tastes better than this."

Aeden was blessedly alone. He took his time putting his shirt and tunic on and made his way into the common room to eat with the others.

Conversation seemed a bit strained during breakfast. His friends probably were trying to figure out what they could talk about without setting him off. He hated how that felt.

"Listen," he told them. "I appreciate you trying to make neutral conversation so you don't hurt my feelings, but there's no need. I'm done sulking. The master gave us valuable information, probably preventing us from wasting our time on things we shouldn't concern ourselves with. Let's act like my reaction never happened, please. No use in guarding your tongue. How often have we been able to eat breakfast with a roof over our heads and in chairs at a table? Let's enjoy it. I'm sorry for overreacting."

That loosened things up a little, but there was still a pressure, a tension hanging over them. So be it. It would pass. Most things did.

They talked of less serious—safe—things for a time, but

they did so with no fervor, only mild complacence. When the topics of conversation swung around to more serious matters, like what they would do and where they would go, Aeden was not surprised. In fact, he was almost relieved. Better to rush in to attack than to wait for one's enemies to lie in wait for you.

"I'm sorry if this is too forward of me, since I am such a recent addition to the group," Jia said, "but what will we do? It almost sounds to me as if we will split up, going our own ways, leaving the dangers and the fate of the world to others. I hope I'm mistaken in that."

Fahtin looked at Aeden, then down at the table. The others seemed content to wait for him to speak.

"I don't know," he said. "All we did before was based on the belief that I was the Malatirsay and that I had the responsibility, and the right, to fight on behalf of humans. As we've found, that is not the case."

"Aeden," Tere said, "you shouldn't take what that master said so hard. For that matter, I'm not entirely sure you should take it as fact. He could be mistaken. He's only a man."

"He's the Master of Prophecy at the Hero Academy, Tere," Aeden said. "If there were one person in all of Dizhelim who would know about the Song and about the Malatirsay, it would be him."

"I suppose so, but people have been wrong for thousands of years about the prophecy. I'm not willing to disbelieve all we've seen just yet."

Aeden put his head in his hands and grunted. The story Dannel had told them flashed through his mind, the one about the false Malatirsay. Weren't almost all the masters wrong about that one?

He shook his head, dispelling the thought. Best to come right out and say it. "I never really believed I was the one anyway. It all felt too convenient, too contrived. After the initial shock, it's really a relief. A blessing. I don't have to carry the weight of the world on my shoulders. As it turns out, the world is heavy."

Tere chuckled. "Yes. I know."

"I don't buy it," Lily said. "I was never accused of being some prophetic hero, and I don't think any of the rest of us here were. It was never about prophecy or responsibility for me. When I learned there were monsters trying to kill every person in Dizhelim, I decided I would fight. Not because some dusty book told me to, but because if I can save one good person who does not deserve to die, it would be worth it. It's what"—she looked to Tere and then away quickly—"heroes do. Not that I am one, but I want to act like one, at least."

Tere studied the woman for a moment, then gave a satisfied nod.

"There is that," Aeden said. "I promised Fahtin I would do everything in my power to fight the animaru, until either the threat was ended or I was. On my honor as a warrior, I cannot back down from that. *I* have no choice. I must help. The Academy will not accept my contribution, but maybe someone else will."

"Someone?" Fahtin asked.

"Anyone."

Aila smirked. "Anyone is a lot of options. We'll probably need a little more detail before we go haring off on some quest or another."

Aeden fixed his gaze on her, silent.

"What? Do you think I'm going to let you go off and get killed without me around to pull you out of the quicksand? Not a chance."

"Yeah," Raki added. "We're with you, whatever you decide to do."

The others nodded, all except Urun. Aeden watched the

young man as his eyes darted toward the ceiling, then the door, and finally to meet Aeden's.

"Osulin told me I was to accompany you," the priest said. "She didn't tell me you were the Malatirsay, just that I was to help *you*. That's good enough for me. She isn't...communicating with me right now, but until she does and tells me to do something else, I will not abandon my friends." He clasped his hands together in front of him and began to study them.

"I appreciate that, all of you," Aeden said. "But it doesn't get us any closer to figuring out what we'll do. I'm telling you, I have no idea. All the plans I had ended when the Academy refused my offer of help."

"Warn the people," Fahtin said.

"What?"

"The people. It doesn't seem like the Academy is taking the animaru threat seriously. They don't believe the darkness has come. Their job is to aid the Malatirsay, yes, but it's really to do what they can to save our world from the threat."

"That's right," Tere said. "Their whole reason for providing training for the Malatirsay is so that he can do his job in beating back the animaru. No one person could do that, so that means the Academy was meant to be an extension of him."

"Right," Fahtin continued. "But since they don't believe, no one will know and the animaru will be able to roll over half the world before anyone takes the rumors seriously. We need to let people know what's out there, that they need to prepare, to fight."

Aeden knew she was right. No one person could fight all the enemies.

Khrazhti had sat silently through the entire morning, nibbling on her food and watching the others during their conversation. Aeden almost forgot she was there. She spoke now.

"I have heard from your tales that the people are divided into nations or kingdoms." She said the words with strange inflections, obviously unaccustomed to them. "With one or a few powerful people leading them. It is like with the animaru and our battle groups. I myself had many under my command, but if I wanted to wage war on a powerful lord with more numerous troops, I would seek an alliance with another lord or battle leader, thus strengthening my army.

"Perhaps our goal should not be to warn all people, but to gather allies to our side. Maybe we should approach these leaders and then they will rally their own people."

Aeden's face broke out into a wide grin. "Khrazhti, you are wonderful. You hit it right on the head. That's exactly what we need. If we can get kings or ruling councils or other leaders on our side, we can build our own army."

"But," Fahtin said, "what about Benzal? He's going to bring more animaru over as soon as he can make another portal."

"She's right about that," Tere agreed. "He does need to be taken care of, if we could ever find him. Maybe we should focus on both. Convince the kingdoms of the threat so we can prepare, but also try to find where that rat is hiding and flush him out. If we start with heading east, gathering allies along the way, we'll have more eyes to try to find him. He may be able to open another portal or two, but we'll get him eventually. Hopefully sooner rather than later."

Aeden considered everything that had been said. He felt a small seed of excited energy sprout within him. Maybe he could still fulfill his promise and do some good. It was too late for his clan, but maybe not for all the other people of Dizhelim.

"That sounds like a good plan to me," he said. "It will be

difficult to get kings and other leaders to listen to us. If we had someone they would pay attention to, someone they respected, to start things off, it would be much easier. Someone like a famous hero." He planted his eyes firmly on Tere's face.

The archer put his hands up in front of him. "Oh no. That won't work. Look at me. I'm a blind old man. No one would believe who I was. I'm only Tere Chizzit now, and I won't be able to convince anyone differently."

"You could show them," Lily said. "Prove it to them by giving them a demonstration."

"No, girl. I'll not be a show pony, performing tricks for stuffy old kings. There are better uses of my time. Leave that dead man out of all your plans. I'll do what I can, but I'll do it as plain old Tere."

Aeden thought to try to convince him, but the look on Tere's face told him it would make things worse. "Fair enough. We have a plan, then. We can head out for the king of Rhaltzheim right away, then move east from there. I don't know how we'll get in to see him, but we can figure that out on the road."

With that matter done, the group finished up their breakfast. Aeden's heart felt lighter, a little at least, but he knew the task they had set for themselves was as hard, or even more so, than what they had originally thought to do. There was nothing for it, though. If the Academy would not support them, they would do what they could without the masters.

He hoped their plans did not run afoul of the real Malatirsay's. If that happened, things might get interesting very quickly, in a dangerous sort of way.

❧ 34 ❧

The party headed east after their meal, following the road they had taken barely over a day before. The plan was to stop in Dartford one more time before beginning their routine of camping as they traveled. One last night with a real bed and a warm bath, and then who knew how long it would be before they would enjoy those things again.

As they walked, Aeden became wrapped up in his own thoughts, not paying attention to the others and their various conversations. He simply moved along, thinking ahead.

How was he going to get an audience with the king of Rhaltzheim? How would he even be able to talk to the mayor of a city or a lord overseeing a relatively small parcel of land? He was a failed Croagh and an adopted Gypta, neither of which lent themselves to mingling with those in power.

He pondered, and the longer he did so, the darker his mood grew. It had all seemed like such a good idea that morning, when he was talking about it with his friends. Then, the common sense of the whole thing hadn't really been prominent in his mind. He'd seen an opportunity to become a hero, something he desperately wanted, but what chance did he really have of doing what they proposed?

Maybe they had all been too optimistic. Maybe they—

"Get out of the way, boy!" someone said, seemingly right above him.

Aeden blinked and jerked away from the massive, hairy form scraping alongside him. "What?" he said.

It was a horse, large and chestnut colored with a woman in its saddle. A woman with long, red hair.

"You're lucky I didn't run you down," she said, sneering at him.

He was on a narrow stretch of the road, the trees on either side crushing in on the packed dirt. There was barely room for three people to walk shoulder-to-shoulder. His friends had moved to the side, but he'd been too caught up in his thoughts.

"Sorry," he said. "I guess I was caught up in my thoughts."

"That's no excuse," she hissed. "Watch where you're going."

"Marla, it's fine," a blond-haired young man on a horse behind her said. "No harm done. Let's go."

The woman—Marla?—pulled on the reins and stopped the horse, still glaring down at Aeden. "Well?" she said.

Aeden looked to his left, to his right, then behind him. There was no one else there. "Well what?"

"You have nothing to say for yourself, boy?"

He felt the heat rising in him, starting from his center and spreading throughout his body. "I said all I need to say, *girl*. I was preoccupied. I apologized. Go on your way."

"Girl?"

"You're not much older than me," he said. "Maybe younger. If I'm a boy, then you're a girl. I can explain the words if you like. If you don't understand them."

The woman bared her teeth at him. What was wrong with her? Did people really act like this?

"Don't give me lip, *boy*, or this *girl* will kick your ass."

Aeden couldn't help it. He laughed. It felt good to do so, lightened the anger that was building in him a little. At the same time he did it, though, he realized it probably wasn't the best response.

"You find that funny?" she said.

"Marla, please," her companion said. He was slender, with a friendly face. Aeden thought he was probably a decent person, even if he did ride around with the red-haired shrew. "Let's just go. He apologized."

"No, Evon. I've had it. These past days have rubbed me raw. I could use a little exercise to blow off some steam."

Her companion gave Aeden an apologetic look, then turned his attention to Aeden's friends. His casual glance had the appearance of someone scanning for danger. That was not something he had expected from the innocent-looking man.

The crazy woman leaped out of her saddle, landing right in front of Aeden.

"So, how about it, boy. You want a duel?"

"A...did you say a duel?"

"I did."

"We're not in Arania." He didn't know quite what to make of the situation. "I don't duel."

"Then I guess I'll just whomp you for a little while, trying to build up a sweat."

Aeden met the eyes of the young man. "Is she serious?"

He sighed. "I'm afraid so. She's a little...intense sometimes."

Aeden laughed again, then barely sidestepped the punch she threw at him. He pivoted, ready to strike her, but he restrained himself. "Is that your idea of a duel?"

"No, that was my idea of the start of a brawl. Duels involve weapons."

"You're mad," he said.

"I am," she retorted. "Mad that you won't duel me like a man. I guess you *are* only a boy."

"Marla."

"Oh, shut it, Evon. I won't injure him permanently, just knock him around a little until he learns some manners."

Out of the corner of his vision, Aeden saw Tere twitch, and suddenly an arrow was nocked on his bowstring and drawn back to his cheek.

"No, Tere," Aeden said. "It's fine. I could use some exercise, too. Besides, someone needs to show this *girl* why she shouldn't be so rude. I hope she can still sit her saddle when I'm done bruising her arse." He showed all his teeth to her. "It is a nice arse, though, I'll give you that." It was true. She did look good in her tight clothing.

That was apparently not the correct thing to say, either. She growled at him and drew her sword with her right hand and a long knife with her left.

Aeden put his hands up. "Hold on, hold on. Let's move away a bit. I don't want my friends to get hurt when you swing those blades wildly trying to hit me."

"I won't cut anyone but you," she said. "I hit what I aim for."

"Fine, then let's move away a bit so that when I throw you to the ground, you won't trip any of them as you roll across the dirt."

She braced to charge, but Evon put his hand on her shoulder. "Marla, if you insist on doing this, at least be respectful to those who moved out of the way without you screaming at them."

She grunted, but pushed past Aeden to the point where the road widened a bit, just beyond where her horse was standing, looking at her. Aeden almost chuckled. The horse seemed to have a long-suffering look on its face. If horses could roll their eyes at the antics of humans, he thought the equine would be doing it. Smart animal.

He followed Marla and faced her. Without a warning, she charged, slashing at him with her sword.

Aeden twisted at the waist, letting the weapon whiz past him. He pushed her shoulder with his left hand to upset her balance and drew one of his swords with his right hand.

But she didn't lose her balance. She moved like a snake, wrenching her body to turn the blade in its path and come back as a backhand blow toward him. The clang of metal sounded as he deflected the strike, then another came a fraction of a second later as his newly drawn sword in his left hand parried a slash from her knife. He kicked out at her, not a real attempt to strike her, and she hopped backward, giving him some space.

A slow smile crept onto Aeden's face. Maybe this would be interesting after all.

She came at him again with a perfectly coordinated combination of slashes, her sword and knife cutting at him from five different angles, moving so fast they were a blur. He defeated each one and swept a kick at her lead leg. She, predictably, lifted it out of the way just as he shouldered her, trapping her blades while he rammed her chest. She backed up, slightly off balance and definitely angrier.

They circled, eyes locked. Hers were an emerald green. That made two women he had met in as many days that could have Croagh blood in them. Red hair and blue or green eyes were common in the highlands, but rarer in the rest of Dizhelim.

"Not bad, boy," she said.

He nodded his head, but didn't return the compliment. Her eyes blazed at the slight, as he knew they would.

Marla charged again, this time starting with straight-line attacks like those used by many of the duelists in Arania. Aeden used short, swift motions with his blades to parry them aside, but then she was suddenly whirling like someone from one of the monk orders in northern Shinyan.

He immediately adapted his own style, spinning his blades around him, an impenetrable wall of whirling steel. The clangs and clinks of the blades rebounding off each other came faster and faster until it sounded like one continuous hum. In the midst of all of it, he felt more than saw the attacks coming and dealt with them. At this close range, it was impossible to track the motion of all four blades.

Marla shifted again, this time to the hammering blows of the Clavian Knights, though her weapons were not well suited to that style. Neither of them had struck the other yet, but then, he hadn't counterattacked, either.

Her breath huffed as she struck. She controlled her breathing well, but she couldn't keep up the frantic pace for very long. It was too taxing. He, on the other hand, put forth as little effort as possible, utilizing the entire length of both blades to deflect or, very occasionally, block her strikes.

Soon now, he would end this match.

Her eyes flashed in the sunlight. He saw the color even though he was focusing on her waist, using his peripheral vision to track the movement of her limbs. At any moment she would...

There. She kicked out at him in between attacks. It was done skillfully, barely breaking her form, but it was enough. Aeden took a half step back, pivoted, and slammed his pommel into her kicking leg.

The strike threw her into a spin, and the only way she could recover was to roll with the fall and come up again several feet away.

Aeden heard gasps, at least two, but he couldn't look to

see who issued them when he was facing so skilled an opponent. Marla recovered quickly—she really was very skilled—and came back up into a ready stance, spitting a few strands of hair from her mouth.

Then she muttered a few low words under her breath and Aeden found himself being thrown back several feet.

"Marla!" a male voice said. It had to have been Evon.

Aeden adjusted his body posture and rolled his back, letting it contact the ground so he smoothly came back onto his feet after a somersault, blades out to the sides so he didn't cut himself with them.

This time he growled. She had used magic on him, the bitch.

She bared her teeth and motioned with her sword for him to attack.

Instead, he decided to fight magic with magic. He sheathed his blades and quickly described the motion of Saving Force—the original Raibrech spell and not the enhanced version—then immediately started another spell. He wasn't able to finish the second one. Instead, he saw something glimmer and come at him with great speed.

He ran toward it.

Halfway to Marla, the magic struck his shield. Aeden had already started spinning, though, expecting the force she had used before. It glanced off his shield and pushed him slightly to the side, but didn't stop him. Marla's eyes went wide.

Just as he slammed into her with a flying kick.

Her abdomen curled itself around his foot and the red-haired warrior flew back from him as if someone had tied a rope around her waist and pulled. The force was enough to knock both her weapons from her hands.

"Uff," she gasped as she left her feet, followed by an "Ugh," when she hit the ground. She recovered nicely, rolling backward and coming into a ready stance with fluid motion.

P.E. PADILLA

She took a few deep breaths, or tried, and then started wheezing out more words of power.

"Enough, Marla!" Evon screamed and threw himself in front of the crazy woman. "Enough. It's getting out of hand. If you two continue, someone is going to die. What are you going to tell the masters about that? You can't just go around trying to kill people." He looked back and forth between the two of them. "Besides, I'm sorry to say it, but he beat you fair and square. You know magic isn't part of a weapons duel."

Marla glared at Aeden, then at Evon, but finally picked up and sheathed her weapons. Aeden did the same.

"Here," Evon said, handing Marla a water skin. "Are you all right? that was some kick."

She snatched the skin from his hand and took a drink. "I'll be fine. Kicks like a damn horse, that one. Surefoot has kicked me and it didn't hurt that much." Her horse whinnied. Yes, a very smart horse.

The woman was plain crazy. Aeden couldn't get out of there fast enough. He dusted off his clothing and started walking toward his friends. They were standing there, mouths wide. What was wrong with them? He looked back, expecting to find Marla in midair launching herself at him. She was still standing near her friend, drinking from the skin.

"Gods," Jia said. "I've never seen anything like that, and I've been training since I was three years old. What are you?"

"I'm a failed Croagh and an adopted Gypta. Nothing more. Come on, we still need to make it to Dartford before day's out."

"Hey," Marla shouted. "What's your name?"

"Aeden. Aeden Tannoch."

"A Croagh?"

"Aye. What of it?"

"Nothing." She took another drink. "Listen, I may have been a bit rude—"

"*Gealich claidhimh d'araesh slaoch*. A bit rude? You gave me the impression of trying your best to kill me."

"Only after I saw that you weren't so easily harmed. I'd have never attacked anyone else like that." She cocked her head, looking thoughtful. "Damn, you know, that's actually true. I would never have attacked anyone else like that. Not anyone I didn't want to kill. But I knew you could take it. Where'd you learn to fight like that?"

"I was born a Croagh aet Brech, of the Tannoch clan."

"I've fought Croagh before. Sparring, mind you. None of them could fight like that. And the Raibrech isn't strong enough to block the spell I used on you."

"I've been through a bit more than the average highlander. I've picked up a few things along the way." He turned and started heading up the road.

"Wait." She jogged up to him. He took wicked pleasure in seeing that she moved carefully. That kick he landed was going to leave a nasty bruise. Like on her entire midsection. "Maybe we can start over. I was a jackass. After the last few weeks, even Evon is lucky I didn't kill him."

"She came close," her companion said from behind her.

"Yeah. It's been rough. My best friend was killed and I... anyway, I was wrong. I'm usually not such a bitch. Please, can we start over, be civil?"

"*I* was civil," he said.

"You were. I admit it. It's all my fault. That bad energy, that anger, it's gone now. Beat out of me, as it were. Plus, I'm exhausted and sore. Just a little bit of your time. We're near Dartford and you seem to be heading that way. How about I ride ahead, have a meal waiting for you all when you arrive. I'll pay for it. I'd just like to talk a bit."

Aeden wasn't sure it was worth the trouble. Fahtin, of course, looked hopeful, eyes wide. Aila gave a little shrug. Tere put his arrow back in his back quiver and faced Aeden, not really giving any indication of his preference. The two assassins—former assassins—studied Marla in a way that either meant they were formulating opinions about her or they were going to dissect her later. Raki nodded vigorously. Khrazhti, under her hood, was expressionless, taking it all in. Urun was humming to himself, looking Marla over.

"Fine. We'll be there in a few hours."

"Great. It'll be closer to two, I think. I'll see you there."

Raki stepped forward. "Masters?"

"What?" Marla said.

"That one, Evon? He said you wouldn't want to explain killing someone to the masters. Are you a hero, from the Academy?"

She scrutinized him, then slowly nodded. "Yeah, we both are."

"I knew it," Raki said.

"We'll tell you all about it when we eat, okay?"

The boy nodded so firmly Aeden thought he might hurt his neck.

Marla got on her horse and Evon on his. The young man kept glancing at Fahtin, almost as if he knew her. Fahtin only met his eyes once, and quickly looked away. Aeden supposed he was simply interested in her. She was gorgeous, after all. He sometimes overlooked that because she was like his sister. In everything but blood, she *was* his sister.

"Anyway," he said. "Let's get moving. The reward of free food when we get to the inn is a good enough incentive to pick up the pace, don't you think?"

He left them staring at him, half of them with their mouths open, until it probably occurred to them they should hurry and catch up before he ate all the food set out.

35

Aeden was the first through the door to the inn's common room. Josef, the innkeeper, spotted him and came over.

"Marla has reserved a private dining room for you and your friends. Please follow me."

Aeden raised his eyebrows and did as asked. The others filed in behind him, wending their way through the tables and chairs, down a hallway with four doors. The inn keeper stopped at the second door on the left and opened it, stepping aside so they could enter.

"I will have Daphne come to you immediately. Bread and ale are on the table already. Let me know if you need anything else."

"Thank you," Aeden said as the man walked back toward the common room.

Inside, Marla and Evon were sitting by the fire, a mug in front of each of them. She stood.

"Welcome," she said, sounding much more jovial and calm than she had earlier. "Help yourself to what's here. We can order some food when Daphne comes."

Everyone moved around the table, choosing a seat and sitting. A few grabbed mugs, others of them tasted the bread.

No one spoke.

"I really do have to apologize, Aeden," Marla said. "I'm difficult to get along with sometimes, but I am rarely that rude."

Evon, standing next to her, nodded, though he seemed distracted, looking at Fahtin but trying not to appear to be looking.

"It's no excuse, but it's been difficult, aggravating, and dangerous for me lately. I let it sour my mood and I'm sorry I took it out on you. In a way, I'm glad, though. If someone else had raised my ire, I would probably have given them some serious bruises. Instead, I have the bruises and have learned a lesson from it all."

"What lesson?" Aeden asked, still not sure if he wanted to simply sit and chat with this woman.

"Don't judge a warrior by his appearance, maybe? You have armor, but you dress like a Gypta. Who'd have thought one of the People could fight like that, let alone use magic."

"What do you know of the Gypta?" Raki asked, a bite in his voice.

"She wasn't clear," Evon said. "It's just that the Gypta are known for their craft, not their combat prowess. I've made something of a study of the People. I greatly admire your families." Again, his eyes flashed toward Fahtin, who dropped her eyes. She had been watching his mouth just a moment before. Evon cleared his throat.

"What I'd like to know," Marla continued, "is how you took a simple spell from the Raibrech and made it that powerful."

Aeden's suspicion was triggered. "How do you know about the Raibrech? My people don't exactly make it a secret, but it's not openly talked about with outsiders, either."

She raised her mug to him. "Evon has his fascination with the Gypta, and I have done my fair share of research into the Croagh."

"Why?"

"Look at me, Aeden. I have red hair and green eyes. Can you tell me that you haven't suspected that I have some Croagh blood in me? For that matter, your barely clad companion there"—she gestured toward Lily with her mug —"looks to be at least part highlander as well."

"I had noticed," Aeden said.

"As had I, with myself. I wanted to know what my possible ancestors were like, what their culture was, how they lived."

"Your *possible* ancestors?" Aeden said.

"Yes. I...I'm not sure what my ancestry is. I was found in front of the gate at the Academy when I was an infant. I've no idea who my real parents were."

A flash of an image brightened in Aeden's mind. Rain, fire, a baby crying. The reason he rarely spoke when he was a child.

"That's terrible," Fahtin said. "Someone just put you there where an animal could have eaten you?"

"I hardly think that was the case," Marla said, "though I can't know. I would assume if they went to the trouble of bringing me to Sitor-Kanda, they probably watched until the groundskeeper found me and brought me inside."

"The groundskeeper?" Tere asked.

"Yes. The Academy has no use for infants. The groundskeeper took me into his home, adopted me, raised me as his own. At least until I was able to be accepted into the Academy. But none of that is important. The point is that I think I have highlander blood in my veins, so I learned what I could about the Croagh."

An awkward silence reigned until Daphne came in to ask

them what food they wanted brought. Of the choices, the roast chicken sounded best to Aeden. The others asked for stew, mutton, or fish. The inn was a major waypoint and this was their high season, so they prepared great quantities and varieties of food.

After Daphne left, Aeden studied Marla. She did look like a Croagh. The hair, the eyes, even her body, they all seemed so familiar. She would have fit into any of his clan's meetings without a doubt.

"Would you like to get a room upstairs and take her there," Aila whispered in his ear, making him blink. He hadn't realized he had been staring at the woman for as long as he had.

"Marla," he said, doing his best to ignore Aila, "do you remember anything? Anything at all from before you were left at the Academy?"

"Psht," Aila said. "People don't remember things from when they were an infant. That's ridiculous."

"I do," Aeden said. "I used to dream it. It repeated often when I was a child and I still experience that dream occasionally."

"Yeah," Marla said. "I have a dream, too, like that. I've had it since I was little also."

Aeden leaned forward. "Will you tell me?"

Marla actually looked uncomfortable. "It's nothing, just a silly dream."

"I'd like to hear it."

"What about yours?" she asked. "Will you tell us?"

"I will."

"Then you first."

He sighed. "Fine. It was when I was just an infant myself. I was swaddled in a rough cloth. It was raining, but I wasn't cold. A giant man—he seemed that way to me, anyway—was holding me and we were near a fire. There were others around, all giants compared to me. They were making sounds, talking in a language I didn't understand yet.

"Then there was a flash of lightning and a boom that shook my entire body. A squealing cry rang out nearby, the screeching I understood better than the language of the adults. My head lolled and I blinked to focus, finally seeing another person, this one a woman, holding another bundle of cloth. That bundle was crying, scared by the thunder, no doubt, but probably cold, too. The rain fell on all of us, but the other bundle wasn't near the fire.

"The man holding me and the woman holding the bundle talked in soft, sad tones. The bundle cried again and the man spoke more harshly. The woman took the bundle away and I never heard from or saw it again.

"For much of my young life, I was quiet, rarely speaking unless absolutely necessary. The dream seemed to tell me that if I made noise, I would disappear, too. In my child's mind, I equated making noise with death.

"I often wondered what it all meant, what happened. The man, of course, was my father, our clan chieftain, and the woman was my mother. The other bundle, well—"

Marla's face had gone white. Her green eyes were liquid and she blinked at Aeden, a twisted look of understanding and dread on her beautiful face.

"It can't be," she whispered. "It can't...I can't." She stopped speaking abruptly and looked around, suddenly embarrassed to find everyone staring at her.

She took a deep breath and let it out slowly. "My dream. I too was near a fire, but too far to feel its warmth. Something was going on, something that felt like doom, but I couldn't understand it. Why couldn't I tell the one holding me that I was scared? The shadows seemed to close in on me and I felt things falling from the sky on me. A loud boom shook me and I cried, trying to tell the giant person how scared I was. She brought her face close to mine, red hair framing it and blocking out everything else, and made comforting noises.

"Then I saw a face in the arms of another person. It looked at me and blinked. I tried to reach out, but my arms wouldn't work like they should have. For a moment, I met eyes with the other one like me, wrapped in cloth and being held, then harsh, guttural words made the one holding me respond with sadness. Soothing whispers reached my tiny ears and we were suddenly moving, farther from the fire. I continued to cry, but it did no good.

"I only felt the abandonment as I lay there on the stone step with huge doors in front of me. I knew somehow that time had passed, but didn't understand enough to judge how long it had been. The only other thing I knew was that I had been found lacking, unworthy of being loved."

The dining room was silent, only the popping of the fire breaking the silence. Marla sniffed and Aeden looked up, focusing on her.

"It's impossible," he said. "I found, after suffering through the dream and my thoughts for many years, that there was an obscure law in my clan. If the clan chief sired twins and one was female, that one would be sacrificed because she would leach power from her brother, who would eventually become clan chief. Though they tried to keep it secret, I found out that had only happened once in the entire history of our clan.

"With my father. With my...sister."

Marla's composure broke completely. Tears streamed down her face. She seemed unaware or unconcerned that the others were there.

Aeden found he was crying, too. He stepped over to her and tentatively put his arms around her, bringing her into his embrace. She stood motionless, but then brought her arms around him and returned the hug. As she shuddered in his arms, he said to her, "You look like her, you know. Our mother."

❧ 36 ❧

In the middle of their emotional time, Daphne came in bringing the first of the food. She started and almost dropped the platters of chicken she was carrying when she first saw the two embracing and then noted the tears in Marla's eyes.

The two siblings held each other for a time, until the tears slowed and then finally stopped. Marla pulled away from Aeden and wiped her damp face.

"I haven't cried like that since...no, I've never cried like that. Daphne will be going straight to Josef to tell him. You can expect him to poke his head in and check on us shortly." She laughed, and the sound of it was like a breath of wind over a fire on a winter's day.

"Miera," he said. "That was our mother's name."

"Fire beauty," Marla said. She obviously knew at least a bit of the Chorain language.

"And father, our clan chief, was called Sartan Tannoch."

"Great Strength," she said, smiling. "Clan chief, eh?"

"Aye. Oh, Marla, I wish you'd have known them. Father was the perfect image of a highland chieftain. Strong, wise, fair, and honorable. Mother was strong, but she was also kind and gentle. She could kill someone, but always tempered her judgment with her caring heart. They were the perfect complement to each other."

"Were?"

Aeden dropped his eyes and frowned. "Yes. I'm afraid they're both dead. I'll tell you about it later. It's a very involved story. For now, let me introduce you to my friends and family.

"Here is Fahtin Achaya, my adopted sister. She's the one who found me, nearly dead, and nursed me back to health. Her father, the leader of our family, took me in as a son. Raki Sinde is like a little brother to me. He has been with me since we first left the caravan."

Marla nodded to them, and readily accepted Fahtin's hug. "I'm Marla Shrike, as you may have heard."

"I always wanted a sister," Fahtin said. "In addition to the bratty brother I already have." She made a show of sticking her tongue out at Aeden.

Aeden smiled. He'd known Fahtin would take to the woman as soon as she saw the tears.

Raki waved at Marla, then looked down immediately. He had become better at dealing with people, but he was still shy when confronted with a beautiful woman he didn't know, especially a hero of the Academy. Now that the venom had left Marla's actions, Aeden saw that she was indeed beautiful, as much so as his mother, who had been the envy of everyone in the clan, before and after her marriage to his father.

"Oh," Marla said, "This is my friend and, increasingly my conscience, Evon Desconse." He stood then bowed to Fahtin and Raki. "*Mei sain avar, avar sai ik.*"

Fahtin smiled and clapped her hands. "*Jai avar sai ik, ais bhi mei sain ik.*" Raki did so as well, actually looking the other young man in the eye.

"It's rare for outsiders to care enough to learn the greetings," Aeden said.

"I have a preoccupation with the People and have studied them a fair amount. I read a bit of Dantogyptain as well. Fascinating language." He turned to Fahtin, finally looking at her in a non-furtive way. "I'm glad to see you escaped safely and appear to be unharmed."

"Escaped?" she asked.

"Yes. From the animaru who had you as a prisoner. I have to apologize for leaving, but—"

"She's *that* girl?" Marla said. "I knew she looked familiar. Damn. I'm sorry, Fahtin. Evon wanted to stay and find you, bring you to a safe place, but I told him we had to move on, that you had already crawled away and you could take care of yourself. It was true, but I regretted the decision after we had gotten a few hours away."

Fahtin's eyes lit up. "Oh! You. The red hair. Aeden, these are the ones who attacked the group of animaru who held me captive. These are the ones who saved me."

"No, no," Evon said. "We only provided a diversion. You had already slipped your bonds and were well on the way to freedom. I just wanted to apologize for not helping more."

"You saved my life, no matter what you say. Thank you. Both of you."

"Curious," Aeden said, "that we were so close to meeting but didn't."

"Maybe it wasn't time yet," Evon said.

Conversation paused. Aeden thought about what Evon had just said, and apparently the others did, too. After a moment, he cleared his throat.

"This one here," Aeden said, "is Tere Chizzit. He's also—"

"The oldest one here, by far," the old archer said, giving Aeden a look that said in no uncertain terms he didn't want his other name bandied about. "It's an honor to meet you,

Marla, Evon. Any family of Aeden's is a friend of mine."
Under his breath, he added, "It's a good thing he stopped me
or I'd have put a hole in your head."

Aeden continued to introduce his friends, one by one,
until everyone knew each other. Both Evon and Marla looked
curiously at Khrazhti's cloaked and hooded form when Aeden
introduced her, but they forgot about that when, as
predicted, Josef the inn keeper entered the room, bringing in
the last of the food. He raised an eyebrow at Marla and she
waved his concern away.

"Josef here is a friend," she said. "We go way back. Josef, I
would like to introduce to you my twin brother, Aeden."

"Oh," he said. "Oh! Twin brother? Gods, I can see it, now
that you mention it. Why didn't you tell me when you were
here before? For Marla's kin, I'd give you a special rate on
rooms."

Aeden laughed. "Thanks, I appreciate it."

"We're fine for now, Josef," Marla said. "Thank you so
much."

"It's no problem, Marla. Let me know if you need
anything else."

They began eating and chatting when Evon gasped. All
eyes went to him. Aeden thought he might be choking. "I just
figured it out, Marla. Oh, I wish Master Aeid had lived to see
this."

"Evon gets excited by apparently trivial things," Marla
said. "A lot. What are you going on about Evon?"

"I realized the mistake we've been making with the
Bhagant."

"The Bhavisyaganant?" Aeden asked.

"Yes, the...how do you know that name?"

"It's kind of a long story," Aeden said. "I'll tell you about it
later."

"Oh, right. Anyway, we've been wrong all this time. Marla,

I've told you for years that you're the Malatirsay, but I was wrong."

Marla continued chewing her food as if what he said wasn't anything of consequence. "I told you that you were. It doesn't feel right somehow."

"Yes, yes. I'm telling you, though, I figured out our error. The plurality, it's not meant to signify importance or honor, or not only that, anyway. It's plural. The Malatirsay isn't one person, but two."

"Two?" Fahtin asked, getting wrapped up in Evon's excitement.

"Yes, two. Marla and Aeden are the Malatirsay. Together."

Aeden nearly choked on his food, but managed to drink a gulp of water to wash it down. "No. The Master of Prophecy at the Academy told me yesterday I wasn't. He said he already knew who it was."

"Do you remember the name of the master you talked to?"

"Umm, it was Marn something."

"Marn Tiscomb?" Marla asked.

"Aye."

"He's a moron. Gods, he's barely a master. They should have pushed him out a third-story window years ago."

"Marla," Evon said. "Be nice." He turned to Aeden. "She's partially right, though. Marn was made master when the other one was murdered a short time ago. The pool of qualified candidates was a bit shallow."

"There was even talk of asking Evon," Marla added. "His specialty is prophecy, and he was the old master's First Student, *assector pruma*." She leaned in close and whispered, "Don't tell Evon, but our nickname for that title is First Ass."

Evon rolled his eyes at her, but otherwise ignored the last part. "I wouldn't have taken it. I'm too young to be a master."

"You'd be a better choice than any of the others, especially Marn."

Evon glared at her. "You're distracting us, Marla. Aeden, if you read the Song, you'd see there are criteria upon which to recognize the Malatirsay."

"Oh," Aeden said. "You mean like the ninth and the twelfth quatrains?

Golga ua rotta aun utta
Malatirsay mortiyu dutrota sain
Deh morita sain ma tutta deh stirota sain
Sunha jintoka deh apruta sain

MALATIRSAY, SAU DEH KATATA SAIN
Ik do dah baneta sai, ma ik dah adata sai
Alaga ma laya paru
Dvara dabana agni deh joddita dara sain

ARE THOSE WHAT YOU'RE TALKING ABOUT?"

Evon's mouth dropped open and he stared at Aeden. "Uh, yes. Exactly those things. How did you know?"

"Aeden has the entire Song memorized, in Dantogyptain," Fahtin said. "You should hear him sing it. It's beautiful. That's how he does his magic, with the words of power from the Song..." She trailed off when she caught sight of him shaking his head at her.

"Oh, come on, Aeden," she said. "It's your sister. You can tell her."

"I'm sorry, Evon," Aeden said. "You were saying?"

"Do you know what those words mean?" Evon asked.

"Roughly," Aeden said, "though my translations may not be completely accurate.

Hero from the east and north

Malatirsay faces death
Dying but living still
Learns the secret to prevail

MALATIRSAY, SPLIT ASUNDER
One to two, but back to one
Separated but brought whole
Welded by the fire's touch

"THAT'S ABOUT AS CLOSE AS I CAN GET."

Evon sputtered, then cleared his throat. "That's...very good."

"Thank you," Aeden said. "I didn't mean to interrupt you. Please continue with what you were saying, Evon."

"I...oh! Well, there were phrases in there that didn't seem right. I've always had problems with them, even when it was generally recognized that Marla was the Malatirsay. She's the most accomplished student the Academy has ever had and, well, it was just thought she was the one. Not by everyone, by any means, but a lot of people believed. But it didn't seem to fit completely. Now it does. You two, together, are the ones we've been waiting three thousand years for."

Aeden noticed Tere nodding his head. All he could think was that the master had told him he wasn't the one. He wasn't sure if he was more disappointed by the master's statement or disheartened by Evon's.

"Incidentally," Evon Desconse said, "why did you go to the Academy?"

"There were several reasons," Aeden answered, "but the main one was to tell them I was told I was the Malatirsay."

"Told by whom?"

Aeden ran his hand through his hair. "Uh, maybe it would

be better if I just told you our whole story. Things are going to get complicated unless you know it all."

"That sounds good to me," Marla said. "After we get that out of the way, I can tell you what we've been up to. I think it would interest you."

❧ 37 ❧

Aeden told the tale of his life; being cast out of his clan, then being found and nursed back to health by the Gypta. He described finding his clan slaughtered and how his father told him the secret of harming the animaru, then his subsequent departure from the family. He only hit the highpoints, realizing that if he told the tale in its entirety, they'd be listening to him all night. The others jumped in with details now and then, but the tale they told was in no way complete.

When Tere told his part of the story, Lily couldn't resist telling them who Tere really was. Aeden supposed she had to or there would have been questions about why the two assassins had so easily switched sides.

It was another surprise when he told how Khrazhti was the leader of the animaru but then realized her honor demanded that she follow the laws her god had given her, even if he didn't do so himself. Aeden nodded at the blue woman to doff her cloak, and the eyes of the two Academy heroes widened.

"And that pretty much brings us up to where we are now."

Aeden reached for his mug. His throat was dry from talking so much.

Evon and Marla stared at Tere, seeming to be at a loss for what to say.

"I'd appreciate it if you'd keep that little secret," Tere said. "Let the dead man remain dead."

Evon blinked twice at the archer and then nodded. Marla's mouth grew into a huge smile.

"Damn, how I loved those stories about Erent Caahs when I was younger. Oh, who am I kidding. I still love them. It's an honor, sir. It really is."

"Oh, don't make a big deal of it," Tere griped. "Most of the stories were wildly exaggerated."

Aeden caught Marla's eyes and shook his head, mouthing "no." She winked at him.

"I can see you, Aeden," Tere said.

"Anyway, that's our story," Aeden said. "Your turn."

Marla told what Aeden realized instantly was a barebones version of her story.

"It all started with the death of Master Aeid, the Master of the School of Prophecy. Because the other masters needed to—by tradition—focus entirely on replacing him as soon as possible, several of the upper level students were allowed to investigate the murder.

"We probably don't need to talk about specifics, but we were led on a merry chase that almost killed us and did kill our friend Skril. We found the one responsible, but each time we got close, he escaped from us. We were heading back to the Academy when we met you. I'd been captured, chained, beaten, cut, suffered the death of my friend, attacked by bandits, and came out of the whole thing with nothing to show for it.

"Oh, and we met some of those animaru. Obviously." She nodded toward Fahtin. "They're tough bastards to kill without using magic." She winced and looked over at Khrazhti. "Uh, sorry."

Khrazhti looked at Aeden, obviously confused as to why the woman was apologizing to her.

"She's saying she's sorry for calling the animaru bastards," Aeden clarified.

Khrazhti nodded. "She is not using the term literally but in a pejorative sense."

"Right."

Marla shook her head. "I still can't get over meeting you, Khrazhti. If it weren't for me meeting my twin brother today, and finding out Erent Caahs was still alive and sitting across from me, that would have been the highlight of the day, the year. I thought all animaru were mindless beasts, rampaging and just trying to kill."

"They are," Khrazhti said with a straight face. Marla froze. Aeden laughed, then Khrazhti smiled at him. "Was that correct?"

"that was fantastic," he said. He shifted to speak to Marla. "She's been trying to get her mind around our humor. I'd say she's got it."

Marla chuckled awkwardly, letting it build into an actual laugh. "I have to say, you had me fooled. Nicely done."

"Thank you." Khrazhti bowed her blue head to Marla. "To be truthful, however, the seren animaru you have mostly seen are as you describe. They are the lesser troops, the ones sent in first to fight face-to-face in large groups. The other classes have their own qualities. All have one thing in common, however. They want to turn Dizhelim to a dark world with no life, like Aruzhelim."

"I see," Marla said. "So, Aeden, you went to tell them you're the Malatirsay and to try to get help with beating the animaru troops."

"Essentially. We also wanted to warn them of the animaru

threat in case they hadn't heard. The creatures have been attacking villages, wiping them out so that no one escapes to report their presence. They did it with my village, wiping out our entire clan, including Mother and Father."

Marla gritted her teeth. She had sufficient reason to hate the dark invaders already. Ensuring she never saw her parents was just another log on the fire of her hatred.

"You need to come to the Academy with us," she said. "We'll talk with the masters—the competent masters—and see what we can do to help. Will you come?"

Aeden only had to consider it for a moment. He had no desire to go back to that place after the reception he had gotten, but if they could help him, it would be worth it.

"I will, but we have to hurry. The animaru are gaining numbers quickly and they need to be stopped."

Marla took a long drink from her mug. "I'll tell you what. You come with me to meet the masters, and I'll go with you to try to stop them. It'll at least make me feel like I'm doing something. We're at a dead end on our own mission. We lost track of the one we were chasing."

"That sounds great. In the morning?"

"That'll work."

"Wonderful. Maybe we can chat a little. You know, about our home. I wish I could show it to you..."

"I'd like that," Marla said. "Then you can come to see my home. I *can* show you that."

They were on the road early the next morning, heading back the way they had come the day before. Marla and Evon held their horses' reins and walked alongside the beasts.

Aeden and Marla had talked until late the night before, Fahtin, Raki, Evon, and Khrazhti staying with them while the others moved to the common room to relax. He couldn't learn enough about his newly found sister and her life in the Hero Academy.

Instead of stopping in Bridgeguard, they crossed the bridge and pushed through to arrive at Sitor-Kanda shortly after nightfall. They had no trouble getting in. Everyone, it seemed, knew Marla and Evon. Aeden's sister ran ahead to try to get a few of the masters to meet with them and Evon led them to a meeting room the two students had agreed on.

While they waited, Aeden chatted with his friends, especially Khrazhti, who looked even more isolated than normal.

"Are you okay?" he asked her. "You look nervous."

"I am fine," she said, too quickly.

"Khrazhti?"

Her eyes met his and then skittered away. "This place. It was built to train those who want to kill the animaru. I understand and I agree with having training facilities for warfare, but I am animaru, Aeden."

"You're half animaru," he said.

"What if the masters want to kill me or to capture me and pry information from me?"

"I won't let them do that."

"I am not afraid of them doing so, but if they try to capture or kill me, I will fight. I do not want you or any of my other friends to be hurt if that happens."

"It won't come to that," he said. "You can keep the cloak on and the hood down so they can't see that you're different. Stay on the edge of the room. It'll be fine."

"I will not be captured," she said. "I must help you to defeat the animaru, but I will not let them take me. I will never be a prisoner again."

He patted her shoulder. "You won't. If they try, we'll fight together."

She nodded and adjusted the hood so it shadowed her face.

Marla came into the room, leading three of what Aeden assumed were masters of the Academy. She hadn't even stopped walking as she rattled off the names of those standing there.

"...and you know Evon, of course. This," she gestured toward Aeden, "is Aeden Tannoch. Among other things, he is my long-lost twin brother.

"For the masters, let me present to you Isegrith Palus, our Master of Fundamental Magic."

Isegrith was a tall woman in green robes that had no sleeves. Instead, the arms of her tunic poked through, dark brown with circles cut out to show the white linen below them, the same linen that poked out of the sleeves at the wrist and ended in a bit of lace. She nodded her head toward Aeden, her hair a mixture of grey streaks and the original dark brown color. Her angular face caught the light of the torches set around the room, but in any light, this woman would look dignified. She seemed to have the presence of a master, unlike the one Aeden had met before.

"Yxna Hagenai is the Master of Edged Weapons," Marla said, indicating another woman, this one a bit shorter than the previous master. Her eyes crinkled as she smiled.

"It is a privilege to meet you, Aeden. All of you. Marla is at once the bane of my existence and the love of my life. The reason for my grey hair and my greatest triumph." She smiled fondly at Marla, who suddenly found her hands fascinating.

Yxna wore a simple leather jerkin and—of all things—snug britches. Her grey hair was pulled into a tail behind her with parts of it braided along her head, and there was no trace of what color it used to be. Marla must be a terror to turn the woman's whole head grey like that. The most disconcerting thing about her, though, was that around her steel-grey eyes, her face was as smooth as Marla's. She had to be older—you didn't become a master when you hadn't seen many decades of life—but her oval face made her seem much too young. If it wasn't for the hair, he would have guessed she had seen less than thirty years.

She stepped up to clasp wrists with Aeden in greeting and he found himself mesmerized by the fluidity and grace of her movements. He found himself staring at her and quickly said, "It is an honor to meet you, Master Hagenai."

"And this," Marla said, "is our headmaster, Master Qydus Okvius."

The whip-thin man stood with feet spread apart and his arms crossed in front of his chest. He didn't wear robes, but loose pants and a tunic with wide cloth shoulders and a narrowing waistline. The top of his head was completely bald and seemed to come to a point, offsetting his sharp chin. At least, from what Aeden could see, it was sharp. He had a bushy mustache and a beard that left his cheeks bare but which hung down to the middle of his chest, where it was banded together with a gold ring. His sharp brows were drawn down into what seemed to be a perpetual scowl, crinkling the skin around his dark, small eyes.

He didn't look very friendly to Aeden, but he put his hand out anyway. The man wrapped his sharp, bony fingers around Aeden's forearm as Aeden did the same for him. He had a firm grip.

"It's an honor to meet you as well, Headmaster."

The master nodded, but Aeden could see no change in expression under the white hair on his face.

"So," Marla began.

"Where is the animaru?" the headmaster asked, his voice smoother and more soothing than Aeden had imagined it would be. He was looking right at Khrazhti.

"The cloaked one," Marla said.

He stepped up to her. "Please, remove the hood and cloak, child. I would see you with my own eyes."

Khrazhti's head swung toward Aeden, who tensed. Would

they have to fight their way out of this place? He shifted his weight in preparation, but found Yxna staring at his movements. He gave Khrazhti a slight nod.

She took the hood down, then unwrapped herself from the cloak.

The headmaster's face went through a shocking and immediate transformation. His eyebrows shot up and the mouth beneath his bushy mustache jumped up into a smile. He gently took Khrazhti's hand.

"You are magnificent," he said to her, bringing her hand up to kiss it lightly. "And so beautiful. I had not imagined the dark creatures of the prophecy to be so enjoyable to look upon."

Khrazhti's confusion was palpable. Her face darkened to a deeper blue. "I thank you," she said.

It was only then that Aeden realized the headmaster had been speaking the animaru dialect of Alaqotim, or at least close enough to be almost indistinguishable.

"Ah," he said, releasing her hand. He began speaking in Ruthrin so the others could understand. "So it is as I deduced. You *do* speak classical Alaqotim. Marvelous, marvelous. You understand Ruthrin as well, I am told?"

Khrazhti smiled and nodded. "I do. Aeden has taught me much, as well as my other friends."

"Very good. Come, let us sit. There is much to discuss."

The tension seemed to break in the room as the masters took seats and the others followed suit.

Isegrith Palus sat ramrod straight in her chair, as Aeden had expected from her posture and poise thus far. She cleared her throat softly. "We are to understand that you are Marla's twin brother, raised by your parents in the Cridheargla?"

"That is partially true, Master Palus—"

"There is no need to be so formal, Aeden. You may call me Isegrith, or Master Isegrith if you insist, and I am sure the other masters would agree that stuffy titles will do nothing but distract."

The other two masters nodded.

"Thank you, Master Isegrith," Aeden said. "I was only raised to adolescence by my clan."

"Where did you go then?"

"I...failed the test of magic and was sentenced to be beaten to death. Our father, the clan chief, had the obligation to strike the fatal blow after I had been beaten nearly to the end. He struck me unconscious, but did not kill me."

"It was a mistake?" Qydus asked.

"No, sir. My father was a supreme warrior. He did not want to kill me. They left me, however, and I most likely would have died if Fahtin had not found me and nursed me back to health. Her family adopted me and I lived to adulthood with the Gypta."

"The Gypta, you say?" Isegrith asked.

"Aye. I am as much Gypta as Croagh, maybe more so."

"The Gypta are a fascinating people," Qydus said, nodding toward Evon, "as some of our students know. There is magic in Gypta blood, more than most."

"I found that out. Raki's grandmother taught me the Bhavisyaganant, and when I began learning it, I discovered how to use my clan's magic. The magic I failed to use in my trial."

"I notice you have both tattoos," Master Yxna said. Aeden was beginning to think these people knew everything. How did she know about the sacred tattoos?

"We found my father," Aeden said. "The animaru had wiped out my clan. As he lay dying, he asked me to perform some of the spells of the Raibrech. When I did so, he, as clan chief, marked me as having completed the trial."

"I see," she said, grey eyes surprisingly sympathetic. "I am sorry for your loss. Your mother?"

"She lay near where we found my father, already dead. Torn apart by dark claws."

"Excuse us for a moment," Qydus said, stepping over to one wall. Isegrith gestured with her hand and the room immediately became silent, even the footsteps of the masters not making a sound.

"What was that?" Aeden asked. His voice sounded normal. Could the others hear him?

"A minor spell to keep us from hearing what they're saying," Marla said.

They only conversed for a few moments before returning.

"You were born to the Croagh," Qydus said, "were rendered virtually dead, became a Gypta, learned magic, fought animaru, and were reunited with your twin sister whom you didn't know existed?"

"Aye."

"And you were able to harm these animaru?" Yxna asked.

"Yes. I found that many of the spells of the Raibrech are life magic, which harms them."

"And your friend, Khrazhti?" Qydus pressed.

"We fought and with the help of my friends, especially Urun, who suppressed her magic, we defeated her. When she realized that her god S'ru had been false, she gave up her position as his high priestess and joined us. She doesn't want them to destroy our world any more than we do."

"I see." Qydus rubbed his beard, eyes going from Aeden to Khrazhti to Marla. After what seemed to be a long time, he continued. "We have been mistaken. Marla told us Evon's theory and we agree. I believe you and Marla together are the Malatirsay." He winked at Evon. "And I believe we should have been more forceful in our argument about who should have been named Master of Prophecy, age conventions and technicalities be damned.

"You have our support, Aeden, and Marla has always had

it. It may take a time for us to convince the other masters, but I believe it can be done. For now, please take my assurance that we will help you in whatever way we can. You two are the reason this institution exists."

Aeden's knees grew week and he knew he would have fallen if he wasn't already sitting. Marla beamed, her green eyes afire, and his friends all seemed to be happy for the statement as well, if the smiles were any indication.

"Thank you, Master Qydus. Knowing we have your support is an immense help. We would also like to describe to you all we know about the animaru and their plans. Khrazhti especially will be vital for this."

"Of course," Qydus said. "Also, once we can arrange it, it would be advantageous for you to receive what training we can provide. Marla has trained here most of her life, but you had to learn on your own. We would like to help supplement the skills you already possess, which I hear are considerable." The old man winked at Marla. She must have told him about the duel.

"That would be great," Aeden said, "but there is something we need to do first."

38

The masters left, Master Qydus promising he would discuss them with the other masters and do all he could to help. As soon as the door closed behind them, Aeden turned to Marla.

"We'd like to stay, but we have something that needs to be done. There's someone we need to track down and stop from bringing more animaru over to Dizhelim."

"I'll help in any way I can," Marla said.

"Aeden," Fahtin said. "We still don't know where to find Benzal. Maybe Marla can—"

"Did you say Benzal?" Marla asked. "As in Izhrod Benzal?"

Aeden's heart skipped a beat. "Yes. Do you know him?" He hadn't named the man when he was telling his tale, not seeing it as important.

"Izhrod Benzal is an arrogant, pretentious fop who believes he is the culmination of all the gods' blessings on Dizhelim."

"And a ruthless and petty bastard on top of that," Evon added.

Aeden smiled at them. "So you do know him. Well, we're going to kill him."

Marla put her hands up. "Whoa, whoa. Let's take a step back. Maybe it's time you told us the whole story of what's going on. It sounds like you skipped some details before."

"Yeah," Lily said. She'd been relatively quiet the entire time, as if she actually respected the masters. "I've only heard bits and pieces, too. It would be nice to know exactly what we jumped into the middle of."

"Fine, fine," Aeden said. "I'll give you more details, but it's going to take some time."

"Then we better get comfortable," Marla said.

Everyone seemed impressed when he explained more fully how Khrazhti reacted when she found out that humans die forever and that S'ru had ignored his own precepts. Jia and Lily smiled at her, and she returned the expression in kind.

The interaction with the Epradotirum—something he had glossed over completely before—got some raised eyebrows. Aeden hadn't even told Tere and the others about the ancient hunter and a few got thoughtful looks over the account.

Marla and Evon were interested in the assassins who had graduated from the Academy, especially Darkcaller. Lily and Jia gave more information about the Falxen, and then Tere took up the story with his group's experiences in Praesturi.

Finally, Aeden explained how they battled and killed Khrazhti's own father, though he didn't state what Suuksis was to the blue woman, and how when they were finished, Benzal spoke to them from the other tower.

"And then he stepped through the doorway and the device next to it started to smoke and melt and eventually stopped working. When we reached the other tower, it was little more than a pile of slag and there was no doorway any longer."

"Did you see through the doorway?" Marla asked. "Were there any details that might help?"

"We couldn't see through it from where we were."

Aeden's sister shook the red hair from her face and tapped her finger on the table. "Teleportation hubs are very costly, both in magic and in supplies. They can transport people and things almost anywhere, but identical devices have to be built on either side and activated before they can be used. Once activated, they last a short time before the magic they channel builds up and overloads them, destroying them. Because of that, they are rarely used except in time-critical operations. Even then, the planning involved is complex because of how long it takes to build them and to place them at either location.

"There is only one reason I can think of for Benzal to use a hub: he wanted to get to another favorable location to open a portal to Aruzhelim before the time period elapsed. Using a hub, he would have been able to open a portal in one location, then transport to another and open another portal there."

Evon expounded, "You see, opening rifts to other worlds are very precise and prohibitive activities. As Khrazhti explained to you, certain times and locations are favorable for opening a portal. You wait for months to open one, then there is a limit to how many animaru can be brought over. The number and magical potency of the ones brought over are dependent on the total magic possible for any individual rift point. But if the portal opener can be in two favorable places in the same day..."

Aeden sighed. "Then they can essentially bring twice as many animaru over. *Andorin recoat du acci rudis flagranti.* We not only missed out on killing Benzal, but he probably opened another portal that same day."

"That's my guess, too," Marla said, a wry smile on her face at Aeden's curse.

"Then you see how important it is for us to stop him. He's been bringing them over for more than half a year."

Khrazhti nodded. "As more powerful animaru come over, they will focus on destroying the Gneisprumay. It was my primary responsibility when I led the animaru who were here."

"Gneisprumay?" Evon said. "First enemies?"

Khrazhti nodded. "Or primary foe. It is the one in our prophecy about this time. Aeden is the Gneisprumay."

"Hey," Marla said. "No fair. You're not allowed to be mentioned in a prophecy without me." She showed all her teeth to him.

Aeden laughed. "You can be mentioned in all the others. I've found that being part of prophecy is a good way to get lots of people to try to kill you. She's right, though. Already, Benzal is focusing on bringing over more important, more powerful, animaru. Soon, they'll have enough here so that even with the Academy's help, it may not be enough."

"Oh, come on," Marla said. "You're not giving us enough credit. I mean, how many animaru could there be?"

Khrazhti looked grave. "Some have been destroyed since we came here, something we did not know was possible except by S'ru himself."

Marla gave the blue woman a wary look. "Khrazhti, about how many were there when you first started coming over to Dizhelim?"

She answered without hesitating to think. "Three hundred fifty-two thousand, one hundred twenty-four."

The entire group sat in stunned silence until Marla finally spoke.

"The gods help us. Even if they were all those simple beasts, we couldn't stand up to that many."

"There are many that are not seren," Khrazhti said. "Many that can use magic or have skills that are inherently magical themselves."

"Now you see why we have to stop him from bringing more over," Aeden said. "If we can't, then we're lost. We don't even know where to start looking for Benzal."

"Whew!" Marla said. "I guess it's a good thing I know where he'll be."

"You do?" Aeden asked.

"Almost completely certain. Anyone who was in close proximity to Izhrod Benzal for more than an hour or so could probably guess. You have to understand the little prig, but once you do, he's not so hard to predict.

"He fancies himself just short of royalty. His parents are both high-level priests of Surus in Kruzekstan, as were several generations of Benzals. He drones on and on about it. One of the things he likes to talk about is an old fortress that has been in his family for ages. Iscopsuru—it means 'rock of Surus'—has been abandoned for longer than he has been alive, but for some reason he thinks it makes him sound important. He told me about it when I first met him and he was trying to get me into his bed." Marla shuddered. "Ew. As if.

"I'm betting that's where he has set up his operation. He's trying to be a ruler in his own right, and to really feel like a ruler, you need a castle, or at least a fortress that makes you feel like you're in a castle. I'm betting that's where we'll find him."

"And it's in Kruzekstan?" Aeden asked.

"Yes, not too far from Nanris, but far enough so that the fortress has held no interest for anyone else. It's in one of the mountains, foothills to the Aerie Mountains, really."

Aeden nodded, rubbing his chin. "That would fit with the

direction we were going before Khrazhti lost her ability to sense him."

"Yeah," Marla said. "We're going to talk about that. Khrazhti and Tere felt strange effects in the magic of the world. We felt something, too, but not at the same time. It may all be related."

"That sounds good, but Benzal is our first priority. We don't know when the next time window when he can open a portal will come. We need to take him out now."

"I agree," Marla said. "I can get us supplies and we can borrow horses from the Academy. It should help us to move faster than we can on foot."

"Let's not take this lightly, though," Evon said. "Benzal is an arrogant blowhard, but he is an accomplished mage. Besides mastering the school of fundamental magic, he's also mastered fire magic and had advanced training in several other magical disciplines. He has adequate combat skills as well."

Tere looked thoughtful. "You know him that well?"

"Not so well," Evon said, "but everyone here knows everybody else's education and achievements."

The others around the table looked confused, and Aeden didn't think he was following what Evon was saying, either. "Can you explain that a little further?"

"Oh. Sure."

"It's like this," Marla said. "Sitor-Kanda is separated into forty-nine schools. There are certain subjects all students must study—history, scholarship, fundamental magic, language—but there are no strict requirements for what a particular student pursues for mastery.

"A student can gain competency in subjects, but in order to truly graduate and be considered a representative of the Academy, each student must gain mastery of at least three schools. It's an infrequent enough occurrence that when someone does gain mastery of a school, everyone else knows about it."

"And you're saying that Benzal has mastered his three already?" Aeden asked.

"Yes," Evon said. "He's mastered preparation—pretty much everyone masters that one—fundamental magic, fire magic, and magical transmission. As I said, he's a competent combatant as well, mainly with the sword, but those are the four he's mastered."

Fahtin raised her hand to get Evon's attention and he smiled at her. "Four. Does that make him average or better or worse than most students?"

Marla tsked. "It's better than most. Many of the students take nearly their whole lifetime to master three or four schools. Some students never get their three."

Evon laughed. "Yes, and some students have mastered more than anyone in history, even though they're younger than most who get their first mastery."

Marla's mouth turned down into a frown, but she didn't respond.

"Really?" Aila said. "That's pretty impressive. How many schools and what age?"

Evon showed a mischievous smile and looked right at Marla. "Oh, I don't know. How many and how old are you, Marla?"

Aeden wasn't surprised in the least Evon had been talking about her.

"It's not important," Marla said. "We have other things to discuss."

Evon laughed again. "Not quite twenty years old and seventeen schools mastered...so far. Our histories show that the most schools anyone previously mastered was fourteen, and that was by a renowned student who came close to being proclaimed the Malatirsay. He was sixty-seven at the time he mastered his fourteenth school, however, and argued success-fully that if he had been the Malatirsay, the darkness would have come decades before."

"It's not seventeen," Marla said. "Yet. I have three I need to take the final test for, so technically it's only fourteen."

"Those are just formalities," Evon said. "You've already passed all the other requirements and only need to perform the practicals. You've never failed one of those."

"Anyway," Marla said, "the point is that though Benzal is laughable in many ways, he is competent, especially when it comes to magic. Best not to underestimate him."

"We won't," Aeden said. "But the man has to be stopped. He's bringing over more animaru every time there's a window of time during which he can do so."

Marla stood up. "I'll go and start getting what we need. The masters have authorized all of you to use guest rooms for tonight. I suggest you make use of them. Tomorrow morning, we'll leave. Even by horse, it'll take us ten or more days to get to Kruzekstan. We can do all our talking on the road."

Before she left, Aeden grabbed her shoulder and pulled her aside. "I want to thank you for everything you're doing."

She smiled. "Anything for my little brother."

"I don't know which of us was born first," he said.

"I know. But I like the sound of that better than 'my older brother.'"

"Okay," he laughed. "Seriously, though, thank you."

"Aeden, we have a job to do. Together. I'm sure we don't know everything that's going on right now, but I'd bet that Benzal is a big part of it. It's the right thing to do, chasing after him. We'll show that bastard what a real Malatirsay can do."

"Oh, did you know?"

"Know what?"

"That he thinks *he's* the Malatirsay? He told Khrazhti

when they were working together, and he told me before he went through that doorway."

Marla's smile grew wicked. "Of course he does. We'll have to convince him he's wrong then, won't we?"

"Aye." Aeden matched her smile. "That we will."

❧ 39 ❧

Evon showed the travelers to their rooms while Marla prepared for the trip. It had been an eventful few days, and it seemed the others felt as worn out as Aeden did. He lay down and was asleep in no time.

Marla knocked on his door the next morning. The world was still dark outside his window, but the unmistakable lightening of pre-dawn crept through the blackness. He was introduced to his horse Snowmane, a dark chestnut stallion with a mane of bright white hair, and set about checking the girth straps and adjusting the stirrups.

Khrazhti stood nearby, eyeing the horse she'd been given to use. Twilight was a grey mare and she stood stiffly, one huge eye watching Khrazhti carefully. It looked like a standoff if ever Aeden had seen one.

"You've never ridden before?" Aeden asked.

"I do not climb upon beasts when my legs work well enough," she said. Marla had given the animaru a primer on how to ride, assuring them that Twilight was gentle and mild. "Must I do this?"

"I'm sorry, Khrazhti, but we're going to be traveling fast. You need to ride her."

"Very well. Give me a moment to try to reason with the creature."

Aeden's eyebrows raised at that, but he nodded and prepared his own mount, watching the blue woman from the edge of his sight.

She spoke her own language to the horse, almost too softly for Aeden to hear. "You will cooperate with me," Khrazhti said, "and I will not tear out your throat and leave you for others to eat you. Do not test me in this."

Her voice had a pleasant tone but what she said was as blatant a threat as ever Aeden had heard. He chuckled, making sure he was facing his own horse so Khrazhti didn't see him. If it worked out for her, he didn't blame her one bit.

Before the sun had more than cracked the horizon, they were riding out of the stables toward the front gates of the Academy. Khrazhti sat her saddle stiffly, but she'd loosen up eventually. Twilight occasionally turned her head to glance at her rider, but plodded along behind Marla's horse without complaint.

They were on their way.

The miles passed more quickly than Aeden would have believed. They stopped each evening—either to camp or to enjoy the rare rooms in an inn—but made steady progress eastward. They passed near Drugancairn and through Hosen —Tere sighed and looked longingly toward the northern edge of the town—and continued on the North Road. It seemed a different world altogether from the saddle, though the vantage point was not that much higher than walking, really.

As they entered the twisting parts of the road that went near the highlands, Aeden's mood soured. All the memories of the place assailed him, especially the most recent, the ones of finding his clan. Or what had been left of it.

Fahtin seemed to understand. She rode next to him, speaking to him of the family and other times they had passed this place or ones that looked like it, trying to take his mind off what had happened so short a time ago. Ever glancing to his left, to the north, he listened and nodded, but his heart was still darkened and his breathing labored.

Soon, the very northern edge of the Aerie Mountains appeared off to their right, the indication that they were coming to the end of the Cridheargla and entering the borders of Kruzekstan. They would be getting close to where they would find their prey, and then they could end all of this. Aeden thought of what had happened to his family because of Benzal and his fingers itched to draw his swords.

A man appeared suddenly out of the brush to the right of the road. He spotted the horses and ran toward them, a shambling gait that Aeden figured was caused by an injury. Sure enough, when the man was close enough, the red along his leg was visible, staining the tan color of the cloth.

"Please," the man said. "Please. Monsters attacking our village. We're not fighters, most of us, but even the ones who are can't seem to kill them. They are struck down and they simply get back up and attack again. Help us."

Aeden hesitated for a moment, but only a moment. His mission to end Benzal was important, but this man's friends and family were dying right now.

"Where is your village?" Aeden asked. The man pointed and Aeden prodded his horse into the vegetation, following the obvious trail the man had blazed in his escape. He didn't wait to see what his friends would do; he didn't need to. If they came, they could help, but if they didn't, that was fine, too. The villagers wouldn't be able to defend themselves from monsters that could shrug off blows of normal weapons.

Just a day before, Aeden had gone around to each of his friends and cast the spell to endow their weapons with life magic. It was a foregone conclusion that they would be fighting the dark beasts eventually. He was sure Benzal had surrounded himself with them. The Croagh was glad of his preemptive action now, as he plowed through the vegetation, because he didn't need to stop to make their weapons suitable now.

It wasn't a great distance until the tips of roofs rose above the squat trees, and then he was out onto a cleared area, the structures visible in front of him. All around them, dark bodies swirled, slashing at every person they could find.

Aeden growled and leaped off the horse before it had stopped completely. His forward momentum caused him to land with his weight shifted ahead of him, so he let his leg collapse, turning it into a roll. As he came out of the somersault, he drew both his swords and charged the nearest animaru, a group of three chasing after a woman.

By the time he stopped, three dark bodies lay on the ground, one still twitching. Aeden turned in time to evade swipes from two more of the monsters. He spun, cutting the arm off one and slashing down the side of the other. They both screamed at him and rushed to attack him again. An arrow sprouted from each of their heads. Aeden waved to Tere and Lily in thanks and moved on, working toward the largest concentration of animaru.

Barely registering that his friends had all joined the attack and were carving a path through the monsters, Aeden slammed into a group of more than a dozen animaru ahead of him. They seemed to be focused on one thing, but Aeden couldn't see what it was because there were too many of the creatures blocking his vision.

He cut, spun, slashed, and dodged as he made his way to where they had all been looking, finally breaking through to get a good look.

A man was there, attacking and defending, trying to keep

the animaru from getting past him to a group of children huddled together, all trying to hide behind a woman holding a sword.

Aeden stopped cold, stunned. The man was obviously skilled, though his weapon couldn't kill the beasts in front of him. He must have realized that, but he continued fighting his desperate battle, trying uselessly to protect the children. Aeden watched for a moment, nearly falling prey to claws raking at him from the side. His reflexes saved him, guiding his sword to cut down the attacking monsters, but he never took his eyes from the man.

He recognized that fighting style, knew it as well as he knew his own. When the man made gestures with the hand not wielding a sword, it threatened to shatter Aeden's focus completely.

Aeden shook his head. The middle of a fight was not time to lose track of what was going on around him, something he knew better than to let happen. He cut down two more animaru near him and pushed on to get closer to the man.

"Light to Conquer Darkness," he yelled. The man's head snapped toward Aeden, but then his attention was taken by the four enemies in front of him doing their best to tear him apart. One of them scored the man's shoulder with its claws.

"Light to Conquer Darkness, Codaghan damn you. Cast it. Cast it on your sword, now!" Aeden's voice cracked at the end, his eyes inexplicably blurring with tears.

The man's eyes widened, but he did as Aeden had commanded. The motions were not the ones Aeden used currently since he had found a more efficient way, but seeing them broke the dam in Aeden's eyes and the tears flowed freely so he could barely see the slight telltale glow of the magic taking effect.

Both men seemed to gather strength and speed and began to cut down the animaru in earnest. Aeden moved closer so that they stood side-to-side, a little more than sword-length away, and they set about trying to destroy all the remaining foes.

"How did you know?" the man said in the predictable brogue.

It made Aeden smile, but this was not the time for it. "Later," he said, and continued.

It was over soon after that. Aeden's friends eventually made it over to him and the man he fought beside, and the last of the animaru was killed—interestingly enough—by Khrazhti as she headed toward Aeden.

The man slumped, exhausted. He said a few words to the woman and she assured him the children were safe. Aeden waited to see what would happen.

The man took a breath and stood up straight. He walked over, his eyes locked onto Aeden's. The man narrowed his and inspected Aeden's face, then his eyes went wide and he gripped his sword more tightly.

"Aeden?"

Aeden answered calmly. "Greimich."

"I...you...how..." He gritted his teeth and stared at his boyhood friend. "You're dead."

"That's news to me, "Aeden answered. "I could say the same of you. The animaru slaughtered our clan. I found my father as he died, the last of us."

"But you...it was years ago. You were to be killed for failing the trial of magic."

"Aye, about that." Aeden pulled the sleeve up on his right arm and showed Greimich his tattoo. "I was a bit late, but my father had me demonstrate the Raibrech as he died and he gave me the mark."

"Then you're not cast out? You're of the clan?"

"I'm not sure how that works, but my father, our clan

chief, marked me and gave me his blessing. I'd say that makes me part of the clan."

Greimich nodded, stunned. Then his face scrunched up and tears started to flow. He threw his sword on the ground and wrapped his arms around Aeden, squeezing for all he was worth.

"I can't believe it," Greimich said. "I thought everyone in our clan was dead. I thought you were dead, but here you are. My Bratharlain. Not only that, but my clan chief as well."

Aeden returned the hug. "I had thought all the Tannochs were dead as well, but you survived somehow. I'll need to hear that story, but that's for later. The villagers will be needing us to help. My friend Urun is a priest of Osulin and he can heal. Are you injured?"

Greimich released his friend and stepped back, wiping at his eyes. "I'm not hurt much. Have him work on the others. These little cuts are nothing compared to what we got in the trials—what *you* gave me in the trials."

"Ach." Aeden slipped easily back into how he used to speak with his friend. "So you remember that bit, do you?"

"Always." Greimich noticed that everyone was standing around him and Aeden, staring at the two of them as if they had lost their minds. He turned to the woman who had been helping protect the children. "Aeden Tannoch, my blade brother, I want to present to you my wife, Catriona Ailgid Tannoch."

"Catriona *Ailgid* Tannoch. It's my privilege to meet you. I'll need to hear the tale of this marriage. I don't think I've ever heard of an Ailgid marrying a Tannoch. No doubt it's an interesting story full of danger.

"As for you, Greimich, I would like to introduce my friends to you, but perhaps it can wait until we see what aid we can give these people."

"Aye. I only just got here a few weeks back, but these people have been kind to me. I'll meet you later."

"Yes." Aeden clasped wrists with his friend, smiling as widely as he could remember since...well since he found out about Marla.

Almost half the village's one hundred and four residents were dead or seriously injured. Urun was able to help the worst of them, and Aeden used his own minor healing spells to aid others. Evon knew a little healing magic as well and aided as he could. Those with field medicine skills—Aila, Jia, Tere, Lily, and Marla—helped others. The rest of Aeden's friends, including Khrazhti, dragged the bodies of the animaru outside of town and burned them. Though the burning created a great cloud of billowing smoke, the wind carried it away from the village.

They finally all sat down as the sun was setting. The villagers cooked a large meal and everyone sat around in the village center eating and sharing tales of the day. Those who had lost people mourned, prayed, and talked with those who remained to them.

Greimich found Aeden slumped on a chair one of the villagers had brought out for him.

"How did you know?" Greimich asked him. "About the Raibrech and how to harm the monsters?"

"My father. As he lay dying, he told me they had figured it out right at the end. Life magic can destroy the animaru. They're not alive. They're more magic and unalive. Because of that, the life magic is one of the only things that hurts them. Other magic can harm them, but not destroy them."

One of the villagers offered Greimich a cup. It smelled like the same ale Aeden was drinking. Greimich took it with a smile and a "thank you."

"How did you survive, Aeden? The warriors came back to the village, all of them in a dark mood. It's never a good thing to have to cast anyone out of the clan, but a dark cloud seemed to hang over the village for a week. I found out much later, after I had become a clan warrior and taken part in one of the *daodh gnath* what it was all about. I mourned you all over again. Up until then, I had thought they had simply cast you out and you were living in the wilds. You had the skills."

"My father, again," Aeden said. "I puzzled over it for a long time. But there was no way he could have made a mistake and not killed me. He was a warrior, our best. He didn't want to kill me. He went through the ritual because he had to—he was chief—but he didn't want to.

"I was found by—" Aeden's attention was taken when Fahtin walked up. She looked exhausted, even more tired than Aeden felt. He immediately took her hand, stood up from his chair, and led her to sit in it. Then he sat on the ground beside her. "I was found by this beautiful woman here. Greimich, this is Fahtin Achaya. Her family's caravan was in the area and she found me, near to death. She nursed me to health and I was eventually adopted into the family."

"A Gypta family?" Greimich asked.

"Watch yourself," Aeden said in a dangerous tone, eyes locking onto his friend's. "The Gypta are an honorable people, more honorable than most, and kinder than almost all. They took me in when my clan did their best to kill me."

Greimich raised his hands. "I meant no offense. It's just surprising."

Aeden relaxed. "Aye, it may be at that, but I learned to sing and even to play an instrument, in a fashion. It was that music that opened my mind to finally grasp the Raibrech, and more. In any case, Fahtin is my sister and she is one of my favorite people in the world."

"Then I'm glad to meet you, Fahtin. Codaghan knows Aeden needs someone to look after him."

Fahtin smiled and shook Greimich's hand. "As do you,

apparently." She nodded toward Greimich's wife making her way over to them.

"You're right there," he said.

"An Ailgid, Greimich?" Aeden said.

"Watch yourself," he said, winking.

Aeden laughed. "Fair enough. But what's the story there?"

Greimich's wife sat on his lap, waving to Aeden and Fahtin. It appeared the two women had met earlier.

"I won't go on at length about how we met and fell in love. I know you don't like romantic tales. The important part is that I was away from the clan, meeting with her, when those creatures attacked our village and killed everyone. I was gone for several days—there's a cave we used to meet in between our clans' territory—and when I got back, I found everyone gone, a great pyre nothing but ashes. The corpses of these dark monsters still lay where they had been defeated, the few that there were.

"We headed for her clan, but those monsters had already reached them as well. Only a few lived, ones who were able to escape. One was a clan elder, who married us. We're essentially the only ones left of both our clans. Some of the other clans weren't attacked at all. It almost seemed like something else caught their attention and they left to chase it."

"Aye," Aeden said. "It was me. They've been chasing me ever since. I think they may have gone to the clans looking for me in the first place."

"But why, Aeden?"

Before he could speak, Aeden spotted Marla, Evon, and Aila walking toward them.

"Marla," Aeden shouted. "Can you come here, please."

She joined them with a wave for Catriona and a nod for Fahtin.

"Marla," Aeden said, "this is my boyhood friend, Greimich. Greimich, do you remember all those rumors when we were children, the ones about a twin sister who was sacrificed as per clan law when we were only babies?"

"Yes. I hated those rumors and only found out later that there really is such a clan law, as obscure as it is."

"Well, the rumors were true. Partially. Greimich, this is Marla. She is my twin sister."

Greimich's mouth dropped open. "Your what?"

"My sister. My mother took her off as I was being accepted by the clan, supposedly to end her life, but she couldn't. Just as my father couldn't end my life. My mother took Marla to Sitor-Kanda, the Hero Academy, and left her for them to raise. She grew up there and has done very well for herself."

Greimich shook hands with Marla, studying her face. "You look like her. I always thought Miera was the most beautiful woman in the world. I had the strongest childhood crush on her."

Greimich's wife cleared her throat loudly.

"Until I met Cat, of course."

Marla belted out a laugh. "I thank you, Greimich, though I'd advise against saying such things to other women in front of your wife." She winked toward Catriona.

Greimich waited for his wife to smile at him before continuing. "So there are three Tannochs still alive. Maybe the clan is not lost yet."

"Maybe," Aeden said, "though if we don't stop these animaru, there won't be hope for anyone. We're actually on our way to trying to put an end to them now. There's a man who has been making magical gateways so they can come from their dark world. We're going to stop him."

"I'll come with you, then," Greimich said. "I've nothing left in the highlands."

Aeden reached out and put his hand on his friend's arm. "No. You need to do something else. Even with the man dead, there are the animaru he has brought here already. We'll need to warn people, prepare them. You saw how they can't be killed unless you have the right kind of magic. You have to go and warn the clans. You're the only one who can do it. They won't listen to outsiders."

"They might listen to outsiders before they'd listen to us. We're from different clans, and you know how clans react when a different clan comes to their territory."

"But they have to know what has been happening. They will let you speak, and once you tell them about the animaru, maybe they'll listen. Some have to. It's been months since the Tannochs were slaughtered. I'm sure they sent scouts to look."

"He's right, Greimich," Catriona said. "You saw what they did here. These people aren't warriors, but warriors might as well be as these when it comes to fighting the monsters. If we ever plan on living in the Cridheargla again, we'll need to have a clear conscience that we tried to help the others. We're all Croagh, no matter the clan. Even if they won't listen to anything else, we can tell them how to hurt the creatures, give them a chance."

"Aye," Greimich said. "You speak sense. Okay, Aeden, we'll go warn the clans. You make sure that bastard suffers for bringing these monsters here."

"Oh, I plan on it, my brother. I plan on it."

❧ 40 ❧

arla drank wine and ate the food the villagers had been nice enough to prepare for them. She'd seen some hard fighting in the last several months, but nothing so one-sided as the villagers trying to fight the animaru. If these creatures were to move en masse through the countryside, they would obliterate any and all humans they found, whether they be simple villagers or Clavian Knights. How does one beat an opponent that can't be killed? They don't, not unless they have the magic necessary to kill them.

She had almost corrected Aeden and Greimich when they spoke about Benzal being the end to the only one bringing animaru over from Aruzhelim. It didn't add up. The dark creatures were getting to Dizhelim in some other way, not only through Benzal.

Fahtin's voice caught Marla's attention.

"Maybe you can answer a question for me, Greimich," the young Gypta said. "When asked if he was skilled as far as his clan was concerned, Aeden says that he was cast out because he lacked the skill to be approved. Personally, I think he's twisting words around. Was he a skilled warrior in relation to the rest of the clan, or was he an incompetent warrior, as he seems to claim?"

Aeden shook his head at Greimich. Marla was at an angle that allowed her to see it, though most of the others probably couldn't. She wanted to hear the answer to the question as well. If he was one of the lesser warriors in his clan, then she had a long way to go until she could match one of them in combat. At least, if she didn't use her magic.

"Aeden?" Greimich chuckled as if someone had told a good joke. "Incompetent?" He laughed out loud this time. "Aeden was the finest warrior anyone had seen since Raisor Tannoch. He once skirted a clan law that said he had to kill his opponent by demonstrating such skill, he brought his foe to the edge of death and then brought him back when the bout was called. He could beat anyone in the clan, probably his father included. We were shocked when he failed the trial of magic. He mastered everything he set his mind to."

"Wait," Catriona said. "You told me the only trial where the combatants fought to the death was the level four combat trial."

"Aye."

"But you told me you fought Aeden in that trial."

"Aye," Greimich said, smiling.

"You mean to tell us," Jia said, "that Aeden killed you and brought you back to life?"

"Something like that. The point is, that man sitting there is the perfect fighting machine. He probably could have fought his way out of the warriors who brought him to the edge of our territory and beat him nearly to death, except his honor wouldn't allow him to do that. Is that right, Aeden?"

"There's no reason to talk about that part of my past. I don't like to think on it."

"He's right," Fahtin said. "Let's talk about something else, like how I was right that Aeden was the best fighter."

Marla smiled as the conversation devolved into tales of a young Aeden fighting, excelling in his trials, and defeating bullies. She got up to walk around, not quite ready to settle into a sleepy stupor.

As she wandered around the village, seeing the children with their parents, it gave her a sense of satisfaction. They had saved these people from the animaru. These families, though many were affected by the deaths of other family members or close friends, would see the next day and eventually be happy again.

that was what the Academy should mean to its students. It was created to train the Malatirsay, but all but one who had ever gone through its doors were not the Malatirsay. Shouldn't those who graduated be applying themselves to being heroes as well? Those who used that knowledge to betray humankind, like Benzal, were abominations and deserved to die.

A man passed by her as her mood turned sour thinking about Benzal. He was carrying a small round item with little moving parts all over it. It looked kind of like an egg with little colored pins and knobs sticking out in all directions.

The sight of it made Marla's heart stop for a moment, then ache as it started up again. There couldn't be two of those in all of Dizhelim. It had belonged to her friend Skril, who had made it himself. He always carried it with him and was always fiddling with it.

"Excuse me," she said. "May I ask where you got that?"

"This here?" the man said, holding the item up. "Sure, it was off near Arcusheim. I don't live here in this village. I'm a messenger, though my horse was killed by those creatures so I'll need to get another before I can deliver anything. Anyway, I was looking for a place to stop for the night in a remote area to the southeast of the city and found the remains of a campfire. Scattered around it were bits of cloth and a few ruined items. This one wasn't damaged too bad. I plan on taking it back home, getting it shined up. Maybe it'll be worth something."

"Would you take three gold marks for it?"

The man's eyebrows shot up. "Three gold? There's no need for that. I'll give it to you." He handed it over.

She took it, reverently, and pressed the gold coins into his hand. "Take it. It'll help you in getting another horse. Thank you."

"No, ma'am, thank *you*, and not only for the gold. If it weren't for you folks, I'd have lost more than a horse. Anything I can ever do to pay you back, you let me know."

"Could you tell me exactly where this campfire was?" she asked.

"I surely could, can even draw you a map, if you like."

"That's very kind of you. I'd appreciate it."

He took out a sheet of paper from his messenger bag and sketched out a simple map with a few directions. "That should get you there." He didn't even ask her why she wanted to know. "Thank you again for saving us all. It was a good thing you were near."

She nodded as she looked over the map, then folded it and put it in her pouch. "It was my honor and responsibility to help the village. It's what we train for at the Academy."

"The Hero Academy? You're from there? Oh, it's a real pleasure to meet a hero, ma'am, no doubting. Thank you, thank you." He was still ducking his head as she walked away.

She caught Evon's attention and motioned for him to come to her. He did so, excusing himself from the group and stepped over.

She held up the map the messenger drew for her in one hand and the little toy in the other. "I know where Quentin is."

❦ 41 ❦

Aeden saddled Snowmane in the chill morning air. He had risen early, as normal, and gone through some of his exercise forms. He stole a bit of precious time to try to work through one of the Raibrech movements, attempting to find the more powerful spell locked within the common one he already knew.

He failed to determine the enhancement. Just as almost always.

He really didn't understand why the steps he had gone through to learn enhancements for other spells didn't work for the rest. It was as if he had to develop an entirely new way to learn with each spell. At this rate, it would be years before he improved his magic significantly.

He sighed, huffing a cloud in front of him. All he could do was to continue trying to improve. What had Evon said of the Academy? Most students worked day after day for most of their lives and didn't master more than a scant handful of the schools there. It took labor to become better than you were. Aeden knew that. He would keep trying.

Marla was up and checking on her own horse. She smiled at him from a dozen feet away, and he returned the expression, adding a wave.

She had come back to the fire the night before looking thoughtful. She was good at keeping her expression neutral, but Aeden was accomplished at perceiving subtle changes in facial features and body language. Maybe it was because she was so familiar to him, even though they had just met. Many of her mannerisms were eerily like their mother's. He would not press her about it, though. If her concerns affected the rest of them, she would tell them. At least, he thought so.

"Up early." She patted her horse's side and walked over.

"Aye. Habit. I like to train early, start the day with a bit of movement."

"I always hated early morning training sessions," she said. "I like evenings myself."

Aeden laughed.

"What?"

"Mother was like that. She was not fond of waking up before the sun had already cleared the horizon." His smile faded.

"I wish I had been able to see them before...you know."

"I wish the same. At the end, father showed pride in me. His belief had been vindicated. I don't doubt that mother had always been proud, too. They'd be proud of you. A hero in your own right, like Raisor Tannoch."

"Like Fiona Seachaid, thank you very much. I'm no hairy, sweaty mountain of a man."

"No, that you're not. You are a fierce, beautiful, imposing woman. Just like your mother. But really, a Seachaid?"

She winked at him and their conversation trailed off.

"We should get an early start," she finally said. "We've still a way to go yet, but we're getting closer."

He considered her for a moment, the very image of his mother standing before him. Like his mother, she kept her deep thoughts hidden. A wonderful, complex puzzle.

"You don't agree with sending Greimich to gather the clans?"

Her eyebrows widened a little but immediately went back to normal, her schooled expression placed again carefully. "It's not that. I agree it's a good idea, but not for the reasons you gave him."

"Why then?"

"Izhrod will not be the end of this. We will stop him and he will no longer bring animaru over, but I don't believe that the only task remaining will be to clean up those animaru that are left. I'm not sure what's happening, but I think it's deeper than just him. The very magic of Dizhelim seems to be changing. I think we're in for a war, not just a battle with Izhrod Benzal."

"Aye, I've had that feeling, too, but I don't want to share the news yet. People need to have hope. It's hard to hope when it seems everything you do doesn't matter."

She took his hand and squeezed it in both of her own. "I am so glad I met you, Aeden. My brother, my twin, my only family."

He brought his other hand up to wrap around hers. "Me too. All this Malatirsay rubbish aside, I am glad to have found you. Let's get the others up. We have some traveling to do today."

Aeden watched her walk toward where the others were starting to stir before following a few seconds later. It was true, what he told her, but there was more. All the talk about the Malatirsay really was something he'd rather not deal with.

At first, it was exciting when Jehira told him about it. Scary, yes, but exciting. As time went on and he realized how much of a responsibility it was, he became afraid that it might be true, then afraid that it might not be. He actively sought things to busy himself with so he didn't have time to go to the Academy. It had been better not to know.

To be the one named in prophecy, the one on whom the entire world relied, that was not something he desired. He never had felt right about the role, and that alone suggested he wasn't suited to it. It was a relief when Master Tiscomb told him he wasn't the one.

And now he'd found Marla, and it was clear that he was the Malatirsay, or at least half of it. It did feel more comfortable, sharing it with his twin sister. He was confident she and Evon and the masters were correct. He and Marla *were* the Malatirsay. They were responsible for saving the world from the animaru invasion. That somehow felt right. When he thought of his friends, those who had stuck with him through danger and difficulty, it increased his desire to fill the role he'd been given.

Yes, he had finally found his place. Not a Croagh, not a Gypta, but someone from both worlds, half a hero along with his sister, who he never knew existed, but had hoped did. A warm feeling washed over him, an assurance that things would be all right. He only needed to do his part—with his friends behind him and his sister beside him. He finally felt as if he could accomplish what was required.

A slow smile crept onto his face as his sister gently shook those still slumbering. He headed over to help her. They had a job to do, and they'd best get to it.

Greimich intercepted Aeden before he reached his friends.

"Cat and I are leaving. We're anxious to get to the clans and to share with them the information you gave us about those monsters. Especially how to kill them."

Aeden clasped wrists with his friend. "Good luck. Be careful, Greimich. Even with things changing, there will be many in the clans who won't welcome a Tannoch or an Ailgid."

"I know, but we have to try. Don't go and die again, Aeden. We still have a lot to talk about when this is all done."

"I'll do my best not to disappoint you," Aeden said. "I'm not sure what I'll be involved in after I finish off Benzal, but a good guess would be that I'll be most easily found at the Hero Academy. I'll look for you when I can, but I'm thinking we'll both be busy."

"I think you're right. Be safe. You can tell me the glorious story of your victory when we next meet."

"Aye," Aeden said. "And you can tell me of yours, how the clans made you king and united under your banner."

Aeden pulled his friend into a hug as Greimich laughed at the statement.

"You keep an eye on him, Cat," Aeden said. "He has a knack for getting into trouble and not being able to get himself out."

"I know it." She ruffled Greimich's hair. "I plan on keeping him around a bit longer, so I'll make sure to get him out of any pickles he finds himself in."

"Good, good." Aeden put his arms out and gave her a hug as well. "Both of you be safe. I have stories to tell you of when Greimich was young. Embarrassing stories. You won't want to miss out on those."

Catriona smiled as Greimich rolled his eyes. The friends locked gazes for a moment longer, then Greimich hitched his pack and the couple headed to the north. Aeden watched them until the foliage swallowed them up, then he joined his friends.

"Come on, now. Let's go. We've some traveling to do today."

Fahtin laughed. "I haven't heard that accent from you in years. Talking with your kin brought it back out in you."

Aeden shrugged. "It was nice hearing someone speak correctly for a change." He dodged Fahtin's playful swat and headed for Snowmane.

❧ 42 ❧

Urun was slow about getting up and getting ready to leave. He didn't much feel like traveling. Of course, he didn't feel much like staying in one place, either. The fact was, he wasn't comfortable doing anything. His days had been up and down since Aeden had talked to him and encouraged him, but today was definitely a down day.

He had gone off and prayed for more than two hours the night before, settling himself in a part of the forest near the village that had been untouched by the battle or the animaru. It was taking a risk being all alone with the dark monsters in the area, but he figured he would be safe enough. He could still make a shield and he would draw attention to himself long before any of the animaru could get through it.

And he needed to talk to Osulin.

He had prayed and begged and pleaded for her to speak to him, all to no avail. She was still silent. Aeden had convinced him that he shouldn't give up his service until he was sure he had been abandoned, but he was beginning to doubt even that. Yes, he was still able to wield the power she had given him, but why would she not give him direction?

The young priest had come back to camp more troubled than when he had left. He sat and listened to his friends talking, telling stories, seemingly unaware that he was suffering. Unaware or uncaring.

No, that was not it. They did care for him. They'd shown him that much. It was so hard to go on, though. Most of the time, he felt as if there was no reason to do so. If it weren't for how much he had grown to care for his friends, he probably would have gone back to the Grundenwald and waited for his goddess to give him direction, one way or another.

But he had stayed, and he would help Aeden and the others as much as he could, at least until Osulin removed her power from him or told him to do something else. How he hoped that wouldn't happen when they needed him most.

"Come on, now," Aeden said. "Let's go. We've some traveling to do today."

Urun strapped his bedroll to his horse and hefted himself into the saddle. They would find Benzal soon, and when they did, they would battle once again. They would win or they would lose. In either case, the mission they had been on for weeks would finally be over. What then? He was almost afraid to ask.

Villagers waved at them as they rode toward the main road. Many had thanked him personally for healing them the day before. He smiled and tried to act as if he were happy for the opportunity. The fact was, he did enjoy helping others, but each time he used his healing magic, it reminded him that his goddess had spurned any attempt at communicating with her. By the time they had left the village behind, his face hurt from forcing that smile and he wanted nothing more than to scowl at the road ahead of him.

His friends chatted around him, asking questions and

answering them, telling stories, and engaging in light-hearted banter. Not Urun. Better to be silent than to speak and betray his dark mood. So he rode alone at the back of the group and kept to himself. It had worked so far; no reason to change what was successful.

Time slipped away and Urun found himself blinking at the lengthening shadows around him. He had stopped his horse by reflex, but hadn't done anything else. He simply sat as all those around him dismounted and moved around what would obviously be their campsite for the evening.

Jia and Marla glanced at him, concern in their eyes, but only Aila approached him.

"Come on, Urun," she said. "You and I need to go find some wood for the fire. Let your horse rest. You can unsaddle her and brush her down when we've got the fire built."

He mechanically dismounted and followed Aila. Motion in his peripheral vision assured him someone had come to take his horse in hand, but he didn't care enough to see who it was.

After bringing several armloads of wood to the center of camp and taking care of his horse, Urun set up his bedroll near the edge of the little clearing his friends had found. He sat on it, eating the food handed to him and drinking from his water skin. Aila came and checked on him, and Aeden sat next to him to talk for a few minutes, but his companions knew enough to recognize when he wasn't going to engage. He felt a prick of conscience, but couldn't muster up the energy to even apologize for his behavior.

As normal of late, the sound of the others talking ebbed and flowed, rising in its pitch and energy and then retreating to a more subtle level. It was like the waves of the sea, he thought, and it mesmerized him, made him drowsy.

He didn't remember falling asleep, but a sudden jolt of realization hit him sometime later. The others were all lying down around him—all except Evon, who kept watch—and the soft sounds of deep breathing and the occasional snores or whistles spun in the air where conversation had such a short time ago. The sudden waking didn't concern him; probably just his subconscious mind telling him he needed to move around.

Urun got up, waving at Evon's raised eyebrows, and headed into the brush surrounding their campsite. The Academy student would probably assume Urun needed to answer nature's call, and he was right, but not as he probably thought. He needed neither to urinate or defecate, but to answer the burning need in him to commune with the natural world and to try, once again, to communicate with his goddess.

He found the perfect place a quarter mile away from the camp. It was far enough that he couldn't see the light from the low fire but close enough that he should be relatively safe from things prowling in the night. A flat, moss-covered stone had kept the area clear of vegetation, and he could see the quarter moon and the stars winking at him from the black velvet of the sky through the hole in the branches above him.

Before his knees even rested on the rock, he was praying, mostly internally, but also softly speaking the words. It had always been like that for him. Osulin could hear him without the sound, but speaking, even in low tones, seemed to deepen the connection for him.

"Osulin, my goddess," he said. "Please, I beg you, answer me, give me some sign. I fear I have disappointed you in some way, that I have failed you. Please, tell me what I have done and how I can correct it. I wish only to please you, to do your will. I..." his voice broke and he found himself weeping. "I...live to serve you. Please. What have I done wrong?

"I try, but I am weak. I can feel my sanity, my very self, slipping away from me. Soon, I fear, I won't be able to think clearly enough even to serve in the unacceptable way I now do. I need you."

A slight breeze rustled the nearby leaves. Urun continued to kneel, his head hanging down and tears dripping onto the moss beneath him. He felt so weak, as if he wouldn't even be able to make the short walk back to the camp. Maybe it was better that he stayed here, not eating or drinking, until he became part of the vegetation around him. The thought brought him a tiny piece of solace, that at least he could be part of nature in that tragic way.

Through his blurry eyes, he saw the shadow of his head on the moss-covered rock. It was as if the moon had suddenly become full, lighting the little area that was at this moment his whole world.

"Oh Urun," a voice came. He wasn't sure if it was in his mind or if he actually heard it.

His head snapped up to see, not the moon gone full, but a softly glowing apparition.

One that was familiar.

He put his head to the moss, tears streaming from his eyes anew. "My goddess."

"Urun," Osulin said. "Do not hide your eyes from me. Meet my gaze."

He did as commanded, raising his head to look at her. Even the soft glow made him squint and hurt his eyes even with the tears blurring his vision, but he blinked them away and in a moment, he grew accustomed to the light.

She stood on air, a few inches from the ground. Tall, beautiful, and powerful. Her dress seemed both made from leaves and vines and also part of her body itself. Long blonde hair, tinged with green, framed those forest green eyes, eyes that had seen thousands upon thousands of years.

Eyes that seemed both tired and sad.

"You see," she said. "You see the heaviness that weighs

upon me. I have had...difficulties of late, my one and only precious priest. I have had trials difficult even for the divine, and I am yet unsure if I can match them.

"I have seen you, Urun, and the troubles you have had. I have seen, but could do nothing, and for this I am sorry. I have been unable to use any of my energy to do so simple a thing as to speak to you, and you, for your part, decided I had abandoned you.

"That is the furthest from the truth of things, my priest. The guilt of it assails me constantly and causes me pain. I would have you know, first and foremost, that I will always be with you, my faithful servant.

"However, it has been all I could do to maintain the link to my power that you feel. Any more effort, and I feared I would have been lost, defeated by the forces arrayed against me. Please understand, precious one, that it was of necessity."

Urun nodded, too overwhelmed to speak at first. He was finally able to gather the strength and opened his mouth. "My lady Osulin, my goddess, what is it that assails you and how can you speak with me now if it might mean your defeat?"

"My tribulations are not for you to know. Not yet. As for the other, there are changes in the magic of the world. Have you not felt it? I have sipped a small excess of the magic from the world, new power I have not had access to for some time. I gathered it, cherished it, held it for use in speaking with you, my beloved priest.

"I cannot know if the changes will be for the good or for the ill, so far as you and I are concerned. Some of this magic, it seems, is natural, and other magics, unnatural. The balance of the world's power is a tenuous thing. Therefore I cannot tell you if I will be able to speak with you again soon. I needed to risk using the power, however, for you have come so close to the brink of damaging yourself. Your mind.

"Know that I am always with you, though it may seem I

am not. I will do what I may to speak with you again, but do not take my silence as disapproval. You must be strong, Urun Chinowa. You must do the things I currently cannot. You must carry on my work."

Urun lifted his chin. "I will. I'm sorry for being weak, for doubting."

"No," she said. "I'll not hear it. You were ignorant of events and acted acceptably. It is I who am to blame. But you know, now, you are precious to me and I will not leave you. Put away your doubt and your dark feelings and do my work."

"I will."

"I have puzzled out a way to harness an infinitesimal portion of the changing magic, how to grant you access to it. It will not steal from my own power, which I desperately need at present, but it will make you more powerful. Will you accept this gift, use it to continue my work?"

"Yes, my goddess, gladly and thankfully."

"Very well. Use it to aid the Malatirsay. There is more at stake than losing your world to darkness. Continue to faithfully serve, as you have always done."

She swept her hand toward him and an icy chill struck his skin. Then it sank into him, warming as it went, until it reached the very center of his being, both body and mind. The warmth grew and he noticed the shadows retreating from him. A soft light blossomed within him. It lasted for only a few moments, then faded. In the place of the warmth was a tingling, an energizing of all the smallest parts of his body.

He didn't feel tired. His doubts, so crushing minutes ago, evaporated like water sprinkled on a burning log.

Osulin smiled at him. A sad smile, he thought, but a smile nonetheless. "It is done. Please, continue to pray to me, to speak with me. In my own darkest times, knowing that you are faithfully doing my work has strengthened me, even if you do not know it. Continue, and I will speak with you again when I may."

She floated to him, took his hands in hers, then leaned in and kissed him. The warmth from those divine lips made the warmth he had felt before seem like a cold winter breeze. His body trembled and his eyes threatened to leak tears again.

"Be well, my priest," she said, her smile becoming more sincere. "I will come to you when I can and tell you what I am able. Keep me in your thoughts."

Urun swallowed the lump in his throat. "Always, my goddess. Always."

Urun got to his feet immediately after Osulin faded from his sight. The tears on his cheeks hadn't even dried as he slipped through the foliage back toward camp, brushing his outstretched hands along the leaves as he went. He gave no thought to how to find his way back; he sensed it.

He felt more connected than before. It was a sense of wonder he had not felt since Osulin first chose him to be her priest. Though the additional power she had granted him was small—in her own estimation—it felt as different as it had when she gave him his power originally.

The priest entered camp without a sound, the foliage refusing to allow his passing to be noticed. As he entered the edge of the clearing, however, Fahtin's head snapped toward him. Apparently, Evon's watch had ended and hers had begun.

"Oh," she said, slipping the knife she had drawn back into its sheath. "You startled me." The Gypta girl narrowed her eyes at him and looked him up and down. "Urun, you're glowing."

He grinned at her, the first genuine smile he could remember in a long time. "Yes. I've emerged from my dark mood. Osulin finally spoke to me. I am...better, now."

She shook her head. "No, you don't understand me. You are *glowing*. You are literally putting off light."

"Huh?" He looked down at his arms. He was lambent. "Osulin infused me with a little more power. It will probably fade."

"I hope so. No offense, but if it doesn't, we're going to have to cover you up when we're trying to travel at night. You're like a beacon."

"A beacon of hope, I hope." He chuckled.

"Get some sleep," she said. "We're starting early tomorrow. The final push to get to Benzal."

"I will. Thank you Fahtin."

"And Urun?"

"Yes?"

"I'm glad you're feeling better. We've all been worried for you."

"I'm fine, now. I won't let it happen again."

"That would make me happy."

"Me, too." He lay on his bedroll, covered himself with his cloak, and faded off to sleep, dreaming of long, green-tinged hair made of moonlight, and of twin emerald eyes.

❧ 43 ❧

"The way I see it," Evon said, "the two of you have magic that is emerging."

Fahtin cocked her head at him. "We have what?"

"Emerging magic. Latent power that has never been identified or nurtured. It happens occasionally, even now. It was much more prominent in the Age of Magic, but it can still happen."

They had stopped for the night, one day closer to finding Benzal.

"But," Raki said, "we never showed any sign of it until lately. Not in our whole lives. Why now?"

Evon leaned in toward Fahtin. "I've been thinking a lot about it, and about you." His eyes widened and he verbally stumbled, rushing through the next sentence. "You both, I mean. Uh, what's happening to both of you...and the magic."

Marla laughed and slapped Evon on the back. "Calm it down there. Slow your breathing and tell us what—*what*, I said, not *who*—you've been thinking about."

He eyed his friend, but took a breath as she suggested.

"Yes. Well, in their history, the Gypta people have been particularly well disposed to magic. Since the time of their wandering, the incidence of magical talent has been many times higher than the population at large."

"How do you know that?" Aeden asked.

"Oh, I have studied the Gypta for a long time. They are one of the most mistreated and misunderstood groups on Dizhelim. The history is fascinating, and I think the..." He trailed off as Marla rolled her eyes.

"Anyway," he continued. "Let's just say that I have learned a lot about them. Even how to speak Dantogyptain."

"Really?" Aeden said. "*Subajuta dara sai dantogyptain?*"

Evon smiled. "*Mo bajuta dara son chute dantogyptain, ma turah nahin.*"

"Very nice," Aeden said.

"I have a question for you now, Aeden," Evon said. "How is it that you, an adopted orphan, can speak the ancient language of the Gypta? Raki has admitted he can speak a few words, and Fahtin has said she can't speak any at all."

"Raki's nani, Jehira, made me learn it before she would teach me the Bhavisyaganant."

"You recited part of it before, but you know more? The whole Bhagant?" Evon asked.

"Aye."

The young man hopped on his seat with nervous energy. "Would you...could you recite it for me?"

"Uh..."

"Oh, Aeden," Fahtin said. "Go on. You sang the whole thing for Dannel. I, for one, can't hear it enough. Each time, it gives me chills and seems to affect me more strongly."

Aeden put his hand behind his neck and rubbed it. "I suppose I can."

"Wonderful," Evon said, clapping his hands.

Fahtin looked at the Academy student and smiled. Clapping like that was something she normally did. She hadn't met anyone else before with that habit.

Aeden cleared his throat, took a sip of water, and began to sing.

As with the other times she heard it, Fahtin felt as if she was caught up in a swirling windstorm, as if a warm breeze circled around her, carrying with it the softest silk. It caressed her, nearly massaged her, and generated in her such a sense of peace, her eyes welled up with emotion.

But there was something else this time, too. She felt a stirring inside her chest, like something coming alive. It vibrated to the rhythm of Aeden's voice as he sang, kept in time with the complex cadence of the Song.

Before she knew it, he was done and the power that had buoyed her up and carried her along faded, easing her back to her place on the log she was sitting on. She sighed, and suddenly felt like she could sleep for a week, but she also felt strangely energized.

She glanced around the fire. Everyone had been mesmerized by the Song. It was if they were slowly coming out of a trance, hesitant to let go of the feeling. Khrazhti stared wide-eyed at Aeden, her mouth open.

"that was fantastic!" Evon said. "Your pronunciation was perfect, so far as I can tell, and the meter. How did you learn that?"

"I heard Jehira sing it and I sort of picked it up," Aeden said.

"You *sort of* picked it up?" Marla asked. "I haven't studied the language, but I know it's one of the more difficult to master, mostly because it is probably the purest expression of magical power in existence. I could feel the power as you sang."

"that was nothing," he said. "You should see what it can

do when the words of power from the Song are paired with the correct gestures."

"I think I have seen," she said, rubbing her abdomen absently. "Or do you forget?"

"Oh. Aye."

"But back on subject," Evon said. "That gives you an indication as to the latent power some—including I—believe is in the Gypta blood. After all, Dantogyptain was their language." He turned back to Raki. "To answer your question from earlier, I believe the magic in the world is changing. Maybe only slightly, but changing nonetheless. Maybe that change is promoting your inherent magic. Have any of you felt anything strange lately, like something shifting?"

"We have," Aeden said. "We've told you about Khrazhti and myself feeling something different, when she lost her ability to sense Benzal."

"We've felt it, too," Tere said. "At least the one time when I lost my powers, but probably at least one other time, as well. But we've figured out the timeline and it didn't happen when the others felt theirs."

Fahtin shook her head. "Raki and I have talked about it and we didn't feel anything when Aeden and Khrazhti did."

"Ah," Evon said, "but I think you would feel it now, if it were to happen again. Start trying to pay special attention to what you're feeling. If something that you can't explain happens, let one of us know. When we get back to the Academy, we can study it properly, maybe help you two to develop your abilities further. You, too, Aeden. After all, the Academy was built for you and Marla. Our resources are yours."

Fahtin put her hand over her belly and took a breath. Her heart, or her tummy, or some part of her in that general area, had fluttered.

"Are you all right?" Evon asked.

"Yes," she said. "It just hit me that my adopted brother

and his twin sister are really the ones prophesied thousands of years ago. It's a little overwhelming."

"Tell me about it," Aeden said.

"It takes a little getting used to," Marla said. "I've been dancing with the idea that I'm the Malatirsay for years. I mainly tried not to think about it. This new thing, though, Aeden and me being the Malatirsay together. It...feels right."

"It does," Aeden said. "And it also feels right that Fahtin and Raki, my family and closest friends, would also have magic. I'd have been lost without them."

Fahtin reached over and hugged Aeden and he returned the embrace quickly. For some reason, Evon's cheeks seemed to color in the firelight. It was probably just a trick of the light.

She released Aeden and took Evon's hand in hers. "Thank you for your insight. I'll let you know if anything else happens or if I feel any magic. I can't wait to learn more about it."

"You're welcome," he said. His cheeks *were* reddening. It was probably all the excitement and the effects of the Song. Her own face grew warm. Why was Aeden looking at her that way, with that wry smile of his?

"I'm tired," she said abruptly, dropping Evon's hand. "I think I'll get to sleep. I have the second watch tonight."

❧ 44 ❧

Tere Chizzit had kept mostly to himself during the ride from the Academy. He still wrestled with what he had been forced to tell the others. With what they had figured out for themselves. He hadn't been careful enough, not nearly as cautious as he would have had to be with Lily around. He had to face it, he would never have been able to fool someone who had studied every little thing about his former life.

It seemed to be working out. Urun had been in the dark place where he'd spent the last few weeks, and the attention of most of the others was on him. Tere rode along, silently counting down the time until they got to Benzal and he could lose himself in mindless combat.

Urun had had some kind of revelation the night before last and now, today, he was back to his old self. Maybe he was even a bit more balanced than he had been before. It had been so long, it was hard to tell. It wouldn't take too much time until his friends started noticing how reserved Tere was.

It probably didn't matter. They knew who he had been.

Even the newcomers knew, the Academy students. Aeden's sister and her friend.

That had taken him by surprise, the existence of a twin for Aeden, and even more so when the arguments they made for the two of them being the Malatirsay together lined up perfectly. Tere had believed Aeden to be the hero from prophecy already, but this seemed even more likely.

But where did that leave him? He was still a failed hero, a coward who ran from his life and hid in the forest for decades. He was still running, not wanting to admit or remember those days. It still hurt after all this time.

It seemed while he was lost in thought, he had lagged behind the others. He sighed and clicked his tongue at his horse to speed up. What to do?

"Are you all right?" Lily asked from next to him. She rarely left his side, probably hoping he'd tell her some kind of secret that would instantly make her a famous hero. But that was too harsh. She was a good person, as far as he could tell, her former profession as an assassin notwithstanding. As she had pointed out, he had been essentially the same thing.

"Just thinking," he said. Better to keep it short.

"About what?"

"About how people always ask me stupid questions, like 'what are you thinking about?'"

She flashed her teeth at him. They were white and straight and perfect. He felt a smile trying to force its way onto his face, too, but he ruthlessly crushed it and maintained his sour expression. Gods, the woman was beautiful, though. How had she kept those perfect teeth when she ran around and played the hero—or assassin? She was good, that was how. She used her bow and she kept out of face-to-face combat, for the most part.

So she was smart, too. Of course she was; she idolized him. The smile slipped through and he cursed under his breath as her smile grew wider. Best to keep his thoughts where they belonged: on how horrible his life was.

"Do you want to talk to me?" she said. "It may help you work out whatever it is you're thinking about."

"No."

"Okay."

They rode on, silent and side-by-side. How long had it been since he'd been able to enjoy that, the speechless camaraderie? He shook his head, dispelling the thought. Time to focus on the future, on finding that bastard Benzal and putting an arrow through his eye.

He was still wrestling his considerations under control when the group stopped for the night.

The fire was burning, everyone had eaten, and they sat around jabbering. Tere didn't want any part of it. He figured he'd get to sleep early so he wouldn't have to pretend he was interested in conversation.

"Story time," Raki said, bouncing on his toes as he normally did when there was some sort of adventure to be described. "It's Tere's turn tonight."

Damn. He had completely forgotten that silly ritual. During story time, he had paid little attention for the entire trip, counting on getting to Benzal before they rolled around to his turn. Now, he was the last one to have a go at it.

"I can't think of a story I haven't told already," he said.

"How about a story about Erent Caahs," Evon said, eyes alight. "Archers always have stories about the hero. I know Lily had dozens of them. You must——" He stopped mid-sentence. "Oh, gods. I'm sorry, Tere, I...um...forgot for a moment."

Tere stared at the young man so intensely, Evon seemed to shrivel before the onslaught. He knew the boy hadn't done it on purpose. He guessed it was good in a way that he had forgotten who Tere was. Had been.

He sighed and deflated. "What the hell. I do have one story. A story that none of you have heard. Not even Lily." He nodded toward the beautiful redhead.

"I find that highly unlikely." She settled herself to listen.

"We'll see," Tere said. "This is the story of how it all caught up to Erent, and how he showed his true colors in the end. It's the truth of what happened to Erent Caahs."

It was as if everyone was frozen in place. Even Raki, ever excited about stories, screwed up his lips as if he might vomit. Aeden looked at Tere doubtfully, his expression seeming to say *you don't have to do this*.

But he did. He did. It was about time he got this weight off his shoulders. Maybe if they heard the truth, they would leave him alone. Lily would decide he wasn't worth emulating. They may even ask him to leave. That would be fine. He wanted to help them, truly he did, but he was so tired of playing the role he'd created all those years ago, it would be a relief to just be himself. If he could remember who he really was.

"I've told you about Raisor Tannoch, Toan Broos, and Lela Ganeva. At least, I've told Aeden, Raki, Fahtin, and Urun. Lily told some of it the other day." How had he remembered that? Wasn't he daydreaming at the time, not paying attention?

"Well, the three heroes traveled for several years together. Sometimes one or the other was missing, but Erent Caahs was always there, always traveling and trying to do what he could. And yes, earning a bit of money from some of it, too.

"Lela, of course, was still in Delver's Crossing, but he would stop by as often as he could to see her. Whenever he was within a hundred or two miles of her, he would visit, and with each visit he grew to love her more and more.

"She didn't press him to stop his wandering life, and it wasn't practical for her to join him because he would constantly fear for her safety. So they continued on, seeing each other when it was possible, but it was never nearly enough.

"Somewhere along the way, Toan Broos also fell in love with Lela.

"Now, Toan was more handsome than Erent. He had the form women seemed to like. Erent was blocky and large, malproportioned. Because of this, Toan proposed to Lela that she give up the waiting for Erent and marry him instead. Of course, he did this when Erent was off with Raisor on another adventure.

"Lela, for her part, had always been cool toward Toan, perhaps sensing his ambiguity. She told him she would never want to be with him, no matter if the entire world burned and they were the only two people left alive.

"Toan was unused to rejection. In his own mind, he explained it away. She had only told him that because she thought someone else could hear, or because she thought he was testing her for Erent. He knew she wanted him, could tell by the way she looked at him. He only needed to pave the way.

"So it was that while he traveled with Erent, and when he did not, he searched for a way to finally make Lela his own. All he needed to do was to give her the opportunity and he would enjoy the body he had come to dream of.

"Finally, he struck upon a plan. Several months he worked on it, fine-tuning the details, until he was ready to strike. He did so when Raisor went back to the highlands to visit his clan.

"Erent was on his way to Delver's Crossing when he got the message. Lela was in trouble and needed him right away. He followed the instructions in the message, knowing it was a trap, but not caring. The woman he loved might be in danger, and he would gladly give his life for her, if need be.

"He made it to the place described, a small clearing near the edge of the Greensward. There, he found Lela, hands bound and eyes covered with a blindfold.

"Erent searched the area before he stepped into the clearing, but detected no one else. As he stepped from the foliage, a racket on the other side of the clearing caught his attention and he nocked an arrow and drew it back, ready to loose.

"It was Toan Broos, rushing into the area like the fool he was.

"'Toan,' Erent said. 'I nearly skewered you. How many times have I told you not to rush into danger like that? It could have been a trap.'

"Toan looked down, abashed. 'I heard Lela was in danger and rushed here. Have you found anything?' Erent shook his head and stepped nearer Lela to free her. He didn't understand what was going on, but with his friend there to guard his back, he relaxed his guard.

"Toan got close to Erent, then cleared his throat to get the archer's attention. When Erent turned toward him, Toan Broos splashed a concoction in his face.

"Erent's eyes burned as if they were directly over the hottest flame. The pain was excruciating. Erent screamed as he jumped backward, tripping and landing on his back.

"Toan pulled the blindfold from Lela's eyes and she screamed. Erent's blue eyes, the ones Lela loved to look into, had been destroyed. They had turned white and no longer worked or moved. They were dead.

"'Come on, Lela,' Toan said. 'Now we can be together. We no longer have to pretend. He can't see you anymore, and you won't have to worry about those blue eyes following you. Come. Leave him to do what he will. We will be together.'

"Lela's full-armed slap split Toan's lip, but he wasn't fazed. 'Yes,' he whispered, 'make him think you don't want to be with me. It will make you feel less guilt.'

"'Erent,' she screamed. 'Oh, gods, Erent.' She tried to go to him, but Toan Broos pulled her away, dragging her out of the clearing.

"Erent Caahs felt like his face was on fire, that he would die, his brain boiling in his skull. But the woman he loved was being taken away and he feared for her life. He went down deep within himself and blocked out the pain, at least to a level he could form complete thoughts.

"He had always been able to see through the magical matrix; it's what gave him the ability to never miss his target. Now, though, with his regular sight ruined, his senses blossomed and he saw what had been possible the whole time. He could see as well as he had before. Better. It was strange, trying to move around and use only his magical sight, but he wasn't blind.

"And that bastard Toan was dragging away the woman he loved.

"He picked up his bow and the arrow he had nocked. He drew back, but the world spun crazily. His body was trying to adjust to his new sight. It was too much of a risk to try to shoot Toan. He would have to do it another way.

"'Toan!' he screamed, drawing his knives. 'Toan, how could you? You were my friend.'

"Toan laughed. 'We were never friends. I was always better than you, but you always got the glory. We'll see who is the great hero now. You won't be helping anyone. You can't even help yourself. Now you'll see that all the glory and the affection always belonged to me. Lela loves me, wants me, and now she's free.'

"This time, Lela balled her fist up before she struck him. He wasn't prepared, and the blow made him stumble. He touched his mouth and brought his finger back bloody.

"Then he slapped Lela across the face, sending her sprawling.

"'Fine,' Toan said. 'I was merciful because we have been traveling companions, but no more. It's probably better that you're dead. You wouldn't want to live your life as a blind man.' He drew his sword and stalked toward Erent.

"Erent had never trusted Toan completely for some reason. Maybe it was his senses telling him the man was false. In any case, Toan Broos didn't know about Erent's magical sight, and he had been far too wrapped up in himself to notice the things Erent had done around him. That proved to be advantageous to Erent Caahs now.

"Erent was still unsteady on his feet, but he evaded or deflected all of Toan's blows. The man was strong and agile, but he couldn't hit the more experienced man—one he had blinded—so he began to get more and more angry. His swings became wilder and wilder, and he was able to give Erent a few small gashes, though nothing serious.

"Toan took it as a sign he was about to gain victory and he continued relentlessly, hacking and slashing at his former friend. Erent saw his opening. Toan wound up for a powerful swipe and Erent stood, acting dazed, luring the man into his trap. As the blow descended, Erent shifted his feet, twisted the knife in his left hand slightly, and gripped his right-hand knife tightly.

"The sword came down, and Lela jumped in front of it to save Erent's life. The blade bit deeply into her shoulder, angling down into her chest and back, reaching halfway to her waist before stopping.

"Lela Ganeva died almost instantly. She had time to put her hand on Erent's ruined face and mouth *I love you* before her legs gave way and she slipped lifelessly to the ground."

Tere took a drink from his water skin, his mouth going suddenly dry. Ten sets of wide eyes stared at him, waiting. He cleared his throat and continued, barely able to keep his voice steady.

"Erent flicked his knife and cut a nerve in Toan's sword arm. The limb instantly went dead and his hand slipped off the sword. Erent twisted and bashed the pommel of his other knife into Toan's temple and the man dropped to the ground like a soaked rope.

"Lela was already dead. Erent held her, wanting to weep over her but unable because of his burned-out eyes. He kissed her face, still perfect but for the swollen lip Toan had given her. After a time, he laid her gently on the ground and arranged her arms to look as if she was simply resting. Then he turned his attention to Toan Broos.

"The man took a long time to die. He had chosen his ambush location well, for after many hours of screaming, no one had detected that the betrayer and his judge were there. Erent Caahs, the man people hailed as a hero, took Toan Broos apart, piece by piece, cutting or tearing—whichever would cause the most pain—and all the while keeping him alive. Erent knew field medicine, how to heal, and he used those skills to bring Toan back to consciousness over and over, simply to take more pieces and cause him more pain.

"It was his bone-weary fatigue and the knowledge he had still to build a pyre for his love that caused him to let Toan Broos die. He was sorry, in a way, that he didn't have days more to cause the man pain. If he did, still he wouldn't feel the tenth part of what Erent felt. Not from his ruined eyes, but from the beautiful, perfect corpse he could still see lying on the ground with his magical sight.

"He built a pyre and burned Lela Ganeva's body. Then he scattered his clothing, his gear, and the pieces of Toan Broos around the clearing and burned the entire place with tinder and oil he found stashed nearby, obviously the possessions of the betrayer.

"When Erent Caahs walked away from the clearing, he swore that the hero was no more. That man was dead and would never darken the landscape of humanity again. In his place was a blind, broken man he decided to call Tere Chizzit.

"After treating the burns to his face, minor compared to what the liquid had done to his eyes, he set off. Wandering for a time, he—I—entered the Grundenwald. It was, after all, where it all had started. A young boy, following his father into the forest to hunt, was how it all began. Perhaps if I died in that forest, it would close the tragic circle of my life.

"Unfortunately, I underestimated my ability to stay alive, like the stubborn old bastard I am, like the man who became my mentor when my family moved to Arcusheim. And so, when another young man who reminded me of my friend Raisor Tannoch showed up in my back yard, I was curious, and I introduced myself. I have no idea if it will work out for good or ill, but I do know one thing: Erent Caahs died many years ago, died along with any thoughts that the world could be a happy place to live. Died with any notion that the man was the spotless hero in all the stories. I'll fight—and hopefully die—for others to try to find their own happiness, but I'll never suffer to be called a hero again."

Tere Chizzit took another drink from his skin, trying to wash down the bile in his throat. It was silly, but one of the things he missed most was the ability to cry. He thought it might help in this situation. It seemed to be the choice of everyone else there, silently weeping for a man they didn't even know.

"With that, I think I'm going to sleep. Enjoy your evening." He shuffled to his bedroll and turned his back on the others.

Tomorrow would be another damn day.

45

Aeden didn't have a watch during the night, but he barely slept. He turned in his bedroll, staring at the sky, dozing occasionally, but never fully achieving slumber. Tere—Erent—and that story. How did the man continue on day after day? That alone made him a hero, as far as Aeden was concerned.

He wasn't the only one who hadn't slept well. After Tere had gone to his bedroll and fallen asleep, the others engaged in muted conversation for a short time. It didn't last, though. No one seemed to want to converse and one by one, they wandered off to their own sleeping place, all except for Lily, who had first watch.

Aeden observed the archer out of the corner of his eye for some time. She sat on a rock, back straight as a sword, eyes darting to the surroundings and to Tere's back, in turn. Those eyes glistened in the firelight, and in the silence he occasionally heard her breath catch. It was a mercy when Evon took the next watch. Lily curled up in her cloak and lay on her bedroll within an arm's length of Tere. She became motionless, staring at the back of the man she had idolized since childhood.

Aeden noted the change of the watch once again, several hours later, a tired Jia taking Evon's place. Even the quintessential assassin had been tossing and turning, disturbed by what she had heard. He wondered if what Erent Caahs had done to Toan Broos concerned her or if it was the shattering of a good man's spirit that troubled her. For him, there was no doubt. Toan Broos received what he deserved, probably less than he deserved. It was the loss of the great hero that bothered him.

That, and the hurt his friend had felt and continued to feel. Damn the world to do something so horrible to so honorable a man.

Dawn approached and Aeden got up to train. He wasn't going to sleep anyway, so he might as well get some exercise in. Khrazhti, who didn't actually need sleep, grabbed her swords and followed him to an area just out of sight of the others. There, they exerted themselves, Aeden performing his routine exercises and Khrazhti following along.

She joined him more than half the time now when he trained in the early morning. At first, she had watched, sometimes trying out a movement or two on the side. Soon, she had more or less learned his sequences, at least the ones he performed most often, and she tried to keep up with him as she mimicked his actions. Recently, she had become smoother in her movements and she could nearly match the speed at which she went through the exercises. He didn't do them at full speed when she trained with him, but it was impressive that she did as well as she did. He thought he might teach her some of the other routines. She'd like that.

By the time he finished, he had a sheen of sweat on his skin and his muscles were comfortably warm. Khrazhti, of course, didn't sweat. He still wasn't sure if that was a good thing or bad. It was definitely cleaner, but there weren't many things as satisfying as perspiration earned through hard work.

Without a word, Aeden nodded to his blue friend and they walked back to camp. It was amazing to him that they could be in each other's presence for so long without uttering a sound. She didn't try to force him to talk, didn't batter him with words. She was just there, sharing the quiet and the rush of wind as they moved quickly doing their exercises.

Most of the others were up and around, only Urun still in his bedroll. They were getting close to Benzal. Aeden could feel the anticipation rising, could almost taste it in the magic surrounding him.

"Good morning, Aeden," Marla said. "Already been exercising?"

"Good morning. Aye, a little movement before sitting the saddle for hours at a time does me good."

"Did you sleep?"

He frowned, eyes lowering to the ground. "No. You?"

"Not much. That was...quite a tale."

He raised his eyes to hers, narrowed his. "You don't believe it?"

"Oh, I believe it. What's unbelievable is that that man has kept sane after that, and for all these years."

"I agree." Aeden shuffled his feet, not quite knowing what to say next. "I'd better eat something so we can get started."

"Uh," Marla said, "I wanted to talk to you about something."

"About what?"

"Magic."

"What about it?" he asked.

"How much do you know? I mean, about magic in general, and how it works?"

He thought back to the only real training he had in magic, the Raibrech he was taught when he was a child. "I was taught specific movements, that they had to be precise to channel the energy. The words of power brought forth the magic, and the gestures focused it for the intended use."

"Did your training include where the magic actually came from or why the specific motions did what they did?"

"No. I practiced the forms, said the words, and the magic was supposed to happen. It didn't, not until many years later, after I had first heard the Song."

"Hmm." She waved Evon over. "We'd like to tell you a little about magic. It may or may not help you with the Raibrech, but it will at least let you understand how others' magic works."

Aeden looked between the two Academy students. They had the formal education in magic that was designed to help the Malatirsay in his or her task. He had none. He would be stupid to pass up the opportunity to learn some of what they knew.

"That sounds like a good idea. Thank you." He thought for a moment, and added, "Do you mind if Khrazhti listens in? She has been doing magic for thousands of years, but it might be different in Aruzhelim. She may learn something, or we may learn from what she knows."

"That would be fantastic," Evon said, answering for both of them. "The opportunity to learn about another world's magic is very exciting."

Marla gave Evon a side-eye. "You know, you sound like a stuffy scholar sometimes."

The young man shrugged, smiling. "What can I say? I'm a stuffy scholar at heart."

"Okay, well, let's get started. Aeden, the first thing you need to know is about the *qozhel*."

"The what?"

"The *qozhel*. It's the base magical power every type of casting relies upon. Look at it this way: everyone's body runs on some kind of power, right?"

"I suppose," he said.

"Okay. It doesn't matter how each person gets their power, either. They could get it by eating meat or vegetables, or it could be stored from things they ate yesterday or the day before.

"The thing is, we all need that energy to move around, to think, to do things. We can perform thousands of different actions, but they all use that power we get from eating. The *qozhel* is like that. It's formless and doesn't have any particular affinity. It's raw magical power. You with me so far?"

"I am, but where does it come from?"

"Ah, good. It's here, on Dizhelim, surrounding us and infusing everything. You could probably say it's what makes things alive."

Khrazhti was frowning.

"Then how does Khrazhti cast magic? She's not alive, or at least, not all the way. Wait, forget about her for now. The other animaru, how do they cast spells? They're not alive, and things that are life-based hurt them."

Marla was stumped, her brows drawn down as she considered it.

"Khrazhti," Evon said, "how do you use magic? Where does it come from?"

Aeden first thought that maybe she hadn't understood the question. Before he could clarify, though, she opened her mouth to answer.

"We have always been taught that magic comes directly from S'ru, that it was his own great power he allowed a few to drink from. I know now that cannot be."

"Why would you say that?" Marla asked.

"S'ru disapproved me, marked me with that disapproval so that the other animaru hunted me to destroy me. If the power came from him, he would have declined my wish to use it to fight him. I would have no magic. Even disapproved, however, I can still use the spells as I always have, though my magical sense decreased lately. I do not believe that was S'ru's doing, however."

"I see what you mean," Marla said. "Maybe you use *qozhel* like the rest of us."

"The word is familiar to me," Khrazhti said. "We have it in my language, but it simply means power. It has no grander application."

Evon jumped in. "Even without defining it, you could be using it. Look at Aeden. He hasn't ever heard the term, but he uses magic, and when he does, he's using the qozhel from the surroundings. It's why we can feel him using it, though the feeling is weaker than what we would sense of someone using magic that powerful by conventional means."

Marla put her hands up. "We won't solve this today, nor is it the point of this conversation. Just remember that the *qozhel* is the fuel to the magic you cast and it comes from the surroundings."

"Can it be used up?" Aeden asked.

"Another good question. It is believed that it cannot. There seems to be some limiting factor of how much a person can use, but that may just be a personal limit. Plus, it's spread across the entire world, so the likelihood of too much being drawn is low. It would just disperse more thinly around the world.

"On the other hand, it is much weaker than it was during the Age of Magic. That doesn't mean it was used up, but that something went horribly wrong back then and severely reduced the *qozhel* available on Dizhelim. That and the loss of so much magical knowledge due to all the deaths in the War of Magic leaves us with the magic-poor world we live in today. Some believe the Malatirsay will help to bring back magic to the world, but that is not explicitly stated in the prophecy. Others believe the gods took magic with them when they left."

"So the *qozhel*," Evon said, "can be used in any of the many branches of magic. There is magic categorized by its nature—life, fire, light, etcetera—and there are types of magic based on what they do, such as enchantment, conjuring, and things like that. From what you've said your masters told you, Raibrech spells are primarily based on life magic."

"But how is the magic of the Song itself classified?" Aeden asked.

Two blank faces stared back at him. Khrazhti leaned toward them as if she didn't want to miss the answer.

"Uh, we don't know," Marla said. "None of the masters at the Academy have ever made it a point to treat the Song of Prophecy as its own kind of magic. What you describe doing with it is unknown in the Academy."

"So, you can't really help me to learn how to use it better? You can't tell me how I can figure out the enhanced versions of the spells I've already learned?"

"I'm afraid not, but we can try to help you work your way through the process. Maybe we can figure it out together."

"It's worth a try, I suppose," he said.

"Great. Cast one of the spells you know. Wait. Choose one you know the enhanced version for, then cast the original followed by the enhanced. We'll watch. Maybe we can pick something out."

Aeden thought for a moment and decided what he'd do. He picked up a nearby kettle, one they'd used to bring water from the stream. It was half full of the liquid, but would be used to douse the fire when they got ready to leave. He set it on a piece of wood someone had been using as a seat.

"Okay," he said. "This one is the third Raibrech. It's called Ice in Spring. It can make things colder, slowing an enemy down, but with a slight change in the gestures and the intonation of the words of power, it can also heat. I'll cast the original spell I learned with the clan first."

He had the others stand back a few feet and he took up a light stance in front of the kettle. He rolled his left wrist, circling his hand up from left to right, then down the other way, continuing to make small circles. As he did so, he focused his mind on generating the magic within himself. Slowly, in time with his motions, he pronounced the words while he pointed toward the kettle with his other hand.

"*Vasant. Parat. Ushma.*"

Aeden stopped and looked at the others. Marla raised an eyebrow.

"That's it?" she asked.

"It is."

"Did it do something?"

"It did."

"What did it do?"

He gestured to the kettle. When no one moved, he put his hand near the outside of the metal container, not quite touching it. That prompted an "oh" from Marla and she put her hand near the kettle, too.

"You heated the water," she said. "Almost to boiling. Okay, good."

"Now the enhanced version," he said, moving another large piece of wood from beside the kettle so it was away from all the others by at least a foot.

Again, Aeden took up a stance that allowed him to bounce on the balls of his feet rather than to root on the ground. He rolled the wrist again in the same manner, though with a slight flourish he hadn't used before. In his mind, he sang the third quatrain of the Song of Prophecy, but only actually pronounced the three words of power out loud, again while he pointed to his target, this time the piece of wood.

"*Vasant. Parat. Ushma.*"

The wood exploded into flame.

Marla put her hand up to shield her eyes, as did Evon. Khrazhti stared into the flame.

"Did you see the effect this time?" Aeden asked, waving at Tere, who had cursed at being too close when the wood flared up.

"Kinda hard to miss," Marla said. "What's interesting to me...well, there are several things, but one is that I sensed more magical power in the first spell than the second."

"Me, too," Evon said. "You also seemed to pronounce the words differently."

"No," Marla said. "Not differently. The cadence in your pronunciation was different, or the intonation. It almost sounded like you were singing them the second time."

"I was," Aeden said. "I find that getting more in touch with the Song itself helps to cast the more powerful spells. My frame of mind matters, too. This one had essentially the same gestures for both, but the others I've figured out don't. It isn't ever the same trick twice."

Khrazhti was still staring at the burning wood.

"Khrazhti?" he said.

"I felt something," she said. "Not magic, or not magic I am accustomed to. I have not noticed this before."

"Is that good or bad?"

"I do not know, but it resonated in me. I felt the power going to the wood before it caught fire. With every magic I have experienced, I could sense when magic was used, but could not interpret its purpose unless I recognized the gestures or words. This time, I knew. I do not know what it means."

"Hmm," Marla said. "I didn't experience that, though I did sense magic, like I said. What I felt was not nearly strong enough to account for either of these effects. I'm more confused now than I was before."

"What process do you use to try to find the movements for the enhanced spells?" Evon asked.

Aeden's face grew hot. "I don't really have a process. I try different things, see if I can feel anything, and then start over and try other new things. Eventually, I stumble upon what works. It takes a long time."

"Have you tried using the same type of changes for the next spell after you've figured one out?"

"I have, but it doesn't do any good. If I change the angle of my hand for one spell and that makes me feel a change in the magic, I'll continue experimenting until I get the right gesture. If I try to change my hand position in the same way with another spell, it won't do anything at all. No two seem to work out the same."

"How do you know what to do, then?" Marla asked.

"I don't. That's the problem. I can sense when I'm heading in the right direction, but it still takes a long time to get to the point where the spell is stronger. Also, the enhancement isn't always more powerful. Sometimes, it seems, the effect is different than the one for the normal spell of the Raibrech.

"One thing I have noticed in the spells I've been able to enhance, though, is that the new motions seem smaller, more easily done while I'm holding weapons or doing something else. It gives me hope that I can one day develop the ability to cast the spells without gestures."

Marla rubbed her temples. "Hmm. That makes things difficult. I'm not sure if I know anything that could help.

Maybe the masters could suggest something. Which spell are you working on right now?"

"Life to Unlife. It's the fifth spell in the Raibrech."

"What does it do?"

"It's the only healing spell I know. It works well enough, but it's weak. I want to enhance it so I can heal my friends better. Plus, I think, since it's life magic, I can actually use it to harm animaru.

"And you're trying to figure out the enhancement for this one?" Marla asked.

"Yes."

"Any luck so far?"

"Not really. I've felt some changes when I play around with the hand positions, but nothing promising. I have a feeling it has more to do with the internal part, how I think and feel while I'm casting it, or maybe how I use the words."

"What will the enhancement do?" Evon asked.

"I don't know. I never know until I've done it. Sometimes I don't even know everything it can do after I have done it. It's frustrating."

Tere called out to Aeden. "Are we going to leave soon? We're burning daylight here."

Aeden waved and said to those with him, "We better get on the road."

"Ride with me for a little while," Marla said. "I have some things you can do, exercises to try to see if you can get a better understanding of your magic. Who knows, it might even help unlock more of your enhancements. Keep at it. You could have a breakthrough where suddenly it all makes sense, but it may be after a hundred hours of practice, or a thousand, or ten thousand."

"That's not very encouraging."

She winked at him. "I'm not here to encourage. I'm here to help you in whatever way I can."

They doused the fire, packed their saddle bags, and headed off. Aeden listened carefully to Marla and Evon and promised to try out the exercises more fully when they stopped again. If it meant making his magic more powerful, he would try anything they suggested. They were getting closer to Benzal all the time, and he could always use another weapon.

✢ 46 ✢

Khrazhti had been watching Aeden in the day and a half since they had left the last village. It was fascinating to see someone so powerful stumble around wielding power that many of the animaru lords could not match. What he did seemed to surprise Marla and Evon as well, and they had been studying such things all their lives, albeit short ones of only two decades or so each.

She looked forward to seeing if what they suggested helped him to understand his power better. So many new and unexpected things!

Twilight drifted toward the side of the road again to eat the grass there. "Do not forget our earlier conversation," she said to the beast in her own language. It was intelligent, as far as beasts went, but it didn't seem to care that she spoke in pure Alaqotim to it. Like the desid, it responded more to the tone than what was actually said.

It angled its ears back, but Khrazhti made a growling sound in her throat. The ears perked up again and Twilight moved back toward the center of the road.

"Vosyn is up this way four or five miles," Marla said.

"We can get supplies and maybe sleep in the inn. We'll have to ask around for Iscopsuru. Benzal never said exactly where it was, but I'm sure the locals will know. A large, abandoned fortress? There must be ghost stories about the place."

Many of the humans seemed obsessed by sprits of one kind or another. They could be strange sometimes. Much of the time.

An hour and a half later, they reached the village.

Or what was left of it.

The buildings mostly consisted of charred beams and stone chimneys. There were no humans left, dead or alive.

The party split up, searching the relatively small expanse of the settlement. Khrazhti followed after Aeden toward what seemed to have been a farmhouse. She would—

Khrazhti.

She recognized the voice echoing in her head.

Khrazhti.

"S'ru?" she said, wincing at using his name without a title or honorific.

Khrazhti, my loyal one, what has happened?

"Do not speak to me, father of lies."

You have abandoned me. After all I have given you.

"You have not given; you have taken. After all the centuries of service, you lied to me, sent me to this world to destroy others permanently in violation of your commandments."

A mere oversight. You would not have understood it had I explained it to you. Perhaps I should have done so, but it is past now.

"My service to you is in the past. I am not longer your follower. I have found a better way."

Come, now, Khrazhti. You are animaru, meant to be my priestess and to lead my followers. You are meant to prepare the way for my transference to the world you are in.

349

"I will not. You will not destroy this world so you can caper in the ashes. I will not let you."

You are my priestess. You will—

"I will not. You have disapproved me. You sent my father against me, gave him some of your power to defeat me."

I will give you such power. The world is more welcoming to me now. Even at this time, it is being transformed into a suitable location for me to enter. I can provide more power even than I gave Suuksis. You could easily crush all the other animaru—after the world is secure for us—and become second only to me. I will make your friends *lords in the new world.*

"No," she said. "I will not listen to your lies. I will aid my friends. I will fight you. You will not have this world, will not destroy all life and make it a place of darkness like Aruzhelim."

You will come to me and accept my rewards, or I will destroy you utterly. The voice sounded strained, angry. *You and all your friends. You cannot fight a god.*

"I can and I will. You are not a god here, not yet. We will put an end to your human associate who has been bringing the animaru here. You will not have this world."

Think on this, Khrazhti. Once you have, you will change your opinion. You will see that there are only two choices. You can choose to aid me and be showered with power and glory, or you can rebel against me and I will destroy you slowly over a hundred years, giving you pain you have never felt before.

"Begone, liar. You are no god. You are simply an evil child striving for a new toy."

So be it. You will regret your decision when you see that I gave my power to another in your place.

The voice fell silent. Khrazhti couldn't help but to look around to see if there was any manifestation of the dark god visible. There wasn't.

"Khrazhti?" This time it was a normal voice, not one in

her head. She turned to see Aeden riding up to her. "Are you all right?"

"I am. Somehow, S'ru contacted me. It may be as he said and the bars to his coming to this world are weakening. He tried to offer me power to betray you and this world. As if I could believe a word he says."

"Then, you're okay? He didn't hurt you?"

"No, he did not. Even if he can speak to me here, I do not believe he can cause harm. Yet. We must get to Izhrod Benzal and prevent him from sending more animaru over. The fewer are here, the fewer S'ru will have with which to try to pervert the world."

"Good. I'm glad you're okay. It doesn't look like there's anything of use in the village, and no one has found any sign of the people who lived here. It would probably be best for us to continue on for a time before making camp."

✖ 47 ✖

Lily Fisher watched Tere Chizzit as the party split up to search the burned village they had found. Tere Chizzit. Why had the great hero Erent Caahs chosen that name? Did it mean something? Maybe he'd tell her one day.

It wouldn't be today. He was still quiet and moody after the story he'd told them all. Out of habit, she had put on her expressionless mask, the one she had cultivated from her lifetime of tragedy and trouble. Only later, after the others had settled down to sleep and the soft, rhythmic breathing of Tere just a few feet away from her brought relative silence to the campsite, had she allowed her face to screw up into what she knew must be an ugly configuration while she silently cried.

Why? It had been years since a tear had dampened her cheek. Did she cry for the loss of the greatest hero the world had ever known, or at the thought the one she idolized wasn't always the shining bastion of honor and right she had always believed?

No, that was unfair. No one was perfect, and no matter

that she held Erent Caahs up as an ideal for her to measure herself against, she had known there was a side of him hidden from the light. He was human, though as close to a perfect human she knew of.

It wasn't the world's loss or her own loss of the image she had imagined. It was Tere himself. To suffer such a betrayal and loss was unthinkable. Her tears were not for herself or the world; they were for the man who was once called Erent Caahs. A man who, against all belief, acted as a force for goodness and honor, only to be quite literally blinded by his trust.

In the present, Tere cocked his head and turned to see her observing him. She forced a smile, but he simply shifted his gaze to the surroundings, pretending he hadn't noticed her looking.

She wished she could help him. Somehow. But he wouldn't avail himself of the offer to listen. He had lived alone for so long, he wouldn't seek solace in someone else, no matter how much she wished it.

She would be there if he decided he wanted to unburden himself further. In the meantime, she would try to make him see that she was his friend, that she wanted to help. And she would learn from him. He had so much experience to share.

Aeden and Khrazhti rode toward them on Lily's left. Others were coming, too. She guessed they were done here. Nothing to find, nothing important enough for them to remain.

As she swept her eyes across the burned husks of simple structures, she sighed. Though much smaller, this village reminded her of her own hometown, the place she had lived before her family moved to Arcusheim. To the big city, where her father and mother thought to make a better life for their little family.

Just like Erent Caahs, she had been transplanted—against

her will—to the capitol of Sutania. It was one of the things that had endeared the man to her and made her crave stories about how he had taken tragedy and turned it into the fuel and raw material for a great hero.

But she had always missed her town. Did he? She wondered if he had dreamed as a child of going back to his own home village. Maybe she could ask him. That seemed a safe enough topic.

"There's nothing here," Aeden said to those assembled, cutting into her thoughts. "We might as well leave. We can ride out a few hours and make camp. I'd rather not do it here."

Lily agreed with him. The smell of ashes and char was not something she had ever grown fond of, despite her penchant for fire arrows. Better pine needles and the scent of grass and leaves.

Aeden led with Marla, Evon, and Khrazhti. Urun, Raki, Fahtin, and Aila followed behind, with Jia moving up to speak with Aila. Tere preferred to be in the rear of the group so he could search for enemies as they rode, both to the sides and behind them. Lily agreed with the philosophy, though it was probably because she had heard and read about how Erent Caahs had the preference.

It was probably a good thing, too, because their position allowed them to see the first of the attackers.

Lily clenched her abdomen, leaning a bit forward and blinking several times rapidly. Was that a...dog?

A massive four-legged beast charged the lead riders from the right, the same side Lily was riding on. After her blinks didn't make the creature disappear, her tightened stomach radiated a sour feeling. That thing was huge, and it was already opening its mouth wide, showing its long fangs.

She leaned over so she could draw her bow. It wasn't a short horseman's bow but a long archer's weapon, more like a hunter's bow. She held it out of habit, knowing she couldn't use it efficiently from the saddle, but one shot should do.

Lily pulled an arrow from her quiver in a smooth, practiced motion, nocked it without having to look at the string, drew it to her cheek, sighted for a fraction of a second, and released.

A thump resounded in the air immediately after the slap of the string against her forearm guard. An almost imperceptible sliver of time after, a twin sound followed.

She blinked again. No, her eyes were not mistaken. Two arrows jutted from the beast's head as its legs collapsed and it slid toward the group, almost tripping up Evon's horse. Both shafts struck the same left eye of the creature.

Lily whipped her head around to find Tere standing on the ground four feet in front of her horse. His own mount was tossing its head beside hers. "How?" she said before the foliage on either side of the road exploded with motion. Had he really leaped from the saddle, drawn and loosed while in midair, and landed on his feet? The furrows leading up to his legs seemed to indicate that he had. Gods!

Something with wings, though shaped like a person, swooped down in the midst of the confusion, aiming for Jia. Lily nocked another arrow, but didn't shoot it. Too many people; while she trusted her aim, a deflected arrow could kill one of her allies. She cursed inwardly, but continued watching even as she took in the tableau in front of her.

Jia flipped out of her saddle, twisting in the air to narrowly evade the winged beast. Impossibly, in the middle of her twist, while she was upside down, she flicked her arm out. Something dark zipped from her hand and cut into the attacker. It screamed its rage and dipped its shoulder, where the sharpened piece of metal Jia had thrown was embedded in the flesh. It wasn't enough to keep the monster from flying, but maybe it would keep it occupied until Lily got a clear shot.

Another of the same type of beast—it looked like a dark human with wings on its back—zoomed in toward the front group of riders. Again, it was too close to the others before she noticed it, so Lily couldn't fire upon it.

There was really no need, though. The target seemed to be Khrazhti. The blue woman calmly hopped from the saddle, made a small gesture with her hand, and the flying attacker spun off to the side as if it was hit by a boulder.

A mix of dark shapes converged on the travelers, along with more recognizable figures. A quick count showed nearly three dozen attackers, mostly human-shaped, but less than half actually human, with the two-winged monsters she had seen, and three more of the giant dogs. The rest were dark humanoid creatures with claws.

All of her friends leaped or slipped from their saddles, drawing whatever weapons they had. It was a maelstrom of limbs and weapons, horseflesh and twisted attackers. In the midst of all of it, there were no clear shots that wouldn't endanger her friends. She could use Erent Caahs's ability to see future movements in the magical field at this point. Then again, Tere Chizzit could use that also. He was cursing under his breath about not being able to take a shot either.

The humans among their attackers had a variety of weapons, but mostly swords or other edged weapons. The dark, twisted creatures loping on their hands as well as their feet didn't have weapons, but even from a distance she saw how sharp their claws and teeth were. Two of the attackers were a bit lighter in color, and taller. They glistened slightly, as if they were covered in fine scales, and they both readied weapons for their attack. One had a sword and the other had a long pole with a wicked blade on the end of it.

These last two didn't delay in choosing their opponents.

Though they weren't the closest, Aeden and Khrazhti seemed to be priorities.

Lily continued looking for an opening as the ambushers slammed into the ranks of her friends. The human attackers —all wearing some kind of armor or another—didn't appear to have any compunction about cooperating with the dark creatures.

The humans split up, two each attacking Khrazhti and Aeden along with those snake things, three going for Marla, two rushing to Fahtin—though thank the gods Evon stood with her with sword and shield already in hand—and one hesitant as he decided where to go.

The dark humanoid creatures similarly split up, attacking in twos or threes. Jia and Aila got the most attention, with Aeden and Khrazhti getting their share as well.

Raki! Where was the young Gypta? Lily hadn't seen him since the commotion started. She looked around carefully for him, hoping against hope that he hadn't been trampled by a horse. A flicker of dark movement at the edge of the general melee resolved itself into Raki's clothing as he appeared, slashed at one of the dark monsters, and left a line of dirty brown on its body before disappearing again.

She had been looking right at him and he simply vanished.

She shook her head and regained focus. The other dog things had decided to come visit her and Tere. They were large, much bigger than any dog she had ever seen, and they were twisted, as if a regular dog had been expanded, taken apart, and put back together not quite the way it should have been. Their malformed bodies kicked up dirt from the road as they growled their way toward her.

Finally able to attack something, she drew the arrow she had nocked and launched the missile at one of the animals. In a flash, she had another arrow out and on the string, but there was no need. The other two were already fallen, arrows in their eyes, care of one Tere Chizzit. She glanced at him and saw what could have been a grimace or teeth gritted into a wicked smile.

Movement close to her, just at the edge of her peripheral vision, triggered a reflex and she drew and fired her arrow, putting the shaft through the throat of the undecided human. Apparently he had finally decided where to go. Toward her.

It was a bad choice.

As the horses screamed and ran off in all different directions, Lily wondered what kind of men the humans attacking them were. They were betraying their entire race. Were they doing it for money, for promises of being excluded from the slaughter that would occur when the animaru snuffed out all life in the world? She shook her head and watched for another opening to shoot an arrow. If she had to wait too much longer, she'd rush in and join the combat with her knives.

Aeden was in the thick of things, his dark red hair flying loose. He slipped around an attack by that snake creature with the pole blade and twisted to slash at one of the animaru while blocking another human's sword. He didn't kill the animaru, but he placed a nice gash along its shoulder and arm, making it stumble in its attempt to put some space between itself and Aeden's sword.

The Croagh ducked under Khrazhti's blade, timing it perfectly so that the blue woman's sword cut through another animaru at the same time she threw her empty hand out toward the second snake thing, the one with the sword. A blast of invisible force picked it up and threw it back a half dozen feet.

As Aeden came up from his duck, he spun, kicked aside a sword thrust, then reversed his motion as fast as lightning, launching a backhanded strike that cut the human swordsman from crotch to neck. He continued his turn, using the momentum of his strike and adding power to it from his body's torque, and came down with the sword in his other hand to lop off the arm of an animaru trying to take advantage of the chaos.

Then the winged beast streaked across the area, just above the combatants' heads, heading for Khrazhti. Quick as thought, Lily loosed an arrow at the erratically flying monster. It banked, faster than anything should have been able to change position in the air, and continued on for a few feet before another arrow sprouted from its face. Lily saw Tere nock another arrow from the corner of her eye.

Evon was still doing an admirable job keeping the two humans from attacking Fahtin, catching one's sword on his shield and slashing to keep the other on defense. Meanwhile, Fahtin worked her knives, keeping the animaru from gashing her with its claws and giving it some cuts in return.

A flash of dark called Lily's attention to the remaining flyer. It zoomed in, almost skimming the heads and shoulders of the fighters—too close to them for her to try to shoot it— heading straight for Urun, whose attention was on Fahtin. The winged animaru slammed into an invisible barrier and twisted enough that its wing didn't crumple against the magical shield. It rolled in midair and pulled out of its dive just in time to avoid Evon's swinging blade.

Marla, bright red hair making her look like fire in a darkened field, worked her sword and knife, parrying, blocking, and cutting at enemies all around her. The blades flashed in the afternoon sun as she dropped her right shoulder to miss being skewered by a sword thrust from one of the humans, then bent her elbow and thrust upward with her own blade, ramming it through the attacker's armpit and into his chest and neck. At the same time, she straightened her other arm, guiding her long knife into an animaru's belly. She spun, tearing both blades from her opponents, and moved onto the next while they dropped to the ground.

Though Lily took all the detail in from her friends' fights, little time had passed. She continued to look for an opening, but there was no need for her to rush into the fray with her knives. The scene before her was probably the single most intense and masterful demonstration of martial skill she had ever seen.

She was glad she was on her friends' side. She wouldn't survive a fight against them. Not on her best day.

With the death of several enemies, the battle started to widen out. Soon she would be able to help with her bow. As it was, she hadn't seen anything more than shallow cuts to her friends.

To her right, Aeden parried a human-wielded sword while slashing downward with his other blade to cut into the neck of an animaru. In the same smooth motion, he spun and swept the feet out from under the creature whose arm he had recently taken. He continued his spin, angling his sword down and driving it into the creature, pinning its head to the ground. Until he violently ripped it out and barely dodged the butt of the pole blade wielded by the snake animaru. Obviously expecting the blow, Aeden jumped back so the follow-up slash with the blade on the other end of the pole merely scored his breastplate instead of splitting him open.

In front of Lily, Jia rolled under the claws of an animaru. Mid-roll, she lashed out with her knife and cut the thing's belly open, dumping its entrails to the ground. She finished her roll on her knees, weight shifted forward, thrusting both knives in her hands in front of her and punching them through the head and chest of another animaru starting a slash at Aila's back.

Blue flashed as barely clothed Khrazhti blocked a sword and jumped forward to ram another human before he could complete his swing. Inches from him, she spun, pulling her sword in toward her chest and raising her elbow high only to swing it down forcefully along with her spin, striking the man so hard on the jaw, Lily heard it break from fifteen feet away. She made a lopsided figure eight with her sword, then struck a powerful backhanded blow with her sword that sheared the man's head cleanly from his shoulders.

But the former leader of the animaru wasn't done. She used her momentum and hopped to perform a kind of wind-milling motion, gathering enough force so that when she uncoiled her other sword arm, her blade cut halfway through the other human's torso, leather armor and all. Before her feet were even firmly on the ground, she moved her other sword at an awkward diagonal angle, blocking the blow from the snake thing with the sword. She pulled the blade in her left hand free of the human and struck at the snake, but it clanged against the monster's blade.

The remaining winged creature dove at Jia, but the former Falxen dove under the only horse still in the area. She rolled underneath it and came up on the other side, sweeping her hand out. Three spikes zipped through the air and stuck in the animaru's shoulder, unbalancing it and causing it to land in a stumbling run. It hadn't even stopped yet before Raki appeared and slashed its throat with his knife, fading again into the dappled shadows on the edge of the road.

With Jia on the other side of the horse from the two dark creatures that had been attacking her, Aila took the opportunity to swing those strange chain-blade weapons of hers. One placed a long cut along the arm of one of the animaru, but the other sheared off part of the second animaru's skull. Before the creature could so much as blink its one remaining eye, Jia had rammed her blade through the back of what was left of its head.

Urun had been in the middle of the formation when they

were attacked, and when everyone dismounted, he remained surrounded by his friends. He made a few gestures, but Lily couldn't see any effects of the spells he cast. For now, though, he appeared to be safe.

Fahtin, to the side from Urun, slipped under a swiping claw and rammed her knife through the monster's throat at the same time Evon punched his blade into the belly of one of the humans trying to attack her.

Another of the humans broke off and charged at Lily. She didn't even bother to draw her bow, noting Tere next to her almost casually loosing an arrow already. It entered the human attacker's eye and went through the back of his head. He slid to a stop a few feet from where she and Tere stood.

He looked over at her with his white eyes and flashed a fake smile as if he was winning some kind of contest with her.

Aeden was in full battle with the snake thing with the bladed pole at the edge of the battlefield, where there was more room. It moved so quickly, it was hard for Lily to follow the movements. Worse, it moved in ways contrary to what a body should be able to do. Aeden parried a blow a little late and received a cut on his arm for his mistake. His curses were loud enough to be clear even from where she was standing.

Aeden pressed in, launching flurries with his swords. The snake blocked and evaded them at first, but then couldn't keep up. Aeden's blades carved small cuts in the monster's flesh. He spun, feinting a high slash while uncoiling his leg for a powerful kick to the thing's midsection. The force of the blow knocked the creature off its feet as Aeden turned one more revolution, lashing out with his sword to take the snake's left hand while it was still falling backward. Without both hands, it couldn't wield its staff properly and promptly lost its head.

The other snake was trading blows with Khrazhti until she threw magic at it, burning part of its face away. The pain distracted the creature enough to allow her to slap its sword aside and shove her blade through it. She spun, tearing her sword outward from the thing's middle, dropping it to the ground in a bloody heap.

Urun finally cast something with effects she could see. Nearly invisible objects, pointed and about the size of his hand, streaked out and blasted through two of the animaru, burning holes through their chests.

The battle was winding down, the humans finishing off the last of the attackers. Lily breathed out and turned to Tere.

And saw what looked like nearly three dozen more ambushers charging in from behind them.

❧ 48 ❧

"More incoming," Lily yelled and launched three arrows in succession. Tere did the same, and between the two of them, three human attackers and two of the animaru dropped to the ground, slowing those behind them and tripping two other humans.

"*Gealich claidhimh d'araesh slaoch,*" Aeden shouted. Lily decided she needed to ask him what all those things he said meant. Later, when they were safe.

The attackers got too close to shoot with arrows. There were more than a dozen humans, almost as many of the dark creatures like the ones they had fought before, and six monstrous, wolf-like beasts with spikes jutting out from several locations on their bodies. They also had spiked tails and swung them around like weapons.

A knife whizzed past her and embedded itself in a human's chest. Before the man went three steps, Raki appeared and punched his knife into the injured man's lower back, simultaneously ripping Fahtin's knife from his chest before disappearing again.

Tere got two more arrows off, killing one of the wolf-beasts, before he swung his bow like a polearm and cracked it against the head of one of the humanoid animaru. He dropped it to draw his knives and cut into the arm and shoulder of two more humans.

Lily tossed her bow off to the side and drew her own long knives. They were similar to Tere's, and it was no coincidence. Besides his iconic bow, Erent Caahs was known for his long knives. She turned to put her back to the man and found herself face-to-face with one of the wolves as it soared through the air at her.

She twisted and ducked, slashing upward with her blades. It howled as she cut two deep furrows into its underside as it passed over.

The maneuver put her in a position facing her friends. Raki stepped from the shadows and handed Fahtin her knife back. Near her, Khrazhti motioned and two of the wolves were thrown backward from her. Aeden had charged in past Lily and blocked two sword strikes that were aimed for Tere's head. The archer lashed out with his knives, tearing the throat from a human and punching his other knife through the eye of another man next to him.

Lily was in a pocket of calm in the midst of the battle. Aeden and Marla commanded the most attention, whirling around each other, him with twin swords and her with her sword and dueling knife. Somehow, in the midst of their acrobatics and complex movements, they never got in each other's way or harmed any of their friends.

By the time they stopped their furious attacks, Aeden and Marla stood in the middle of four dead humans, one dead animaru, and one wolf that had nearly been cut in half.

"The pilae!" Khrazhti shouted, drawing Lily's attention. She thought the blue woman might have been speaking her own language. It made no sense. "The pilae. Get them before they escape."

No one else seemed to understand what she was trying to tell them.

She growled in frustration, shaking her head as she cut down another human attacker. "The little balls of shadow, over there." She pointed one of her swords toward an area just outside where the fighting was taking place. "Kill them. They are spies. They will go to Izhrod Benzal."

Lily scanned the area Khrazhti had pointed to and finally saw them. Two bundles of shadow without anything to cast them were near the foliage. They were roughly ball shaped.

She dove at her bow, lying on the ground nearby. She snatched it up, nocked an arrow, and launched it. At the same time, a flash of steel rushed toward the other shadow. Both struck true, right in the center of the shadowy creatures. They quivered and then deflated.

Had that knife come from Tere? It wasn't one of his long knives, but a shorter throwing blade. She had never heard of him using thrown weapons. He was already moving on to his next victim, knives flashing.

One of the wolf-things was bearing down on Fahtin, spikes bristling and tail lashing. Evon jumped and slammed his shield into the thing, forcing it back. It turned on him, bunching its muscles to pounce, but Evon's sword came around and cut deeply into one of its front legs. The beast shifted its weight just in time for Evon's backswing to take the other leg. As it fell forward, the Academy student bashed it with the edge of his shield and buried the point of his sword into its head.

Lily turned to attack a small group of the attackers, but found Jia and Aila working together to draw the enemies into range. By the time they were done, two more humans and two of the animaru no longer moved.

Lily killed one more human and one animaru before her friends had surrounded and cut down the rest. With no more attackers apparent, she let out a long breath and stepped over to pick up her bow where she had tossed it aside again.

"It would seem that Benzal knows we're coming," Tere said, retrieving his own bow. "Or, at least, he knows we're in the area."

"Aye," Aeden said. "We'll need to take advantage of his lack of current information and get to him quickly before he realizes his ambush didn't work."

"Did you see any more of those spies, Khrazhti?" Fahtin asked, inspecting a gash in her tunic and skin.

"The pilae? No. That does not mean there were not more. It is safer to assume Izhrod Benzal knows we were not killed."

Urun was busy going from person to person, inspecting them for serious wounds. Almost everyone was injured in one way or another, but Lily didn't think any of them were serious. It was a miracle they hadn't lost one of their number. Even skilled warriors could be injured or killed in such chaotic battles. She was surprised to find a tear along her belly, probably from that wolf thing.

Urun stepped up to her. "May I?" He put his hand over her injury, not quite touching her but close enough for her to feel his hand's presence. A shock of cold hit her and traveled through her abdomen. Urun nodded and moved on to the next person.

Lily wiped the blood from her skin. The wound had closed and the skin looked like it had never seen any damage. All these heroes...it was going to take some getting used to.

The young priest continued to heal minor injuries on the spot, not looking to be exerting much power at all. For the deeper cuts, he seemed to take more time and do things a little differently. Still, they were soon all healed, if tired.

It took some time to gather up the scattered horses. Remarkably, only one of them was injured, the poor scared beast that had remained in the area out of pure panic and confusion, the one Jia had used as cover. Urun bit his lower lip as he contemplated healing the creature, but when he finally tried, the gash in the horse's side disappeared. It sighed and shook its head, whickering softly.

"He has brought over aliten, colechna, and kryzt," Khrazhti said, though it didn't appear she was speaking with anyone in particular.

"What's that?" Aeden asked.

The blue woman blinked at Aeden as if surprised. "I was merely pondering. Izhrod Benzal has brought over animaru more powerful than the seren. The aliten, the winged animaru, are very useful as spies and scouts. The colechna, those with the scales and weapons, are very often officers in animaru forces." She pointed toward the spiked wolf-creatures. "The kryzt are used at the front of an assault to batter the other forces and throw them into disarray."

"What about these?" Aeden said, kicking one of the huge, twisted dog things. "What are they called?"

"Gulrae."

"And then there's those...what did you call them? The little balls of shadow?"

"Pilae," she said. "They are useful as spies as well. No doubt they were given orders to observe and report back. They have few offensive capabilities."

"So, there are more than those seren animaru," Tere said. "Wonderful. Those are bad enough. How many types of animaru are there?"

"Sixteen basic types."

"*Cachten siolach peitseag.* We better get going if we want to use Benzal's ignorance to our advantage."

"But we don't know where we're going," Raki said. "We were going to ask the people at Vosyn. How are we going to find Benzal's fortress?"

Aeden grumbled something else under his breath. He looked toward his hands, clasped in front of him, forearms resting on his knees. His eyebrows shot up and a slow grin appeared on his face.

"Tere," he said. "You can't track through the magical field, right?"

"Yeah."

"But knowing you, you never relied completely on the magic. You had to have learned to track like everyone else, right?"

"Yeah."

"And again, knowing you, you probably got pretty damn good at it."

"Yeah. So?"

Aeden pointed to the torn-up ground where part of the battle took place, but then he moved his finger to the side, toward where the second group had come from.

"Ah," Tere said. "Give me a moment." He got up and began walking, following the furrows the spiky wolf-things had torn in the ground, but then stopped, turning toward Lily. "You coming? You tracked us well enough. A bunch of spiked monsters should be no problem."

Lily smiled at him—earning a frown—and jogged to catch up.

❧ 49 ❧

A eden felt a little better than he had a few moments ago when he thought they'd lost their chance to find Benzal. Tere was following the trail as it wended around the ambush site, Lily by his side.

"We're counting on those attackers coming from where Benzal was. Even if they didn't, it'll let us find more of his minions and eventually we'll get to him. It's better than wandering around the countryside trying to locate a fortress that may be so overgrown we'd never find it."

"Somehow, I doubt it would be like that," Marla said. "If Benzal is using it, he would have cleaned it up. He's not one to engage in hardship, and to him, hardship is not having a dozen servants and manicured grounds."

"All the better for us to find him, then."

It wasn't long before Tere and Lily came back.

"They split up over there a ways," Tere said. "The trail from when they were still together is pretty clear. That's a big group. Even if they weren't clumsy and stupid, we'd be able to track them on a night with no moon and all of us half drunk. You want to start now?"

"Definitely," Aeden said. "The sooner we find that bastard, the sooner this whole thing is over."

When he said it, Marla shifted her eyes toward Evon and he did likewise.

They followed Tere and Lily, who were following the trail. The group of attackers had stayed on the road about half the time, but spent a fair part of the journey off-road as well. Aeden wondered what dictated the path to take. It probably didn't matter. All they needed to do was to follow where it led and hope they'd find Benzal at the end of it.

The day wore on and despite what Tere had said, they agreed to stop when darkness had fallen. They were tired and no one wanted to take the chance they'd miss something traveling at night. Aeden was pretty sure Tere wouldn't miss anything in the darkest part of the night, but it was better to be safe.

In general, the party was subdued and abnormally quiet, though whether because of the battle earlier in the day or anticipation of what lay ahead, Aeden didn't know. They went to bed early after setting up two people for the first watch.

They were up and on the trail again before the sun was fully up. *Today*, Aeden thought. *Today is the day we'll finally finish Benzal.*

How he was looking forward to the end. It seemed like he had been running for years, either chasing after something or fleeing. He wasn't sure what the future held for him, but stopping, being able to look around and enjoy his life, was something he desired. Putting all this hero stuff behind him, at least for now, sounded like a very good thing.

Early in the day, Tere brought them to a path heading up into the foothills between the Aerie Mountains and the Vasmorvin River. It was barely large enough to be called a path, but there were signs it had once been something more. A loose stone now and then that was too regular not to have been cut and placed there, a flatness that didn't match the surrounding terrain, and other small things. They were on what had been a road once, long ago.

"I think this is it," Tere said.

The path had obviously been trod recently. The crushed vegetation wound its way up the hills, turned to the right, and disappeared. Somewhere up there was Benzal and the fortress he had bragged so much about to his fellow Academy students.

Aeden rubbed his chin, wondering how far it was. He scanned the hills and didn't see any structures, though that didn't mean anything. His view was obstructed not only by folds in the hills but also by the trees surrounding them. There were mainly spruce, beech, and pine, but he saw the occasional oak or elm. It wasn't too different than many of the other forested areas they'd passed through in their travels.

"Let's head up," Aeden said. "No use standing out in the open where lookouts can spot us." He put his right foot forward to head up, but Marla grabbed his arm.

"Hold on. There's something...stay here. Give me a moment. Evon?"

The blond-haired young man put his head together with her and they conversed for a few seconds. He nodded, then closed his eyes, muttered something under his breath, and swept his hand out in front of him.

His eyebrows shot up and he nodded to Marla. The two of them walked slowly forward, Evon still waving his arm ahead of them. After a few steps, they went to the left and then forward again.

After what seemed like a long time, they came back to Aeden and the others.

"There are magical beacons," Marla said, "spread out along the trail. They're a type of detection magic. If we go up that way, they will no doubt alert Benzal that he has visitors."

"Can you disable them?" Aeden asked.

Marla shared a look with Evon. "We should be able to, but if we try, they may signal him anyway."

"Do you think they're in the trees, too?" Tere asked. We can go that way if it'll prevent us from running across them."

"Beacons like that take time to make," Evon said. "Izhrod wouldn't have put them everywhere. He'd get constant false alarms from animals. It's worth a try to see if there's a path through the trees."

The archer nodded. "Good. Let's try that way." He pointed toward the left, where the trees didn't seem quite as tangled as those on the right. "Will you come with me so we can search?"

"Sure," Marla said. "If we can—"

"Traps," Jia said.

"What?" Marla said.

"Traps. There will be traps, maybe even sentries. If Benzal is as arrogant and intelligent as you say he is, he is no doubt paranoid, too. He won't rely completely on magic. There will be physical means of keeping trespassers out."

"The girl has a point," Tere said.

Jia smiled at the archer. "I'm good at traps. I can look for them and...neutralize any sentries."

Marla, Evon, and Tere all turned to Aeden, waiting for a decision. "Do it," he said. "The rest of us will go over there, just off the path so we're not in the open."

Lily joined the other three and headed off slowly into the bushes. Once they were off the path, Fahtin began to chat softly with Aila. Raki and Urun began a conversation, and Khrazhti came and sat next to Aeden on a rock.

"This way of detecting others, it is typical in this world?" she asked.

"I don't know if I would say it's typical, but it's not all that rare. Did you not have fortresses and walls in Aruzhelim?"

"We did. We also have animaru that specialize in infiltration and assassination, but the normal way of doing things is to attack the enemy without subterfuge. Eventually, the outcome will be decided by the skill and power of the winning army. There is no reason to waste time and energy in sneaking a small group into an enemy camp."

Aeden narrowed his eyes. "That doesn't sound like you take advantage of all you can. Some of the greatest victories in history were decided by small groups doing spectacular things."

"It is your imagination and creativity. The animaru are set in their ways and have continued doing things since they were created twelve thousand years ago. Besides me, you will not find more than a few animaru who innovate. We do not experiment and discover. It is one of the most fascinating things about humans, to me."

"You're right," Aeden said. "We do enjoy learning new things, or creating them. If we're not innovating, we're improvising. I've noticed that the longer I fight a particular animaru, even one more skilled than me, if I hang on for a time, I am able to see their pattern, their habits, and then beat them."

"It is a great advantage, I think."

"One you share."

She leaned away from him to focus on him more fully. "What do you mean?"

"When I fought you, you were not as predictable as any of the other animaru. If Urun hadn't suppressed your magic, I don't know if I could have beaten you."

A slow smile appeared on her face. "I am pleased. And honored you would say that."

"Just telling the truth. There are few people I would rather have by my side in a battle. Even without magic, you're very skilled."

The flattering words seemed to make her uncomfortable. Her cheeks darkened and he realized that, yes, she did blush, though it was more subtle than on humans. He chuckled to himself, thinking of the hard-as-iron animaru general she had been when he first encountered her. She seemed to have softened up quite a bit since then, showing emotion that he at first thought she didn't possess.

What had caused the change? Magic had shifted, but he thought it was more than that. It was as if she was discovering and revealing her human half, like being around them caused her to act more human. He liked it, but wondered if she realized it was happening. Already, she displayed more facial expressions, and even body language, than any other animaru he'd ever seen. Granted, he'd only associated with the others long enough to kill them, but still, he knew she was different.

He found himself staring into her glowing blue eyes, not focusing on anything, his mind just processing thoughts subconsciously. Someone clearing their throat made him blink and look around.

Fahtin was standing next to him, Aila next to her.

"Aeden," the Gypta said, "what do you think we'll find when we get to the fortress?" Her eyes darted back and forth between Aeden and Khrazhti, the latter still blushing slightly.

"No telling," he said. "I'd guess he's got a lot of troops up there, both human and animaru, though the trail doesn't indicate that they used this route. Maybe there's another path up. Either way, you can bet there'll be a fight. Benzal won't be giving up and letting us kill him. I hope he's there and hasn't left again."

"Do you think it's a real fortress or just some old shack surrounded by a leaning wooden fence?" Aila asked.

Aeden laughed. "I don't know. Marla seems to think it's a

legitimate fortress. She knows Benzal better than we do, so I'll trust her on that."

"She's great," Fahtin said. "I like her."

"Sure," Aeden said. "Once you get over the whole trying-to-kill-me-the-first-time-we-met thing."

Fahtin winked. "That's one of the reasons I like her so much."

Aeden laughed again, as did the two women. Khrazhti looked around, trying to work out what was funny. She didn't laugh, but the crack of a smile did steal its way onto her lips.

The others soon returned. Tere thumbed back toward the area they had scouted, and Aeden and the others fell into line behind him.

"We found a few more of those beacons," he said, "as well as some sentries. That Jia is skilled. I mean, she's so good it's scary. A person would have to be stupid to turn his back on her if they were enemies."

"Yeah," Aila said, "but she's our friend. We don't have anything to worry about." She sped up and joined Jia at the front. The former assassin's face lit up when Aila joined her and they put their heads together and immediately started chatting, though Aeden couldn't hear anything.

He shook his head and continued on.

They reached a small, flat area where they could see both the path below and traces of it up ahead. More importantly, it gave them their first view of the fortress itself.

Iscopsuru was truly a fortress, though different in shape than others Aeden had seen. He contrasted it with the one at Broken Reach. Whereas that stronghold was tall, with high walls—though parts of them had crumbled over time—Iscopsuru was sprawling and squat. It stretched out over a large hill, commanding a great view of the surrounding area, but blended into the hillside so well, they may have actually been looking at it when they were lower and never knew it.

Even now, closer to it, parts of it seemed to blend into the terrain.

Part of that was the vegetation that had grown around it, but it was also obvious that Benzal had commanded his servants to cut back some of it. The result was an impressive compromise between rugged wilderness and timeless defensive structure.

He whistled softly. With the terrain and the moderate walls—fifteen to twenty feet in most places he could see—they might have trouble getting in if there were troops stationed there.

"There aren't many," Marla said, as if she was reading his mind. "We scouted close. That's the only path up there, as far as we can tell, and there just isn't enough damage to the vegetation to be consistent with a lot of men—or animaru—moving."

"Unless they teleported in," Evon added.

"Yeah," she said. "Or that. I think this is about as far as we're going to be able to take the horses. We should tie them up so they can graze out of sight."

They did as she suggested and were soon closer to the fortress, though they still hadn't seen any movement.

"Come on," Marla said. "Let's get closer so we can decide how we'll get in."

Benzal had done an admirable job clearing the vegetation from within a dozen feet of the walls. It wasn't much of an alley, but it would allow any sentries to see if someone was skulking about.

But there were no sentries visible. They watched the main gate and the battlements within sight and didn't see any movement at all.

"Are they hiding and watching?" Fahtin asked.

"I don't know," Aeden said.

"It would be unorthodox to do so," Marla pointed out.

"Their field of vision would be restricted and they would have a hard time attacking anyone who did show up. Maybe we were wrong about him being here."

"No, we weren't wrong," Evon said. "People don't clear away brush and clean a place up like this without using it."

She nodded, still scanning the wall. "Then why isn't anyone around?"

"Maybe he doesn't have many minions with him," Tere said. "Which will be good for us. Why don't we get inside and then we can see what we're up against? I can probably get a grapple over the wall where the vegetation is closer, over there. If I can—"

Jia glided toward the wall. "I'll be right back."

❧ 50 ❧

The others stared, mouths agape, as the small woman with the bluish-black hair scurried up the wall like she was some type of squirrel.

Aeden caught Tere shifting his gaze back and forth from the rapidly ascending form of Jia and Lily, who was standing next to the older archer. The red-haired woman had a proud smile on her face.

"She's good like that," Lily said.

A few minutes later, the sally door within one of the doors of the main gate opened and Jia stepped out, waving for them to join her.

Aeden laughed. He did so enjoy his friends.

"I didn't see anyone, but the place is not abandoned," Jia told them in a soft voice when they gathered inside the walls. "I can smell smoke, and a lot of these tracks are recent." She pointed a few out.

"Good enough," Aeden said. "Anyone have an idea where we should go? Marla?"

"I haven't been here, but the layout is a classical fortress style that was popular seven or eight centuries ago. I'd guess that if Benzal were here, he'd be in the central part of the main keep. The other structures there are utilitarian outbuildings."

"Let's get moving, then," Aeden said. "I want this done."

There was no sign of anyone else as they made their way across the bailey to the keep. Aeden didn't like it. He had a feeling like someone was speaking to him but not quite making sense. Like they were communicating their intent clearly, but he wasn't smart enough to understand what they were saying to him. What was he missing?

He allowed Marla and Jia to go first, his sister scanning for magical traps and the former assassin looking for those of a more conventional nature. With every step, Aeden felt the pressure building. It would have to blow soon, and when it did, he wasn't sure they'd survive it.

He forced the thoughts from his mind and simply paid attention to where he was going. He had faith in his own abilities and those of his friends. They needed to find Benzal and finish him. Then they could go home. Wherever that was.

Jia put her hand up as they approached another door in the wide hall. The others stopped, but she and Marla continued on ahead.

First, she inspected the door, all the way around the frame. Then she turned her attention to the latch, looking at it from all angles that she could. She put her ear so close to the door, Aeden could feel splinters tickling his own ears from the anticipation. She finally opened the door slowly, crouching down low, and put her head in so she could see.

The hallway was silent as death. The others must have been holding their breaths, too, like he was, afraid to even add the sound of air going in and out of their bodies to the quiet.

Jia stood up and entered the corridor beyond. A collective sigh came from the others.

They traveled slowly until it seemed they should be at the center of the keep. There, they found a large trapdoor in the floor. It was closed.

"I hardly think Benzal would be down in the depths of the earth," Marla said. "His pride couldn't handle it. I say we leave the trap door alone."

"No," Aeden said. "Not alone. Bar it. I'll not have troops hiding below us come up from behind as we find Benzal."

"I agree," Tere said. "No telling what's down there. Whatever it is, let's make sure it stays down there for now."

Tere and Aeden found a bar meant for a door a few rooms back and managed to wedge it against the iron ring on the trap door and the nearby wall. It would have to do. With a nod toward Jia and Marla, Aeden took his position again in the group and they continued on.

Eventually, they found a ramp going upward. This led to a set of stone steps going up. Marla cocked her head and shrugged. Aeden nodded to her. He agreed with her. With what he knew of Benzal, he figured the man would like to be up high.

At the top of the steps was a vast hallway. It seemed out of place, especially above the ground floor. The party spread out. Aeden searched the ceiling for murder holes and the walls for arrows slits or openings of any kind. He saw none.

He was about to say something when a click echoed in the cavernous space.

Jia threw her hand up and everyone stopped. What had that sound been?

All eyes turned to Urun, who had frozen before Jia's hand had reached for the ceiling. His face was pale and he was beginning to sweat. He had been to the far left of most of the others, a couple of paces from the wall.

"Daeann daedos ist."

Jia stepped up to the priest and knelt in front of him.

Below his left foot was a loose stone, indistinguishable from other stones in the floor.

Except that it was half an inch lower than those around it.

"Get back," she said. "Slowly go back, using your exact steps if you can. Go all the way through the door onto the steps. I'm not sure what this will do."

Aeden waited as the others all filed out, back from where they had come. Marla stopped next to Jia and did her own inspection of the floor.

"Any ideas?" Marla asked the assassin.

"No. It's obviously some kind of device, but I have no idea where the trigger is attached or what it does."

"Leave me," Urun said. "Go on ahead. I'll stay here as long as I can. When you're safe, it won't matter if the trap goes off."

"We won't be doing that," Marla said. "You're not going to be the heroic martyr today, priest. Any chance your goddess can help?"

"No," he said. "She has problems of her own right now."

"Pity."

Aeden still hadn't moved. "What's your best guess for what the trap might be?" he asked both women. "If you had set it, what would you have made it do?"

"Me?" Jia said. "I'd have had it do something that would wipe out everyone in the hall. Some kind of big sweeping blade or rolling stone cylinder or something like that."

"That sounds like the most effective way," Marla said.

"Urun," Aeden said, "just how strong is your shield? Could it withstand something like that?"

"I...I don't know. Before, probably not, but Osulin gave me more power when she came to me. It might hold up against something like that."

"Any other options?" he asked the women.

"I can't think of any," Marla said.

"Me either," Jia said.

Aeden ran his fingers through his hair. "Well, then, I guess we have a plan. What do you think, Urun? Are you willing to give it a go?"

"Only if you all three go back with the others. If my shield doesn't work, then we'll only be losing me. We can't lose you or Marla."

"I'm not leaving you to—" Aeden started.

"He's right, Aeden," Marla said. "Don't be stupid. You can't do anything to help. Especially since we don't know what the trap will do. Come on. Let's get out of the way and let Urun do his thing."

The priest was sweating profusely now. He was also tense, so much that his leg trembled. Still, Urun forced a smile and nodded.

"Go on, Aeden. I'll see you in a couple of minutes, once we figure out what happens."

"*Aruna recipia dui.* Make the shield as strong as you can, Urun. Osulin is not done with you yet. Neither are we. We need you."

"I'll do my best," he said. "Go on. My leg is shaking and it's going to give out in a minute. You need to be gone when it does."

"Osulin be with you, my friend." Aeden carefully retraced his steps and headed toward the others.

As Marla and Jia followed him, Urun started chanting and Aeden felt a slight tingling. Could he feel Urun's nature magic now? Was that new or had he simply missed it in the middle of fighting before? He hoped he had an opportunity to see if that was a normal occurrence.

The nature priest kept his eyes glued to Aeden and the two women. As soon as all three were through the doorway, he closed his eyes, took a breath, reopened his lids, and lifted his foot.

A louder click than the first one sounded and a lump that had lodged itself in Aeden's throat dropped to his belly. He watched Urun and the rest of the corridor, but nothing seemed to be happening.

Then, abruptly, the floor of the entire hallway dropped out from under the priest.

"No!" Aila said, still with the presence of mind not to shout. As if anyone within a mile of the fortress wouldn't have heard the commotion of the entire floor falling into the darkness.

The stone blocks making up the floor tumbled downward, raising up a cloud of dust as they crashed and crumbled against their siblings. For a moment, all Aeden could do was to stare into the obscured hallway, not quite believing what he had just seen.

The dust settled slowly over the next few seconds, during which everyone in the party stared speechlessly at where their friend had been.

A cough pierced the silence that followed the rumble of

the stones falling and settling on the floor of the grand hall some thirty feet below.

"Urun?" Aeden frantically searched for his friend.

The entire floor had not collapsed. A small ring around the walls, maybe half a foot wide, still remained. From the section near where Urun had been, two hands clung desperately.

"Urun!" Aeden sprang into what was left of the hallway. He skittered along the edge, almost slipping twice before he was standing above the hands. Urun's dusty face looked up at him, eyes wide.

"I...can't hold on, Aeden," the priest said. "I can't—" His left hand slipped and Aeden watched in horror as the right began to lose its grip as well.

Aeden, face to the wall, squatted as low as he could, his rear sticking out into the open air above where the floor was. "No," he said. "I'll not have it." His hand shot out between his feet and grabbed the wrist of Urun's right hand, locking it in an iron grip. The priest dangled precariously, eyes even wider than before and mouth open, gasping like a fish on land.

Aeden grunted and straightened his knees, hauling Urun up until the priest was resting his elbows on the ledge. Without the need to hold Urun's entire weight up, Aeden stepped to his right. Getting into another solid squat stance, the front of his body pressed as tightly against the wall as he could, he reached over, snatched Urun's arm with his left hand, and pulled the priest up.

Urun's feet scrabbled on the stone as Aeden nearly lifted him with one hand so he could stand on the ledge. He looked down and gulped, breaths still coming in rapid gasps.

"We're going to move along the ledge, Urun," Aeden said. "Okay? We need to move to the end of the room."

Urun nodded and looked toward the others.

"Not that way," Aeden said. "We've already been back there. We're going forward."

Urun nodded, hugging the wall.

"You're going to need to breathe. If you hyperventilate, you'll pass out and I may not be able to keep you from falling. Control your breaths or this damn trap may get you after all."

The priest closed his eyes for a moment—and teetered precariously—then opened them again and made an effort to take long, slow breaths.

"Good," Aeden said. "Let's go. Every step gets us closer. Just slide your feet along the edge. Keep your weight as much toward the wall as you can. I'll keep one hand on you, but I need you to do the work. I can't carry you."

"Okay."

They scuttled down the hall, one sliding step at a time. It seemed to take hours, and by the time they finally stepped onto the threshold at the other end of the hall, Aeden's left arm was shaking and his legs felt like lead. It took several tries to release his grip on Urun's robes.

Urun dropped to the stone, breaths shuddering again briefly. He trembled like a sapling in a windstorm.

"Thank you, Aeden. I thought I was dead."

"You're welcome. That was some fine work, grabbing that ledge. Did you jump for it when the floor dropped?"

The priest chuckled, a nervous, shaky thing. "No. As the block I was standing on fell, it pitched me toward the wall. My hands struck the stone and somehow, I grabbed on out of reflex."

"that was a lucky thing. I'm glad of it."

"Me too."

The others slid their way along the ledge to join them, Jia lightly dancing across the lip on the other side of the room as if it were five feet wide, the others helping those who needed it. Soon, they all stood next to Aeden and Urun, who had stood up and stopped shaking. Fahtin and Aila took turns hugging the priest, making his face go crimson.

"Well, whoever is here knows we're here now," Aeden said. "We might as well continue. Let's try to be more careful of traps."

Jia cast her eyes to the floor.

"I'm not blaming anyone," Aeden said quickly. "All I'm saying is that we should be extra careful. We know now that we might run into more little tricks. If I'm going to die, I want it to be in battle, not because Benzal played a joke on me." He nodded to Jia, who firmed her jaw and nodded back.

She and Marla took up the position in the front again, heading down the smaller corridor, searching for anything else that might kill them.

Their path took them up a ramp through several major corridors, and up another set of stairs. The two women at the front stopped them three times, twice resulting in nothing, but the third allowing Jia to discover another trap.

"I'm not exactly sure what it does," the former assassin said, "but we know it's there. Let me check on the place where we would go around it."

She did so, and found another trigger, the same type as they had found before: a stone slightly looser than those around it. Jia and Marla spent an hour checking the rest of the room meticulously before proclaiming that if the party followed Jia's exact footsteps, they would be safe.

By the time they arrived at the large room, something like an audience chamber by the look of it, Aeden was fatigued from being on the edge of anticipation for so long. The chamber was bent, shaped like an L, with the only other door barely visible after the room turned to the right. He scanned the tables at the edges of the room and the few chairs beside them, but his eyes almost immediately found the figures at the far side of the chamber.

It looked like two dozen people standing silently, watching to see when the party would notice them. No, not all people. Of those not truly human, most of them were man-shaped, but wore either no clothes or strange ensembles displaying their scales, fur, or thick twisted flesh.

They surrounded a man in a fine black coat and pants, a bit of lace at his neck and cuffs and hair that, though wild and curly, still appeared fashionable. He lifted his chin and looked down his nose at the newcomers.

"Izhrod," Marla growled.

"Ah, Marla, and dear Evon," he said in a cultured, slightly whiny voice. "So good of you to visit. Such a pity I can't give you the welcome you deserve. This will have to suffice." He waved his hand in their direction and his minions charged.

Aeden drew his weapons. Before they even cleared the scabbards, Tere and Lily had fired several arrows, taking down three of the enemies; two animaru and a human man with chain mail. Unfortunately for the man, his mail didn't cover his eyes, one of which received an arrow.

"This is going to be quick," Aeden said, running toward the animaru.

Benzal smiled. "Not for you, it won't be." He reached over to the wall next to him and pulled a small lever.

The floor dropped out before him. This time, the entire room's floor didn't disappear, only about fifteen feet of it. One of Benzal's human minions hadn't been fast enough and lost his balance as the floor dropped away. He followed the stone, screaming the whole way. It took fully two seconds until the thump that signaled the end of his life replaced his screams. That had to be close to sixty feet. Aeden definitely didn't want to end up falling into that pit.

Four of the animaru running at him were those snake things. What had Khrazhti called them? Colechna? He hated that type. One holding two-foot sticks with another foot of sharp steel blade attached to them came at Aeden while the others spread out to attack.

The battle with the colechna was fast and furious. The thing was so quick, it was able to use the hardened wood to parry blows as well as the steel parts of its weapons. It pressed Aeden the way all the snakes did, with speed and a flexibility no human could match.

It slithered aside and parried a whirlwind of blows from Aeden's swords. Unable to score a strike, Aeden kicked and managed to partially land his foot on the thing's midsection. It curled back over itself, almost doubling over completely, and then whipped its body back to strike at Aeden again.

But Aeden wasn't where it had expected. He had collapsed the leg he was standing on after he kicked, sliding forward on his knee. When the colechna struck out, Aeden chopped upward with both of his swords, cutting deeply into the thing's upper arms. It screamed until Marla came along from behind Aeden and took its head.

"Thanks." Aeden hopped back onto his feet.

"Don't mention it." She whirled to block the attack of another colechna.

Aeden spared a moment to look at Benzal. The Academy graduate was smiling. He caught Aeden's eyes, gave a little shrug, and walked toward the door.

It seems that Tere had seen as well because two arrows streaked toward Benzal, one right after the other.

They never made it to the man. They swerved in midair, striking some kind of machine nearby with a snap as if it was a powerful magnet and the arrows were made of metal. Tere fired another with the same results.

Benzal's smile grew wider as he got closer to the room's exit.

"No," Aeden spat. "Not again. Your trick worked before,

but not this time." He stepped forward to run after Benzal, but Marla, still battling with the colechna, spoke to him.

"Aeden, you can't jump that. It's got to be more then fifteen feet."

"I'll do it. I'm not letting him get away again. I've been here once before. He's not escaping this time."

She spun, slapping the colechna's sword away, cutting into its belly and its neck simultaneously with her sword and dueling knife, then finishing her rotation with a thrust that impaled the scaled creature.

"Don't leave," she said.

Aeden narrowed his eyes at her. Her voice sounded strange, almost needy. He looked toward Benzal's retreating form then back at her, then around him.

"They can handle this lot. Come on." He sheathed both his swords in a lightning-quick motion and put his hand out. "Together. Let's do this, brother and sister."

She stared as his hand for a moment, unconsciously ducking a blow from another animaru, this one of the seren type. Evon slammed the creature with his shield, and it spun away to fight with Marla's friend.

She sheathed her own weapons and grabbed Aeden's hand. She followed where he was tugging her.

Away from the battle.

Toward the chasm in front of them.

✳ 52 ✳

A few feet from the gaping pit, Aeden and Marla
released each other's hands, picked up speed, and
leaped out into the empty air. Aeden glanced down
and saw broken stone fifty or sixty feet below him. If he
didn't make this jump, he was dead.

His foot struck the stone half a pace from the edge and he
let his knee go loose. He smoothly rolled on his shoulder and
back and came back onto his feet, barely stopping his
momentum before striking the wall.

Marla did a fantastic job of landing and rolling to dissipate
her energy as well. Probably a better job than him, if he was
honest. He smiled and nodded toward the door Benzal had
gone through.

"Let's finish this."

Aeden cast one last glance at his friends, hoping they
would be all right fighting without him and Marla. Part of
him felt like he was abandoning them, though he knew that
each of them would have encouraged him to go after Benzal.
The Academy graduate was the most important thing at the
moment.

He swung his head around as he crossed the threshold into the room beyond. Just as something slammed into his left shoulder, hitting him with such force it spun him, causing him to career off the door frame.

"Agh. *Andorin recoat du acci rudis flagranti*," he yelled out. Looking down, he saw half a crossbow bolt sticking out of his shoulder. Benzal was two dozen feet away, frantically working the crank on a crossbow so he could take another shot. Luckily, it was a smaller weapon. A typical crossbow at that range would have launched a bolt through Aeden's shoulder and probably into Marla behind him.

Benzal wasn't smiling now. Aeden growled and launched himself from the wall toward the man before he could get off another shot.

Two other figures lunged toward him from the side of the room. One of them was another snake animaru and the other was...Suuksis? Marla charged the two, giving Aeden a moment to realize that the sickly grey animaru wasn't Suuksis, just another like him.

"Take care of Benzal," Marla said, slashing at the colechna. "I'll handle these two."

"The grey one is a magic user," he said, continuing his sprint for Benzal. He wasn't certain that was the case, but Khrazhti had told him that most of the semhominus types could use magic. Better safe than surprised.

Aeden reached Izhrod Benzal just as he finished loading a bolt into the crossbow. He brought it up, finger on the trigger, but couldn't quite get it leveled before Aeden's right shoulder slammed into him. The crossbow flew off in one direction—its bolt zipping across the room in a wild shot that clattered harmlessly against a wall—and Benzal fell the other way.

The pain of the impact made Aeden's vision go black at the sides. He reached over so he could grasp the bolt in his other shoulder and yank it out. Luckily, it wasn't barbed, and it tore free with a splash of blood and fire that traveled all the way down his arm. He shook his head, trying to keep from blacking out, and drew one of his swords with his right hand. He grunted at the pain and turned toward Benzal.

The man was smiling again. Codaghan, how Aeden hated that smile. He would be sure to eliminate it from the world.

Benzal drew his sword with his left hand, putting his right up as if he could use it defensively against Aeden's weapon. "You went through so much trouble to come see me," he said. "Only to die here. I'll make it quick for you. I've no time to deal with pests."

Something inside Aeden clanged like an alarm bell. Without really knowing what he was doing, he jumped to the side. A burst of flame rushed out from Benzal's outstretched hand, washing over the area Aeden had vacated.

Right, Aeden thought. *He's a mage.* He lunged with his sword, but he couldn't close the distance fast enough. Benzal swiped his own blade outward and with a clang, Aeden's sword was forced away. Marla also said he was a fair swordsman. Not a good combination when Aeden had only one usable arm and was losing blood. Best to end it quickly.

Another gush of flame roared toward Aeden. This time, he didn't have time to dodge. Instead, he made the gestures out of reflex and spoke the words of power in a fast, clipped voice. The flame spread out before him, describing a ball around him. Aeden's shield held, though it was weaker than he was capable of making.

Benzal's eyes grew wide as the flame had no effect on Aeden and the Croagh counterattacked with his sword. He scored a shallow cut on the mage's sword arm, but it was nothing that would end the battle.

Uncertainty entered Benzal's eyes, and Aeden grinned.

"Quit playing around with her and kill *him*," Benzal said in

Alaqotim. From the sides of Aeden's vision, he saw the two animaru break off from Marla to race toward him. She slashed at the colechna, but only struck a glancing blow.

Aeden stepped in toward Benzal, but even if he killed the man, the other two enemies could cut into him as he did so. He had no desire to sacrifice himself in that way. Instead, he turned to the side, placing himself so that Benzal was on his left and the animaru charged toward him from his right.

His left shoulder was too weak to hold a sword, but he could move it, though it was painful. His mind went to the movements he had been practicing. He closed his eyes for a fraction of a second, centered himself, and let his body flow into a routine he had been searching for, but not quite grasping.

His feet spread apart slightly more than his normal stance, dropping his body down a few inches.

Just enough that the sword the colechna swung at his head whizzed over the top, shearing a few hairs in its passing. His arms—the right one still holding a sword—swung out to the side, but not as widely as he was used to. A small, compact movement, a tight circle.

The clang of Benzal's sword on his surprised him, but did not affect his movements or his thoughts. He chanted words of power under his breath, each one a bit louder and more distinct than the other.

"*Fantim*." He could feel the semhominus animaru begin to cast a spell against him.

"*Lishant*." Benzal looped his sword around while he brought his other hand up, ready for his magic to flare to life. The colechna reversed the position of his sword and cut deeply into Aeden's back, nearly causing him to lose his concentration completely.

"*Katha!*" The colechna swung its sword around again,

aiming it toward Aeden's neck. The Croagh would not be able to duck under this one.

But then, he didn't need to.

Power flared out of Aeden as his hands pushed outward. A bright light blasted in every direction, throwing the animaru ten feet away from him and staggering Benzal. He fell backward, his magic fizzling out on his hand.

Marla was not affected by the blast, as Aeden knew would be the case. Instead, she caught up to the colcchna and slashed it savagely before it could even hit the ground.

Aeden narrowed his eyes at Benzal. He had climbed to his feet, blinking as if dazed.

Aeden charged, sword making a figure eight in the air in front of him.

Benzal dropped his sword and put both hands up, calling up a shield. Aeden slammed into it, his sword deflected to the side. He hit with enough momentum to knock Benzal back once more.

"What—" Benzal said, but Aeden wasn't in the mood to hear the other man's voice. He hacked downward, cutting into whatever shield was protecting Benzal. With each blow, the sword got closer and closer to striking the one who had betrayed the entire human race.

Aeden gritted his teeth and growled, losing track of what Marla was doing completely. He trusted her not to let the other two get him. He had eyes only for Benzal.

Some sense in Aeden warned him once again and he brought up his own shield. Saving Force came almost without thought now, and as it snapped into place, power from Benzal buffeted it. It was a half-hearted attempt, though. The man was panicking.

He knew what came next.

Aeden's blade cut through what remained of Benzal's shield, but it was still deflected enough that he only scratched the other man's chest. It had been a mistake to not wear armor, counting on his allies and his magic to keep him safe. Nothing could keep him safe. Not anymore.

Aeden spun, kicking with all the force the rotation generated. His foot connected with Benzal's face and Aeden felt the jawbone break beneath his heel. He continued his movement and lashed out with his sword, cutting a deep furrow in his opponent's belly, not quite enough to spill his entrails, but almost.

Another spin and there was nothing Benzal could do. Unable to mouth words of power, his sword on the floor where he had dropped it, he put his hand up to try to stop what he knew was coming. It didn't matter.

Aeden once again harnessed his momentum and slashed horizontally. His blade cut through Benzal's upraised arm like it wasn't even there, then continued unerringly to the man's neck, slicing through and separating his head from his body. Stylish hair tumbled in the air until it struck the stone floor with a dull thump.

❧ 53 ❧

The Croagh stopped his spin and turned the opposite way, bringing his sword up to a ready position in time to see Marla ram her sword through the semhominus's chest. She pulled it out quickly and slashed downward, burying it in the animaru's head. The colechna already lay defeated a few feet away, its torso split open and leaking mud-colored blood.

Aeden slumped, scanning the area for more enemies. There were none.

"The others." He took a step back toward where they had come from.

And promptly fell to his knees. Why did he feel so weak?

"Oh, gods, Aeden," Marla said. "You're bleeding out. Here, let me help. We can check on our friends in a moment."

She tore the clothes from Benzal's body and started ripping his robes into strips.

"Stay with me," she said, expertly bandaging him while she spoke. She pulled out a small vial from her belt pouch. "Drink this. It'll slow the blood loss and kill the pain a little."

"You...seem to be good at that...treating wounds," he said. Things were starting to get fuzzy.

"Drink," she said, putting the vial to his lips. He drank down the contents. "Yes, I've studied healing. Not magical healing, though, not yet. I planned on getting around to it, but...not yet. Evon can do a little, but not enough. We need to get you to Urun."

She finished bandaging him and slid his sword into its scabbard.

Then she put her arms under his legs and across his wound and picked him up.

That only lasted for a few seconds, though. The pain the position caused him, even with the elixir she gave him, was too much. He screamed in pain. She had also underestimated how heavy he was, or how tired she was. While he was impressed she picked him up at all, it was not to be.

"I'm sorry, Aeden." Tears made tracks through the blood that had splashed on her face. "I can't do it. I'll have to help you walk. Come on."

The distance—covered in seconds just minutes before— seemed as great as any trek he had ever taken. As they entered the room where Benzal had caused the floor to drop, they passed by the contraption that had drawn Tere's arrows from the air.

"Hmm," Marla said. "I'll have to inspect that once we get you squared away."

Aeden looked to his friends across the chasm, afraid of what he might see. A jumble of bodies littered the floor. Darker brown blood mingled with red, though there was much more of the former. When humans stood at the sound of Aeden and Marla coming around the corner, he let out a sigh of relief. The first person he saw was Fahtin. The second was Khrazhti. She moved over to the edge of the chasm, fixing her gaze on Aeden.

Raki hovered near the wall, half in the shadows. Tere batted away Lily's hand as she tried to clean a wound over his eye. Evon looked disheveled but remarkably uninjured. Jia and Aila stood near each other, the former assassin with animaru blood on her clothing and face, but no red that Aeden could see. Aila favored one leg, a slash down the other one that had been bandaged, but that still leaked blood.

Urun. Where was Urun?

A mound of dark clothing lay near the others.

"No," Aeden said. "Urun?"

"Shhh," Fahtin said. "He's injured, but he'll live. One of the snakes got his leg before he could put his shield up. He fell and hit his head."

"No concussion," Evon said, "but he lost a lot of blood before we were able to finish off the others and bandage him. We were hoping you could heal him." As he said it, he raised his eyebrows. Aeden was barely standing.

"He won't be healing anyone anytime soon," Marla said. "We were hoping for Urun to heal him. They're both too weak to heal someone else. The effort may well kill them. Damn it, I wish I'd tackled the magical healing school. I always put it off."

"I can help a little," Evon said, "but I'm exhausted, so I can't do much."

"How are you going to get back here?" Fahtin asked. "No one is going to be jumping that gap now. We—"

A blue streak passed at the edge of Aeden's vision. It landed on his side of the gap. Khrazhti straightened up from her landing and rushed to his side.

Marla lowered Aeden to the floor, where Khrazhti helped to support his head. "Stay here. I'll find a corridor going back to the others. There has to be one."

Aeden nodded. "Be careful. There may be more of them."

"I doubt it, but I'll be careful just the same." She took off at a jog toward the room where Benzal and his animaru still lay. Khrazhti's eyes never left Aeden.

Fifteen minutes later, Aeden limped into the room to join the others, Marla on one side of him and Khrazhti on the other, supporting him. Tere and Fahtin got on either side of Aeden and took the burden from Marla. Evon had healed Aeden partially, enough that they didn't have to worry about him dying, but couldn't repeatedly cast his healing spell because he was exhausted from the battle.

"It's done," Aeden said, sitting down near Urun. "Benzal is gone. We did it, stopped the animaru invasion."

Evon and Marla looked at each other.

"Uh, not so fast," Marla said.

"What?"

"There's more to this than just Benzal. In fact, Evon and I have to leave now."

Aeden blinked. "Leave? What do you mean?"

Marla knelt next to him. "We were on a mission before we met you. It had reached a dead end and we were going back to the Academy. But in that village we saved, I got information that told me where the one we're after is hiding. We helped you with Benzal, but now we need to go finish our own job. We'll meet you back at the Academy, okay?"

"No," Aeden said. "No, it's not okay. If you have another mission, I'm going with you."

"You're in no condition to do anything but slowly make your way back to the Academy. If it wasn't for the chance of animaru showing up here, I would say you should stay here until you heal. In either case, you can't come with us. You're injured too badly."

"Wait for me to heal, then we'll do it together."

"No, Aeden. I've postponed it long enough. If we don't act soon, our enemy might slip through our fingers again. I can't let that happen. I'll tell you all about it when we meet again at the Academy."

"But," he said, "we can't just show up at the Academy and expect them to take us in."

"You'll be fine. The masters met you, at least some of them. They'll vouch for you. Even if they didn't, they won't turn away someone in need of medical treatment."

"Oh," Fahtin said, "we also know Dannel. He might be there by now. He can vouch for us, too."

Evon cocked his head. "Dannel?"

"Yeah," she said. "Dannel Powfrey. We've met him twice in our travels. He is fond of us."

"Who is Dannel Powfrey?" Marla asked.

The Gypta girl narrowed her eyes at Marla, then turned her head to meet Evon's eyes. "He's an Academy graduate, maybe thirty years old, a historian. He's kind of thin, about the same height as me, brown hair."

"No one by that name has graduated, or even attended, the Academy in the last twenty years. Whatever scam he was running, he's not one of us."

"Oh," Fahtin said, looking a bit troubled by the news. "Well, the masters will do."

"This mission you're going on," Tere said, "it has to do with the animaru?"

"It does," Marla said. "I'll explain it all when we meet again. We need to get going."

"I'll go with you," the archer said.

"No, you won't. The group needs you, both for protection and for directions, if necessary. You need to keep my brother safe, get him back to the Academy. And Urun, too. They need you all for protection. Who knows if there are more animaru out there, or some other danger."

Tere grumbled, but had no real argument.

"Listen," Marla said. "I know some of you might be

thinking about going with us, but please, it's much more important to me that you're strong enough to get Aeden and Urun back to Sitor-Kanda. Evon and I will manage our task and will see you soon. Okay?"

Aeden hung his head. "Be careful, Marla. I just found you. I don't want to lose you."

She smiled at him, face still splattered with animaru blood and hair wild and tangled. It was the most beautiful thing he had ever seen. "Oh, you're not going to lose me. I won't stand for it. Take your time, be safe, and heal. We may even beat you back to the Academy and be waiting with a feast and some new clothes to replace the shredded rags you have now."

Aeden chuckled, but cut off abruptly as fire raced across his back. "Fair enough. At the Academy, then."

Marla hugged him gently, kissed his forehead, and headed down the stairs, Evon in tow. The blond young man looked back over his shoulder toward Fahtin, almost tripping on the top step, and then he disappeared after Marla.

"Well, then," Tere said. "Why don't we move to a room without bodies in it and clean up our wounds the best we can. We can probably get a night's sleep if we bar the door and keep watch. Then we can leave in the morning."

Aeden nodded, too tired to do anything else. Fahtin and Khrazhti supported him on either side as Tere picked up Urun. The bruised and beaten group shuffled across the hall and down the stairs to find a suitable room to rest in.

❧ 54 ❧

Fahtin brushed a lock of Aeden's hair off his face. He was sleeping now, as was everyone else but Aila, who volunteered—like Fahtin—to take first watch. The room had a brazier and even an oil lantern, so there was light enough to see. The heavy wooden door was barred, enclosing them in the safest place they'd been for quite some time. There may still be animaru out there, but they wouldn't get into this room easily, even if they found it.

Aeden's face was pale, but his breathing was regular, aside from the occasional catch when he unconsciously shifted in his sleep and aggravated his wounds.

They were bad, but not life-threatening. Hopefully, after some rest he could heal Urun to the point where the priest could in turn heal Aeden. It seemed too coincidental that the only two of their party with healing magic were too injured to use their powers, but sometimes, that's how it went.

But they would be fine. Eventually. As Marla had asked, they would travel slowly back to the Academy, using the roads for ease of travel and going at a snail's pace. At least until one or both of those who could heal were strong enough to do so.

Overall, she was happy no one was killed. For what they'd been through, it was purely a miracle the injuries weren't worse.

But, oh, poor Aeden. It wasn't only that he was injured—he'd been there before—it was that he had to let Marla go off on her own to take care of her dangerous mission. Fahtin knew Aeden as well as anyone. Being left behind when his newly found sister went into danger hurt worse than any physical wound he could have taken.

Khrazhti hadn't left Aeden's side since he had come back to them. She volunteered to keep watch all night since she didn't need sleep, but Fahtin offered to let her take a long third watch instead so she and Aila could do their part. The animaru accepted her words without complaint. She merely sat, watching Aeden, occasionally scanning the room for danger as if something could get in without the others knowing.

Fahtin hoped Marla would be all right. She smiled at the thought of the fiery-haired—and fiery tempered—woman. She already looked at her as a sister and hoped she would have the chance to get to know her better.

A tap on Fahtin's shoulder drew her attention. Tere had awakened and was standing behind her. Lily was talking softly with Aila.

"Time to switch."

She nodded.

"How's he doing?"

"He's fine. A little thing like almost being cut in half won't slow him for long." She showed her teeth, trying to make it look like a smile.

"Yeah," Tere said. "He's a tough one, all right. Get some sleep. Lily and I will take over now."

Fahtin leaned down and kissed Aeden's forehead. He grunted and shifted but didn't wake. She was pleased that his skin was cool. He didn't have a fever, though infection probably wouldn't have set in so quickly.

She moved over a couple of feet and lay down on her cloak. It wasn't very much padding, but it was the best she could do. She wanted to stay near Aeden in case he needed her. Tere walked over to Lily as Aila found her own spot to lie down. She cast a look at Fahtin and nodded to her.

Fahtin was asleep almost instantly, plunging into the deep blackness of slumber.

A fine mist spread across her vision. She blinked, but knew as she did it that her eyes weren't open. She must be dreaming, but it didn't feel like a dream.

A flare of red light from her left caught her attention. She turned and saw a familiar boxy shape surrounded by darkness. A wagon. Her family's wagon.

And it was on fire.

There were no people around, but as she watched, the flame enveloped the entire wagon, casting light on the surrounding trees. They seemed stretched and twisted, unlike any trunks or branches she had ever seen.

It was too late to help, even if she hadn't been rooted to the spot. In the space of seconds, the fire flared up and completely consumed the place she had always thought of as home.

She gasped, and the scene disappeared.

Fahtin looked down on a room, a large table at its center. Dark shapes in cloaks sat around the table, speaking in a language she should have understood, but couldn't. There were thirteen of them.

Try as she might, she could not pierce the shadows around them to identify their faces. She wasn't entirely sure they were even human, though their silhouettes seemed to indicate that they were.

A flash of light and she was standing outside a great city

on a bright, clear day. She recognized it: Ebenrau, the capitol city of Rhaltzheim. In front of her was the mouth of a cavern, a splotch of darkness so deep it seemed impossible in the bright sunshine.

Something stirred in the depths of the blackness, but she couldn't tell what it was. Motion to her right pulled her eyes to the form walking toward the gaping hole.

It was Tere Chizzit.

Fahtin tried to open her mouth to warn him away, but the picture dissolved into broken fragments of darkness and color.

The pieces rearranged themselves into a grand stone hall. A glowing doorway dominated the middle of the chamber. As she watched, dozens of animaru at a time came through. Dark, grotesque bodies intermingled with scaled, furred, and clothed figures. Hundreds of the creatures entered the chamber and marched past Fahtin through the huge double doors.

That image disintegrated and remade itself. She was now on a hill overlooking a vast plain. Groups of shapes were scattered as far as she could see. Some, ordered in ranks, were obviously human, though shadows streamed off them like dark steam. Less organized were animaru of every shape and size. Some, she knew, were the same she had just seen. It wasn't clear how she knew this, but she did.

In addition to those, however, were all of the animaru she had seen before—the seren, colechna, semhominus, all of them—and others she didn't recognize. Some were huge, standing twelve feet high or more. Others were small and oddly shaped. As she watched, some of them blurred into dual images and, after a few seconds, fuzzed back together.

There had to be thousands of them, and they were all facing the same direction. Toward the Hero Academy. A much smaller all-human army stood between them and Sitor-Kanda, seeming small and weak.

Fahtin sat up with a gasp, shaking droplets of sweat from her forehead.

Aeden started, sitting up quickly himself, then moaning at the pain it caused his injuries.

"What?" he said. "What is it? Fahtin, are you okay?"

Tere had jumped to his feet and come over.

"A dream, girl. It was just a dream. It's all right. Breathe."

"It's not," she said. "It's not just a dream. It felt...different. Like the other ones I had. It's something more."

Aeden put a hand on her arm, grabbing her attention. Her eyes met his. They calmed her, as they had always done. So confident, so in command of everything.

"Tell us," he said.

She did, explaining every detail she could remember. Tere raised his eyebrows at the part where he appeared, but said nothing. When she was finished, she took a deep breath and deflated as she let it out.

"Well, then," Aeden said. "We'll need to get back to the Academy. I had hoped Benzal would be the end of it, but Marla has already told us he wasn't. Now we have another piece of evidence that we're not done."

"Just like that?" she said. "You take it as a sign of something important?"

"Of course," he said. "We don't know what's happening to you, Fahtin, but I trust you. I think it's more than a dream, like you do. We'll talk to the masters when we get to Sitor-Kanda and see if they can help. We just have to get there."

Fahtin's breath caught at the emotion gathering in her throat. "Thank you. Thank you for not thinking I'm silly or crazy."

He patted her arm. "Never again. Let's get a bit more sleep. We'll leave in the morning. The sooner we depart, the sooner we'll get to the Hero Academy and any answers it can give us. I've a feeling that there is much more to do, and I think you will help us to figure out what."

She went to hug him, but then remembered his injury, so changed her motion to kissing his cheek. "That sounds like a good idea."

Fahtin Achaya settled back onto her cloak, her eyes heavy. She was no longer afraid of dreaming, even if the confusion and anxiety about what she'd seen hadn't left her completely. She looked forward to getting back to the Academy to get answers. Like Aeden, she sensed somehow they had more to do. Their adventures had just started.

HEROES' SONG GLOSSARY

Following is a list of unfamiliar terms. Included are brief descriptions of the words as well as pronunciation. For the most part, pronunciation is depicted using common words or sounds in English, not IPA phonetic characters. Please note that the diphthong *ai* has the sound like the English word *Aye*. The *zh* sound, very common in the language Alaqotim, is listed as being equivalent to *sh*, but in reality, it is spoken with more of a buzz, such as *szh*. Other pronunciations should be intuitive.

Abyssum (*a·BIS·um*) – the world of the dead, Percipius's realm.

Aeden Tannoch (AY·*den* TAN·*ahkh*) – a man born to and trained by a highland clan, raised by the Gypta, and able to utilize the magic of the ancient Song of Prophecy.

Aesculus (*AY·skyoo·lus*) – the god of water and the seas.

Agypten (*a·GIP·ten*) – an ancient nation, no longer in existence.

Ahred Chimlain (*AH·red CHIM·lane*) – noted scholar of the first century of the third age

Aila Ven (*AI·la ven*) – a woman of small stature who joins the party and lends her skills in stealth and combat to their cause.

Ailgid (*ILE·jid*) – one of the five highland clans of the Cridheargla, the clan Greimich Tannoch's wife came from.

Alain (*a·LAYN*) – the god of language. The ancient language of magic, Alaqotim, is named after him.

Alaqotim (*ah·la·KOTE·eem*) – the ancient language of magic. It is not spoken currently by any but those who practice magic.

Aliten (*AL·it·ten*) – a type of animaru that is humanoid but has wings and can fly.

Alvaspirtu (*al·vah·SPEER·too*) – a large river that runs from the Heaven's Teeth mountains to the Kanton Sea. The Gwenore River splits from it and travels al the way down to the Aesculun Ocean.

Animaru (*ah·nee·MAR·oo*) – dark creatures from the world Aruzhelim. The name means "dark creatures" or "dark animals."

Arcus (*ARK·us*) – the god of blacksmithing and devices.

Arcusheim (*AHR·coo·shime*) – a large city on the southern shore of the Kanton Sea, the capital of the nation of Sutania and the home of Erent Caahs before he left to travel the world.

Arto Deniselo (*AHR·toe day·NEE·say·low*) – a dueling master in the Aranian city of Vis Bena who taught Erent Caahs how to drastically improve his combat abilities.

Aruna (pl. Arunai) (*ah·ROON·ah; ah·roo·NIE*) – a citizen of the tribal nation of Campastra. Originally, the name was pejorative, referring to the color of their skin, but they embraced it and it became the legitimate name for the people in Campastra.

Aruzhelim (*ah·ROO·shel·eem*) – the world from which the animaru come. The name means "dark world," "dark universe," or "dark dimension." Aruzhelim is a planet physically removed from Dizhelim.

Atwyn Iaphor (*AT·win EE·ah·fore*) – a student at the Hero Academy, a companion of Quentin Duzen when he was still on campus.

Bhagant (*bog·AHNT*) – the shortened form of the name for the Song of Prophecy, in the language Dantogyptain.

Bhavisyaganant (*bah·VIS·ya·gahn·ahnt*) – The full name for the Song of Prophecy in Dantogyptain. It means "the song of foretelling of the end," loosely translated.

Biuri (*bee·OOR·ee*) – small, quick animaru that recall the appearance and movements of rodents. They are useful as spies because of their small size and quickness.

Boltshadow – one of the Falxen sent to kill Khrazhti and her companions. A former student at Sitor-Kanda, he is skilled at wielding lightning magic.

Brace – the term used by the Falxen for a group of assassins ("blades").

Braitharlan (*brah·EE·thar·lan*) – the buddy assigned in the clan training to become a warrior. It means "blade brother" in Chorain.

Brausprech (*BROW·sprekh*) – a small town on the northwest edge of the Grundenwald forest, in the nation of Rhaltzheim. It is the hometown of Urun Chinowa.

Bridgeguard – the small community, barely more than a guardpost, on the mainland end of the northern bridge to Munsahtiz

Broken Reach – a rugged, unforgiving land to the southeast of the Grundenwald. There are ruins of old fortifications there.

Campastra (*cam·PAHS·trah*) – a tribal nation in the southwestern portion of the continent of Promistala

Catriona (Ailgid) Tannoch (*CAT·ree·own·ah ILE·jid*) –

the wife of Greimich Tannoch. She is originally from the Ailgid clan, but now has taken the last name Tannoch.

Ceti *(SET·ee)* – a higher level animaru, appearing aquatic with small tentacles, even though there is no water in Aruzhelim. They are very intelligent and have magical aptitude. Some of them are accomplished with weapons as well.

Chorain *(KHAW·rin)* – the ancestral language of the highland clans of the Cridheargla.

Clavian Knights *(CLAY·vee·en)* – the fighting force of the Grand Enclave, the finest heavy cavalry in Dizhelim.

Codaghan *(COD·ah·ghan)* – the god of war.

Colechna *(co·LECK·nah)* – one of the higher levels of animaru. Theyappear to be at least part snake, typically highly intelligent as well as skilled with weapons. They are usually in the upper ranks of the command structure. Their agility and flexibility makes them dangerous enemies in combat. A few can use magic, but most are strictly melee fighters.

Cridheargla *(cree·ARG·la)* – the lands of the highland clans. The word is a contraction of Crionna Crodhearg Fiacla in Chorain.

Crionna Crodhearg Fiacla *(cree·OWN·na CROW·arg FEE·cla)*) – the land of the highland clans. It means "old blood-red teeth" in Chorain, referring to the hills and mountains that abound in the area and the warlike nature of its people.

Croagh Aet Brech *(CROWGH ET BREKH)* – the name of the highland clans in Chorain. It means, roughly, "blood warriors." The clans sometimes refer to themselves simply as Croagh, from which their nickname "crows" sprang, foreigners not pronouncing their language correctly.

Dannel Powfrey – a self-proclaimed scholar from the Hero Academy who meets Aeden on his journey.

Danta (*DAHN·ta*) – the goddess of music and song. The language Dantogyptain is named after her.

Dantogyptain (*DAHN·toe·gip·TAY·in*) – the ancestral language of the Gypta people.

Daodh Gnath (*DOWGH GHRAY*) – the Croagh Ritual of Death, the cutting off of someone from the clans. The name means simply "death ceremony."

Dared Moran (*DAR·ed·mo·RAN*) – the "Mayor" of Praesturi. Essentially, he's a crime boss who controls the town.

Darkcaller – one of the Falxen sent to kill Khrazhti and her companions. A former student at Sitor-Kanda, her specialty is dark magic.

Dartford – a small town on the mainland near the north bridge to the island of Munsahtiz.

Darun Achaya (*dah·ROON ah·CHAI·ah*) – father of Fahtin, head of the family of Gypta that adopts Aeden.

Desid (*DAY·sid*) – a type of animaru. They're nearly mindless, only able to follow simple commands, but they are fairly strong and tireless. They are about five feet tall with thick, clawed fingers useful for digging. They have the mentality of a young child.

Dizhelim (*DEESH·ay·leem*) – the world in which the story happens. The name means "center universe" in the ancient magical language Alaqotim.

Dmirgan – a town in Kruzekstan, where a young Erent Caahs killed a man he thought was a murderer

Dreigan (*DRAY·gun*) – a mythical beast, a reptile that resembles a monstrous snake with four legs attached to its sides like a lizard. The slightly smaller cousin to the mythical dragons.

Drugancairn (*DROO·gan·cayrn*) – a small town on the southwest edge of the Grundenwald Forest.

Ebenrau (*EBB·en·ra·oo*) – the capital city of Rhaltzheim, one of the seven great cities in Dizhelim

Edge – one of the Falxen sent to kill Khrazhti and her companions. A former assassin and bodyguard in Teroshi, he is skilled in the use of the Teroshi long sword and short sword.

Encalo (pl. encali) (*en·CAW·lo*) – four-armed, squat, powerful humanoids. There are few in Dizhelim, mostly in the western portion of the continent Promistala.

Erent Caahs (*AIR·ent CAWS*) – the most famous of the contemporary heroes. He disappeared twenty years before the story takes place, and is suspected to be dead, though his body was never found.

Erfinchen (*air·FEEN·chen*) – animaru that are shapeshifters. Though not intelligent and powerful enough to be leaders among the animaru, they are often at higher levels, though not in command of others. They typically perform special missions and are truly the closest thing to assassins the animaru have. A very few can use some magic.

Espirion (*es·PEER·ee·on*) – the god of plans and schemes. From his name comes the terms espionage and spy.

Evon Desconse – a graduate of the famed Hero Academy and best friend to Marla Shrike

Fahtin Achaya (*FAH·teen ah·CHAI·ah*) – a young Gypta girl in the family that adopted Aeden. She and Aeden grew as close as brother and sister in the four years he spent with the family.

Falxen (*FAL·ksen*) – an assassin organization, twelve of whom go after Aeden and his friends. The members are commonly referred to as "Blades."

Featherblade – one of the Falxen sent to kill Khrazhti and her companions. He is the leader of the brace and his skill with a sword is supreme.

Fireshard – one of the Falxen sent to kill Khrazhti and her companions. She wields fire magic.

Forgren (*FORE·gren*) – a type of animaru that is tireless and single-minded. They are able to memorize long messages and repeat them exactly, so they make good messengers. They have no common sense and almost no problem-solving skills

Formivestu (*form·ee·VES·too*) – the insect creatures that attacked Tere's group when they were on their way to Sitor-Kanda. They look like giant ants with human faces and were thought to be extinct.

Fyorio (*fee·YORE·ee·oh*) – the god of fire and light, from whose name comes the word *fyre*, spelled *fire* in modern times.

Gentason (*jen·TAY·sun*) – an ancient nation, enemy of Salamus. It no longer exists.

Gneisprumay (*gNAYS·proo·may*) – first (or most important) enemy. The name for the Malatirsay in the animaru dialect of Alaqotim.

Great Enclave – a nation to the west of the Kanton Sea and the Hero Academy.

Greimich Tannoch (*GREY·mikh TAN·ahkh*) – Aeden's close friend, his braitharlan, during his training with the clans.

Grundenwald Forest (*GROON·den·vahld*) – the enormous forest in the northeastern part of the main continent of Promistala. It is said to be the home of magic and beasts beyond belief.

Gulra (pl. gulrae) (*GUL·rah; GUL·ray*) – an animaru that walks on four legs and resembles a large, twisted dog. These are used for tracking, using their keen sense of smell like a hound.

Gwenore River – a large river that splits off from the Alvaspirtu and travels south, through Satta Sarak and all the way to the Aesculun Ocean

Gypta (*GIP·tah*) – the traveling people, a nomadic group that lives in wagons, homes on wheels, and move about, never settling down into towns or villages.

Heaven's Teeth – the range of mountains to the east of the Kanton sea, in between that body of water and the Grundenwald Forest.

Ianthra (*ee·ANTH·rah*) – the goddess of love and beauty.

Iscopsuru (*ee·SCOP·soo·roo*) – the name of Benzal's fortress outside of Nanris in Kruzekstan; it's over eight hundred years old. The name means Rock of Surus in Alaqotim.

Isegrith Palas (*ISS·eh·grith PAL·us*) – the Master of Fundamental Magic at the Hero Academy.

Izhrod Benzal (*EESH·rod ben·ZAHL*) – a powerful magic-user, one who has learned to make portals between Aruzhelim and Dizhelim. The dark god S'ru has an agreement with him so he is second to none in authority over the animaru on Dizhelim.

Jehira Sinde (*jay·HEER·ah SINDH*) – Raki's grandmother (nani) and soothsayer for the family of Gypta that adopts Aeden.

Jia Toun (*JEE·ah TOON*) – an expert thief and assassin who was formerly the Falxen named Shadeglide. She uses her real name now that she has joined Aeden's group of friends and allies.

Jintu Devexo (*JEEN·too day·VEX·oh*) – the high chieftain of the Arunai during the time of the false Malatirsay.

Josef – the owner of the Wolfen's Rest inn in Dartford, a friend of Marla Shrike

Kanton Sea (*KAN·tahn*) – an inland sea in which the island of Munsahtiz, home of the Hero Academy, sits.

Kebahn Faitar (Kebahn the Wise) (*kay·BAWN FYE·tahr*) – the advisor and friend to Thomasinus; the one who actually came up with the idea to gather all the scattered people and make a stand at the site of what is now the Great Enclave.

Keenseeker – one of the Falxen sent to kill Khrazhti and her companions. He is a huge, strong warrior who wields a massive battle axe.

Khrazhti (*KHRASH·tee*) – the former High Priestess to the dark god S'ru and former leader of the animaru forces on Dizhelim. At the discovery that her god was untrue, she has become an ally and friend to Aeden.

Kruzekstan (*KROO·zek·stahn*) – a small nation due south of the highland clan lands of Cridheargla.

Leafburrow – a village in Rhaltzheim, north of Arcusheim off the River Road, the location of a bandit ambush where Erent Caahs demonstrated his special spinning arrow technique.

Lela Ganeva (*LEE·lah·gahn·AY·vah*) – the woman Erent Caahs fell in love with.

Lesnum (*LESS·num*) – large, hairy, beastlike animaru. These sometimes walk around on two feet, but more commonly use all four limbs. They are strong and fast and intelligent enough to be used as sergeants, commanding groups of seren and other low-level animaru.

Lilianor (Lili) Caahs (*LI·lee·ah·nore CAWS*) – Erent Cahhs's little sister; she was murdered when she was eleven years old

Lily Fisher – an archer of supreme skill who was formerly the Falxen assassin named Phoenixarrow. She uses her real name now that she has joined Aeden's group of friends and allies.

Malatirsay (*Mahl·ah·TEER·say*) – the hero who will defeat the animaru and save Dizhelim from the darkness, according to prophecy. The name means "chosen warrior" or "special warrior" in Alaqotim.

Manandantan (*mahn·ahn·DAHN·tahn*) – the festival to celebrate the goddess Danta, goddess of song.

Marla Shrike – a graduate of the famed Hero Academy,

an experienced combatant in both martial and magical disciplines.

Marn Tiscomb – the new Master of Prophecy at the Hero Academy. He replaced Master Aeid, who was murdered.

Mellaine (*meh·LAYN*) – goddess of nature and growing things.

Miera Tannoch (*MEERA TAN·ahkh*) – Aeden's mother, wife of Sartan.

Migae (*MEE·jay*) – the god of magic.

Moschephis (*mose·CHE·feess*) – the trickster god, from whose name comes the word mischief.

Mudertis (*moo·DARE·teez*) – the god of thievery and assassination.

Munsahtiz (*moon·SAW·teez*) – the island in the Kanton sea on which the Hero Academy Sitor-Kanda resides.

Nanris – the unofficial capital of Kruzekstan, more important than the actual capital of Kruzeks because most of the wealth of the nation is centered in Nanris.

Osulin (*AWE·soo·lin*) – goddess of nature. She is the daughter of Mellaine and the human hero Trikus Phen.

Pach (*PAHKH*) – in Dantogyptain, it means five. As a proper noun, it refers to the festival of Manandantan that occurs every fifth year, a special celebration in which the Song of Prophecy is sung in full.

Percipius (*pare·CHIP·ee·us*) – god of the dead and of the underworld.

Phoenixarrow – one of the Falxen sent to kill Khrazhti and her companions. A statuesque red-haired archer who had a penchant for using fire arrows.

Pilae (*PEEL·lay*) – a type of animaru that looks like a ball of shadow

Pouran (*PORE·an*) – roundish, heavy humanoids with piggish faces and tusks like a boar

Praesturi (*prayz·TURE·ee*) – the town and former military outpost on the southeastern tip of the island of Munsah-tiz. The south bridge from the mainland to the island ends within Praesturi.

Preshim (*PRAY·sheem*) – title of the leader of a family of Gypta

Promistala (*prome·ees·TAHL·ah*) – the main continent in Dizhelim. In Alaqotim, the name means "first (or most important) land."

Quentin Duzen – a Hero Academy graduate, the antagonist against Marla and Evon.

Qydus Okvius (*KIE·duss OCK·vee·us*) – the headmaster of the Hero Academy, Sitor-Kanda.

Raibrech (*RAI·brekh*) – the clan magic of the highland clans. In Chorain, it means "bloodfire."

Raisor Tannoch (*RAI·sore TAN·ahkh*) – a famous warrior of Clan Tannoch, companion of the hero Erent Caahs.

Raki Sinde (*ROCK·ee SINDH*) – grandson of Jehira Sinde, friend and training partner of Aeden.

Rhaltzheim (*RALTZ·haim*) – the nation to the northeast of the Grundenwald Forest. The people of the land are called Rhaltzen. The term Rhaltzheim is often used to refer to the rugged land within the national borders (e.g., "traverse the Rhaltzheim")

Ritma Achaya (*REET·mah ah·CHAI·ah*) – Fahtin's mother, wife of the Gypta family leader Darun.

Ruthrin (*ROOTH·rin*) – the common tongue of Dizhelim, the language virtually everyone in the world speaks in addition to their own national languages.

S'ru (*SROO*) – the dark god of the animaru, supreme power in Aruzhelim.

Salamus (*sah·LAHM·oos*) – an ancient nation in which the legendary hero Trikus Phen resided. It no longer exists.

Sartan Tannoch (*SAR·tan TAN·ahkh*) – Aeden's father, clan chief of the Tannoch clan of Craogh.

Satta Sarak (*SAH·tah SARE·ack*) – a city in the south-eastern part of the continent of Promistala, part of the Saraki Principality.

Semhominus (*sem·HOM·in·us*) – one of the highest level of animaru. They are humanoid, larger than a typical human, and use weapons. Many of them can also use magic. Most animaru lords are of this type.

Seren (*SARE·en*) – the most common type of animaru, with sharp teeth and claws. They are similar in shape and size to humans.

Shadeglide – one of the Falxen sent to kill Khrazhti and her companions. She is small of stature but extremely skilled as a thief and assassin.

Shaku (*SHOCK·oo*) – a class of Teroshimi assassins

Shinyan (*SHEEN·yahn*) – a nation on the northern tip of the western part of Promistala, bordering the Kanton Sea and the Cattilan Sea. Things of Shinyan (such as people) are referred to as Shinyin.

Sike (*SEEK·ay*) – a class of Shinyin assassins

Sitor-Kanda (*SEE·tor KAN·dah*) – the Hero Academy, the institution created by the great prophet Tsosin Ruus to train the Malatirsay. The name means roughly "home of magic" in Alaqotim.

Snowmane – the horse the Academy lent to Aeden, a chestnut stallion with a white mane

Solon (*SEW·lahn*) – one of the masters in Clan Tannoch, responsible for training young warriors how to use the clan magic, the Raibrech.

Srantorna (*sran·TORN·ah*) – the abode of the gods, a place where humans cannot go.

Surus (*SOO·roos*) – king of the gods.

Tere Chizzit (*TEER CHIZ·it*) – a blind archer and tracker with the ability to see despite having no working eyes. He is Aeden's companion in the story.

Teroshi (*tare·OH·shee*) – an island nation in the northern part of Dizhelim. Things of Teroshi, including people, are referred to as Teroshimi.

Thomasinus, son of Daven (*toe·mah·SINE·us*) – the hero who banded the remnants of the troops of Gentason together to create the Great Enclave. Once they elected him king, he changed his last name to Davenson.

Toan Broos (*TOE·aan*) – traveling companion of Erent Caahs and Raisor Tannoch

Trikus Phen (*TRY·kus FEN*) – a legendary hero who battled Codaghan, the god of war, himself, and sired Osulin by the goddess Mellaine.

Tsosin Ruus (*TSO·sin ROOS*) – the Prophet, the seer and archmage who penned the Song of Prophecy and founded Sitor-Kanda, the Hero Academy.

Tuach (*TOO·akh*) – one of the masters in Clan Tannoch, responsible for teaching the young warriors the art of physical combat.

Ulfaris Triban (*ool·FARE·iss TRY·ban*) – a Hero Academy graduate, companion to Izhrod Benzal

Urtumbrus (*oor·TOOM·brus*) – a type of animaru that are essentially living shadows.

Urun Chinowa (*OO·run CHIN·oh·wah*) – the High Priest of the goddess Osulin, a nature priest.

Vanda (*VAHN·dah*) – a modern god, claimed by his followers to be the only true god. It is said he is many gods in one, having different manifestations. The Church of Vanda is very large and very powerful in Dizhelim.

Vatheca (*VATH·ay·kuh*) – the headquarters and training center of the Falxen. It is a mixture of two Alaqotim words, both meaning "sheath."

Vincus (pl. vinci) (*VEEN·cuss; VEEN·chee*) – Aila's chain blade weapons.

Voordim (*VOOR·deem*) – the pantheon of gods in Dizhe-lim. It does not include the modern god Vanda.

Whiteshadow – one of the Falxen sent to kill Khrazhti and her companions. She is a master swordswoman and has no fewer than four swords strapped to her at all times.

Yxna Hagenai (*IX·nah HAG·en·eye*) – the Master of Edged Weapons at the Hero Academy.

LETTER TO THE READER

Dear Reader,

It was awesome you could join me in experiencing the dangers and heroics in the Song of Prophecy series. I hoped you enjoyed the stories. If you would be so kind, **could you please leave a review for the book** so not only I, but others will know what you thought? It means a lot to get feedback from readers and I'd love to hear from you. Thank you in advance.

Finally, we have solved some of the mysteries of the Song of Prophecy, but not all. There are a lot more questions that need answers and more actions that need to be taken by our heroes. We've been introduced to Marla Shrike and the Hero Academy itself, so where are we to go now?

Yeah, I know, that's a leading question if ever you've read one. The answer is simple. The Song of Prophecy series may be finished, but the story continues in the Hero Academy series. If you're reading this, I have already finished the first three books in the HA series, along with not only a companion novel for that series, but also one for the Song of Prophecy series. They may or may not already be available in the stores as you read this, but rest assured that they're written. You don't have to worry about waiting a long time to see the next book.

Though I'm presenting them as two different series, they're essentially just one big story, and when I say big I mean BIG. Let's put it this way, at this point, I have four books written in the series (if you count the companion novel, a type of prequel), have planned out and structured three more, and will start writing the fourth book in the main series within a month of when I'm writing this. So, if you enjoyed sharing Aeden's adventures, you'll love what happens next, and you'll be able to get your hands on it in short order.

Thank you so much for sharing with me my world and the heroes I write about. I hope to see you again in Dizhelim!

P.E. Padilla

AUTHOR NOTES

Author's Notes

The Song of Prophecy series is finished, but the story is not. I can't really remember when I decided I wanted to make a long series out of the stories, but I have so much fun in Dizhelim, it was kind of natural that I do so. That's why I'm continuing on in the Hero Academy series.

It's funny how as an author, you get attached to certain characters. I suppose it's just like life itself. Some people enter your life, make an impression, and then leave, while others stick around for a long, long time. With a series this large, and a cast of dozens of what are commonly called POV (point of view) characters, it's not surprising that I'd cherish some more than others. I hope each reader can pick out favorites of their own, ones who they want to see in further adventures.

That was part of the allure of continuing the series. There are so many fantastic people, heroes and villains and mysterious figures that could be either, that I wanted to spend more time with them. What better way to do that than to follow them on their quest to save the world from dark creatures wanting to destroy all life and light? It's exciting just to think about.

So I started to expand my view of what our heroes had to face and what the not-so-heroic people would do to beat them down. With each facet of the overall story, I found myself sinking deeper into the lore, the languages, and the world itself. I truly enjoy writing (and reading!) about the adventures in the series. I hope others feel the same.

I do have an endpoint in mind, and even a path to get there, but it may take a few stories to accomplish it. It took a few years to continue the story from the first book, Wanderer's Song, but there won't be nearly that kind of delay with the Hero Academy series. It's a living, breathing thing now, so I'm doing my best to keep up with it. It won't let me rest if I don't keep up with writing in it. I do have a specific number of books and the adventures they will entail, but I think I'll keep that information to myself for now. Suffice it to say that this will easily be my longest series to date, maybe the longest for quite some time. I'm looking forward to it.

ABOUT THE AUTHOR

A chemical engineer by degree and at various times an air quality engineer, a process control engineer, and a regulatory specialist by vocation, USA Today bestselling author P.E. Padilla learned long ago that crunching numbers and designing solutions was not enough to satisfy his creative urges. Weaned on classic science fiction and fantasy stories from authors as diverse as Heinlein, Tolkien, and Jordan, and affected by his love of role playing games such as Dungeons and Dragons (analog) and Final Fantasy (digital), he sometimes has trouble distinguishing reality from fantasy. While not ideal for a person who needs to function in modern society, it's the perfect state of mind for a writer. He is a recent transplant from Southern California to Northern Washington, where he lives surrounded by trees.

pepadilla.com/
pep@pepadilla.com

ALSO BY P.E. PADILLA

Adventures in Gythe:

Vibrations: Harmonic Magic Book 1 (also available as an audiobook)

Harmonics: Harmonic Magic Book 2 (also available as an audiobook)

Resonance: Harmonic Magic Book 3

Tales of Gythe: Gray Man Rising (also available as an audiobook)

Harmonic Magic Series Boxed Set

The Unlikely Hero Series (under pen name Eric Padilla):

Unfurled: Heroing is a Tough Gig (Unlikely Hero Series Book 1) (also
available as an audiobook)

Unmasked (Unlikely Hero Series Book 2)

Undaunted (Unlikely Hero Series Book 3)

The Shadowling Chronicles (under pen name Eric Padilla):

Shadowling (Book 1)

Witches of the Elements Series :

Water & Flame (Book 1)

Song of Prophecy Series :

Wanderer's Song

Warrior's Song

Heroes' Song (this book)

Order of the Fire Series:

Call of Fire

Hero of Fire

Legacy of Fire

Order of the Fire Boxed Set

Made in the USA
Las Vegas, NV
21 July 2021

26814492R00256